"INTRIGUING . . .

Rice's gracious style and strong visual imagery make this town so believable, the pages almost sweat from the cloying humidity of the South she describes."
Houston Chronicle

"A rich tale about a small Southern town that changes forever . . . Part mystery and part psychological thriller, the novel offers the sharply etched characters and detailed portrait of time and place that often characterize Southern fiction."
The Chattanooga Times

"This is the kind of story that allows you to smell the flowers blooming and the swamp gas rising at night . . . . [Rice] truly creates a world unto itself with her microscopic view of a town under siege."
Ocala Star-Banner

"The savage murder of elderly widow Sarah Roth rocks Essex, a somnolent South Carolina town whose awakening to evil is masterfully dramatized in this first novel . . . . Rarely seen since Faulkner's *Sanctuary*."
The Kirkus Reviews

Southern Exposure

Linda Lightsey Rice

IVY BOOKS · NEW YORK

Ivy Books
Published by Ballantine Books
Copyright © 1991 by Linda Lightsey Rice

This novel is a work of fiction. Names, characters, places, and incidents are either the product of the author's imagination or are used fictitiously. Any resemblance to actual persons, living or dead, events, or locales is entirely coincidental.

The town of Essex, South Carolina, does not exist. The Sheldon Church ruins and the Coosawhatchie Swamp (which is rarely called that now) are real, but certain liberties have been taken with the geography of that section of the South Carolina Low Country.

A small portion of this novel, in altered form, was originally published in *The Phoenix*.

Library of Congress Catalog Card Number: 90-45616

ISBN 0-8041-0935-4

This edition published by arrangement with Doubleday, a division of Bantam Doubleday Dell Publishing Group, Inc.

Manufactured in the United States of America

First Ballantine Books Edition: June 1992

In memory of Ruth Haigler Lightsey
And especially for you, Bob

Acknowledgments

WRITERS ENDURE DREADFUL isolation but have not, thank goodness, been sent to solitary. Thus, I am grateful to be indebted to the following: to the works of Charlestonian Virginia Mixson Geraty on the Gullah language, from which I borrowed the name Maum Chrish; to the scholarship on myth and mysticism and religion by Sir James Frazer, Newbell Niles Puckett, Zolar, Milo Rigaud, Wade Davis, John S. Mbiti, and Zora Neal Hurston; to Special Agent John Denton of the FBI for technical advice; to my cousin Doug Monts Jr. for the jacket photograph of that wonderful old house built by the Lightseys; to the students of my fiction workshops at the University of Tennessee for asking so many tough questions; to Becky Phillips Schneider, who read the manuscript several times and provided insight as well as many laughs, not to mention a few sandwiches and the free therapy. A special thanks also to Pat Conroy for his generous encouragement, to my mother for her belief in me and all those old stories, and to my editor Shaye Areheart and my agent Diane Cleaver for their friendship and enthusiastic creative support.

A note on idiosyncrasies: First, voodoo/voudou is spelled both ways herein depending on the speaker, to separate cultural superstition from cultural fact. (The religion described here is basically Haitian and is not necessarily practiced by any living persons in South Carolina.) Second, the Low Country of South Carolina has never been, to me, the Lowcountry. I don't know why. Perhaps because the extraordinary power of the place is such that I cannot consume it quickly. Finally, there are these three names of mine—Lightsey is my mother's family, Rice my father's. Some people call me by my first name, many now call me Lightsey. When *I* figure out who I am, I'm going to make up a whole new set of names and really confuse everyone.

And finally my gratitude to Tradd, golden retriever par excellence, who lay under my desk and slept blissfully on and never once suggested that I might want to stop talking about this book.

L.L.R.

But one man loved the pilgrim soul in you,
And loved the sorrows of your changing face.

—W. B. Yeats

One

WE LIVED IN a Low Country. Both before and after that summer, but it was never the same.

Like all Southerners, we loved and hated to excess. As we grew tall under the South Carolina sun, the mortar of our psyche was chinked with unequal parts of both. Oftentimes we couldn't tell the difference between them. Which is what we finally learned that last long night, in a darkness shattered by the obscene clarity of light.

Later, when Stoney McFarland became temporary custodian of the paintings that survived, he likened them to the town. "Old paintings belong in old towns," he said with a trace of sadness. "They're faded and cracked and pockmarked with age. But they do endure; if we take care of these, they'll last a long time." Then he paused and added, "I guess only a terrible accident can really destroy a work of art."

We knew then, of course, that he wasn't really talking about the paintings.

Stoney McFarland was a prodigal son. One of several actually, for our town seemed to pull back its outcasts like a choke chain. But certainly Stoney was our favorite. He and his wife Anna, in their mid-thirties, had moved to Essex only two years before and had bought the old McCloskey place, a mammoth white frame house on Laurens Avenue, in the oldest part of town. It loomed behind a low wrought-iron fence with brick pillars, the left wing a massive two-story turret with banks of floor-to-ceiling shuttered casement windows; the adjoining wing was squared off into right angles, the roof pitched on the left and flat on the right. Fully half the structure was round but it affected cubism, fronted as it was on both levels by boxy balustraded balconies that completely encircled the building. It was

1

obviously the life's work of a schizophrenic vacillating between
the Italianate and Queen Anne. With all the Victorian lattice-
work and gingerbread brackets on the balconies, the house was
almost too busy to be attractive. But it was compelling, commanded attention, constituted a deliberate affront to the modest
bungalows it lived among. In a place where frugality and common sense were handed out with birth certificates, this house
was an uncontrolled extravagance, as tawdry as a loose woman,
maybe worse.

Anna McFarland liked the house because it was unlike any
other in Essex. It separated them. Stoney felt just the opposite:
to him, this old house made them more a part of the town's
history.

On an unusually warm April night, Stoney and Anna were
sitting in their back yard. The rear of the McCloskey house concluded with a glassed-in back porch and a concrete pathway that
led to a detached wooden garage, slightly leaning and so
crammed with garden and sports equipment even a Japanese car
wouldn't fit inside. The garden tools had been inherited from
the previous owner, and neither Stoney nor Anna knew what
some of the implements were for. Their grass was neatly cut
but, having been city dwellers most of their lives, they'd done
little other landscaping. Even the jumbles of yellow jonquils
along the sidewalk had been planted by the McCloskeys. The
back of the lot, which was actually two lots deep, ended just
short of a small natural pond about thirty by twenty feet. It was
encircled by fifteen moss-draped live oak trees, stately old sen-
tinels standing guard over the water.

Stoney McFarland was stretched out in the grass on the bank
of the pond, his shirttail loose, his toes freed from the white
Nikes beside him, his back against a stump and his fingers laced
behind his head. He looked as though he belonged exactly where
he was. A large golden retriever named Silas lay at Stoney's
side, the dog's sleeping head pillowed atop the white sneakers.
In a second Stoney leaned forward and picked up a flat rock.
"Stay," he said. The dog opened a lazy eye and watched as the
man pitched the rock across the pond. Stoney was a champion
stone skimmer, a childhood pastime he had perfected on this
very spot. But tonight his stone spiraled only a few feet before
dropping unceremoniously out of sight.

Anna McFarland reclined on a webbed lounge chair several
feet away, her eyes closed. A portable Sony radio tuned to Savannah's classical station sat on the ground beside her glass of

wine. Stoney gazed beyond Anna to the treetops, then higher up to the full moon, hanging heavy and close. He looked back at Anna and wished she would open her eyes and come over and sit beside him. At one time they had always sat close so they could reach out and touch each other easily, quickly. In the early years they had never wanted to travel alone, or be apart overnight. That beginning, however, hadn't saved them from this—this distance.

He patted the dog's rump, then got up and crossed to Anna and leaned down and kissed her lightly on the forehead. He slowly turned the radio volume down. She opened her eyes and he said, "How about some health food?"

"What?" She stared up at the man who once swore he would take "real food" with him the next time he went to California.

"The original health food." Stoney grinned and picked up her glass of wine. He sipped the burgundy, then handed it to her.

She smiled and finished the wine. Then, "It's getting chilly, think I'll go in."

"And leave me out here alone to get mugged or something?"

Anna stood up. Her voice was light but not light enough to muffle its edge. "You couldn't pay a mugger to live here."

Silence. She started toward the house. He hesitated for a second, hands in his pockets, uncertain whether to resume the conversation they'd had earlier that day. "Anna . . . if you'd just give the town a chance."

She stopped, her back still to him. "I have given it a chance. I told you how I feel, I'm not comfortable here. We don't fit in."

"You don't want to fit in," he said quietly.

She whirled around, eyes flashing. "If you mean I don't want to spend my whole life sitting around throwing rocks in a pond in the middle of nowhere, you're right. I sure as hell don't." The dark-haired woman looked down abruptly, remembering when it never mattered where they were or what they did as long as they did it together. She walked back toward Stoney. "I know you needed to come back here; at the time I was all for it." She reached out and touched his arm. "I love you, you know that. You're the brightest man I know. But we can't keep living in the past. We have to go forward—toward something."

Clutching her radio, an IV to the outside world, Anna made her way back to the house in its pool of stark white moonlight. Stoney watched her let herself in. He would happily sign his life away to the first years he and Anna were together. He picked up another stone and sailed it across the pond with a vengeance. It fell in the water with a defeated plop.

Stoney McFarland loved the town of Essex, loved it for reasons that tentacled more deeply to his own childhood than to the fact that his father had grown up there. Descended from the impoverished genteel South, for whom education and culture remained acutely important long after they could afford either, Stoney had had the misfortune to come along a few decades after the Depression. At a time when jobs were scarce, they were scarcer still in a land where world war had decimated the agrarian tradition, and the Southern exodus of the thirties to the Northern cities had cost Stoney an Essex upbringing. By the late forties Stoney's father settled in Washington, as a government clerk who eventually rose to a position of minor authority in the State Department. In the early days Stoney's family lived in a gestating slum on the capital's northwest side. What the boy remembered of that time was a pervasive uncertainty. Tall row houses with broken windows and reeking hallways and old drunks splayed across the stoops. And rules—rules about where he could go, which people on the block he could talk to, the safest way to and from school. As the offspring of small-towners who never fully adjusted to city life, the child inculcated his parents' insecurities with precision. Every summer, however, he was shipped off to South Carolina, to a small town in the Low Country where his grandmother lived. There he was reincarnated in another world; the train that pulled out of Union Station moved between two astral planes. In Essex he could go anywhere he pleased. Alone. Old men patted him on the head and taught him how to fish instead of hissing at him to "Git out the way." Everyone called him by name, not just the few people who lived nearby, everyone. People he saw at the filling station when his grandmother's shiny red Plymouth needed gas and he got a Coke and stuffed peanuts in the narrow-necked bottle, reclining on the hood to watch old man Harris work the white ceramic pump. Everyone at the Lutheran church where he had to sit in the front pew so his grandmother could see him from the choir stall, everyone at the brick post office where she went to pick up her mail every day. And especially all the boys who met at the pond behind the McCloskey place.

For nine months of every year he was pale and strained, but every summer he burst forth like a new plant. He shot up tall and straight; tanned, he looked out on the world in Essex and was pleased.

By the time his father left government service for a private company and they moved to the Virginia suburbs, Stoney was in high school. His grandmother died and he rarely went to Essex after that. In the suburbs of the early sixties he learned that a guy was the clothes he wore, the car he drove, the girls he was seen with. These dictums seemed as oppressive to Stoney as the rules of his city childhood, and so he turned to sports, an arena less plagued by inconsistency and injustice. He excelled at baseball and found that athletics allowed him to satisfy the social requirements of his milieu without ever fully endorsing them.

"You still go down to that hick place in South Carolina every July?" a buddy asked him when he was seventeen. "I hear they lynch niggers down there at the drop of a hat."

Stoney had never heard of anyone even being robbed in Essex, much less murdered. Black or white. No one in his family had ever been allowed to use the word "nigger." But he kept his mouth shut, he did not try to exonerate the town. As race riots were written into the history of the decade, it became increasingly apparent that he would do well to keep his connection to South Carolina to himself. He read the newspaper religiously and tried to figure out which of the people who'd smiled at him when he was seven was likely to beat a man to death because his skin was dark. Harris at the gas station? The fat lady who ran the post office? (Only Harriet Setzler ever said mean things about black people.) Listening to the sudden authorities on Southern prejudice, Stoney never mentioned Essex to anyone for many years. Yet the town lurked beneath his consciousness like a dirty secret. He couldn't cherish South Carolina as he once had, nor could he hate it as the times dictated he should. The uncertainty of his childhood in Washington—of what was true, who could be trusted—now permeated Essex too. Safe harbors did not exist. His best memories of his past lay buried in a place devoured by hate.

The athlete in him finally elected to trust his instinct. He turned his back on the historical record: some parts of the South were different.

For him, Essex was always a physical experience and in its senses he breathed in the elixir of childhood. It was the sticky sweetness of the honeysuckle vines that grew ten feet tall along the wire fence guarding the town cemetery. It was the gluelike coastal humidity, the verdant color and hypnotic redolence of flowers, the opulent sunshine whose superfluity burned into his shoulders and suspended time and gave him back a boy's imagination. Everything about the Low Country threatened the sane and the sensible and for him invalidated adult ennui, from the gnarled live oak trees pressing heavily against the sky to the old black people mysteriously speaking Geechee along the shores of coastal islands. Wherever he walked, on the beach or in a swamp or along county blacktop, what this land gave to him, always, was texture.

Perhaps his love for the Low Country was so intense because it had never truly belonged to him as a child. Much like Silas, who had epilepsy and thus would never be bred. Stoney had not grown up in Essex, nor would he grow old beside his retriever's grandchildren. Both were temporal gifts, yet both somehow made him believe in infinity.

If only Anna felt the same way.

Before heading inside, Stoney looked back at the pond. The scene was just as he remembered from his youth—the water, the trees, the whispers of the night. Soft, peaceful, trustworthy. Then the moon floated behind a cloud and left the yard in sudden shadows. Stoney whistled for Silas and finally went inside.

It all really began, it certainly ended, in the swamp. Leave the town sleeping in its complacency and venture down the swamp road, a deserted two-lane that leads toward the coast. Cool midnight air blankets the hot pavement, steamy squiggles rising from it like rows of stranded ghosts. Hidden here and there in the woods are gray tarpaper shacks, blue paint outlining their screenless windows. Above the road live oak branches interlock in a canopy. The trees part over murky inlets and hunter hawks fly low just as a water moccasin glides by beneath them. Everywhere the veil of humidity lacquers the night with a surreal varnish wherein shapes and forms transmigrate at will. What you see may be what you see—or it may not.

Then the Low Country falls lower, becomes an altitudeless underbelly of earth and water. Its darkness feels like a prehistoric realm of ancient rites, of incantation and exorcism and transmutation. A snaky narrow river, which began in the open marshes of the coast, has slithered inland to form a dense swamp so choked with vegetation that the water barely moves. In the eerie stillness verrucose live oak trees rise from the watery underworld like primitive gargoyles. The tree trunks branch out only a few feet above the black water, crouching low beneath their shroud of Spanish moss. Unable to reach the sky, spidery old branches cleave inward, hang suspended in midair, crooked and twisted and useless.

These are the live oaks of legend. Most are two or three hundred years old, rooted to ancient terra firma stained by the blood of honor and tainted by the smell of witchcraft. Old-timers say that once this Southern tree grew straight and tall: unbent, it reached high into the sky. Legend has it that the live oak began to droop during the Civil War; as blood flowed freely around it, the tree shrank into itself. Shame stunted it forever. In Essex, children had always believed the live oak was haunted, that blacks who practiced voodoo or black magic had put a curse on it. Over time, touching a live oak in the swamps became a mandatory rite of passage for our young. Simply being in the swamps at night sometimes sufficed.

Which is how, that same night, five people chanced to be where only one of them belonged. When the moon Stoney McFarland had seen in town escaped from behind its clouds, it illuminated a house some ten miles away, in the thickest darkest bayou. There a ramshackle wooden cottage perched beside a blackwater inlet. From the rotting eave of this house hung a model of a century-old sailing ship painted bright red. A few feet away a small fire burned and from its center protruded a stationary iron bar, slanted sideways as though it had fallen from the sky. This was the home of Maum Chrish, a black woman of almost six feet whose close-cropped gray head seemed to reach above the trees she lived among. Naked to the waist, her pendulous breasts flopped back and forth in the moonlight, slap-slap-slap in rhythm to the sluck-sluck-sluck of her bare feet as they repeated themselves in the mud. Between the bank of the river and her house were rows of newly turned earth, the black dirt streaked with the white sand of the Low Country. The woman reached inside a burlap bag slung over her shoulder in the style of her ancestors and scooped out tiny brown kernels. She dropped to her knees and tucked the seeds in the ground, leaning over, her long slim breasts grazing the mounds of dirt between the rows. Then she rose and moved farther down, row after row after row, her slapping breasts and feet piercing the nighttime still.

No one knew where she had come from, no one knew exactly when she had first appeared in the swamps. The black people who lived near her and were said to consult her when someone

was sick or had died might have known but they weren't saying.
Rarely did she come to town, but several people took her supplies from time to time, including an inordinate number of live
chickens. Once in a while hunters would come upon gatherings
at her shack, would bring back stories of wild singing and dancing. We didn't ask questions, we didn't particularly care. Not
then.

When Maum Chrish finished with the seeds she paused beside the black water, breathed in, "*Djo-là-passée, djo-là-passée.*
The water to Ilé." Turning, she picked up a Mason jar containing a thick white liquid and carefully poured the filmy material
onto the seeds. Afterward she took a bamboo pole and began
to fish Spanish moss out of the live oaks. The base of each tree
was encircled by a brick pedestal lined with burning candles
which spotlighted her dark face as she passed. She tossed the
moss onto the rows of earth, then moved to the next tree. Again
she removed the gauzy webbing and spread it across the planted
seeds. She went from tree to tree until she had made a full circle
around her house. Now a blanket of gray moss covered the
disturbed dirt like flowers on a fresh grave.

Maum Chrish sat on the ground and intoned a silent prayer
to Cousin Zaca. She did not pray for her garden; she prayed
instead for what she had seen in the white glare of the Dark
Satellite in the sky.

Some distance away, a boy and a girl of about the same stature—slim and tall and taut of skin and sinew—crept into the
swamp. Hand in hand they walked among the great trees, moonlight lighting their way. In a moment they came to a small clearing surrounded by live oaks that shielded them from the rest of
the tangled swamp.

The teenagers paused in the clearing on a small grassy knoll
protected from rain by intertwined branches. They seemed to
know where they were. They embraced. Here the bayou smelled
of rotted riverlife patined with the musk of camellia, magnolia,
azalea. In the spring the flowers always erupt with hot color, the
last remnants of the old rice plantations. Wild and unchecked,
as everything is here, their scent is sweet and lush and danger-
ously sensual. It whispers to the stranger, promises pleasure. If
he lingers, he will know what he has never known before. And
so the boy and girl shed their clothes and knelt down together
on the grass, their tongues and legs entwining.

"Damn, he's doing it to her!"

On the opposite side of the clearing, two boys not yet twelve crouched low, in blue jeans and polo shirts and nylon jackets, flashlights poking out of the back pockets of their Levi's. Little Magellans exploring new territory.

"Damn," the larger boy breathed again. He peeked out from behind the tree that hid him, stared hard at the naked couple a hundred feet away, then turned to his companion. "It's true, they *do* do it out here. He's doing it to a black girl." He stopped, then repeated, "A black girl."

The smaller of the voyeurs timidly looked on. Weren't they freezing? He tried not to notice the spooky trees, the sounds he kept hearing in the water. Snakes? The couple rolled over and now the black girl was astride her companion. How did they do that without breaking it? He noticed her pretty cocoa breasts, but mostly he kept wondering if the swamps really were haunted. And whether his mother would get up in the night and discover he'd sneaked out.

"Lookit them knockers," the larger boy giggled. Then he clapped his hand over his mouth and bent down lower, where his erection was less noticeable. He punched his cohort. "Wish I could get my hands on a set like that. Don't you?"

Seth Von Hocke couldn't have cared less. He only hoped to get out of the swamps before something awful happened. Maybe that old lady out here really was a witch. . . .

"Damn, damn, damn, lookit 'em go! I bet—"

A twig snapped. A great black giant stepped behind the two boys. Out of the corner of her eye she noticed the lovers. She turned her fiery eyes on the boys and they scattered.

In Essex we've told so many stories about that night that almost everyone knows pretty much what happened, even down to what most of us were doing before we went to bed. In a small town you live in each other's pockets whether you want to or not; you grow so omniscient about your neighbors' lives even their thoughts aren't sacred. We're not exactly like that anymore. If what happened then happened now, it's unlikely any of us would know the whole story.

When the phone rang that night in Stoney McFarland's house, he didn't even hear it at first. He was dreaming about an old World War II movie his father had taken him to see when he was nine and he kept hearing air raid sirens. Over and over again. Surely everyone knew by now to take cover. He stirred, flicked open his eyes. The luminous dial of the clock radio blinked "1:33." Suddenly he jumped. The shrill jangle of his dream was on the nightstand.

He picked up the telephone receiver but the voice on the other end spoke first. "Hello? Hello?"

Stoney recognized the crackle. "Mrs. Setzler?"

Some people said she was the oldest lady in town. If not, she was undoubtedly the most controversial. Harriet Youmans Setzler was the reigning Dowager Queen of Essex, the only woman ever to sit on the Essex Town Council—a milestone likely to remain forever intact. For during her tenure as councilwoman, Harriet Setzler wrote a town ordinance, as yet unchallenged, limiting subsequent membership to men only. She liked to make her mark without competition.

"I know it's late, Stoney," she explained, "but I couldn't think of anyone else to call. I tried Jim Leland, he's not answering. Only policeman we have and he takes his phone off the hook, might as well not have one."

Stoney refocused on the clock, wondered what on earth Harriet Setzler wanted this time of night. "What's wrong, Mrs. Setzler?"

"What is it?" Anna mumbled from her side of the bed. Stoney's parents always called immediately when a distant relative was ill. "What time is it?"

"I need you to come over here," Harriet Setzler commanded. "I woke up a while ago and heard something over at Sarah's. A noise, something. Maybe I dreamed it but I can't put it out of my mind. I'd sure rest easier if somebody checked on her. I'd go myself—but you're 'bout as close as I am."

The McFarlands lived five blocks from Sarah Roth's house; Harriet Setzler lived across the street. But in her eyes Stoney McFarland was still a boy who earned money every summer mowing lawns and running errands. So, when he and Anna moved to Essex, into the old neighborhood with more than its share of "widow-ladies," he soon became their resident ladder-climber, heavy-lifter, and checker-outer.

"Mrs. Setzler, did you call Sarah?"

A pause. "No answer." Then, "Course Sarah's snoring could drown out a hurricane. I spent two nights over there when she was sick last year and I couldn't even hear the trains go by. She is an old lady, you know."

Harriet Setzler, at eighty-seven, frequently made it clear that she herself was exempt from the customary ravages of old age.

She was also the only charter member of the Essex Lutheran Church who boycotted the monthly Senior Citizen suppers.

"I'll walk over in a second," Stoney said. "I'm sure Sarah's fine, don't worry." He hung up the phone.

By now Anna's eyes were wide open. "What's going on?"

"It's nothing." Stoney climbed out of bed and pulled on the khakis draped over a nearby chair. "Mrs. Setzler thinks she heard something at Sarah Roth's house, wants somebody to check on her. Leland can't be reached, of course."

"She wants you to come over there at this time of night?" Anna peered at the clock radio, then turned back to Stoney. "Those old ladies think you're their errand boy."

Stoney slipped on a rugby shirt, then went to the closet for his shoes and a jacket. "I know. Mrs. Setzler probably just had a nightmare." He tied his shoelaces, crossed back to the bed, and sat down beside his wife. "Go back to sleep."

She reached out and hugged him. "Stoney, let's don't argue about Essex anymore." He held her and then she leaned back. "Why do you love me anyway?"

He grinned. "Because you're shorter than I am."

"Get outta here." Anna snuggled back down into her pillow. "You be careful."

Her husband stood up. "Now what could happen to me in a hick town like this?" He winked and headed for the door. "I'll be back before my side of the bed gets cold."

Downstairs, in the kitchen, Silas snapped to attention when the light came on. Stoney knelt beside the dog's bed and scratched under the retriever's neck. Silas was a big, goofy dog with serious dark brown eyes whose iris was the same spun-gold as his fur. Anna had given Stoney the pup on their first wedding anniversary in Essex and he was just the sort of dog Stoney had always wanted but couldn't keep in a city apartment. Silas agreeably rolled over onto his back to have his belly scratched, then he jumped up and stretched and shook off sleep. When he saw Stoney reach for the leash hanging by the back door, he shot across the kitchen floor, his tail sweeping wide arcs behind him. Stoney clipped the leash to his collar. "Let's go for a walk, kid." On the back porch Stoney flipped on the outside lights and locked the door behind him. Some people in Essex still didn't lock their doors at night, but the McFarlands couldn't shake the city-bred habit. (The one night they tried, they both lay awake until three in the morning, then got up together and locked every door in the entire house.) Essexians were quite proud of the town's lack of crime: natives were quick to point out that there'd never been any real trouble, not a single murder anyone could remember or even any serious racial unrest. Robberies and vandalism and domestic squabbles, the triple terrors of many small communities, were few and far between. Stoney breathed in the night air. It was still chilly and sometime since midnight a light rain had fallen; the street and the old concrete sidewalks bordering it glistened under the occasional streetlight. On both sides of the road stood the traditional Old Essex house: a one-story bungalow with a pitched roof, always painted white in his youth but now leaning toward pastels with contrasting trim. His grandmother had owned such a house which, in the hands of a subsequent owner, had burned to the ground when Stoney was in high school. Here and there the rectangular shape of the houses rose to two stories or turned squatty and square and featured a bit of gingerbread trim on wide front porches that always sported a swing or wooden rockers.

"Heel, Silas," Stoney called sharply. He had let go of the leash and now the fluffy blond dog was half a block ahead of him. With a resigned air, Silas stopped and waited for his companion, checking the tree limbs above him for squirrels. When Stoney caught up, the dog trotted alongside him for another block and then they turned left and crossed the street, heading toward Aiken Avenue.

Stoney gazed idly at the sleeping houses on his right. In appearance Essex had changed very little since he was a boy. Pictures of this part of town had looked much the same in the 1930s, the 1950s, and the 1970s. Only the condition of the photograph dated the scene. Despite the fact that the town had spread out and now even had a "development" of brick ranchers, there was still no best place to live. When Stoney was young, blacks lived on the outskirts of Essex in all directions with whites in the center. Now three black families owned homes in the center of town and the subdivision was fully integrated. On paper anyway. For change was slow and social interaction still minimal.

Turning right onto Aiken Avenue, the oldest residential street in town, Stoney again noted a sign of progress, the attractive frame home of Marian Davis. A vivacious black woman a little older than Stoney, Marian Davis taught English at the high school. And lived on the street where blacks had once only come and gone as servants. The first time Stoney had ever seen Marian had been on this same street, this time of night, over twenty years ago. Originally named Alma, before Harriet Setzler took her in and changed her name to Marian, she was then a skinny kid who cooked and cleaned for Harriet just as her mother once had.

Late that summer's night, when Stoney couldn't sleep, he had slipped out of his grandmother's house for a walk. It was exciting being out at night, alone. Something he could never do in Washington. Then he heard a commotion in front of the Setzler house, a house he normally avoided, given its owner's reputation for keeping baseballs that landed in her yard. Lights and voices, the sound of a girl crying, the harsh syllables of a baritone. Harriet Setzler standing on her front porch looking meaner than a copperhead, clutching her bathrobe to her like she actually thought somebody might want to *look* at her. Below her, on the sidewalk, the sheriff from Ashton County, a heavyset man in his sixties, seemed annoyed.

"Sorry to bother you, Miz Setzler. I picked this here colored girl up off the highway. Near the swamps." He pushed the girl at arm's length, keeping a hand on the back of her collar. "She shore does stink, drunker 'n sin, I don't know where they git it. This'n 'bout got herself kilt, she was weaving all over the road, I near-bout hit her."

The girl, obviously unsteady, grabbed the sheriff's arm, swayed, then moaned, "Oh please doan carry me to the jail-house. Take me to Miz Setzler."

The large man shook his head. "Damn fool don't know where she's at." He looked up at Harriet Setzler, who was staring at Marian with pursed lips. "She wouldn't tell me where she lives, just kept bawling for me to bring her here."

Hiding in the bushes, Stoney held his breath. He felt sorry for Marian, that she had nowhere else to go. Everybody knew how hard Harriet Setzler was on colored people. She also hated drinking: getting "liquored-up" in her book was the one sure ticket to hell. People said it was on account of how one of her boys took to the bottle real bad, they said she never forgave him.

Harriet Setzler glowered at the trembling girl. "Marian, I'm ashamed of you. Acting like this. No better'n white trash. Come on in here right now."

The sheriff, who didn't live in Essex, stared at the white woman. "You gonna take this girl in your house? Like this?"

Imperious, Harriet marched down her steps and took Marian's arm, daring the sheriff to object. "She lives here." She led the girl back up onto the porch. The Ashton sheriff stared, his mouth ajar; everyone in the county knew of Harriet Setzler's legendary racism. But as the two women disappeared inside the door, Stoney saw a pudgy white arm cradle the girl's thin shoulders as naturally as if it belonged there.

Many years later Marian the college graduate had come home to teach, and she now lived just down the street from the woman she'd once worked for. Stoney stared ahead of him. Sarah Roth's house was two doors down. He reached out and patted Silas, then quickened his pace. Soon he'd be crawling back into bed. Harriet Setzler was probably just imagining things. Maybe a dog woke her up, squirrels or something. Stoney smiled. Anna said he was baby-sitting the old ladies in Essex. Maybe he was. They had done as much for him once.

Sarah Roth's house was a two-story frame structure with a gabled roof. She was the last survivor of one of the oldest families in Essex, the only Jewish family ever to live there. Of the original five settlers of the town, a Samuel Rothenbarger had come to Essex to open a dry goods store. That store, in a post-1865 building, still stood in the middle of the town's business district and passed as its only facsimile of a department store. It had remained in the family through each generation and had been known to many Essexians as simply "Roth's." When her husband was killed in a train accident (they lost their only child in World War II), Sarah took over the store. She was the first woman to run a business in Essex and the strength of her personality left its mark. Now, despite her retirement, the store was known as "Sarah's."

Stoney mounted the wide wooden stairs of her house. A stained glass window Sarah's husband had given her the year before his death was mounted in the oak front door. For years everyone had told her some kid's softball was going to break it but she'd paid no heed. And it was still intact. Stoney knocked on the door softly. He hated to wake her, scare her like this just because Harriet Setzler couldn't sleep.

No answer. Stoney glanced across the street at Harriet Setzler's house and wondered if the old lady was watching him. He turned and knocked on Sarah's door again and waited, motioning to Silas to lie down. The dog ignored Stoney and stood on the edge of the porch staring out at the street. When Sarah Roth still didn't answer, Stoney hesitated. This is silly, he thought. He ambled to the edge of the porch. "What do you see, boy?" Silas looked up at Stoney with soulful eyes but didn't move. Stoney gazed out at the street. Everything was perfectly still. He studied the knifelike shadows the live oaks left on the sidewalk, then shivered and went back to the door and knocked again.

Sarah Roth still didn't answer. God, she must sleep soundly. What if she was sick, had a heart attack or something? Why didn't he think of that before? He turned back to the wooden door and tried the lock. It didn't budge. She probably didn't use the front door, many Essexians didn't.

Stoney scrambled around to the back of Sarah Roth's house. He strode toward the back porch and jerked open the screen door. Looking down, he saw mud on the linoleum in front of the door. It had rained during the night but not until after he and Anna had gone to bed. Surely Sarah hadn't been out this time of night.

Abruptly Stoney remembered Silas and turned around. The dog was sniffing the steps. "What is it, Silas?"

Head still down, the retriever growled, his body rigid.

"Stay, Silas." To himself Stoney intoned silently, calm down. If she's sick, you can take care of it, it'll be all right. He crossed to the wooden door, yanked the rusty metal doorknob and pushed. "Mrs. Roth?" he called when the door opened. "It's Stoney McFarland. You okay?"

The silence inside felt wider than an ocean.

"Mrs. Roth?"

Stoney stepped inside the kitchen; he felt like a prowler. He licked his lips. Where the hell was her bedroom? Quietly he made his way through the unfamiliar rooms. If she was okay and he woke her like this in the middle of the night, he'd probably give her a heart attack. He passed an old china cupboard with glass doors. He'd only been in this house a few times and he had no idea where the light switches were.

"Mrs. Roth?" he called loudly. "Mrs. Roth, it's Stoney."

God, could she sleep through anything? Stoney's heart hammered in his chest and he lurched down the hallway, found the light switch and snapped it on. The glare blinded him momentarily, but even the light didn't wake her.

He rushed into what looked like a breakfast room, then into a smaller room furnished like a den: a television, a treadle Singer sewing machine, a small desk piled high with papers. The living room would be at the front of the house; at her age she probably didn't use the second floor, so that left two rooms, both with their doors closed. Stoney threw open the first. Double bed, starched white chintz curtains, cotton throw-rugs. No Sarah.

"Mrs. Roth?"

Stoney pivoted, burst into the other room. "Mrs. Roth, wake up. Are you—"

Everything stopped.

Years later he would remember it as he remembered the only hurricane he ever witnessed. He was eleven, visiting his grandmother one August, when a storm came inland and left thousands of decapitated trees in its wake. Through a crack in the plywood nailed over his grandmother's windows, he had watched the malevolent wind reach out and viciously sever pine trees, leaving behind nothing but ragged stumps.

There was blood everywhere. On the walls, on the spindles of the headboard, on the sheets, even on the carpet. Like someone had taken a shower in it. What remained of Sarah Rothenbarger lay nude on the bloodied bed, her face nearly unrecognizable.

Stoney recoiled in horror. Then, suddenly, he saw none of it, no red gashes in the fleshy neck, no lifeless bluing lips. All he saw was an energetic middle-aged woman in a flowered dress, her hair the color of a ripe pumpkin in the strong sunlight; she was hanging wet clothes on a line strung between two live oaks while he maneuvered a push mower across her back yard.

"Gabriel, you want some water?"

The boy winced. Nobody in Essex called him Gabriel anymore. Thank goodness.

"No ma'am." He paused and leaned on the mower's wood handle, deliberately affecting the pose he'd observed in adult yard men like Monkey, the man who worked for Mrs. Setzler and threw a baseball like nobody's business. "Mrs. Roth, uh, ma'am, people don't call me Gabriel anymore."

Sarah Rothenbarger gazed at the boy and her tiny brown eyes came to a point, folks around town called her "shrewd" when she looked that way, said that was how she kept the store going when she lost her husband. "Your grandmother calls you Gabriel. That's your name."

"That was when I was a baby. Everybody calls me Stoney now."

"Stoney?"

"Yes ma'am. On account of how I skip rocks on the McCloskey pond. I've had big ones skim clear across and land on the other side. I win at ducks and drakes every time. All the kids know." It was only a slight exaggeration.

"Don't you like the name Gabriel? In your Bible Gabriel is

the angel who brings good news, isn't he? I believe he's considered a guardian and a protector.''

Stoney refrained from telling her that the Bible made it even worse, as if being stuck with a sissy name wasn't bad enough. It would be many years before the irony of this conversation would occur to him—that Sarah Rothenbarger knew so much about his religion when he knew nothing of hers. "I just think a fella oughta be called what he likes.''

Sarah smiled and got that shrewd look again. "I guess you're right. I guess a fella oughta. I won't forget, Stoney.''

And she hadn't either. Not in all those summers he'd cut her grass, not when he'd come back to Essex to live as an adult either. At seventy-five, she had pronounced his nickname in such a way—crisp as the first fall apple—that it always felt like a gift. He'd never had a conversation with her about anything more significant than the weather, but all her life she had touched him. Just by the way she spoke his name.

Stoney turned and ran. He ran through the house, into the kitchen, out the back door, down the porch steps, into the yard. Silas jumped up and chased him, barking playfully. But Stoney dropped onto the ground, covered his face, rocked back and forth like a wounded child. Finally he opened his eyes. Moonlight still streamed weakly through the branches of the live oaks in Sarah's yard. The clothesline was gone now and suddenly he couldn't remember which trees had supported it. In this fading light the live oaks became misshapened monsters, the swamplike tree of legend, stunted, knurled up like ancient arthritic hands whose disease lives within and lays waste to the whole.

Silas whimpered and lay down by the man he loved.

Two

SOMETIME AROUND FIVE in the morning a sharp noise startled Marian Davis and she couldn't get back to sleep. She tossed and turned for an hour, fighting it out with her pillow. Finally she gave up, opened her eyes and gazed around her bedroom in the semidarkness. It was a light and airy cocoon filled with white wicker and unbleached muslin, each wall dominated by an Impressionist. She stared at her favorite print for a second: Degas' *Two Dancers*. This painting always conjured up the image of a young girl dancing along a highway in the middle of the night, her scrawny arms aloft as she struggled to rise to her toes in a pair of secondhand shoes. Then the girl fell on the hard dry pavement, her face scratched by loose gravel, reality in her throat.

"Ain't no nigger ever been no dancer," her sallow-eyed mother had once proclaimed. "You big as a hoss, lookit them feet." And the mother had gone back to the biscuit making, a coal-tar woman up to her elbows in white people's flour.

Marian's eyes rested on the pale dresser across the room. Atop it sat a black-and-white photograph of a girl named Alma. The woman in bed and the girl didn't look much alike. Alma had nubby pigtails all over her head; Marian's face was framed by the "relaxed" softness of a hairdresser's curls, cut short and stylish. Alma was born with a flat nose, her flaring nostrils as wide as airplane wings; Marian's nose was slim and tapered, a surgeon's creation. Nothing in Alma suggested opportunity— nothing in Marian suggested she'd ever been without it. Yet the two females did share the same skin: honey-gold, high yellow, a chocolate milkshake heavy on the cream. And their eyes were identical, mahogany with a cedar center, a goblet of warm sherry held to the light, full-bodied and complex.

18

In a moment Marian glanced at the pastel linen suit hanging on the back of her closet door. If Mama could see me now, she thought. Next to the closet a rocking chair cradled a large briefcase stuffed with term papers. These days she was a black woman who worked with words, who would never roll biscuits again. She stretched her long frame luxuriously. Spring. The best time of the year. What teacher didn't feel like a kid this close to a three-month date with freedom? Summer was the advantage to teaching: your life was always a cycle, you always had closure, rest, and a new beginning to look forward to. Always starting over, you never had time to grow old.

And she knew a lot about new beginnings, didn't she?

Not that she didn't love her "babies," as she privately called her students. When I walk in a room, Mama, the kids look up expectantly. Do you know how many teachers walk into a room and the kids don't even notice? Not me. I make words dance for them, I choreograph futures. I take a black kid who can't speak real English, not the English that'll let him do things in this world, and I show him how the words in a sentence fit together like a puzzle, how they go together one way smooth as silk, how they get pushed together another and make sandpaper. I tell him it's okay to talk our talk at home, but to use what I teach him everywhere else.

She wished her mama knew how people in Essex respected her now, how they stopped her on the street to ask about Johnny's spelling or Susan's essay, how they waved and said why didn't she come in for a cup of coffee? Hardly anyone looked at her anymore and said, "There goes the black English teacher." Now they said, "Why there goes Marian, who used to live with Harriet. Lost her folks but she made something of herself after all." Mama didn't know that a black woman could get respect in a white world if she worked hard enough, persisted, didn't give in. Didn't run away.

Marian got up, went down the hall to the kitchen and put the coffee on. Her house was small, shotgun style, all four rooms emptying into a central hallway. Coming back down the hall, she reentered her bedroom and made the bed. As she was crossing to the bathroom, her eyes fell on the picture of Alma again. She turned and walked over to the painted white dresser and picked the photograph up. Alma, who had looked so much like her mother.

They had lived in a shack on the outskirts of town. Two rooms and a dirt yard that was always swarming with stray chickens and mangy dogs and flies. The house was constructed of un-painted gray wood, and burlap flapped at the open windows bereft of glass. Behind the structure was an outhouse and the unkempt garden that provided all their food in the summer. And on both sides stood carbon-copy houses, crowded so close that hands stuck out of opposing windows could touch.

When she came home that day, it all looked the same. Chickens scratching in the dirt for imaginary feed, the neighbor's baby squalling on the porch next door. Alma sat down on the rickety wooden steps of her house, looked at the wilted circles of petunias in the yard, and took off the shoes she wore only to school. It was spring, almost time to put them up again. An old dog of uncertain extraction ambled over and nuzzled her knee and she picked fleas out of his eyes. Then the animal lay down beside her and vomited. ''Dis dog be sick,'' she muttered and went inside to tell her mama.

Something seemed odd the moment she walked in the door. It wasn't the silence, for often she came home to an empty house. It was more the absence of any expectation, as though the house knew it needn't wait up for anyone else. Also, it was scrupulously clean. The floor had been scrubbed, the dishes were all stacked neatly in their orange crate, the bed pillows had even been fluffed. A legacy of cleanliness, her start in the world. She ran from the parlor to the bedroom where her mama slept. No clothes in the closet, the hairbrush gone from the mantel, the Bible no longer under the bed. Even her smell was gone. She'd washed it away before she left.

Alma went back out and sat down on the steps. She sat there until dark. She sat there until daybreak. Then she went to tell the white lady that her mama wasn't coming to work.

She was eight years old at the time.

Five years ago Marian had been certain that someday she would see her mother again. It was the memory of her mother, or more accurately the lack of it, that had driven her to give up a good job in Columbia in order to come home. Maturity—and a successful adult life—had tempered the pain of abandonment somewhat, had made way for a curiosity once deadened by resentment and loss. Lonnie must have had a good reason for leaving. Marian wanted to see her mother again, to get to know her finally. Black people who left the South always came back someday, sometimes to show off, often to die. Her mother had departed in a sudden flash, without warning or explanation. No doubt she would return the same way. And Marian wanted to be there when it happened; she did not want to risk missing whatever time they still had.

When she'd first come back to Essex, she'd promised herself she'd only stay for one year. During those months she hounded blacks and whites alike for information about Lonnie Davis—surely someone had heard from her, knew something about why she had disappeared all those years ago, recalled her favorite color or whether she'd finished high school. The older blacks, who remembered a scruffy kid named Alma, took one look at this new black woman in her fine suit and tapered nose and didn't say much. But Marian kept at it, went back to them again in shorts and sandals, and gradually they said just enough to make her decide to stay a second year. They didn't know where Lonnie was or why she'd gone away but they did know her favorite color was red, and that was enough for Marian, and the second year began. And a third, a fourth, a fifth. The black woman thrust by chance into a white world stayed on . . . and waited.

A sudden knock on the door startled Marian. She looked up, slipped on her polished cotton bathrobe, and padded toward her front door. It was early for company. On her front porch stood Elsie Fenton, a white woman in her sixties whose most distinguishing trademark was her refusal to abide by daylight savings time. From April to October she was perpetually late. Moving time forward one hour, she maintained, put her one hour closer to her death. And besides, that extra hour of sunlight burned up her grass.

When Marian opened her door, she knew something was wrong. "Morning, Elsie. You okay?"

"Oh Marian—have you heard about Sarah?"

"Heard what?" The black woman backed inside. "Come on in, it's chilly out here."

The other woman didn't move, just wrung her hands together. "I had to talk to somebody, it's so awful. I can't believe it. Nothing like this has ever happened here. Not to anybody we know. I don't know what to do."

Marian stared at the shorter woman. "What's wrong with Sarah?"

The older woman held up her hands helplessly. "She's been murdered. Found dead in her bed. Stabbed to death."

They stood in shocked silence for a few seconds, Marian watching her neighbor's distraught, lined face.

Then Elsie Fenton added, "Stoney McFarland found her early this morning. The Ashton sheriff was here too. They took her away in an ambulance."

"My God," Marian said finally. Was that what woke her earlier? "Do they know who did it?"

Her visitor's eyes filled with dread. She shook her head. "They don't have a clue." She looked down the street suspiciously, lowered her voice. "I guess it could be somebody we know."

"Has anyone told Harriet?"

"I think so. I saw Stoney go over there after the ambulance left. I'd better get on back home, I just thought you'd want to know."

Marian reached out and patted the other woman on the shoulder. "I appreciate your coming over; I'd better check on Harriet. They'll find who did this. Try not to worry."

Rushing back inside to dress, Marian felt sorry for her frightened neighbor. Violence was unheard of in Essex, she should be scared stiff herself. Yet her hands were steady, she wasn't even in shock. Her race, her sex, lived with the omnipresence of brutality, it was forever there beside you, a shadow, a second skin, a prickly awareness. You knew the price of freedom might very well be pain.

Quickly Marian dressed, in loose slacks and a sweater. This might be the rare day she missed school, or was late. She grabbed her purse and checked to make sure her wallet was inside. Absently she fingered the zippered inner compartment of the leather bag; within it lay the loaded single-shot derringer she'd carried for twenty years.

Sarah Roth's house was full of people. A dazed Jim Leland, the thin and wispy symbol of law enforcement in Essex, trailed behind the Ashton County sheriff like a child learning the rules of a new game. The lab team from Ashton County with its fingerprinting apparatus and tape and cameras moved back and forth between the rooms. Only the county coroner had left, bearing Sarah Roth's body on its final journey. Stoney sat at the kitchen table sipping the strong coffee someone had brought over. People milled about, speaking to themselves but not to him, and he had the strangest sensation of being invisible, of being a ghost in a house full of the living. They were animated but he was still. Like Sarah.

"Stoney, maybe you oughta go home. There's nothing you can do here," Ed Hammond said as he crossed to the table; he was still clad in the pajamas and tartan robe he'd been wearing when Stoney got him out of bed.

The only doctor in Essex, Ed Hammond was also the medical examiner for Ashton County; he had an office in Essex and also practiced at the county hospital outside town. "I guess I'd better get going myself," he went on, yawning. "They'll need me at the hospital."

"You'll do the autopsy," Stoney said.

Ed Hammond nodded. "Maybe we'll know more after that."

The doctor reached back and massaged his shoulder blades with his fingertips. He was a short, thick man with the neck and torso of a bulldog and, at forty-six, was already totally bald like his father, the Essex doctor when Stoney was a boy. Ed nodded at Stoney again. "I'll see you later."

"Ed, wait." Stoney gazed at the other man. "I just don't understand this."

"Neither do I." The doctor headed for the door. "Go home, get some sleep."

Stoney watched the bald man disappear into the morning light, then he closed his eyes.

He had raced down the street after he found Sarah, had covered the ten blocks to Ed's house in less than two minutes. It never occurred to him to get Jim Leland. Instead, he banged on the doctor's front door, shouted, set the neighbor's cats to howling. When a startled Ed flipped on the porch light and opened the door, Stoney yelled, "You gotta come. It's Sarah. I don't know what happened. *For God's sake, come on.*"

In Ed's car Stoney told him, briefly, what he'd found. After that they didn't speak. They jumped out of the car at the curb at Sarah's house and ran around to the back door. Stoney led the way to her bedroom. "I—I can't—"

"Stay here," Ed whispered.

Stoney paced back and forth in the kitchen. He leaned over the counter and turned on the water in the sink, cupped his hands together and splashed the cold liquid on his face. Then he slammed his fist down on the cabinet. What in God's name *happened*? He turned around, whirled back to the cabinet and kicked the door. "Craaccck!" His foot went right through the wood. Pain shot up his leg and tears rose in his eyes. He limped over to the kitchen table and sat down. Then he got up again, paced over to the sink and stared out at the moonlight.

This could not be real.

In a few minutes Ed Hammond entered the kitchen, his face

colorless. He crossed to the sink and washed his hands. He turned around and looked at Stoney.

"We've got to get Leland. And the Ashton sheriff. She's been dead an hour or two." He swallowed. "Somebody really cut her up. I haven't seen anything like it since I was a resident in Charlotte. She bled to death probably, her carotid artery was cut in half." Ed walked over to the table and sat down, his voice flat. "There's something else, Stoney. First I thought she'd been raped, since she's naked and all. There's semen all over her. But she wasn't raped."

Stoney gaped at the other man. "What?"

"I'm fairly positive—as positive as I can be now. There's no sign of forcible entry."

For a moment neither man said a word, just stared at each other.

"Aw, Christ," Stoney said after a moment. He got up and paced again. "I don't understand this."

"I don't know what to think either. I'm just telling you what I found. Massive facial injuries. Semen, but no evidence of rape."

Stoney fought the urge to retch. He went back to the sink and stuck his face under the faucet, wiped his eyes with a kitchen towel lying on the counter. Suddenly he turned around. "You think somebody came through town, tried to rob her and she heard them?"

The doctor looked up. "Her TV's still here, I saw it in the den." He eyed Stoney for a second. "What did she have anybody'd want to steal?"

It was true. Sarah Roth had lived modestly, had not been given to buying or hoarding. Her most valuable asset had been the store, which she still owned but paid someone else to run. Stoney sighed. "I've never heard of anyone who didn't like her, who'd have a grudge against her." He sat down at the table again. "It had to be somebody passing through town. Nobody in Essex would do this."

The doctor's image faded when Stoney felt a hand on his shoulder. He stared up at the Ashton sheriff. Buck Henry, whom Stoney had never met before, was a tall man in a khaki uniform. "Mr. McFarland, we're going to have to seal off the house now. 'Preciate you sticking around so long. If you think of anything else, please contact Chief Leland or get in touch with my office."

It took Stoney a moment to realize he was being dismissed. He stood up awkwardly. "Did you find anything?"

"Unfortunately not much. No fingerprints or footprints. We think he came through the yard by way of that stone path and wore gloves in the house. Knew what he was doing, I'd say."

"What happens now?"

"You go home and get some rest. We'll take a complete statement from you later. Don't worry, a full investigation will be under way."

As Stoney was leaving Sarah Roth's house, Marian Davis was heading in the opposite direction.

Harriet Setzler lived a block away from Marian, in a light green clapboard house with a sleeping porch jutting out to one side. The town's foremost eccentric, she was also the axis around which this neighborhood rotated. She had angered nearly all of us at one time or another but we rarely confronted her. Most of us, although we didn't admit it, were afraid of her, had been ever since enduring her English classes at Essex High. She had come to town in the early 1920s as the second wife of the town clerk, a gentle blue-eyed man whose artistic wife had died in childbirth, leaving him four small children to raise. Afterward, Harriet moved in, with her domineering schoolteacher ways, and took on the prefab family like a clean-up campaign. That she loved the father, to whom she never bore any offspring herself, was never questioned; when he died young, she remained loyal to his memory and faithfully put fresh flowers on his grave every Sunday, even in the rain. When all her children moved on, she stayed behind in the house her husband built for his first wife. If she was lonely, we never knew it—displays of emotion were alien to her. Which made what she did when her husband died all the more legendary. When his first wife died, William Setzler had bought a family plot in the town cemetery, saving a place beside her body for him and later adding additional room on the other side for his second wife (death arrangements being a perpetual preoccupation among Essexians). However, when William also died early, he unaccountably ended up on the far side of the triple plot. Harriet Setzler made sure she would eventually occupy the middle space, keeping the other two apart for eternity.

The graveyard incident was Marian's favorite gossip about her former guardian. When the black woman got to the corner, she turned and went around to the back of Harriet's house, letting

herself inside the high wooden fence and walking up the concrete back steps. She entered this house the same way she had
twenty years earlier, always through the back. She pulled open
the door of the screened-in back porch. Coming in the back way
in Essex meant you were either a servant or family. She certainly
wasn't Harriet's servant. Was she family? She felt like she was,
yet the lack of the adoption she'd prayed for so fervently as an
adolescent, despite the odds, kept the question unanswered. She
knocked on the back door. Through the thin fabric covering the
glass panes she could see the old lady sitting at the kitchen table,
her rounded shoulders uncharacteristically slumped, her head
resting in her hands. Marian knocked louder. Harriet's hearing
was finally going. This time the older woman looked up, squared
her shoulders, got to her feet slowly and let Marian in.

"You heard?"

Marian nodded. The white-haired woman looked so lost she
wanted to reach out and embrace her. Instead, she went to
the counter and busied herself making coffee. As she poured the
brown liquid into two ceramic mugs, she noticed a Mason jar
of blackberry preserves on the counter. For a moment it took
her back to the first day she'd ever set foot in that house. Six
years old, on the back porch steps eating her lunch in the blis-
tering August sun after five hours of scrubbing and sweeping,
drinking her iced water out of a Mason jar so white folks—as
her mother explained later—wouldn't have to throw their kitchen
glasses away.

When they had their coffee before them and were seated at
the round claw-foot table in the center of the room, Harriet said,
"Now they're almost all gone."

The younger woman knew what she meant. Sarah Roth had
been one of the old guard, one of the few who remembered
William Setzler. Marian gazed at Harriet's massive hands. They
were wrinkled and liver-spotted, and her veins bulged like the
mole tunnels she often found in her garden. When Marian was
a child, Harriet's hands had fascinated her: their size, their
strength, the amazing things they accomplished. Powerful hands,
capable of molding bread dough or public opinion. She'd always
wanted to grab hold of one of those hands and swing from it.
Harriet's hand would keep her from flying into space, would
protect her. Impulsively she reached out now and covered the
white hand with her brown one, felt the shaking beneath her
palm. Slowly the white trembling stopped. Harriet was staring

at Marian's hand as if she didn't see it, or didn't realize it was touching her.

"Must have been some drifter," the older woman cried vehemently. "Some no-count trash coming through town in the middle of the night. Probably a—" She halted, noticed the dark hand atop hers. "Nigra" died on her lips.

Marian heard it anyway. She withdrew her hand.

"Stoney came over first thing this morning," Harriet covered quickly. "The Ashton sheriff wanted to know if anything was missing, they couldn't tell by themselves. Sarah's jewelry—the good pieces as well as that costume stuff she loved—was all gone. And some little trinkets she prized, a porcelain box someone sent her from England, her spoon collection, worthless sentimental things. Why would anybody take those? They got the silver too. But most of the house was untouched, like Sarah'd just gone on a trip. Mud on the back porch and on a chair, but nothing else. They didn't take much at all, just killed her. And—defiled her."

The other woman looked up abruptly. "She was raped?"

"I heard Ed Hammond, he was there too, talking to the sheriff. About . . . semen." Harriet could barely get the word out. She cleared her throat. "Then Ed said she probably wasn't raped. I don't know what he meant. They kept the door to Sarah's room closed, I didn't see her."

Marian coughed. The room felt airless all of a sudden. She swallowed, tried to get her breath.

"Oh I just can't talk about it anymore," Harriet said, her voice unsteady. She got up and headed toward the rear of the house and its one bathroom. Marian crossed to the sink and rinsed out the coffee cups, glad for something to do. A hundred disturbing possibilities flooded her now. To quell them, she walked over to the telephone and called the high school secretary, to explain she'd be late to school. The secretary, who lived in the newer part of town, had not yet heard the news.

Was Harriet all right? Marian wandered into the breakfast room where built-in china cupboards rose to the ceiling and walked through the adjoining door into the dining room that was never used. It was a mammoth room with a twelve-foot mahogany table, ten large oil paintings on the walls, two oak china cabinets guarding Haviland china and Fostoria crystal, and a brick fireplace framed by brass andirons. In the early years when Marian and her mother had come to Harriet's to cook the Thanksgiving dinners, Harriet's burgeoning relatives had always been squeezed in around the small table in the breakfast room. Packed in so tight the food had to be brought in by rounds: first the turkey, ham, and roast; then the sweet potatoes and creamed corn and fried okra and five or six other vegetables; next the breads and coffee and tea; finally the pecan pie, the tiny lime pies, the ambrosia, and the fruit and pound cakes. Every bit of it, she thought, would have fit on this one table. Was this table used when William Setzler was alive?

Through the double-wide doorway she passed into the old-fashioned living room which hadn't changed in twenty years: black upright piano, overstuffed armchairs upholstered in a floral print, glass bookcases housing dusty volumes of the Harvard Classics, and a small mahogany table with a glass top displaying Harriet's glass figurine collection. It was also the room where a black girl had been married. Marian smiled. Harriet loved shocking people. It was one thing to take in a black orphan, it was quite another to publicly present her. So when Harriet gave a wedding in her own parlor for a colored teenager, it had set the town's mouths on fire for a year.

Marian closed her eyes, became eighteen again. It had been years now since she'd come to live with Miss Harriet. Now the white woman had sewn her a long white dress with a veil. And up the steps they came that summer day. Black and white together. Staring at each other. Standing on different sides of the room. Integration before its time, those who remembered said of it now. They didn't know it was the first time the silver chest in that house had ever been under lock and key. All they recalled was that Harriet Setzler opened her doors to the colored, and presided over Marian's wedding as if she were mother of the bride. They missed the symbolism of the reception afterward: one table set up in the breakfast room, another in the kitchen. Marian smiled again, ruefully. God knows what color you had to be to get served in that dining room.

The marriage didn't last, of course. The groom had been a handsome bum who was kind to Marian as no man had ever been; but a year later, when she realized she didn't love him and that he really only wanted a maid, she was off to college, Harriet's check in her purse. After the divorce her ex-husband had drifted toward Florida; she had never heard from him again. What she recalled most about her wedding day was not the groom or her white dress but the way Harriet Setzler had fussed over her in public.

Marian walked out of the living room. The center of Harriet's house was a bedroom which the elderly lady called "the front room," to distinguish it from "the back room" behind it. The latter contained a brass bed, a mirrored armoire, and in one corner, a small ceramic sink behind a Japanese screen. Company slept there, as had Marian on the rebellious night she had drunk so much whiskey she couldn't make it upstairs. And on one other night, a much worse one. Even now she still remembered the softness of the satin-covered down quilt on that bed. The front room, where Harriet slept, also led to the sleeping porch, a patterned linoleum expanse half the length of the house and wainscotted with windows overlooking Harriet's garden. Marian peered inside the doorway. Three single beds lined the walls. Harriet's boys had slept here when they were small, and even now Mr. William's hospital bed with its manual steel crank remained in its place, high enough to catch even the briefest breeze through the windows. No one but Marian knew that after the children left home Harriet Setzler had often, on long listless summer nights, left her own bed in the early hours and spent the rest of the night in the last place her husband ever slept.

The black woman recrossed to the center of Harriet's room, stopped and gazed at the closet door. Inside the square walk-in closet a ladder nailed to the wall led up into the attic, where only the roof vents admitted light and fresh air. A mattress had been lugged up there by Monkey the yard man, along with a washstand, a trunk for her clothes, and later a small desk. Marian stared at the door, again saw herself sweating on a damp mattress in the middle of a summer night, her body striped by vertical lines of moonlight shining through the attic vent as she listened to the three o'clock train whistle by. Essentially alone in the world but not really unhappy. She wondered if her bed was still up there. Did the smell of her childhood linger in that close, humid air?

Two days after her mother left, Marian told Aunt Posey down the street (who was nobody's aunt but everybody in town called her that) and Aunt Posey told everyone she knew. Lonnie Davis was gone and her chile Alma didn't have nobody now. Couldn't a soul find Lonnie's kin, they was all down to Charleston or somewheres. So Aunt Posey moved the girl in with her children. Alma would be a help with the baby if Aunt Posey could just feed all of them. Thus it was settled, would have stayed settled were it not for a big black Ford automobile. The one Harriet Setzler learned to drive after William died. The white matron rolled up to the Negro shacks and climbed out, wearing a silk

Sunday dress and a broad-brim hat and white gloves, and she waited on the sidewalk until the various children ran to find the adults. Negroes from across the street came out and sat on their porches to stare at the lady with the gloves, but Harriet had eyes for only one person in the yard.

"I've come to take Lonnie's girl home with me," Harriet said when Aunt Posey appeared. "I think it's best if she comes to live with me. Mind you, this is not charity. She'll work for her keep, she knows that already, but she'll live in a nice house, eat regular meals, and have clothes on her back. I'll see that she gets an education. I'll take care of her."

Marian heard Harriet in the kitchen again and she walked back toward it. The older woman was straightening the cloth calendar on the pantry door. Marian watched her. This woman had taken care of her. Always. It had been Harriet who'd marched over to the high school principal five years ago and demanded to know why a properly certified teacher, black or no, couldn't get hired in her own hometown. Still, Harriet had yet to visit in Marian's home, the way she visited Sarah or her other friends on Aiken Avenue. All of Marian's life, Harriet had pulled her close and then pushed her away.

"When's the funeral?" Marian asked.

Harriet crossed to the sink and absentmindedly began filling it with clean dishes. "Don't know yet. They're calling Sarah's cousin this morning." She ran water into the sink, as she stared out the bank of windows above it. "I keep thinking about . . . about years ago," she stumbled.

Marian turned sharply. She knew instantly what Harriet meant, although they hadn't discussed the matter in two decades. "Why?"

"I can't help it, Alma. It was the last time something so awful happened."

The black woman marched over to the sink. "Stop it. And don't call me Alma."

The creased old face regarded the other woman with genuine surprise. "I don't know what made me say that. I'm losing my mind, I guess."

The younger woman's shoulders relaxed. "One thing has nothing to do with the other. Absolutely nothing." Marian stopped. She felt short of breath again; she had to get out of that house. "Will you be all right? I should get to school."

Harriet raised her head. "I'm just fine, you go on."

Marian opened the back door. "They'll find who did this,"

she said. She quickly shut the door behind her, raced down the steps, and swung through the back gate of Harriet's house. Outside, she collapsed against the fence. The past, crusted over with time like an old oyster shell, flooded back on a relentless tide. It couldn't be, she told herself again. But all the way home she didn't stop shaking.

Harriet Setzler walked out on her back porch after Marian left and latched the screen door. She had always been protecting something, safeguarding someone, taking care of what needed to be taken care of. One day she was a girl, still living at home and teaching in the country, the next she was mother to four children she didn't know. Too few years with a good man and then one day he walked down the street to the doctor's office only to be told that if he didn't lie down a few hours each day he'd be dead within the year. Angina, a heart so fragile it barely worked anymore. So she bought a hospital bed and installed it on the sleeping porch; she wasn't giving this man up to any anonymous hospital. He rested there and smiled through uncomplaining crystal eyes, brushing back the elegant lanky white hair that arrived twenty years too early. For hours each day she shielded him from worry, from too much family, too many friends, too much excitement. But he died anyway.

"Miz Harriet, you best come down here directly," they called that day on the telephone. "It's Mr. William."

She flew down Aiken Avenue as fast as she could, didn't think to put on a hat, was still wearing her apron and her house shoes. Down the long blocks, past the Tutens and the Copelands and the Goodings and the Folks and the Loadholts and the Brabhams, past the big white houses and the small bungalows with vegetable gardens stretching to the alley. She tore past the fire station and the water tower, took a right toward town, crossed the railroad tracks and dashed through the main traffic intersection. She could see the post office now, people standing all around his car, staring inside it. Lowering their eyes, they backed away as she rushed forward; some secretly anticipated seeing her fall apart. He was lying with his head thrown back, one hand on his chest, the other still on the door handle, his eyes mercifully closed. She did not utter a word. Carefully, with exquisite tenderness, she slid him over to the passenger side. She got in the car. She'd seen him drive hundreds of times, it couldn't be that hard. You turned the key, pulled the choke out, pushed the gearshift lever up, pressed the floor pedal on the right and turned

the wheel. She started the engine. Then she drove him away as
if they were going to the county fair, leaving the gaping sight-
seers in the dust.

In the days that followed no one was allowed to touch him.
No undertaker, no doctor, no one. She washed and dressed him
herself, called his brothers out in the country to come and lift
him into the casket which sat on the dining room table. On the
day he was buried, the town came to see him off; they marched
up the front stairs and stood in the living room in their best
black clothes. He went from no church to the ground: he went
from his own house to his Maker, from her protection to His.
No intermediaries.

Harriet walked into her dining room, making a mental list of
things to do for Sarah Roth. People could come here to pay their
respects, of course. Would there be a Jewish service? Sarah
hadn't practiced her family's religion in years, since she got too
old to drive over to Charleston every week to the synagogue. In
later life Sarah had had funny ideas about religion anyway. Harriet reached in the wooden buffet for a lace tablecloth, while
unconsciously studying a massive oil painting in a gilt frame
hanging above the fireplace. Measuring four by six feet, it was
a panorama of a forest fire, a raging tempest of red and black
and yellow, a funnel column of smoke rising from within the
woods. The youngest trees already lay on the ground, blackened
and still; the old oaks would be next. Harriet turned her back
on the disturbing painting. All her life she'd been trying to protect herself from it.

1922. The leafy gold fall that Harriet came to Essex. The
whole town knew the tragic story of William Setzler and his
bride the lovely Elizabeth. No man had ever been more smitten,
it was fairy-tale love, we just smiled over the new baby born to
them each year. Elizabeth was dark-eyed and exotic. "The
painting lady," we called her as we vied for an invitation to
the new house William had built for her—we wanted to see
all the pictures hanging on the walls. Canvases she'd painted
when she was studying at an art school in North Carolina and
when she taught art at the Essex school. Every room was
laden with massive images of aristocratic hunting dogs; of
white roses and fresh pears; of deer roaming snowy woods;
of cherubic shepherds tending sheep. We flocked to the house
as to a museum, we who had none. And afterward we looked
at Elizabeth crosswise: anyone who could capture a likeness
like that must be touched by God.

But one day William's agonized cry was heard throughout the town. Elizabeth and her fifth baby died in childbirth, as romantically, as tragically, as the heroine of any novel. A half-smocked christening gown for the unbreathing newborn lay in her bureau drawer, and on her easel on the sleeping porch loomed an image of a forest fire. Her very best painting.

Six months later Harriet's life began. William came galloping up to the farmhouse, thinner but just as handsome as the man Harriet had known before he married Elizabeth. He wore a black waistcoat and slapped his horse's reins like a man come back from the dead. A week later he gathered Harriet up, lifted her into his wagon, and cantered back to Essex to whisk her inside the house built for an artist. The door opened for Harriet on that wood-fragrant morning and inside three boys scrambled on the floor, a baby girl lay gurgling in a cradle, and on the walls was written the history of the woman who preceded her.

Harriet walked among the rooms of her new house that day and studied the paintings she'd heard about. Her new husband put his arm around her and said, "As you know, my Elizabeth was an artist. These remind me of her so much. Aren't they lovely?" The bride turned and looked at her husband but his eyes were elsewhere. Glued to a painting of a fire. "There was so much vitality in Elizabeth," he whispered. The new wife stared at her husband and knew that on this, her wedding day, she had already lost the man she loved. In his eyes she discerned one thing she was powerless against: the idealized love of the dead. She drew in her breath, corseted her patience around her. She waited for time to pass, waited for the year to come when he'd suggest they take down some of the paintings and store them in the attic. She waited and waited, she waited almost twenty years. He went, the paintings remained.

So she lived among the visions of her predecessor. She walked each day in Elizabeth's shadow. Harriet saw her children gaze longingly at the canvases on winter evenings and knew their minds were trying to remember, to construct a bridge to the mother they'd hardly known. Harriet was a presence upstaged by a ghost. She got her revenge in the town cemetery. But revenge, like incest, breeds itself. One son sensed her anger at his dead mother and rejected her because of it: he punished her, she finally concluded, by taking to drink and embarrassing her, by becoming a living reminder that she'd failed at stepmothering.

1944. That son's body in the railroad car. The war still going strong. The oldest son also home from overseas, taking care of arrangements, leading her aside at the train station, apologetic look on his face: "They found a note with his things, Mother. He asked to be buried at our real mother's feet."

Elizabeth remained Harriet's tormentor, for Harriet refused to make peace with her. She feigned an interest in the artwork, a fascination with one so talented. When she cleaned out the attic after William's death and found more paintings stored there, she framed them and hung them on the walls of her house alongside the others. To ourselves we said it was a wonder, a mystery, the way Miz Harriet was so taken with Elizabeth's pictures. The truth was Harriet would have slashed every painting in the house in an instant—had it not constituted such obvious proof that Elizabeth had bested her. No, Essex would never see her rage like a second-choice woman. So the paintings stayed throughout Harriet's life, monuments to the self-imposed exile she lived within her own home. When her adult children came to visit and stared at the canvases, she knew they wanted them, wanted to have their mother's legacy in their own homes. Yet she didn't offer the first painting. When she died, the pictures would be divided among them and then they could forget her. But not until then.

Leaving the fire painting behind, Harriet walked slowly to her front door and gazed out the glass panes. Beyond her fence, change had become the prevailing speed of the world. When she'd almost adjusted to automobiles, along came jet planes to confuse her. When she'd figured out how to survive the Depression, along came the Second World War. When she'd stopped shuddering at women wearing men's pants, along came miniskirts. The only thing out there that stood still was the live oak. Strong and sturdy, it was rooted to a past Harriet took comfort in.

Abruptly she stared past the trees to the house across the street. Tacked to Sarah's porch was a sign forbidding entrance. Harriet closed her eyes. All her life the greatest danger had seemed inside her own house. But now? Now it was also outside and had claimed her oldest friend.

Three

I T BECAME THE town's Aaron's rod, this murder. It descended, then turned into a thousand snakes. For years the people of Essex had smugly watched their televisions and dismissed disaster and crime alike: "Sure glad I don't live there. Thank the Lord things are different here." Now things weren't different. And we began to act like people at risk. The local hardware store, a dusty wood-floor emporium, sold out of chain locks within four days of Sarah's Roth's murder and frantically ordered more dead bolts from their supplier. The man on the edge of town who raised German shepherds got so many calls that first week he took his phone off the hook. Families who normally threw their windows open to admit springtime kept the casements shut tight. Parents walked their children to school and kept them indoors during the long afternoons. Old ladies phoned each other and tied up the lines for hours talking about nothing, comforting each other through the interminable phantom nights. No one walked "upstreet" to the grocery store in the evening; they drove or they didn't go at all. And those at home peered out from behind their curtains at the sound of each and every footstep.

On the following Wednesday morning Amos Tumley realized things were different. Retired now, the black man supplemented his income by picking up fresh fruit and vegetables at the large farms outside Essex for delivery to private homes. He took orders every week, then delivered what his clients wanted directly to their doors, as the grocery store had done when Amos was a boy. Since it was early spring, he didn't have much produce this week, other than some early strawberries. He stopped at Miss Pris Bender's house and left some pecans, then went on down Aiken Avenue to the Wallerman's. Soon he was leaving the old part of town, heading toward the brick rancher where the Wilsons lived. The Wilsons were good customers; Amos had always liked them. Schoolteachers, both of them. Mrs. Wilson taught at the school for handicapped children in Ashboro and Mr. Wilson was head of the Science Department at Essex High. They had a daughter and one son. The girl was away at college but the boy had graduated and come home to work. Every week Amos would see that boy head downtown to the bank in his suit. Just like a big shot. Amos grinned. He could remember when that boy wasn't tall enough to get down the back steps by himself.

Amos was thinking about the Wilson boy as he braked his bicycle and laid it down on the ground, carefully lifting the cardboard box of strawberries out of the wire basket. He walked onto the carport like he always did and headed toward the back door. At the back steps he leaned down to set the box of berries by the door. Then he heard the voice.

"Who's there? Who is it?"

Amos looked up as the Wilson boy opened the door. Amos smiled. And stared into a World War II service automatic pointed at his head.

We had always been a simple town, one of an endless paperdoll of small crossroads strung between the sand hills of Columbia and the Low Country of the coast. Along with cattails and palmetto trees, even today these villages line the rusted railroad tracks like failed ballerinas, grown old and stiff now, standing at the barre awaiting instructions, despondent but not defeated yet. Taken together, they constitute a Synaptic South, a skipover between Gothic and Genteel, between Old and New. In Essex elderly ladies still went to the beauty shop every Wednesday afternoon, but there were no Bible salesmen with pornographic postcards, nor any chrome shopping malls with discounted Gucci handbags. In short, we lay in a tundra bypassed by movements and movers.

The town itself contained about two thousand inhabitants and had been settled in the early 1800s by a group of dissatisfied Charleston merchants who'd tired of the city's snobbishness. In Essex they created a thriving railroad town, a convenient cotton stop between the ports of Charleston and Savannah. The community's only claim to fame, however, came a half-century later with its greatest misfortune, that of lying directly in the path of William T. Sherman's famed march to the sea. Thanks to a free-lancing patrol party that preceded the general's contingent of 62,000, Essex became the only "Twice-Burned Town" in the history of the War Between the States.

Double-lighted fires altered the town's landscape forever. No fine antebellum homes graced its streets now; there were no grand public buildings, nothing of Savannah or Charleston. Essex had, quite literally, been rebuilt during Reconstruction, and so most homes were modest, streets were narrow, buildings rarely more than two stories, church spires just tall enough to be seen three blocks away. Thus, the town exuded compactness, a cleanly functional lack of excess. Likewise, its no-nonsense people took pride in their stolid ability to survive. If nothing else, Essex was a tough little devil. It had come back from total devastation and, having done so, nothing much fazed it.

Until now.

The autopsy on Sarah Roth revealed little, except that she had suffered from advanced arteriosclerosis, but the attendant paperwork took a week, and it was another week before Sarah's closest relative arrived from New York to make funeral arrangements. At Harriet Setzler's insistence, a memorial service was held in the Essex Lutheran Church, with a private burial to follow one day later in the Jewish cemetery in Charleston where the Rothenbargers had been laid to rest for over a century. The Essex service was well attended. In our village, as in most like it, funerals were social events; your funeral was the last impression you left on everyone so it had to be good. Which must be the reason we spent so much of life's energy planning for our deaths. Harriet Setzler, for example, had rewritten her funeral plans six times in as many years, her last instruction being that her casket should be pulled through town in a horse-drawn wagon so that people might stand in the street and watch her pass by. Something on the order of the rituals for John F. Kennedy and Franklin Roosevelt would do nicely. Had we known about this plan then, we'd have laughed out loud but, oddly enough, when the time came it happened just like that. Stoney McFarland saw to it. And we didn't laugh. We stood stock-still as the wagon went by.

Of all those who attended Sarah Roth's funeral, the most uncomfortable was Anna McFarland. Sitting in a white frame Lutheran church in a small town mourning a murdered elderly woman she hardly knew, was about the last place Anna had ever expected to find herself. She and Stoney sat on the fifth row listening to the bell in the tower somberly toll Bach's "Jesu."

Anna shifted in the old-fashioned oak pew and stared at the kneeling rail at her feet. The interior of the church was elegantly simple: white walls and white woodwork offset by a rich burgundy carpet down the center aisle which led to the raised chancel with a red-globed eternal flame suspended from its ceiling. Beneath which, draped by a blanket of white roses, sat the bronze coffin. And on both sides of the sanctuary arched stained glass windows were raised to catch the breeze and admitted the hiss of pollinating bees and the pungent musk of honeysuckle.

"Everybody in town must have come," Anna whispered.

Stoney nodded. "I guess so."

He had lines around his eyes, she noticed. Sad lines. Could wrinkles appear on a man's face in just a matter of days? His face looked ravaged, as though he'd lost a close personal relative in Sarah, a family member, someone or something he treasured deeply. He'd only known Sarah Roth casually, as children know their parents' friends, but somehow he felt responsible for what happened to her. Even now he kept going back over to her house and staring at it in silence, as if he were to blame. Meanwhile, the other elderly widows in the neighborhood were dragging him out of bed almost every night to check on a noise or inspect a rusty door lock. They didn't call the Essex police chief, they knew they couldn't count on Jim Leland. Instead, they called Stoney McFarland and he went to their houses at all hours and assured them they weren't about to be murdered in their beds. Or worse.

The service began and Anna sat back. A bee danced through the air and landed on her skirt; as she shook him off, her profile stood out in the sunlight spilling onto the floor through the open windows. People often said she was a study in contradiction; that she was a puzzle which, even when the pieces were put together, still didn't yield an understandable whole. Even her looks didn't mesh predictably. Her features were too sharply defined, like separate entities derived from dissimilar faces. Her curly black hair was still shoulder-length and was tipped on the ends with the silver that would one day overtake it. Her cheekbones were high and strong. By contrast, however, her eyes were palest blue, almost translucent, the delicate eyes more common to a blonde but far too fiery here, too penetrating. She looked out at people with a challenge; she didn't so much *see* what she observed as she recorded it.

It was warm in the church and Anna wished she had worn something cooler than her pleated tuxedo shirt and long, flared skirt over red leather boots. Long and lanky in stature, she usually chose nontraditional clothes. Her bright hand-painted T-shirts and black leather jackets did not go unnoticed, nor unremarked, in a conservative town like Essex. She practically advertised she was "not from around here." But she never looked totally at home in her clothes. Sometimes what she wore was more statement than covering. And like someone wearing an unfamiliar costume, she tended to button up necks designed to be left open, to cinch in waists intended to be left flowing.

As the funeral progressed, Anna gazed at the people around her: pewter-haired women and salt-and-pepper men, young mothers and fathers whose small children were blissfully unconcerned with final departures, in the second row the town council president Heyward Rutherford with his rotund wife, behind them a long string of elderly widows who constituted the garden club and the Essex Library Society, the police chief Jim Leland sitting next to the newspaper editor Stoney jogged with, a few blacks who mostly sat together except for Marian Davis who was alone, and of course Harriet Setzler in her hat towering over Sarah's cousin in the family pew.

Despite two years here Anna had made no real friends in Essex and her least favorite person in town was Harriet Setzler. The octogenarian was the first person in Essex Anna had met. In fact, Harriet had appeared at the McCloskey house while Stoney and Anna were still unpacking; the old lady marched up the steps, tapped perfunctorily on the door frame, and waltzed through the open door as if invited. Anna peered out from behind a stack of boxes as Stoney introduced the visitor, who presented them with a welcoming plate of lime pies. Thanking her, Anna watched the older woman survey their belongings. Then Harriet looked up, said to Anna, "We'll be looking for you in church Sunday. The preacher always likes to introduce new members."

Anna, who referred to aggressive religious solicitors as "Ronald Reagan's God Squad," stepped out from behind the cardboard boxes. "I'm afraid we won't be there, Mrs. Setzler. Thank you anyway, but we don't believe in organized religion."

"You have to go to church," Harriet Setzler insisted. "It's either us or the Baptists." She spat out the last word like diseased phlegm.

"I can't imagine choosing either, to be perfectly frank. As I said, thank you for the invitation, but we don't go to church."

Harriet Setzler gaped at the rudest woman she had ever met.

Stoney stepped toward the old lady quickly. "Thank you so much for coming by, Mrs. Setzler. And for the lime pies. How's your garden coming along this year?" After Harriet left, he turned to Anna with exasperation, "Couldn't you just nod and go along with her? We didn't have to go, but you didn't have to antagonize her either."

All over the church people were shuffling, coughing, shifting. The minister had launched into the eulogy. Anna gazed around the room again. She didn't belong here and she knew she never would. She had spent her childhood in an Atlanta suburb, the only child of a divorced working mother before that was commonplace. Her parents had separated when she was ten. One day her mother loved her father and the next day she hated his guts. "He" had ruined their lives; a smart woman stayed away from men. Soon Anna was allowed to see her father only every other weekend.

As a result, Anna Reston grew to be very independent. She was alone a lot and she learned to rely on herself. Consequently, she often found herself at odds with her peers. In the middle-class suburb where she lived, in the huge high school she attended, Anna always stood out, an initially painful experience which eventually grew on her. A free-thinker stirred by the coming changes in the South, she espoused radicalism before it fully overtook her generation but she never participated in peace movements or protests in college: her allegiance was intellectual; she was not a joiner, a team player. Those who didn't like her said she always covered her rear, talked a game of risk rather than playing one. At the University of Maryland, she no longer cared that she was out of step with her times, that she was studying while others fomented revolution. So she made her way through the late sixties and early seventies quietly, majoring in art history and later developing a passion for photography.

"Don't let some man ruin your life like I did," her mother had warned her repeatedly. After a while Anna noticed that the man "ruining" her mother's life had been gone for years. But the warning went unheeded. By the time Anna realized what it really meant, it was too late, a suave older man had seduced her virginity out from under her while she wasn't looking. But she kept silent about her mistake, swallowed her sixteen-year-old's lesson in misplaced trust. Clearly men did not want to be friends. Men wanted to get inside. And for a while Anna gave them what they wanted.

Then Anna met Stoney McFarland their senior year in college. As usual, she was running into the lecture hall late the first day of class, without the required textbook, grabbing the last seat by the door in a literature seminar. After class began, she found herself studying the student seated beside her. In cutoffs, a T-shirt, and leather sandals, he was broad-shouldered with thick chestnut hair that hung down the back of his neck. His face, small and angular, had the hollowed-out look of a starving poet or constant doper, and his eyes were hazel, at once both ironic and gentle. His chin was short and stubby, like someone forgot to finish his face, but he had the build of a solid athlete, the easy grace that comes to those whose bodies always obey.

At the end of class he nodded shyly and headed for the door. No "hello," no "I'm so-and-so from so-and-so and my major is . . ." Just gone. Anna promptly forgot him. Until later that same afternoon when, coming down the hill from Tydings Hall, she spied him stretched out on an Indian blanket under a willow oak on the mall. Reading *The Rainbow*. That, she couldn't let pass; after all, she was writing her senior English thesis on Lawrence.

"Hey," she called, approaching the nameless classmate. "Do you know the Anglo-Saxon root of the word 'fuck'? I need to know for my thesis, for my argument about Constance Chatterley."

Stoney blanched white. Few women he knew—no matter how bold—used that word. They might do it but they didn't talk about it. Not in Maryland.

"Well," she asked, "do you?"

He laughed out loud. "Who are you?"

By that evening, sitting on the grass, they'd exchanged views on Lawrence and Henry Miller and Hesse and Salinger, on Faulkner and race and growing-up-Southern, on Steichen and Van Gogh and Vietnam (he had a pretty safe number) and Kent State and Woodstock, the Crusades and social Darwinism, the water pipe and how hashish could turn your own dorm into unrecognizable territory, existentialism and Crosby, Stills and Nash, and . . . aren't you hungry? Hours later, still talking, they lay across the bed in his rented room and he kissed her. Simple, quiet, the natural conclusion to the afternoon. Then his eyes twinkled and he said, "Want to fool around or would you rather have a beer?"

What the hell kind of question was that? Anna, nonplussed, realized no one had ever asked her before: they just did it and she went along or she fought it. She voted for the beer, put him to the test. He got up and got two long-neck bottles out of a mini-refrigerator on the other side of the room. She knew what would happen now. He'd gulp his beer. He might pout. Finally he'd tell her what she "really wanted" to do. Then he'd be all over her. She tensed and waited. They talked some more. He finished his beer and got up and got another, smiling at her. He got her another beer, asked her what she wanted to do with her life. And they talked all night long.

Many years later a good friend would say to Anna, "My God, Stoney really listens. When you talk to him he's right there with you. He looks at you like your words are as valuable as gold. Do you have any idea how lucky you are?"

The next morning Anna was still in his room. Their seminar textbook, *Chief Modern Poets of Britain and America*, lay open on the floor; they'd been reading Yeats aloud to each other when they fell asleep. When they woke up, they reached for each other by unspoken mutual consent. Their love was slow and sensual. It was also the first time Anna ever cried aloud with pleasure.

Anna looked up abruptly as everyone in the church stood up. The minister had begun his summation. He was now standing on one side of the draped casket, his right hand above it. "Forasmuch as it hath pleased the Almighty God of His great mercy," he intoned, "to take upon Himself the soul of our sister: we therefore commit her body to His keeping." He began to make the sign of the cross and then stopped, his hand frozen in midair as he stared at the rear of the church.

In the doorway, framed from behind by the morning sun and looking almost celestial, stood the largest black woman Anna had ever seen. Maum Chrish was dressed in a multicolored caftan with a white scarf, an *agouéssan*, draped over her right shoulder and knotted at the opposite hip. Everyone in the church turned to stare at her. Slowly she walked down the aisle, regal, oblivious, staring straight ahead at the casket. On both sides of her, people gawked. When she reached the coffin, the Lutheran minister's hand was still poised above it. Maum Chrish reached inside the pocket of her caftan and drew out an iron asson, a small dagger containing stones and shaped like a cross with tiny arms and downturned hands at both east and west. She rapped it on the metal top of the coffin three times.

"Stop her," someone called out. "That's voodoo blasphemy!"

Two pallbearers stepped forward. Maum Chrish pivoted and strode toward the rear door of the church, where two ushers stood ready to intercept her. Abruptly she hesitated, looked around in terror, then scrambled toward an open window. She jumped up, her skirts flying over bare feet, and climbed through the window and disappeared.

For a moment no one breathed a word; everyone just sat where they were, shaken by the odd turn of events. Finally the flustered minister nodded at the pallbearers. After their exit with the coffin the church emptied quickly, but most people lingered outside to watch as the hearse, bearing Sarah Roth's body to Charleston, moved out of sight.

"What happened in there?" Anna asked. She and Stoney stood on the church steps. "Who was that woman?"

Stoney shook his head. "She lives out in the swamps. People call her Maum Chrish."

"Maum Chrish? What was she doing here?" When Anna realized Stoney was only half listening, she asked, "What's the matter?"

"Nothing. Only that was the worst funeral I've ever been to."

"You've been to one that's fun?"

"You know what I mean. He talked so much about how Sarah died. The one thing everyone wants to forget. What about how she lived?" Stoney started down the church steps. "I wish to hell they'd find who did this."

At the bottom of the steps a tall silver-haired man stepped out of the group around him and put his hand out to Stoney. Stoney took it and nodded. "Heyward. Heard anything about the investigation?"

Heyward Rutherford shook his head no. He was taller than Stoney but narrower in the shoulders, with a lean, patrician bearing everyone in Essex considered one of God's great incongruities. In truth, the man was a first-class thief and so it must have been his incomparable good looks, his affable manner, that made us continue to elect him president of the Essex Town Council. He sold real estate and had made most of his money during the Depression, when he was very young. Then, "landpoor" families had gladly exchanged a few prime acres for shoes and gasoline and a side of beef. Now Heyward built nearly every new house in Essex and gobbled up failing businesses like a starving PacMan. Still, people liked him: he emanated distinguished respectability. We also knew he was full of himself. Everyone laughed about the way Heyward talked; he rarely uttered a sentence in which the word "great" didn't appear at least once. It was a great morning, it was a great town, things were going great in Essex, we would be going great guns come summer, the rain was downright great, he had had a great life, he had surrounded himself with great friends, he was a great judge of character. When he turned sixty, he wrote his autobiography which he published at his own expense, and he presented an autographed copy to everyone in town at the annual Fourth of July barbeque. We had a terrific time with that book for about a year—contests sprang up all over Essex to see who could find the most "greats" in it.

Characteristically, Heyward never answered Stoney's question about the murder investigation but turned to greet Harriet Setzler, who was coming down the church steps. "Mrs. Setzler, I'm so sorry about Sarah. I know what great old friends you two were."

Harriet brushed aside Heyward's condolences; she had never liked the man. He had always treated her like she was fifty years older than he, instead of just ten or fifteen. After Heyward walked on down the steps, Harriet said under her breath to Stoney, "Bet he's not sorry at all. He's been trying to get Sarah's store for years."

"What does he want with the store?"

Harriet snorted disapproval. "Wants to tear it down and put a car wash and a laundromat there. Wants more money for himself is what it is. I ask you, what do we need with a car wash?" Harriet gazed down the stairs and watched Heyward approach Sarah's cousin. "She's not cold yet and he's trying to get the store away from that boy. I guess he'll finally succeed now."

The old lady turned back to Stoney, giving Anna a slight nod that exempted her from rudeness. "Marian says I should get dead bolts put on all my doors. I declare, I never thought I'd see the day. I was wondering if you'd have time to put them up for me."

"Be glad to," Stoney murmured.

Marian Davis came through the church door then, stared at the window Maum Chrish had used, then headed toward Stoney and Anna and Harriet. They all talked for a few minutes about Sarah, about how she had always taken in stray animals. Marian told a long story about a bulldog Sarah had once found that was so ugly everyone suggested she not save this one. People on Aiken Avenue made her so mad about the pup that Sarah not only saved it but raised it and showed it at the annual dog show in Savannah where it won honorable mention for deportment.

For the rest of that year the dog wore his blue ribbon taped to his collar, for all the neighbors to see.

Everyone laughed but in a moment they all fell silent again. "I don't guess anything'll ever be the same again," Harriet said finally. No one disagreed and soon she and Marian headed toward the parking lot.

Stoney watched them leave. Leonard Hansen stopped and said something to them which seemed to irritate both women. Leonard had grown up in Essex and, like both Stoney and Marian, had returned after a long absence. Unlike Stoney, Leonard had had a bad reputation in Essex; as a child he'd been a bully, continually in minor trouble of one sort or another. Everyone said the Marines had really changed him. He had come back to Essex a year ago when his father died and left him the long-abandoned family house. Leonard was still in Essex reportedly because he couldn't even get Heyward Rutherford to buy the place. People who passed it said Leonard was fixing it up in the hope of attracting a buyer. Meanwhile, he was working at the new Nissan factory outside Ashboro.

Anna followed Stoney's eyes to Leonard Hansen. "Why don't you like him?"

Her husband grinned sheepishly. "It's stupid. He beat the crap out of me once." He took Anna's hand. "Let's go home."

They waved to Jim Leland and one or two others as they left; then they passed down the wide tree-lined boulevard that led into town from the north. Along this street sat the largest homes in Essex, seven mammoth Victorian clapboards originally inhabited by well-off Essexians in the 1920s. Some were restored, while others still sported peeling, decade-old paint. Two of them loomed disconcertedly over a brick rancher that had grown up between them upon the demise of one of their own. Passing the large green yards, Stoney breathed in the dogwood and azalea blossoms, a smell he associated with certain Easter mornings of his youth. An old family photograph appeared in his memory— he and his parents and his grandmother standing in front of her favorite white azalea in the bright spring sunshine. He was wearing his first suit and his mother was smiling and his father looked relaxed, both of them happy in a way they never seemed in Washington.

Unconsciously Stoney had stepped up his pace and left Anna behind. When she called out he turned around. "Sorry." He waited until she caught up. "I just can't stop thinking about Sarah," he said suddenly, finally vocalizing his feelings. "You're not supposed to have to be on guard here. But in just one night—everything's changed. Someone crept into town and killed Sarah and robbed all of us of our peace of mind.''

''How can you be sure it wasn't someone who lives here?''

Anna regretted the question as soon as it was out. Stoney didn't answer but began to walk faster. She gazed at him as she quickened her own step. Even though he continually lamented his height (being two inches shy of the six feet he coveted), her husband was strong and solid, still had an athlete's broad chest and shoulders. He looked physically powerful, yet this was a power seldom manifested in aggression. Stoney always endeavored to keep himself under control; when stressed, he would run five or six miles and come home sweating and smiling. One of the few times she had seen him lose his temper had been soon after they were married, when they were bicycling through Old Towne Alexandria one afternoon and an impatient Mercedes had failed to yield and had run Anna down, causing her to crash-land on the median. Stoney had jumped off his bike and hurled a huge rock at the expensive car, then chased it down the street.

Right now he didn't look like the same man who'd thrown that rock. Right now he was hunched over like someone who'd just taken a bullet, his body compensating for what he felt by leaning forward abnormally. Anna surveyed his long thin nose and the slight cleft in his chin. His body was his barometer and it bothered her to see him looking like this. Nowadays his hair didn't extend to his shoulders but it was still lanky and sun-bronzed, a wild mass touching the edge of his oxford-cloth collar. Normally he still reminded her of a college boy but in the past few days he'd looked much older.

His eyes had been different too, so stark and troubled they seemed almost black, since the morning he returned from Sarah Roth's house. He had called Anna sometime during that long night and she had gone downstairs, made coffee, and waited for him to come home. At dawn she could no longer keep her eyes open, so she went back upstairs and crawled into bed and fell asleep instantly. The next thing she knew, some hours later, he was in bed with her, silent and unspeaking. She reached for him, to hold him, to talk about what had happened, when she felt his fingers all over her, inside her, demanding arousal. She was startled, uncertain; they had not made love in weeks and she'd only expected, tonight, to be there for him emotionally. But he never opened his lips, except to take her breasts into his mouth. She wondered how someone could find a dead body and then come home and want to make love, but his passion was so urgent and insistent she didn't question it. If anything, it was a powerful aphrodisiac. He could not seem to stop, he pulled her up off the bed in an act of penetration that was so deep and encompassing she almost lost consciousness. It was, ironically, the best sex they had had in years.

A week after Sarah Roth's funeral, Stoney got a second call from Harriet Setzler in the middle of the night. This time he jumped for the telephone like a man hit by a live wire. He slammed the receiver down, scrambled out of bed, and threw on his clothes. Anna sat bolt upright. "Call Jim Leland. Stoney, please, I'm scared."

"It's probably nothing," he said, trying to sound calm. "She just heard something outside her house."

"You can't keep doing this," Anna argued. "You'll be exhausted at work tomorrow. It's Jim Leland's job."

Stoney was out the door before she finished. Of course it was nothing, he thought on his way down the hall. But when one of the old ladies called, he couldn't not go. What if? Right now, however, he didn't like leaving Anna alone at night. This was no goddamn way to live. He pounded down the staircase, heard Silas whining in the kitchen. "No, boy, not tonight," he whispered as he sped by the expectant dog on the way out the back door.

In three minutes he was standing on Harriet Setzler's front porch and he heard her unlock the door before he knocked. When it opened she was wearing a chenille bathrobe, her hair trapped in a spidery hairnet. "It was just like that night," she cried, staccato. "About this time—I heard something—the same kind of sound—only tonight it was in my yard—back by the sleeping porch."

Stoney had never seen Harriet Setzler so agitated. The tremulous voice was totally out of character, and it took him a moment to respond. Finally he said, "Don't worry. It's probably just a dog or something."

"A dog can't get in a locked gate."

"You go back inside," Stoney assured her. "I'll look around."

He walked back down the steps, paused beside the cyclone fence, and surveyed the yard. Harriet Setzler's way with nature was the envy of everyone in Essex. Her entire front yard, which extended well over half a block, was a flower garden just now at the height of color: azaleas, tulips, daffodils, early roses. Some of the azaleas, which she didn't prune back like everyone else, were ten feet tall. In a moment Stoney reached the side gate that led to the back yard. In the rear lay Harriet's vegetable garden; she'd had the wooden fence built to deliberately bisect her property, so that from the street only the flowers were visible. An aesthetic separation that would later become symbolic to Stoney. He unlatched the gate and the hinge creaked. He followed the edge of the house until he was underneath the sleeping porch, its coated aluminum window covers closed above him in a row. To his right were rows of broccoli circles, strung-up lines for green beans, a large group of young tomato plants, and elevated in a huge cement trough so they were easy to pick, some of the best strawberries a kid ever swiped.

Stoney looked back at the house, beamed the flashlight he'd brought along at the ground, swung it back and forth in a wide arc. No sign of a dog or rabbit or anything. Maybe she'd heard a squirrel in a tree. Stoney walked around to the back of Harriet's house, where the sleeping porch joined the rest of the structure. For a second he remembered when Harriet Setzler had kept chickens in her back yard; as a kid, he'd seen her wring their necks without batting an eye. He moved the flashlight over the ground again, closer to the house. Suddenly he stopped, stared. Then he knelt down in the dirt, aimed the flashlight at a specific spot. There it was. Part of a footprint. Clear as day. Right up beside the house, outside the sleeping porch where Harriet Setzler said she'd heard the noise. Only the one print, where someone had apparently stepped off the thick grass and onto bare dirt.

Of course it could have been made by almost anyone, someone working in the yard, for example; Harriet did still have a man who came once a month. But this looked fresh, recent. Stoney studied the indentation in the ground again. Looked like a fairly large foot, and the tread was deep, like on heavy work shoes. He stood up and moved the flashlight's beam around the edges of the yard.

In a moment Stoney slipped around to Harriet's back gate on the other side of the yard and checked the lock. Tight. He stared at the bolt for a second. The shiny new metal he'd installed three days before gleamed against the weathered old boards. On impulse he pressed against the fence. A lock on a fence you could almost knock down with your bare hands.

He returned to Harriet's front door and knocked again. "Mrs. Setzler?"

In a few seconds she reappeared. "Did you find anything?"

"No," he lied. "Everything's fine. It was probably just a rabbit having lunch in your garden."

The lined face across from him relaxed. The hairnet was gone, she seemed more herself now. "Can you come in a minute? I made some coffee. No way I'll get back to sleep tonight."

Stoney followed the elderly woman inside. Harriet was fully dressed now: a jersey print dress, stockings (tidily rolled underneath her hemline), omnipresent black leather shoes with squatty heels. She wasn't a tall woman, no more than five feet seven, but she was rock-solid; total waistlessness made her girth as intimidating as a Sherman tank. Yet she wasn't fat either; fat would have been soft and Harriet Setzler's cells were made of steel. To Stoney, she always looked like a boxer in drag. But on the street she was always a lady, with her elegant silk dresses and matching hats.

In her kitchen she poured coffee into a china cup and handed it, with a saucer, to Stoney. Then she poured a cup for herself and sat down at the table across from him. He sipped his coffee and studied her face. It was square and loose with excess flesh yet very ruddy, and her close-cropped wiry hair was revived into a perfect alabaster white each week at the beauty shop on Main Street. Her eyes were small and dark gray—intelligent, active, always sizing things up.

"Emma Thomas was over here yesterday," she said, as if continuing a previous conversation. "Her boy Harry wants her to move to one of those retirement places in Florida, he says she'll be safer there. Emma's lived in Essex all her life. . . ." Harriet trailed off.

Stoney was silent. Then he said, "What's happened is truly terrible, but we've got to keep our perspective. Not give in to hysteria. They'll find the killer. Things will be the same again."

Harriet eyed him doubtfully. "Who'll find him? Jim Leland?" A pause. "You don't understand, Stoney. The thing you hope for most is just a good end. Not to be a burden to anyone. Just go to sleep one night and not wake up. Hopefully somebody'll find you, get you looking good before they call anybody. You'll just drift off thinking about good times, old days, old friends, loved ones." Her eyes were distant and Stoney realized she was speaking more to herself than to him. "You don't want to die scared to death, you don't want anyone to take what little time you have left away from you. You don't want—merciful heaven—to be—to have what happened to Sarah—you don't." She stopped, her voice shaking. "You go like that and that's what everyone will remember about you."

Abruptly Harriet got up and carried their cups to the sink. "Used to be there was only one thing I was afraid of." Besides that woman, she allowed to herself truthfully. "Of being made to leave here—leave my house, my town. Of getting so feeble I had to go away. Here I can walk the streets by myself, I know people and they know me, there's a place for me here, I'm safe and at peace. That's what I always thought."

Moved, Stoney struggled to find his voice. He had never known Harriet Setzler to open up to anyone, and he floundered for some word of comfort to offer. But could he tell her this was still a safe place?

Then Harriet turned back around. Her voice was normal now, her face recomposed. She asked if he wanted anything to eat, he said no, he'd better be going. They walked to her front door and he told her not to worry. After she closed her door, he stood outside on the porch listening while she locked it behind him. He looked out at the street for a moment, then went down the stairs and headed home. He noticed that the night was turning cooler, thought briefly about what he had to do at work the next day.

Turning right toward Laurens Avenue a few moments later, Stoney stopped dead when he saw someone in a truck a hundred yards ahead of him. All he could make out was the red glow at the end of a lighted cigarette.

"That you, McFarland?"

Stoney hesitated under a streetlight but the other man was shrouded in shadows. "Yeah," he called and walked toward the voice.

In a moment he was standing beside Leonard Hansen's pickup. "You gave me a scare," Leonard said, dragging on his cigarette.

"Same here." Stoney stared at the man who lived on the outskirts of town. "What are you doing here this time of night?"

"Leland asked me to help him sorta keep an eye on things. Wanted me to ride in once in a while late and check on things— he knows I stay up until all hours working on that house of mine." Leonard flicked his cigarette butt out onto the pavement. "Damn shame about Mrs. Roth."

"Sure is." Stoney gazed at Leonard. The other man had silky

blond hair that fell across his forehead in a boyish manner that
was undermined by the steely cobalt, almost violet eyes below,
the eyes of someone who had not been a boy in a very long time.
Abruptly Stoney thought about the footprint in Harriet Setzler's
yard. "You didn't see anybody else tonight, did you?"

"Naw. Why?"

"Mrs. Setzler thought she heard something, that's all."

"Well, I did see a car take off real fast down by the water
tower when I came by there. Just came out of nowhere, going
real fast, I didn't recognize it at all."

"Might have been Ed Hammond going to the hospital on an
emergency," Stoney suggested, thinking aloud. "He drives a
Buick." A pause. "You weren't in Mrs. Setzler's yard by any
chance, were you?"

"Naw, I just got down here. Well listen, I best get going.
Gotta build some Jap cars tomorrow. See ya. Tell that foxy wife
of yours I said hello."

Stoney watched as Leonard drove off. He wasn't sure he liked
Leonard Hansen calling Anna foxy. He wasn't sure he liked Leonard Hansen noticing his wife at all. Sometimes the man still
reminded him of a bully. Stoney remembered Leonard as being
peculiarly mean, capable of a viciousness that went beyond the
normal mischievousness of most boys. In a fight Leonard had
always tried to humiliate his opponent—he didn't stop at beating
him. No, he ground the other guy's face in the dirt, spat on him,
dragged his pants down around his knees and laughed. Stoney
swallowed. Even now he could still taste the blood in his mouth
on the day he'd been Leonard's target.

But that was a long time ago. Leonard's father had made him
enlist when he was still in his teens and that had apparently done
the trick. He'd had a good service record, everyone said. Although he never went to Vietnam, he trained many of those who
did. By the time he got out of the service, his family had moved
to Birmingham so his father could go into business with a friend.
Leonard had come back to Essex briefly in the early seventies
to see some old buddies but he hadn't stayed long. After that,
someone said he was married and living in Detroit working in
the automobile business. But when he returned to Essex to sell
his father's house, he hadn't brought along a wife and had never
mentioned a marriage to anyone. Yet he was a different man.
Friendly to people, reliable (several Essexians consulted him
now about repairs needed on their cars), minded his own busi-

ness. Most people thought he'd probably go north again where the money was better as soon as he sold that old house.

Stoney put Leonard out of his mind and walked on home. As he crawled into bed again, he was thinking that someone had to talk to Jim Leland. Things could not go on like this.

While Stoney became more and more involved in Sarah Roth's murder, Anna dove deeper into her work. Ever since the funeral, she had been thinking about the black woman called Maum Chrish. Anna had even pumped a neighborhood boy for information about where the strange woman lived. (Children knew absolutely everything in small towns, she'd discovered.) She wanted to photograph Maum Chrish. Which is how it happened that on a cloudy day while Stoney was at work she loaded her Canon F-1 and various lenses and her tripod into the Subaru along with Silas for an afternoon of shooting. She usually didn't take the retriever; he had ruined several shoots in his time but he'd seen her loading the car and had jumped through the open door onto the back seat before she could object, wagging his tail, slobbering all over the windows with anticipation. She didn't have the heart to leave him behind.

Anna was rarely interested in human beings as subjects; normally she found they exaggerated too much for the lens. But the vision of Maum Chrish framed from behind by morning light had stayed with Anna so vividly she'd even dreamed about it twice. And the day was perfect—cloudy, overcast enough that colors would be rich and true, the light would be even, she could shoot at a lower speed.

In Baltimore during the early years with Stoney, when he worked for the state of Maryland and they still lived in a run-down apartment on Charles Street, Anna had trained in the photography department of the city's evening newspaper. She'd served her apprenticeship in the lab and later covered major breaking stories. Even though her photo of Agnew on the day he resigned had won two Sigma Delta Chi awards, she'd felt confined by photojournalism. Eventually, at Stoney's urging, she left the paper to go solo and taught herself all that could be learned from reams of wasted film. Then she began to take her portfolio to D.C. galleries, to send her contact sheets to regional magazines, wildlife journals, art publications. At first she earned nothing but rejection. "Good concept, technically immature," one publication advised her. Stoney said, "Keep at it. You've come too far to quit now." So she reapplied herself to f-stops, studied art books on composition. She submitted new photographs and still nothing happened. One rainy cold October afternoon she trudged from gallery to gallery to gallery. At the last one the slick gay manager suggested she find another line of work.

"I cannot do it any longer," she cried into Stoney's shoulder that night. "I just can't. What if I never get anywhere, what if I spend my whole life chasing some stupid dream?"

He looked at her later over a smoky glass of cabernet. "Would it really be so bad to spend your whole life in pursuit of a dream? Is that any worse than giving up—like most people do—and resigning yourself to a life, a career, you neither like nor believe in? Which would be the greater waste?"

A year later she had a showing in a one-room gallery on M Street. Twenty-five people showed up. Three pictures sold. Anna made $125 and was never to feel richer in her life.

The next year she sold several pictures to magazines, even had one appear in the Washington *Post Magazine*. She had a second showing. This time a hundred people came. That night, when she and Stoney were both a little heady on Gallo and good times (who passed that joint around anyway?), she looked at him and wondered if she would ever have done this well without him. She'd talked for years about free-lancing, becoming an artist instead of a hack. But all she'd done was talk. He had galvanized her to action, encouraged her, reassured her constantly that her work was good. She was grateful to him. But it bothered her that she'd so badly needed his support in order to achieve her potential.

It was one of the great mistakes of her life that Anna always believed her independence to be imperiled. She was constantly fighting nonexistent wars, fending off the enemy before he even appeared. Her obsessive need to be true to herself was an inoperable cataract. Only one person in her entire life had ever threatened her destiny, but that experience had traumatized her for life. She had never really expected to marry but she'd accepted Stoney's proposal because he never made her feel owned. She didn't foresee that she might forget this in time, that out of her emotional chaos she might impute to him another's sins. Or that a hick town like Essex might undermine her individuality by reducing her to "Stoney's wife." In South Carolina, Anna had come face to face with the very thing she'd been trying to avoid.

She had agreed to the move, mostly, to escape Stoney's family. In Washington, Anna and Stoney lived so close to the elder McFarlands (especially after leaving Baltimore and moving to Georgetown), that the new wife found herself caught up in a vortex of family gatherings. (How many cousins did Stoney have anyway?) At first she was entranced. Stoney's parents were so close, so stable; they welcomed her into their fold eagerly and she was initially mesmerized by the extended family life she'd never had. To please them, she tried to conform—played idiotic games at bridal and baby showers for women she didn't know, bought her clothes from L.L. Bean and Talbots so she'd look right at the family picnics, kept quiet about her politics for the sake of harmony, politely pretended to be interested in tennis and bridge. But she noticed that her in-laws, who never asked about her photography, perceived her only as their son's wife. When she and Stoney didn't have children after five years, awkward silences ensued after mention of their childlessness. Little by little Anna began to resent the loss of her privacy and she stopped attending all of the family functions. This earned her pointed criticism from her mother-in-law: not to participate was tantamount to rudeness. In the social South, going your own way was almost as embarrassing as not wearing the right clothes. Apparently being herself and pleasing Stoney's family were mutually exclusive possibilities, and now Anna feared she would leave Stoney sooner or later—even though she adored him—in order to extricate herself from his family.

Stoney had always longed to return to South Carolina and so they moved. Now Anna lived a long way from her in-laws. In a town where she'd imagined she would lead a pastoral creative life—she would free-lance and experiment with rural photography, and she and Stoney would have time to get close again. But neither had exactly happened, and now her career was in jeopardy. She had obtained several commercial assignments from a Savannah advertising company, but her magazine connections had been strained by the move. The fact was she and Stoney had made a mistake; if anything, his allegiance to the town had pushed them further apart. Unlike him, she was ready to go back to a city where you could buy good cheese and see a foreign film.

Anna gazed out the car window as she headed toward the swamps. On either side of the road snaky truncated vines crawled high in cypress trees, and knotted live oak roots bulged out of the silent pockets of water. It was spooky, just like Seth Von Hocke had described it. Nothing moved, not even the lily pads, the still white ink spots that lay on the surface of the moody water. Hardly anyone ever used this road except in the summer, as a shortcut to Beaufort and Hilton Head and the islands.

Before long Anna stopped the car and parked on the side of the road, climbed out, and opened the back door for Silas. "Come on, boy. Let's see if we can find it."

They headed for a footpath and walked into the thick growth beyond it, as Anna studied the shadows on the trees. She never photographed objects, she always shot light. Each photograph she took was an examination of light, its counterpoint and compatibility, the fecund spacelessness of shadows. The subject was secondary. In her work as in her life, she often overlooked the concrete.

Silas growled softly and Anna paused, patted the retriever on the head, scratched behind his right ear. "Brave sucker, aren't you?" They started again and walked into the woods. But in a second the dog froze and barked.

"Would you stop?" Anna gazed into the woods. "There's nothing there."

They walked a few more yards and then Anna hesitated too. Ahead lay a small ancient graveyard, no marked boundaries, just ten or eleven cracked and leaning slabs of concrete gathered together under a stand of pines, slaves maybe, their names lost to the ravages of time, their remains sinking lower and lower with the settling of the ocean-bound earth. Involuntarily Anna shivered. On top of several of the graves were personal items, drinking cups and metal combs, rusted, corroded, splattered with dried mud. Anna pulled Silas closer to her. She was glad she'd brought him. For a moment Anna almost turned around and went home. It was damn eerie in here, so silent and dark. It would be like shooting at night. The image of Maum Chrish flashed across her mind again. Was she crazy like half the town was saying now? Suddenly Silas lurched and the jerk on his leash almost toppled Anna. A doe jumped over a fallen log several feet away and was gone in an instant. Anna pushed her camera strap back up on her shoulder and chided the dog, who finally stopped growling. In a few more minutes they reached a clearing by the river and Anna stopped to swat at the early mosquitoes. She stood very still, and listened. She heard something. Silas growled again, low and nervous this time.

"What is it, boy?"

Anna walked toward the sound. Then she knew what it was. A woman's voice. Relieved, Anna tied the dog's leash to a tree, then moved farther into the clearing. She paused and listened.

She was singing, whoever it was. But the language was odd—
part French, part something else. Some older blacks in the Low
Country still knew Gullah, an African dialect two centuries old,
but Anna had never heard it spoken. Was this it? She listened
again:

Ati Bon Legba, ouvri barriè pou moin, ago yé!
Voudoun Legba, ouvri barriè pou moin, pou moin ca rentré
L'hèi m'a tounin, m'a remercié loa-yo.

Skirting the water, Anna moved closer to the voice. When
she finally saw Maum Chrish, she shrank behind a tree. Sitting
in her yard, staring at her garden, the black woman was singing
at the top of her lungs, her hands raised skyward, a glowing fire
behind her. Her song was an ardent supplication but Anna
couldn't tell if its power arose from a sense of joy or fear. In a
few moments Maum Chrish stood up. Anna swallowed. The
black woman was completely naked. Instinctively Anna looked
away. Then Maum began to sing again and she danced around
in a circle, slapping her hands against her bare heels behind her
back. The intensity of her voice startled Anna. She gazed back
at the other woman's face, then her eyes wandered down Maum's
chest, to her abdomen, her legs, her feet. The dark black skin
was smooth despite her age and, unable to restrain her curiosity,
Anna searched the deep-V between her legs to see if the hair
was gray.
Embarrassed, Anna looked away again, then stared behind
her as if she expected someone to catch her watching the naked
woman. When was the last time she'd seen a female body other
then her own? College maybe. She didn't even look at her own
very often anymore. In college, girls always looked down when
a friend undressed. Courtesy, modesty, whatever, you didn't
stare at your girlfriend's body, it was a given. Consequently,
Anna could not take her eyes off of the uninhibited woman in
the woods.
In a world all her own, Maum Chrish kicked her feet and
hummed. Anna slipped her camera over her head, set the meter,
popped the lens cap off. Through the lens she continued to watch
the naked woman. She noticed the trees behind Maum Chrish;
they were decorated with brightly painted designs reminiscent
of Pennsylvania Dutch hex signs. Anna saw Maum Chrish turn
in her direction and she rested her finger on the shutter button.

Abruptly she imagined the other woman saw her, knew she was cowering behind a tree like a voyeur. She felt the black woman had control of her finger. Anna tried to force it down. It didn't move. Maum Chrish did not grant permission and the shutter never clicked.

Soon the black woman stopped dancing and sat back down on the ground in the lotus position. Then, suddenly, she jumped up again and started toward Anna, who saw her coming just in time. Anna whirled around and sped backward, toward Silas and the car.

Four

STONEY MCFARLAND WAS part and parcel of a generation who never quite imagined itself working for a living. They were a generation of idealists who never foresaw that idealists might have to eat. When government grants and tuition from home began to dry up, the active radicals of the era had pretty much burned out anyway: an Icarus must eventually either abandon the desire for flight or die from overexposure. But people like Stoney and Anna, who had never overtly participated in the social and political movements of their adolescence, actually retained their effects longer. They grew more in tune with their youth as they aged. Which was why Stoney had a job that should have been a career but wasn't. He'd studied engineering before it became fashionable but had chosen the less-lucrative life of public service. He did not like pressure, gamesmanship. If someone had the power to fire you (a company president, for example), he reasoned, then that person controlled you. In government service, Stoney had found the autonomy he needed. He worked for the people—not for a capitalist demagogue.

If he lacked ambition, he had his father to thank. The elder McFarland was a kindhearted man who unfortunately also believed that the way to shape children correctly was to shape them completely. You told them when to come in at night, you told them where to go to college, you told them where to work after college, you told them when to cut their hair no matter how old they were. And if you had any doubts, you checked up on them: you appeared at their dorm room unannounced from time to time to see what was going on, you called them at work late to make sure they weren't going home early, you called them at their apartments at midnight to see if a woman answered. You

58

got them summer jobs and then told the foreman to cut their salary to minimum wage, to make sure they appreciated the value of money. Whenever the children turned around, you were there leaning over their shoulder to tell them what to do next. You let them know that you expected great things from them. With the best of intentions you did what parents did then and you inevitably sabotaged yourself—you alone assured that none of it would work out as you'd planned. A child too controlled early on will often sacrifice anything, even that bright future you had planned for him, just to get out from under.

Thus, during the day Stoney designed roads and bridges, bought right-of-way, and appraised real estate South Carolina needed to acquire for highway construction. But his passions were at home—Anna, athletics, music. He worked to support his free time, this enigmatic man who first attracted his wife by being the unexpected—a jock who liked literature. Yet it took Anna years to accept Stoney's lack of ambition, to stop feeling he was wasting his talent and his intelligence, and she once asked him, "What do you want to have achieved by the end of your life?"

"Knowledge," he said without hesitation. "I want to have learned certain things. Not how to build a better road, that's not important. Real knowledge. Why people react as they do, what it all means in the long run."

Anna concluded, much later, that he was actually the most ambitious person she'd ever met.

As a "professional" in Essex, Stoney commanded no more respect than a good plumber, perhaps less. This fact didn't bother him but it infuriated his superior, District Engineer Brownlow, who was not a degreed engineer but had been hired years ago when all highway department managerial staff were given that title. Brownlow and his generation had "known" what they were going to do with their lives from the outset: they were going to work like hell and get ahead. Sumter Brownlow had done that. He'd begun working for the transportation department right out of high school, when a fellow was darn lucky to find a job, and he had returned there as soon as he'd dispensed with his war service. Eventually he went to college part-time and got a business degree, moved up in the agency, took more management courses as the years went by, and developed a zeal for expediting human beings. His zenith came when he was appointed to the Central Office staff in Columbia. Then he goofed. He tried to expedite someone in the governor's office and was promptly shipped to Siberia.

"Think you could get to work on time just once?" the bird-like man of sixty squawked at Stoney when the younger man came in the door one morning. "We're supposed to be at our desks at eight-thirty. You almost never get here until quarter of."

"Morning, Sump. You trying out for grouch-of-the-year or what?" Stoney smiled and closed the door behind him. The regional office of the South Carolina Highway Department consisted of one room containing two metal desks which sat on opposite sides of the room. Between them were two filing cabinets, two trash cans, several wooden chairs. Behind the desks was a metal conference table with five sets of survey plans laid out on top. All the walls were covered with maps of the counties surrounding Essex, along with the calendar printed every December by JOE'S GARAGE which featured a prominent picture of Joe himself in front of the red 1959 Cadillac he had restored two years ago. The Essex idea of a pinup.

Brownlow didn't smile back. "You lose your coat and tie?"

"For Christsake, Sump, give it a rest. This is not Madison Avenue. I was up half the damn night."

The other man frowned. Laxness in the office irritated him. McFarland was a competent man but his attitude was all wrong, he never took anything seriously. "We got in that Acquisition Stage Report from Columbia over the weekend," Brownlow announced. "Better get right on it."

"I thought the money hadn't been approved yet."

"We need to be ready when it is."

Inwardly Stoney sighed. He hated Acquisition Reports. Taking an individual's land for highway construction, sometimes his house as well, was a loathsome task, even if the owner was usually paid better-than-market price. Stoney despised the procedure all the more because Brownlow, who never did acquisitions himself, stayed in an uproar about them. His theory was to take someone's land real fast, before the owner had a chance to object or to consider court action. At the slightest sign of trouble, the older man was quick to condemn and take property by force. His colleague, on the other hand, had never initiated a condemnation and sometimes advised individuals to sue the state.

Shuffling through various papers on his desk, Stoney looked for a set of plans for a new secondary road through the swamps.

Abruptly Brownlow asked, "What were you doing up all night anyway?"

"Oh, two dogs got in a fight outside Miss Bender's sometime after midnight and she got upset and called. Everyone in my part of town is still scared stiff." Stoney found the plans for the swamp project and studied them for a moment.

The other man noticed what Stoney had in his hand. "You know, I talked to the lieutenant governor the other day, he and I are old friends, you know, and he said we'd be getting a lot more work out around the swamps—what with the development of more of the islands. I had a real long talk with him. He'll probably make a good governor."

Stoney didn't respond. He detested the strip-mining of South Carolina's coastline.

"Of course, you can never tell what will happen to a man when he gets to high office," Brownlow went on, leaning back in his chair, pontificating. "I've been involved in five state administrations now and the pattern's always the same. I saw some things in Central Office, you can be sure of that. Governors, U.S. senators, the developers, all the big-money boys, they were all over there at one time or another."

The younger man interrupted, "Sump, who do you think murdered Sarah? You don't think anyone in Essex did it, do you?"

"Who knows? Small towns aren't what they used to be. I hear some think it's that crazy woman out in the swamps."

Stoney's eyes widened. "Why would she want to kill Sarah?"

"If she's crazy, she don't need a reason. People who've been around here a lot longer than you or me say she's done some pretty funny things. Like at the funeral."

"That was odd. I guess if you live alone out there you're bound to be eccentric. But the killer had to be a guy." Stoney pushed the set of plans to one side of his desk. "That reminds me, I've got to see Leland."

Brownlow gazed at the school clock on the wall. "He's hard to catch at lunch."

"I can't wait until then." Stoney stood up.

"What about that Acquisition Report? We need to get that out this morning."

"I'll do it this afternoon."

Sumter Brownlow shook his head when the office door slammed shut behind Stoney, then he made a note of the time in the daily log he kept.

Out on the street, Stoney walked toward the town hall. An old black man on a bicycle whizzed past followed by a friendly retinue of mongrel pups, and Stoney waved at Amos Tumley, who reminded him of Monkey, the black man who'd taught him to pitch when he was little. Strange, how no one ever talked about Monkey anymore.

Stoney crossed the street. The center of the Essex business district was an imperfect triangle formed by the intersection of two railroad lines and three secondary roads, one to Charleston, one to Columbia, one to Savannah. In the middle of the railroad crossing sat a small red frame depot rarely used nowadays, as the rail traffic consisted of only freight trains now. Across from the depot on one side was the omnipresent brick Piggly Wiggly with its eight parking spaces out front, and on the other side loomed the three-story clapboard library. Down that line of the triangle perched a convenience store which had replaced an old gas station that once sported ceramic pumps, the new video store next door, and the boarded-up movie theater which had been operated at one time or another—at a loss—by nearly every family in town. At present it was closed again, up for sale this time.

Across the street from the movie house stretched a long grassy mall with a white gazebo at one end and a derelict tennis court on the other. Across from the mall a new crafts store had opened beside the barbershop and the beauty shop that had stood side by side for thirty years. The latter was named Venny's for the original proprietor, Venice Estill, whose mother had always wanted to go to Italy. It had plate-glass windows through which the town's older women could be seen sitting under the four steel-helmet dryers, yelling at each other above the noise. Beyond the beauty shop sat Winona's Hat Shoppe, which was a dress store housed in a converted gas station. Next to it was one of the town's two functioning gas stations; the Greyhound buses still stopped under the Texaco sign twice a day except on Sunday. Perpendicular to it were the Noftis Drug Store, the furniture store, and the hardware store with its wheelbarrows lined up out front. At a diagonal, closing up the third leg of the triangle, were Rothenbarger's Department Store with its name engraved in Old English over the door lintel, the two-story frame town hall, and the small brick post office which still had a hitching post out front.

Inside the town hall, Stoney passed down a long hallway paved in black-and-white vinyl squares. At its end he turned right toward an open door with CONSTABLE painted on textured glass in bold, black letters. Inside was a large room that contained one holding cell, a scratched oak schoolteacher's desk, three filing cabinets, a locked gun cabinet with four shotguns inside, and a police radio that was disconnected. Jim Leland, a slender man in his mid-forties with thinning hair, was leaning back in his wooden swivel chair reading a day-old Atlanta *Constitution*.

A native of Essex, the soft-spoken man was the ideal policeman for a town where nothing ever happened. His major responsibilities were confined to traffic violations, vandalism (which he always said no one on earth could do anything about), and theft. Burglaries were his forté: he bustled around all over town when looking for a thief and he did from time to time solve the infrequent Essex heist. As for domestic squabbles, he didn't go near them. Spring-loaded law enforcement clearly wasn't his priority. But he smiled a lot, clucked at children, and generally did whatever Heyward Rutherford told him to do. It was, in fact, the hunting and fishing expeditions Jim Leland took with other town fathers every year that kept him in office.

From the doorway Stoney called, "Got a minute, Jim?"

The police chief put his paper down. He had a bland, vague face; Harriet Setzler said he looked as though he was always trying to remember who he was. "Sure. Come on in."

As Stoney sat down on the other side of the desk, they exchanged pleasantries, views on the weather. Then Stoney asked, "How's the investigation coming?"

Jim Leland's eyes opened wide. "God, Stoney, you wouldn't believe what's going on. It's been in newspapers all over the state. People might not a' heard of this town before but they've sure heard of it now. Bunch a' ladies came over this morning, all worried. Want me to impose a curfew. So nobody can walk around at night." He said the latter as though Stoney might not understand the concept.

"Jim, do we know any more about who *did* it?"

The policeman pressed his fingertips together. "Oh, it's coming along, you know how these things are. Takes time. I went over to Ashboro yesterday. You know they found a fella, a drifter name a' J. T. Turner, who came through Essex that night. But they had to let him go. Wasn't a thing to hold him on. He's working at a HandiMart over there. Admits being in Essex that night but says he was long gone before midnight. Didn't know Sarah, doesn't know anybody around here. No record 'cept a petty theft charge years ago in Georgia."

"They let him go?" Stoney was silent for a second. "What was he doing here that night?"

"Says he hitched a ride from Savannah, got this far. Says he was on his way to Columbia to look for work."

Suddenly Stoney remembered his reason for visiting the police chief. "When did they let him go?" When Jim said he didn't know exactly, Stoney continued, "The reason I ask is—somebody was wandering around Harriet Setzler's yard night before last. I called you about it yesterday, I guess you were in Ashboro. She called me over there because she heard something and I found part of a footprint up by her house. I thought you'd want to have a look at it. It's about the same size as my feet and I wear a ten." Stoney leaned forward intensely. "Jim, if the guy's still out there, we've *got* to find him."

"Well, I'm doing everything I can." The pale man held out his hands, soft palms upturned. "There's just no evidence. No footprints at the scene, no fingerprints, not even a hair or fiber that can be clearly identified. Nothing much stolen except the silver. There was three hundred dollars in a dresser drawer the guy didn't even take, can you believe that? And certainly no reason for anybody to kill her." Jim Leland sighed with exasperation. "The state law enforcement people are sending a SLED agent down the end of the week, to help out."

"We know it was a man," Stoney said. "It's not much of a start but it's something."

"We also know, thanks to Ed, that he used a knife with a seven-and-a-half-inch blade, serrated on one side. Not a kitchen knife." Jim nodded toward the wall behind him. "Likely the same as that Buckmaster."

The other man got up and walked around to look at the knife mounted on a wood plaque on the wall. "What kind of knife is that?"

"Field knife. Lodge gave it to me after I brought down a ten-point buck a few years back. It's for wilderness survival; they claim that back edge will cut you out of a car or airplane."

Stoney stared at the long pewter-bright knife. He believed it. The back of the blade looked like a saw. "So the guy must have been a hunter," he said as he walked back over and sat down again.

"Not necessarily. Some people collect Buckmasters, they cost a fortune." Jim was quiet for a moment, then added, "You know some folks think it's that black woman. Maum Chrish."

"You don't agree with them, do you?"

"Naw. People just don't like her, way they live out there, so strange and all. The talk is she killed Sarah without ever getting near her. Some voodoo thing. And she planted the semen to throw everybody off." Jim laughed. "Let 'em talk. We'll just wait and see what the SLED man finds."

"We *can't* just wait around," Stoney insisted. "The whole town's going to hell. People are afraid to walk out the door at night. Until we find who did it and why, nobody's going to be able to relax. Everybody feels like it could happen again. To them, this time."

The other man stared. "I'll go look at what you found at Mrs. Setzler's. It's my job."

Stoney fell silent. It was Jim Leland's job. Just his job. And everyone in town knew how seriously he took that. Old people were scared witless, were suddenly afraid of their neighbors, were even thinking of moving, but this seemed of little concern to Jim Leland. He intended to sit right there and read the paper until a "real" policeman arrived from Columbia.

When Stoney left Jim Leland's office, he crossed the railroad tracks and headed toward the water tower and the fire station behind the old movie house. The fire house was a two-story white brick building with FIRE emblazoned on its side in red letters. Across from it sat the one-story General Telephone of the Southeast building. Stoney passed it and turned onto Aiken Avenue. Soon the old houses appeared. This was his favorite street in town, where imperturbable institutions like Harriet Setzler and Sarah Rothenbarger and even his own grandmother had withstood the assaults of the twentieth century. It was always the women he remembered, never their husbands, these women who were born old but ageless, with their capable hands and clairvoyant eyes, who could shovel horse manure and then serve high tea, who would send money to the African Missionary Society but deny a black neighbor access to the Baptist church. These were the women who had imparted to his youth the color and texture of contradiction.

It was their smell, too, that flowed through him as he breathed in the spring. Rose water and mothballs and moist loam. Women who were forever digging in the earth lacquered their neighborhoods with the fragrance of newly turned dirt. Damp dirt overlaid with the aroma of gardenias and American Beauty roses, of musky tomato plants ripening in the sun, of sweat and leather baseball gloves and stolen sex. The sensual incense of a childhood lived close to the ground. But when Stoney looked at the houses now, the fragrance vanished. The sidewalk was barren; everyone was at work or safely locked inside. Empty porch swings and wooden rockers mocked him like dead spirits. He paused briefly in front of the Wallerman's house where a new six-foot-high privacy fence had just been erected; it now encircled the entire back yard. Within that fence lay one garden he'd never smell again.

Farther down the street, Stoney suddenly came to an abrupt stop. Three doors down, in front of a large two-story house with dormers, was a rectangular white truck with ALLIED painted on its side. A moving van. In front of Emma Thomas' house, just like Harriet Setzler had said. Stoney walked toward the house. Two men were carrying a loveseat into the van via the steel walkway strung between the truck and the porch. Other pieces of furniture sat on the porch waiting a turn, including five boxes of plants—mostly flowering begonias—safely ensconced inside cardboard boxes whose tops had been cut off.

Stoney walked inside the house looking for Emma Thomas. In a moment she appeared, kitchen utensils in her right hand. They talked for a moment, standing amid the packed cartons in her rose-tinted living room. She always looked like a child to Stoney, with her perfectly round chubby face, a tiny mite of only five feet who had somehow given birth to ten children. Together they stared at the outlines left on the wall by pictures now packed. Stoney remembered those photographs of the Thomas children, how three boys had remained forever young in their World War II uniforms. Emma Thomas crossed to the fireplace and fingered the dented mantelpiece. "Now that it's done, I really don't want to go," she said softly. "My boy Harry says it's best though, I'll be better off, he says. Safe. What with all the children scattered. And . . . well, everything." She paused, turned to look at Stoney. "Did you know I was born in this house? Seventy-three years ago come July. Fred and I always thought we'd move into a smaller house when the last children left but somehow we just never did." She gazed around the room as though memorizing it. "I know every corner like one of my fingers. This old place is my best friend now." Another pause. "They have a gate at the new place they lock every night, and a night watchman stands guard."

The rest of Stoney's day was passed in mindless paperwork that was remarkably soothing for a change. He called and confirmed sales all afternoon, a task he normally disliked but which today was almost a pleasure. In fact, he got so caught up in his work that he stayed at the office a half-hour late, to finish up the sales confirmations. Sumter Brownlow also stayed late; Stoney had never known him to be the first to go home.

When Stoney did get home, he found Seth Von Hocke sitting on his front porch. He had almost forgotten about Seth, to whom he gave guitar lessons once a week. The boy was a thin, gangly child of eleven, with large serious brown eyes that reminded Stoney of Silas.

"Hi, Seth." Stoney sat down on the front steps beside the boy, who was holding a student-size classical guitar.

Seth nodded but didn't answer. Absently he plucked the E-string. He had a lot on his mind these days. Kids around school said the old lady in the swamps killed Mrs. Roth. Seth swallowed, thinking about it again. It was the same night he and Donny snuck out there and saw the white boy and black girl going at it. He wasn't going out there again, not ever, not to see anything.

"Hey, you still on this planet?" Stoney smiled. "We better get to your lesson. You been practicing?"

To prove himself, Seth stumbled through a succession of chords he'd picked out by himself. Then he looked up. "Pretty good, huh? Maybe I should just go on home?"

Stoney threw his head back and laughed. "You're not getting out of a lesson that easy. Come on, kid."

By that evening, however, Stoney had begun to think about Emma Thomas again. During dinner he told Anna about his day and she tried to say something to lighten his mood, suggested that perhaps they should get away for a weekend at the beach. He said that sounded nice, but his mood didn't change. While she was putting the dishes into the dishwasher, he wandered out into the back yard to throw a stick for Silas. Through the back door Anna could hear the dog yelping with joy. Then everything got quiet again. Anna finished the dishes and walked out to join them.

Stoney was sitting on a tree stump beside the pond, Silas right beside him, the dog's head resting on his knee. At Stoney's feet lay several untouched stones. Above him in the indigo sky hung a cradle of a quarter moon. But he stared straight into the dark water at his feet, as if he expected something to suddenly rise from it.

"It's not your fault," Anna said softly when she reached his side.

Stoney looked up. "No, I didn't cause this. I didn't cause

slavery either, I didn't start or perpetuate racism. But as a Southerner I feel responsible for both sometimes. Only I've never really stood up for anything I love or hate. I hear someone say something racist but I don't challenge them, none of us do, we just go along, that's the polite thing to do. And look where that's gotten us.''

''What does racism have to do with the murder?''

Her husband turned to stare at her, his eyes still that eerie black. ''Don't you see? Finally I understand. I didn't do it—but I am responsible. I can't undo what happened to Sarah any more than I can reverse history. But I can do more than just sit by and watch.'' Stoney paused, then added forcefully, ''If Leland won't do anything about this, then I will.''

They talked for a while longer and then they went inside again and locked up. They undressed silently and slipped into bed. Stoney thought about taking Anna in his arms, as he'd once done so often, sliding her silky gown up to feel her skin against his. Half of him wanted to do so but half of him didn't—the tired half did not want to appear to start something he didn't want to finish. On her side of the bed Anna sensed all this, and waited. Except for perfunctory gestures they'd not touched each other since the morning after Sarah was killed. Half of her wanted him to make a move, even as the rest of her knew she'd beg off somehow. In the end they both decided this wasn't a good time, they could always do this later. They kissed demurely and turned over and went to sleep.

The road between Essex and Ashboro, the county seat of Ashton County, followed the railroad tracks. Everyone going to Florida during the thirties and forties had used this highway, so its borders were littered with deserted gas stations and defunct motels. In Stoney's youth it had been a narrow two-lane but recently the road had been widened to four lanes. One of his first projects upon moving to Essex had been to assist in that improvement, and now the new asphalt sparkled in the sunlight as though laid with diamonds. On Stoney's left loomed the new high school—it wasn't that new anymore but it was under construction again, being enlarged once more. Next he passed the Ashton County Hospital, low and white and squatty; the hospital entrance was directly adjacent to the turnoff that led to the Ashton County Law Enforcement Center. On the outskirts of Ashboro a Radio Shack and two car dealerships appeared as well as the only liquor store in the county, housed in what still resembled a tenant farmer's shack.

Ashboro was larger and more imposing than Essex, thanks largely to the two-story courthouse with its cement fountain out front. The town was kept alive by the regional hospital, a small textile mill, a community college, and the Nissan factory five miles beyond it to the south.

In a few minutes Stoney pulled his Land Rover up in front of the HandiMart on the east side of town and went inside. Several people were at the counter, so he waited. A wooden barrel filled with beer on ice sat beside the counter, along with a hand-lettered sign about fishing licenses. Finally a tall man in an apron asked Stoney what he wanted. Stoney told him and the man jerked a thumb toward the door. "Turner works the full-service pump."

J. T. Turner turned out to be the kind of man who inspires people on a bus to stand rather than occupy the seat beside him. They look him over and say to themselves, he's not all there; then they pass on down the aisle. He was short and fat, his fleshy oval face half-hidden by thick glasses and long matted black hair that looked permanently uncombed. Encased in a torn zippered sweatshirt and dirty workpants, he shifted his eyes back and forth as Stoney moved the Rover over to the full-service pump.

Stoney got out and said, "Need ten dollars. Unleaded." As Turner began filling the tank, Stoney studied him. He was probably in his late twenties. His dark tan was odd; he seemed more the type to stay pasty white all summer long. And despite his girth he moved quickly, jumpy and jerky, like a rabbit.

Turner replaced the pump. "Ten bucks."

Reaching in his back pocket for his wallet, Stoney said, "Understand you were in Essex the night of the murder."

The other man's eyes dilated like a teenager on PCP. "I ain't kilt nobody. *Nobody!*" He stopped short. "Ten bucks for the gas."

Stoney handed him a twenty. Sure was a nervous guy. He watched Turner open the door to the convenience store and noticed that the man wore heavy construction boots. The kind with a deep tread. Probably a ten or eleven.

In a few seconds Turner returned with Stoney's change. "Can't a man hitch a ride," he growled, "without gittin' accused a' murderin' somebody?"

"You didn't see or hear anybody that night?"

Turner backed away. "Who are you?"

"Nobody." Stoney smiled. "I live there, I knew the lady who was killed."

"You a cop?"

"No. Honest. I work for the highway department."

"How come you so curious?"

"How come you were in Essex that night?"

"I told the sheriff a hundred times," Turner lashed out. "I caught a ride, the guy let me off there 'cause he wasn't coming this way."

"What was his name, the guy who gave you the ride?"

"He didn't say."

"What time did you leave Essex that night, how'd you get here?"

"I walked, took me all damn night. I stopped and slept in some old barn."

"Were you in the old part of town? You didn't hear or see anyone else?"

"I don't know where I was. All I saw was some stores, old houses."

Turner walked over and started cleaning the windshield of an empty car parked at the next pump. Stoney followed him. "You haven't been back to Essex since you were released, have you?"

The other man looked up, snarled, "I don't have to answer you. They let me go, didn't have nothin' on me."

"If you didn't do anything, why be afraid of answering questions?"

The small round man tensed, crouched against the windshield. He bared his teeth and hissed. "Leave me alone. I ain't the guy."

Stoney gazed at the man's neck. Inside his open collar, draped around his thick neck, lay a shiny gold chain. The incongruous adornment reminded Stoney of Sarah Roth's jewelry and he said, "Nice chain."

Abruptly Turner preened. "Yeah it is, ain't it?" He reached up and fondled the gold links. As he did so the chain shifted.

"Looks like real gold," Stoney added. "Had it long?"

"Naw, it ain't real."

The short man leaned back and the chain moved again. Stoney thought about the white line his watch left on his wrist every summer. Nowhere on Turner's neck was there a similar line. If he wore that chain all the time, on that suntanned neck, it was a recent acquisition.

"My wife likes gold jewelry," Stoney said. "Where'd you get a chain like that?"

Turner looked up, his eyes narrowing. "Had it," he said. Then he turned and went inside the convenience store.

On his way back to Essex, Stoney wondered about J. T. Turner. So skittish on the one hand, downright hostile and defiant on the other—not exactly the hallmark of a stable personality. Why would he kill Sarah though? To steal some costume jewelry (which he was then stupid enough to wear)? If he broke in to steal, would he leave behind three hundred dollars in cash in a bureau drawer? Moreover, where would a guy like that pawn stolen silver? Not locally, it'd be noticed for sure, he'd have to take it elsewhere—on foot apparently. J. T. Turner wore boots with a deep tread. Of course, so did half the men in Essex.

Once in Essex, Stoney stopped by Harriet Setzler's house. No, she couldn't say for sure whether Sarah had owned a gold chain or not. Sounded a bit modern for Sarah. Sarah had had some nice pearls though, that much she did know.

Around one o'clock Stoney returned to his office, which was empty. Apparently Sumter Brownlow had gone to lunch late. While Stoney had been in Ashboro, the plans for two new projects had appeared on his desk. He scanned the letting dates. A year away. Stoney got up and walked over to the coffeepot and poured himself a cup. He peered out the window. Idly he watched Leonard Hansen cross the street; he'd just come out of the Essex Dinnerplate, a family-style restaurant that still brought heaping platters to the table. Odd that Leonard would come all the way to Essex for lunch if he was working. Stoney wondered if the other man was still patrolling the streets at night; he hadn't seen Leonard since the night Harriet Setzler had called. Odd, too, that Jim Leland would ask Leonard to do that, given Jim's nonchalance about the whole thing. Leonard disappeared into his pickup and Stoney thought about J. T. Turner again. Why would he kill Sarah? He broke in, she woke up and saw him, he panicked and killed her that viciously? It didn't make sense. Stoney drained the last of his coffee and was still musing at the window when Sumter Brownlow walked in. Turning, Stoney said, "Sorry I was so late getting back."

Brownlow didn't say anything. But he sat down at his desk with a set face and stared at Stoney for a moment. "McFarland, I've never pulled rank around here. But this thing of disappearing during working hours has got to stop. Except when you're out on a project, I expect you to be here."

Stoney walked toward the other man angrily. "Am I behind on my work?"

"That's not the point."

"For God's sake, Sump. Spring's always slow. Everything we've got going is at least a year or two away from letting. I can't for the life of me see what difference it makes if I leave the office briefly—as long as I keep my projects up to date."

The older man drew himself up in his chair. "I don't run the kind of office where people make their own rules."

"Don't you care who killed Sarah? Don't you care that Jim Leland's not doing one goddamn thing about it?"

"It's not my business."

Stoney slammed his hand down on the other man's desk. "Well it sure as hell oughta be."

Brownlow leaned back in his chair and affected a crafty smile. "You know, if you could muster this much energy about your work, Central Office wouldn't call this the No-Man's-Land district."

The phrase stuck in Stoney's brain. No-man's-land. Something Harriet Setzler had said. About how Sarah felt obliged to shelter all the lost souls from no-man's-land. Stoney whirled around and headed for the door.

The older man gaped at him. "Where are you going now?"

"I'll stay late tonight."

"You just got here."

"I've got to see Harriet Setzler. It could be important."

Brownlow shook his head. "You keep this up and I'll be forced to take it up with someone else. Absenteeism *is* grounds for dismissal from civil service."

Stoney turned sharply. He had always tolerated Brownlow's superciliousness with good humor, but this time he said, one word at a time, "Stop threatening me."

In a few moments Stoney left. When the door closed behind him, Brownlow picked up the phone.

Five

AND SO, LIFE went on. This is not to say that the shock of Sarah Roth's murder diminished in Essex but rather that it became integral to our ethos. We went about our business, yet we still talked of little else. But now much of our talk evolved into outright speculation. Into suspicion. No one could say for sure who first started it but rumors about "that black woman" multiplied like guppies. Some claimed it was Marynell Pittman, that every time the Baptist church ladies took her clothes and food for her children, she began ranting and raving about how she'd seen Maum Chrish performing witchcraft. The Baptist ladies came back home and started asking questions themselves—just what was going on out in those swamps anyway, was it true those people practiced voodoo or something? Langley Thompson got in the act then, told somebody how he was hunting out there one time and saw a bunch of 'em gathered around a fire singing and dancing and, sure 'nough, now that he thought about it, that big woman was right there in the middle of everything. This got back to John Loadholt's wife, who had a sister who lived down near New Orleans, and her sister told her on the phone one night that in Louisiana, where voodooists sacrificed animals all the time, one group had been arrested in 1973 for a murder the police believed was actually a ritualistic human sacrifice. In three weeks time almost everyone in Essex with nothing better to do suddenly remembered something weird he or she had once seen in the swamps.

It was, of course, an easy way to explain the unexplainable. Counter one brand of lunacy with another.

The annual May Day Festival was canceled in Sarah's honor, and April passed into May unheralded, without our endorsement or consent. Spring had failed Essex this year. A few of us, to be sure, endeavored to keep our perspective. Stoney Mc-Farland went to work every day and worked unusually hard, although he bought an inordinate amount of gas every week from the HandiMart in Ashboro, in his continuing quest to form an opinion about J. T. Turner. Heyward Rutherford, for his part, wrote six letters to Sarah Roth's cousin, increasing his offer for the store each time, always claiming this was his final offer. Harriet Setzler was busy cataloging the new books she'd ordered for the town library, which she still ran, and she tried not to notice the FOR SALE sign on Sarah's house when she came home every evening. Jim Leland called the South Carolina Law Enforcement Division in Columbia twice a week to check on the agent they were supposed to be sending to Essex; each time he described the town as being "in a state of crisis." Seth Von Hocke wondered if he'd ever get through the sixth grade. Leonard Hansen used the good weather to put a new roof on his house. Amos Tumley went back to the Wilson's house eventually, but despite profuse apologies from the Wilson boy; now he left the vegetables at the curb rather than on the carport. Marian Davis yearned for the end of the school year more ferociously than normal and seriously considered making this her last year in Essex. Ever since Sarah's death she'd had trouble sleeping too; she was definitely overdue for a change.

On the first Saturday in May, Anna McFarland invited Marian to lunch. Usually Marian went to Charleston on Saturdays but today she accepted Anna's invitation; she and Anna needed to talk about Career Day, so she walked up the steps of the McCloskey house at eleven-thirty. Facing the sun, the house was flooded with light from the azure sky; Silas was lying on the front door mat and he immediately popped up and pointed at Marian, uncertain. "It's okay, Silas. You know me," she assured him. Then the dog decided the black woman was okay and ran over to her and started sniffing.

The front door opened and Stoney came out, in nylon shorts and jogging shoes. "Silas, down," he ordered. He grabbed the dog's collar and pulled him backward. "Hi, Marian. How're you doing?"

"I'm okay. You?"

Stoney nodded at the retriever, who was now standing on the edge of the porch staring out at the sidewalk. "We're going for a run. Something makes me think I'm holding him up." A pause. "I'm glad you and Anna are getting together. She'll be down in a second. Go on in."

"Thanks." Marian hesitated. "Stoney, have you heard anything else about the investigation?"

"Not really. All I'm hearing these days are crazy rumors. Why?"

"Oh, no reason." Marian changed the subject. "Thanks for the locks you put on Harriet's doors. You've really been good to everyone around here since this happened."

Stoney thought about the footprint in Harriet's back yard and wondered if the locks were enough. He'd been back over to her house in the middle of the night several times, on his own, but had found no other sign that anyone had been there. He wished Marian a good lunch, and he and Silas took off running down the street.

Marian walked through the open door into the living room of the McCloskey house. Bookshelves lined one wall, a large brick fireplace another; the third was dominated by the curved bank of windows overlooking the porch outside. Low-slung modern easy chairs around the fireplace, beside them end tables Anna said were made from the cypress beams of old Charleston houses, an abstract modern sculpture in a corner, a Colonial sofa in deep burgundy, and an Indian throw rug over the center of the polished oak floor. The eclectic furnishings had a carefully crafted feel; only the sunlight streaming through the bay window felt accidental. To Marian this room looked more like someone's idea of a contemporary salon than a place where living people propped their feet up on rainy afternoons.

In a moment Anna appeared, in a short skirt and oversized cotton sweater, and she and Marian walked from room to room for a few minutes looking at the newest renovations being made on the old house. Then they got in Anna's Subaru and drove out to Fairfield Plantation, a bed-and-breakfast with the finest restaurant in Ashton County, both housed in the only surviving Civil War estate in that part of South Carolina. The two women walked up the curved stone staircase to the porticoed entrance of the four-story Federal mansion. Inside, a hall laid with Italian marble led to the rear of the brick building where a solarium had been created by uniting a drawing room with two bedrooms. The exterior wall was now glass and overlooked the terraced grounds which bordered the Salkehatchie River. The music of Segovia was playing softly as the headwaiter led Anna and Marian to a corner table with a nice view of the river.

Marian gazed around the room, with its damask draperies and tables set with Irish linen. Somehow she'd suspected Anna would want to come here. To the one restaurant near Essex where a black patron was still uncommon. Marian gazed over at her companion; Anna was smiling like a dictator after a successful coup. That, Marian remembered, was the reason she usually declined Anna's invitations. The two women had seen each other socially fairly often, starting when Anna was invited to talk about photography at Career Day at the high school the previous year. But Marian never felt totally comfortable with Anna McFarland. There was an off-putting edge to the other woman: she was so strident, she always seemed slightly irritated with the world, as though she were having to fight so hard to maintain her place in it.

They ordered the scampi, the Fairfield specialty, and a bottle of chardonnay. When the waiter left, Anna leaned back. "I'm glad you could come today, it's been ages since we talked. How's everything at school?"

Marian smiled. "It'll be better soon. Right now the month of June seems like proof that God is not dead after all."

The other woman laughed and for a while they talked desultorily, about school, new books, the weather. Marian mentioned several changes in the Career Day program and asked Anna if her presentation would be the same as last year's.

"No, I want to expand a little, do more on the history of photography. I think anyone going into the field needs that overview."

The schoolteacher nodded. "Thanks for participating again. It's nice to have a professional photographer in town."

After their lunch arrived and they began eating, Anna broached a different subject. "Sometimes I wonder why a woman like you—with so much to offer—stays in Essex."

The black woman didn't respond at first. It was a very personal comment; Anna often alienated Essex with her city-bred directness. Marian laid down her fork and picked up her wineglass, thinking: why did "a woman like you" sound so much like "you people"? She sipped the white wine. Why was she so sensitive today?

"This is home," she said after a minute. "I lived in Columbia for ten years and I'll probably go back there before long. But over the years I sort of lost touch with my teaching, with what made it mean something, you can do that in the bureaucracy of huge city schools. I needed more one-to-one with kids again."

Anna watched Marian's face and thought about photographing her. She wasn't tall nor bone-thin enough to be a fashion model, but she had a warmly sensual look that was interesting. Marian wore tapered slacks beneath a long tunic in a bold abstract print which was belted below her hips; the bright color flattered her gold-tone skin and the tunic was split at the neckline in a deep V which touched the intersection of her full breasts.

"I guess what I meant was—this must be so tame for someone who was politically active." Anna stared across the table. "Stoney told me about your work in Columbia. It's hard to imagine you could be satisfied here—or that you ever lived with Harriet Setzler, for that matter."

Marian explained no more about her reasons for returning to Essex. "Harriet's a tough old bird. She absolutely thrives on public contention. My mother once told me that Harriet was the only woman in town in the twenties to bob her hair, seems it was a major scandal." Marian smiled. "Can you imagine?"

"No. That woman as daring, as a leader of the avant-garde, no I can't."

The black woman swallowed the last of her shrimp. "Harriet's always been self-sufficient and that's made her more than a little suspect around here. Women were not supposed to survive that well alone. During World War II—by then she'd lost her husband—she helped support herself making baked goods for other people to send overseas to their sons. She got extra ration coupons for the sugar. Before that, during the Depression, when schoolteachers got credit vouchers instead of their salary, Harriet started sewing for people in order to keep her own kids in shoes. She clothed half the women in this town for years." Marian paused. "Black women couldn't afford store-bought clothes so they'd take a dollar and a piece of cloth to Harriet and she'd make them a dress."

"You're awfully generous to her. Considering."

Marian eyed Anna directly. "I've known Harriet for a long time, Anna, and I know what her faults are. She's color-blind. Certain colors blind her: when she sees them, she responds generically, with Pavlovian training, without thinking. That this response is so impersonal makes it even worse." Marian slowed down. "Nonetheless—she has a resilience I admire. Come war or depression or just bad times, she never let anything defeat her. She never once just threw her hands up and said, I can't take any more. She never once let fear of other people talk her out of being who she is. She's nobody's mule and never has been."

Anna was silent for a second. Then, "You can honestly say her racism doesn't bother you?"

For a second Marian regarded the other woman irritably. Thinking of her NAACP days, she snapped, "Of course it bothers me." She hesitated, tried to control her tone. "But as long as I keep defining myself in terms of what bigotry has done to me—it was white men who made slaves of us both, you know—then I remain powerless. Hate keeps me his victim. Victimization is a powerful opiate, you keep coming back for more. You'll win this time. But hate makes you stupid and careless, you don't think things through. Hate is too emotional. Like love. So he gets you all over again, and again and again and . . ."

The black woman stopped sharply, realized what she'd said. What was wrong with her? She looked at Anna. Their eyes locked and neither said anything for a moment.

Marian finally looked away. "The scampi really was good."

"Marian, I understand what you're talking about." The other woman wouldn't meet her eyes again but Anna persisted, "Something like that once happened to me too."

The schoolteacher cleared her throat but didn't speak. Something in Anna's blue eyes saw through her, instinctively recognized what she'd not said. If a mirror could steal your soul, no doubt those eyes could make off with your life story. A story she had no desire to discuss.

Anna let it drop. She took a sip of wine and said, "While I've got you here, I wanted to ask you something else. Do you know anything about Maum Chrish?"

Am I supposed to? Marian wondered. "What about her?"

"Do you think she's crazy? Do you believe that stuff about voodoo? I'm asking because I'd like to shoot some film of her."

Marian laughed. "I see you've been listening to the grapevine." She paused. "I don't know anything about her, Anna. I've heard she's a recluse. The fact that we're both black doesn't make us intimate. As for voudou—voudou's a religion, it has almost nothing in common with Hollywood voodoo. I studied it once in a Black Studies class at the university; it's an archaic pantheistic religion. I gather Maum Chrish is just a superstitious woman caught up in old African customs and beliefs. She lives out there because she can't adapt, I suppose."

Anna described her visit out to the swamps. "That place is scary but sort of fascinating too. You should see all the stuff around her house—the trees are decorated, there's this boat hanging from the rafters."

The other woman nodded. "The boat represents the moon, the goddess Erzulie. In Haitian voudou, anyway." Marian's eyes flickered. "She's a dark-skinned woman because she's been burned by her husband the sun."

"Sounds like astrology."

"A distant cousin, I guess. God is the supreme being in voudou but there are many other gods—loas—and the voudouist interacts with these on a daily basis. Some are ancestral spirits, spirits of the recently dead, spirits of the natural world. Believers draw symbolic designs, called *vèvès*, to call out these gods. A mambo like Maum Chrish—if that's what she really is—serves these lesser gods. Some of whom, they believe, live in the trees until called out."

"That's wild," Anna said.

"Why are you so interested? Because these are the backward superstitions of unenlightened people?" Marian's voice was cold.

Anna looked surprised, gazed across the table for a moment. "No." Then she dropped the subject. They polished off the rest of their wine and drove back to Essex, where Anna let Marian off at her house. Marian waved, walked up her front steps, opened her door, and slammed it behind her. She wished she'd stayed home and done her laundry. For a moment she thought about calling Jordan Taylor, the black lawyer in Beaufort with whom she had dinner once in a while. When she first returned to Essex, she and Jordan had made it a point to be seen together publicly every so often, but she hadn't seen him now in several months.

She had met Jordan Taylor at a lunch counter sit-in in 1968 in Columbia, the first of several civil rights demonstrations Marian participated in both during and after her graduation from the University of South Carolina. He was, at that time, a tall and slim pre-law student at Allen University, the Negro college across town. They sat side by side at the Woolworth's lunch counter on Main Street, rode to the city lockup in the same van, and over time (and subsequent demonstrations and arrests) became fast friends. Seven years later he was a young assistant district attorney and she was a classroom teacher in charge of the Richland County School District pilot program to prepare the city schools for massive desegregation. One night they met for a drink and she found herself confessing the confusing romantic situation in which she was involved. Two days later for the first time Jordan invited Marian to his apartment to meet his lover of three years, a black male jazz musician with long elegant hands and fingers.

Sometimes it seemed to Marian that Jordan Taylor was the only black person she'd ever been close to. She'd never known her father, her mother had deserted her, and her association with Harriet Setzler always stood between her and the black community in Essex. So, when she went away to college, she joined the NAACP and got involved in the civil rights movement. But oftentimes the woman sitting beside her at a lunch counter or in the university administration building was white and it was to them Marian gravitated. Living with Harriet Setzler had changed her speech and often she talked more easily with whites. Finally Marian found herself in a group of Columbia teachers selected to prepare other teachers for massive school desegregation. She sat in an auditorium one morning and listened to the white program chairman, who spoke again that afternoon in a more intimate group discussion. No doubt about it, Marian decided, the woman was brilliant; she knew everything the books had ever said about child socialization. But she was wrong-headed just the same, the whole premise was wrong-headed. Later that day Marian raised her hand. "Excuse me, but aren't we going about this all wrong? We're spending all this time worrying about how to incorporate black children into our classrooms so they assimilate easily. Isn't the way to do that very simple—we treat them like all the other students? We're preparing for them as if they're from outer space, as if they're so weird we have to make special provisions for them. But our goal is to treat the black children as equals—isn't it?"

Two months later Marian Davis was put in charge of the city's entire program, at the instigation of the white woman. She became Marian's assistant and was instrumental in garnering support for the black woman's point of view. For the first time in Marian's life someone believed in her, totally. Eileen Brook nurtured Marian with unequivocal acceptance. And became the love of Marian's life.

A few months later Marian and Eileen moved in together. They ate at restaurants where white people ate, read the books white people were talking about. Marian's few black friends called less and less often. One even accused her of being the only black activist in South Carolina who lived in a white world. Do it with whoever you want, the friend said, but aren't there enough black women in the world to suit you? Gradually Marian became less active in NAACP activities; desegregation came and went and there were problems none of them had even remotely anticipated. Marian found herself having to tell white teachers that seating all the black children on one side of the room was discriminatory. She found herself going to some black homes to beg parents to stop instructing their children to stand up to the white teachers.

One mother, leaning in the doorway of a house without any heat or plumbing, eyed Marian with contempt. "And what kinda white nigger might you be?"

Eventually, Marian left Eileen. A year later she almost married a black doctor but she backed out at the last minute; somehow she knew it would end just like her first ill-fated marriage. The die was cast. Over the years she became involved with more women, including the woman in Charleston whom she saw most weekends. Who was as white as Anna McFarland but softer, more loving. Women like Anna always reminded Marian of the past. So many things, lately, kept doing that.

Stoney and Silas jogged over to the housing development on the east side of town. Willowbrook Estates was Heyward Rutherford's "planned community" which had neither streetlights nor sidewalks like the rest of the town, just four blocks of half-acre lots where sparse grass struggled against sandy soil in front of long carbon-copy brick ranchers. Stoney turned down a street named Partridge Drive, wiping sweat off his forehead with the back of his hand. Silas had his nose to the ground behind him and Stoney called and the dog soon caught up.

At a house with gray shutters, Stoney stopped and turned and walked up the driveway. As he did so a side door opened and a taller man, a little older than Stoney, came out to meet him. Bill Jenkins owned the Essex *Telegraph*, a weekly paper devoted to local news which he had begun when he came back home after college. Large and lumpy as a bear, Bill had a monk's haircut and wore thick wire-rim glasses. Perpetually overweight, he had started running with Stoney soon after Stoney moved back to town.

"You're late," Bill said, stopping to scratch Silas on the top of the head.

"I know. Silas is getting old."

"Yeah, right. Silas."

They began running, keeping an even steady pace. Stoney was clearly the better athlete, and he slowed down from time to time to accommodate the heavier man. "You talk to the Ashton sheriff this week? I don't suppose they know anything new."

"Not that I heard," Bill expelled, breathing hard. "I can't believe how Leland's acting, like the whole thing will just go away. Even Heyward's disgusted. Says we ought to fire him."

"Has Heyward got his hands on the store yet?"

"How'd you know about that?"

"Harriet Setzler, who else?"

Bill slowed down, cast a sidelong glance at Stoney. "You thinking what I'm thinking? What I've been too chicken to say out loud?"

"You mean that Heyward stood to gain by Sarah's death?"

Bill came to a complete stop. "That's the one. You mentioned this to anyone else?"

Stoney stopped too. "Hell no. Men like Heyward don't kill people. I like the voodoo theory myself—murder from a distance."

They began jogging again. "Stoney, they're serious. They really believe that stuff."

Leaving the subdivision behind, they rounded a corner and turned onto a back road that led, eventually, to Savannah. "What do you really think?" Stoney asked.

"Well, the longer this goes on, the less I believe it was random, some stranger breaking in to steal. Sooner or later we may have to face the fact that it may be somebody right here."

"I can't believe that. Maybe I don't want to believe it." Stoney turned abruptly. "Silas, leave those squirrels alone!" When the dog rejoined them, Stoney said to Bill, "Funny thing, though, I saw Marian Davis this morning—she and Anna were going out to lunch—and I had the feeling she was thinking the same thing. But who? And why?"

The other man glanced at his companion. "If we knew why, we'd probably know who." Bill Jenkins hesitated. "I got out my old hunting rifle the other day and cleaned it. Felt like a damn fool but I did it."

"I've thought about doing the same thing," Stoney said. "It's crazy. But I worry about Anna when I'm not there. I haven't touched a gun in years, not since the seventh grade when I thought guns were cool. I shot a bird and felt like shit afterward. A robin." A pause. Then, "We've got to *do* something. Leland's just sitting around on his can. You know, Mrs. Setzler told me something really interesting—did you know Sarah was always inviting strangers home to her house for a hot meal?"

"Yeah, she was like that. I saw her go up to an old drifter sitting in front of the barber shop one day, must have been five years ago, and she asked him if he was hungry. Eventually he went home with her. She took in stray cats and dogs *and kids*— God, the kids, every time somebody ran away Sarah'd let 'em stay with her until they cooled off and were ready to go back to their folks. Sally Wallerman, that Haigler kid, even Leonard Hansen when he came back to town that time. Sarah had a hell of a big heart."

Stoney slowed down again. "Leonard Hansen?"

"Yeah. When he got out of the service. His parents had moved to Alabama by then. Rumor was he and his daddy still weren't getting along, the old man made Leonard join up. You remember his daddy, dontcha? Anyhow Leonard came back to town fresh out of the Marines and he stayed with Sarah for a while, he didn't have a job so he did stuff around her house to earn his keep. Then he left town again."

"I can't picture Leonard Hansen at Sarah's house. Are you sure?"

"Sure I'm sure. Why?"

"In those days Leonard was a real bruiser. I can't imagine Sarah Roth having a kid like that in her house."

Bill pointed at Silas. "Does that dog ever get tired?" The hefty man slowed to a walk. "Leonard's changed a lot. Did you know his father opened an electronics store in Birmingham? Did pretty good, I hear. Apparently he and Leonard never made peace. Leonard's mother must be dead because the old man left all his money to a guy who worked in the store, didn't leave Leonard anything but that shack."

"Why did Leonard's father make him join the Marines?"

Bill Jenkins rolled his eyes. "How would I know? That was a hundred years ago."

Having come full circle, the two men were nearing the entrance to Willowbrook again. "Maybe Leonard killed Sarah," Stoney said, half in jest.

Bill laughed aloud as he came to a stop in front of his house. "She was nice to him so he knocked her over a coupla decades later, huh? That's almost as good as Maum Chrish. Go home, McFarland. And take that dog with you. It should be illegal to have that much energy."

Stoney waved and he and Silas peeled off again. After a few blocks they stopped and Stoney checked the black sports watch on his left wrist. He set the time and said to the retriever, "Okay, boy, now it's for real.'' Each week he took a different route home and increased his distance by a half-mile, at the same time trying to shorten his time. Stoney took a deep breath and then shot out onto the highway; Silas jumped, realized the change in tempo, and broke into a canter to catch up. Air filled Stoney's lungs and he could feel them expand, in and out, in and out; he could see the tension in his quadriceps as each thigh rose up in front of him.

Sweat soon soaked Stoney's T-shirt and ran down his legs. His side hurt but he ran harder. Then harder still. Silas fell behind but they were only six blocks from the McCloskey house and the dog knew the way home. Stoney's legs hurt but he couldn't stop. He swallowed air hungrily. Then he sprinted all-out as fast as he could, panting, gasping.

Until he collapsed on his front steps in a heap, satisfied, sated, one minute ahead of his best time.

That night Anna woke up sweating. She sat up, stared blankly at the naked shoulders of the man sleeping beside her. Now she could escape, she could sneak out of bed and put on her clothes, slip out of the apartment before he knew she was gone. This time she'd get away. She searched the darkness for her underwear. Where was it? She lifted the bedcovers carefully, then stopped suddenly, refocused. Her heart slowed. She was wearing a nightgown. It wasn't him. Instead, Stoney lay sleeping with his fingers laced together under the back of his head, elbows akimbo, a slight grin on his lips. Anna relaxed, smiled with relief. How on earth could anyone sleep that way?

She lay back down. It was all right. Darkness bathed the four-poster in winnowy shadows, the only light the half-concealed moon outside the window refracted on the mirror above her dresser. Pulling the covers up around her chin, she gazed over at Stoney again. He always slept soundly but she was a frequent insomniac. Night made her available for haunting; she was a house full of spooks. Tonight, for the first time in years, she'd been visited by the first man she'd loved, the slick older man who'd opened her sixteen-year-old thighs and whispered, ''You are mine now,'' as he planted the flag of imperialism between her legs.

The year was 1967. Anna Reston was a bookish high school junior with little experience with the opposite sex. Her best friend was a girl named Maria who was soft and curvy and maternal; Maria wanted to be a writer and so she dragged Anna to poetry readings all over Atlanta. One reading took place in a huge bookstore in downtown Atlanta, a new store that was so large it resembled a library. When she and Maria arrived, Anna wandered around in awe: the place had so many books. In one area of the store was a podium with folding chairs arranged around it in half-moons. As people began to gather there, Maria rushed over to get a good seat, but Anna lagged behind, still admiring the oversized art books. She pulled out a volume on Van Gogh and flipped through it to *Starry Night*. Her favorite painting, it symbolized how she often felt at sixteen, as though all the lines of her life swirled endlessly.

Then she heard his voice, a voice so strong and resonant it seemed to emanate from the Van Gogh. It crashed and whorled with the same passion: the hair stood up on Anna's forearms and she turned around, the book still in her hands. She couldn't see the speaker, so she stood on tiptoe. To stare.

He walked out from behind the podium, to be closer to the audience. He stood just a few feet from the first row, leaning toward the spectators, demanding that they listen. Not one of them looked away or even yawned; they seemed to acknowledge the speaker's power to control. If Anna noticed this, it didn't register. All she saw was a slender man of twenty-four with narrow shoulders and a long torso, a body of beguiling fragility. Hair the color of iridescent black ink fell over his forehead and over his ears. His face was long and narrow like his frame, dominated by high cheekbones and the sharp arrogant chin of a man used to getting what he wanted—in art and in life. His stare was penetrating; it caught Anna across the room and willed her to join the others. His eyes were blue-black; one color watched her, the other kept everyone else in sight, like a ringmaster with two souls. Anna had missed his introduction but she would hear it later. Philip Randolph Ayres, called Rand, was the son of one of Atlanta's leading lawyers; his renegade's black leather jacket and riding boots had not come from Goodwill, despite the ragged state of the tight jeans between them. He had defied his family tradition, Anna learned later, by refusing to study law, by taking to literature instead. He had earned his M.A. in English at UCLA and had now come home to write his first novel. Meanwhile, he was treating Atlanta to his skills in poetry.

Mesmerized, Anna sat down in a seat on the last row. The poet kept his eyes trained on her. She couldn't stop staring back and she felt his magnificent voice swirl around inside her, encircling her internal organs like Van Gogh's brushstrokes making love to the moon. He looked only at her. Deliberately. Even Maria would comment on it later. But it would be years before Anna would understand why—because she had dared to linger in the stacks while he performed.

When he finished reading, the crowd just sat for a moment, somehow waiting for his permission to leave. Finally he gave it, with a slight nod and a handshake to the manager of the bookstore, and people got up and milled about. Almost everyone went up to speak to him and he stood at the podium, resting against it casually like a conquering chieftain receiving his minions. He seemed glad to see each admirer but one eye remained fixed on the two teenage girls in the back.

"Isn't he super?" Maria whispered. "Let's go talk to him."

Anna followed her friend to the front of the room. Maria asked Rand Ayres endless questions but Anna stood there quietly. She didn't trust herself to ask him anything, even to speak. But as Rand Ayres patiently answered her friend, he looked at her.

A half hour later, to Anna's amazement, she and Maria were having coffee with Rand Ayres in a seedy bar that smelled of something that might have been marijuana. The poet ordered coffee for the two girls, coffee and brandy for himself, and talked to Maria about his writing. When Maria had talked herself out, she rose to go to the restroom. Rand Ayres just sat and stared at Anna. Then he asked, "If you were going to write a poem, what would you write about?"

"My father," she blurted out without thinking. Then she blushed. She must sound about ten years old.

The poet leaned toward her and she could smell the fine leather of his coat. "What about your father?" When she hesitated, he coaxed her, "If you don't talk about it, you'll never be able to write about it."

Under the man's spell, Anna answered honestly, "I'd write about how I don't really know him. My parents divorced when I was little. I only saw him weekends; we had to start over again every Saturday." Anna heard the anger creep into her voice but she couldn't control it. "He remarried last year and moved to Arizona and now it's too late."

Then Maria returned and she and Anna prepared to leave. Maria thanked Rand and he gallantly took her hand and wished her luck in her writing career. She stammered in embarrassment; Anna knew she had only written two poems ever. Then Rand took Anna's hand and moved his index finger in a circle in her palm as he said, "Come to my reading next month at the library. I'll be reading a poem about my father. I'd like you to hear it."

For months Anna attended Rand's readings, sometimes with Maria and often alone. From the main library to branch locations to bookstores to meetings of literary clubs, she followed the man who became her best friend. After his readings they had long conversations about life and art and Anna often talked about her difficulties at home, how she missed her father and felt her mother regarded her only as a burden. For the first time she talked freely about her parents' divorce. Rand drew confessions and confidences out of her, a diviner who gave none in return. Instead he would recite poetry to her. One evening after a reading, sitting in his MG sportscar talking about the day her father left Atlanta, Anna burst into tears and Rand leaned over in the darkness and traced her tears with his index finger and quoted:

> Though nothing can bring back the hour
> Of splendor in the grass, of glory in the flower;
> We will grieve not, rather find
> Strength in what remains behind.

When he opened his arms to crush her to his chest, Anna felt so safe, so understood. This passionate man in his passionate struggle to express his feelings had become her first confidant in life, the first person she truly trusted. Unlike the insipid high school boys Anna knew, whose conversation was confined to cars and sports, Rand wanted to know who she really was. Unlike them, he never tried to get her clothes off or move his hand up under her skirt.

By now Anna was hopelessly in love with him and she began seeing him between poetry readings, lying to her mother because of his age. She would wait for him on a street corner not far from her house. One twilight he swooped up on a motorcycle and took her for a windswept ride so dangerous she never forgot it. He took her to movies minors weren't allowed to see, treated her as though she were his equal in age and sophistication. But he never touched her, except to comfort and console her. Always he talked to her about her problems, tried to gain her confidence emotionally, and Anna adored the attention. Finally one night they met at his sparsely furnished apartment (which he kept solely for social purposes, as he still lived on his parents' estate). Drinking wine for the first time, Anna was talking about her father again when Rand took her hand and slowly began to trace the lifeline in her right palm. His touch was different, she noticed. So were his eyes. Each time his fingers moved across her skin her flesh quivered; she felt the sensation in her legs, her shoulders, her stomach. "If you were my daughter," he whispered close to her face, "I'd never let a day go by that I didn't see you, talk to you. The same if you were my wife. Or my lover."

Lover. The word reverberated in Anna's brain. Not because of what it meant but because it was such an adult word. Heathcliff and Cathy were lovers, Eustacia and Wildeve, Rochester and Jane.

Still he held her hand. They were sitting on the carpetless floor, listening to a Rod McKuen record. Rand's fingers stroked her forearm and she swallowed, drunk as much on his eyes as the wine. "You'll probably have a lover before long," he said, his voice huskier. His face was now so close to Anna's she could taste his breath. Gently he pushed her onto her back and kissed her. All she could feel was his tongue moving in and out of the dark corners of her mouth. That, and an odd new tightness between her legs.

In a second he had her skirt off. He moved her legs apart, his body as insistent as his eyes had been that first night. "I want you," he demanded. "You are mine now." And he pushed himself against her long before she was ready, met resistance and then pushed harder, backed up a second, and rammed his way in.

Pain shot through Anna, as he bucked and grunted above her. Afterward he told her that he loved her and drove her home, stopping two blocks from her house to let her out. He patted her hand reassuringly, kissed her lightly. Then, as she was getting out of the car, he said, his eyes separated again, "Meet me here on Thursday. About six. I want to fuck you again."

Anna gaped at him, as she stared into eyes that did not take no for an answer. Abruptly he reached out and stroked her chin, like the old Rand. "You're a woman now. Remember, I love you."

For the next two years he ordered Anna to sleep with him whenever he wished. He began telling her how to dress, how to talk, how to walk, which of her ideas were silly. He always did so with kindness, in the manner in which he'd initially captured her trust: "I just want you to grow into the woman you're meant to be.'' She saw Rand whenever he decreed; she gave herself up to the sexual slavery that trust and love had somehow wrought for her.

Penned in by the prevailing morality of the day, Anna *was* tied to Rand Ayres. Hadn't she given him the only thing of value she had? Although she felt no earth move, the lovemaking made her feel close to him and since they were in love it wasn't really wrong. Theirs was, as Rand said, ''a passion beyond morality,'' which meant she could sleep with him and still be a good girl. But she was shocked when Rand would throw her on the bed the minute they walked into his apartment and say, ''Pull up your skirt and open your legs.'' She would hesitate, wanting him to talk to her tenderly as he usually did or at least kiss her, but he'd only shout, ''I said, spread your fucking legs.'' Then he would reach down and jerk her legs apart, taking her without foreplay, without speaking, without even removing his leather jacket.

At other times he was gentle, brought her flowers, let her read part of his novel. But he withdrew his kindness whenever she did something he didn't like, kept her continually off-balance emotionally. He told her not to apply to the University of Maryland where her father had gone to school; he wanted her at Emory or Agnes Scott. For months Anna didn't tell Rand she'd won a scholarship to Maryland. She yearned to escape from his sexual bondage. When Rand learned of Anna's scholarship, he acted pleased for her and she almost regretted her decision to go away. That night, her eighteenth birthday, he took her out for an elegant dinner and made love to her so savagely she was exhausted afterward. The next day, however, when Anna came home from school, his car was pulling out of her driveway. It was the last time she ever saw him.

Rand Ayres never yielded control. He had told Anna's mother everything—that Anna had chased him for months and had finally worn down his resistance, that he was tired of the lies. He gave her mother dates and times, even down to excuses Anna had given the older woman in order to see him.

This revelation ruined the already-shaky relationship between mother and daughter forever. Anna went off to college more alone than ever before. Chafing from Rand's virtual ownership, she spent the first two years of college sleeping indiscriminately with whomever she ran across. She became the kind of woman her mother, who never questioned Rand's honesty, already said she was. She let other men sleep with her but she would not let them get close. Her desire for sex and her desire for love never shook hands again until she met Stoney McFarland.

Completely awake now, Anna padded over to the window to look at the moon, then she tiptoed out into the hall and down the stairs to the first floor. At the bottom of the landing she paused and stared into the living room, her eyes resting on the Aztec design of the rug in front of the fireplace. She'd put that rug there, with a thick pad underneath, thinking it would be a nice place to make love. But it had yet to be used for that purpose. Anna headed into the kitchen and poured herself a glass of wine. Silas stirred and ambled over to her sleepily and she knelt down to hug him; the huge dog felt like a warm teddy bear. She walked through the kitchen to her studio at the rear of the house. Originally built as a porch, before the McCloskeys enlarged that side of the house, the small room was centered around a large oak desk; originally Anna's father's, it was the one piece of furniture she had brought from her home in Atlanta. Adjacent to it sat a pine worktable piled high with photographs, above it was a bulletin board with more photographs tacked to it haphazardly, and inside a nearby closet that had once been a bathroom lay a fully equipped darkroom. Anna sat down at her desk, clicked on the swing lamp. Two signed originals by Ansel Adams were framed on the wall opposite her. Through the bank of windows on her left, she could also see the live oaks that encircled the pond in the back yard. They blocked off her sanctuary from the prying eyes of the rest of the town. Sometimes she worked when she couldn't sleep—brought her journal up to date, selected shots she wanted to submit, studied others she felt were flawed, read the photography magazines. But tonight she surveyed it all with disinterest. Instead, she just stared at the outline of the trees. What had made her dream about Rand tonight? She leaned back in her swivel chair and her eyes narrowed. Maybe the lunch with Marian, that speech about being used.

In a moment, on impulse, Anna unlocked the bottom drawer of her desk, pulled it out, and reached far in the back to withdraw a sealed envelope. She slit the envelope open and took out a set of photographs she hadn't looked at in a long time, black-and-white enlargements of a nude woman on a bed. Thirty or forty pictures in all. In some the woman's eyes were half-masted, veiled. Tension stood out in her facial muscles and her eyes focused in intense concentration above tightened lips. In the later photos the lips became noticeably softer, the cheekbones relaxed, and the eyes took on a suffused dreaminess, as though a light were shining through them.

"I love to watch your face at the end," Stoney had told her in bed a year after they were married. "It's like I can finally see inside you."

She'd begun taking the pictures sometime after that. Tripod and time lapse. He knew what she looked like but she didn't. She knew what he looked like, the way his eyes closed and his shoulders shook. Did women and men look the same? What right had he to know something about her she didn't know? Anna studied her younger face, unfettered and unprotected. Was that woman her? Had it ever been? She put the photographs back into the envelope, shoved them into her desk, and locked them away again. To this day Stoney did not know about them. She knew he'd enjoy seeing them. She also knew, sadly, he probably never would.

Women envied Anna McFarland for her marriage. Friends said she and Stoney were perfect complements: he was calm and intelligent where she was artistic and tempestuous. When they still lived in Washington, Anna would sometimes tell a friend about the three hours she and Stoney spent over a bottle of wine discussing politics and the friend would roll her eyes and exclaim, "Jesus, I can't imagine Steve spending three hours talking to me. About anything." Then the friend would complain that all Steve ever wanted to do was fuck, that he seemed to think *that* was the way to make their marriage work. Anna would sympathize and then would remember that after she and Stoney had talked for three hours she would have given anything if he'd also seduced her.

What had drawn Stoney and Anna together was intellectual compatibility, laced with enough sexual attraction to keep it interesting. She liked the way he smelled and his athlete's build and he liked her husky voice and the sight of her long dark hair splayed across the white pillow beside him every morning. In their early days they made love often, eagerly, unself-consciously. They experimented with positions and technique and Stoney showed her that sex, like life, need not always be as serious as she took it. Eventually, though, their lives settled into a routine; they slept together and enjoyed it but it did not figure as vitally into their daily lives. After several years, like many married couples, sex became something brought out for weekends and special occasions. As such, it drew attention (and pressure) to itself. Infrequency bred insecurity and gradually their physical love became a question of improved performance; not an expression of feeling or pleasure, but the mechanical execution of an idealized goal.

For Anna, it also began to feel like a command performance, something she owed Stoney, and she began to remember Rand Ayres. Was sex ever beyond power? Then she would rebel at the idea that anyone ''owned'' her like that and say no to Stoney's overtures (as she had never done to Rand). At the same time she yearned for the great art of seduction and thought the way to get it was to complain about it. Stoney thought she had elevated sex to the level of religious conversion and wished she would just once lie back and open her legs temptingly like she really enjoyed it. Neither told the other any of these things, and their physical love lost that which created it—natural instinct.

Most of their married friends were drifting apart emotionally but still having sex on schedule—and this knowledge did little for Anna's confidence. Or her sense of isolation. She had always been so sure she and Stoney were invincible, that because they communicated intellectually (who else spent hours trading ideas on religion and art and why the twentieth century made people so pathologically unhappy?), the rest would follow. What could harm two people who could really *talk*? Which seemed a reasonable assumption until the sex went bad. As it gradually worsened, Anna wondered if her marriage of intellectual compatibility, of shared values, was *too* thinking-oriented. Everything she and Stoney did was thought through so thoroughly—it once took them six months to decide to move to a new apartment—that little energy was left over at the end for spontaneity. Anna listened to other women and searched for a theory to explain why her best of all marriages had soured physically. How did she and Stoney start off so well and still end up here? She found no answer. What had brought the two of them together so perfectly that one afternoon in Maryland had been pure mystery, and now again, what was pulling them apart was shrouded in its own mantle of myopic arcanum.

The eighth year they were married they went for six weeks without making love. Everything else between them was okay, despite the minidramas caused by in-laws and who did the dishes. They still shared ideas and feelings but that year Anna knew something was seriously wrong with a couple just turning thirty who had sex so seldomly. But she discussed it with no one. Because of her free-lancing, their budget was too skimpy to allow for a therapist, and she was too much the anarchist for therapy anyway. To no one would she confess that her husband no longer seemed to want her. The truth was, of course, that he did want her. But having been often rejected now, he did little about it. So he and Anna lived more like tender siblings, emotionally close but physically constrained.

Frightened that she might become as asexual as her mother, Anna began to bring up "their problem" from time to time. She and Stoney sat in the small living room of their basement apartment in Georgetown one evening listening to Miles Davis and she asked, "Don't you wonder why we don't make love more often? Don't you think there's something wrong?"

He wouldn't look at her. "There are lots more important things in marriage than just sex. We understand each other better than most people ever will. Maybe we're not highly sexed."

"You sound like you're giving up. You can't believe that. What good is love if you don't have emotional understanding wedded to good sex?"

His voice was angry. Half the time she said no and now she was complaining? "I don't see what the big deal is."

In short, they did not understand each other nearly so well as they thought. He missed the point that in the South women are conditioned to define themselves through their ability to attract men, that a sexually insecure woman is likely to be even more unraveled by the suspicion that she's lost her sexual allure, the very thing which frightens her. So Stoney would kiss Anna lovingly when they went to sleep but he no longer slipped his hand playfully between her legs. Anna came to miss the gesture that had once seemed an act of sexual proprietorship: he owned her there, like Rand. No one did these days and she wasn't happy now either. For months she and Stoney would live like platonic friends and then, after weeks of abstinence, their passion would suddenly erupt in the middle of the night. The next morning they would not mention the sex and the physical distance would set in again. Lovemaking became a dirty little weakness they gave in to once in a while. If Anna was angry, Stoney was saddened by what had happened; after all, it had been Anna's free spirit which first attracted him. Her zest for life—for college, for ideas, for photography—had always been a sexual high to him. But now sex often felt like just too much trouble, fraught with too many pitfalls (Was it *always* his fault when she didn't make it?); when he felt the urge, he usually talked himself out of it. He had said he would never beg—and he still wouldn't.

She would come to him because she wanted to; he would not force her.

The problem, he thought, was a matter of lust. Anna always wanted an out-of-body experience, sometimes he just wanted to get laid. Occasionally he felt lust for his wife that was separate from his love for her and he got the feeling from her that he shouldn't. She never initiated sex, she was at her most amorous when slightly drunk, and all too often he felt like she was doing him a favor. Their infrequent sex had once driven him astray. When they were in Washington and he was doing field work in a rural West Virginia county, he had to measure an abandoned farmhouse with a female appraiser who had short blond hair and a silly laugh that made him feel about eighteen. They took a lunch break, drank too much beer, and returned to the house all giddy in the summer sunshine. Soon she was kneeling in the grass and her blouse was open to naked breasts and she looked up at him and said, ''Please fuck me.'' A schoolboy's wet dream come true. But when it was over he regretted it; screwing around on Anna was an unnatural act for him. Love in one corner, lust in another, it was too much like high school, good girls and bad girls, you married a good girl but then you wanted to fuck her like a bad girl and both of you knew you should be beyond this prehistoric garbage but there it was, burned into your fanny like a birthmark. Little by little Stoney concluded that the intellectual symbiosis he enjoyed with his wife was more important than the best sex in the world. She gave him a sense of self-worth that no one else had ever provided. All his life he'd wanted a friend like Anna; even without sex, she was the primary focus of his life. She was, in fact, the only woman he'd ever been able to talk to. If he was just patient, this would work itself out.

Since their move to Essex little had changed: Stoney and Anna kept on having intimate moments that should have led to sexual intimacy yet usually didn't. But the new location did affect them differently. Rural South Carolina, so close to earth and water, was inordinately more sensuous than the steel and concrete of Washington. The air in Essex seemed more primordial, the nights hotter, the rhythms of nature more invasive. Here physical sensations felt more overt—colors, sounds, smells were all closer. Anna usually realized when she was ovulating now; before, she'd been too busy or distracted to notice. And the aroma that permeated Essex—that thick musk of loam, of fertilization—always reminded Stoney of the deep smell of a woman.

On a Friday night a week after Anna's lunch with Marian, the McFarlands relaxed on the balcony of the Hilton Head condo they had rented for the weekend and sipped Beaujolais and listened to the surf. They sat at a round café table, in two director's chairs turned sideways from the table to face each other. Below them, on the beach, a couple walked hand in hand in the darkness, a small terrier and two children trailing behind them. Anna glanced at Stoney; he looked more peaceful than he had in weeks. For once he seemed to be thinking about something other than Essex and the murder. Anna gazed back out at the now empty beach. "I wonder why the ocean has such a regenerative effect."

"It's mystical," he suggested. "Unexplainable. Like the moon which governs it. And keeps it always changing, like a woman. Biologically, you and the ocean are both governed by cycles of the moon. That's what makes women fascinating to men—that you're never static, we can never quite catch you."

It was the kind of conversation that had made her fall in love with him. But she said, teasing, "Meaning we're flighty?"

He smiled, caught the challenge. "Meaning you're always tempting. Letting us come close, backing away again like the tide. Your nature is to keep moving. I sometimes think ours is to stand still—like a mountain."

"Unyielding, hard, and implacable?"

His eyes took on a definite twinkle. "Well, maybe one out of three."

They had had sexy conversations in the past but they were usually more abstracted now. He watched her face. Her eyes were soft and sensual. Her hair was tangled by the wind, a mass of wildness, like unchecked vines in a swamp, and her blouse was uncharacteristically low on her breasts. He followed their curve with his eyes. She laid a hand on his arm absently and without thinking he moved his right foot and hooked it on the bottom hinge of her chair, between her bare legs. He wiggled his foot around to get a better grip and accidentally brushed her thigh. Their eyes met.

She closed her legs tight around his and held them there.

Stoney swallowed. He could feel the heat of her legs against his. His pulse hammered. All that existed was the increasing pressure of her legs. He moved his leg slightly. The shift put his leg deeper between hers and he could feel the softness of her thighs against his calf. He leaned over to kiss her and she met his tongue, wet and aggressive. Filled with relief that he had not misread her, he drew her shoulders toward him, ran his tongue down her throat and back up again to encircle her right ear and plunge inside it. He thought of how she would taste and her smell filled his head; he wanted to push her backward across the table and open her legs right there. The thought made him shiver so he forced himself to think about condemnation hearings, anything, to try to keep from going too fast. She always left the pace up to him, almost indifferently, and he never knew whether he was moving too fast or too slow.

She often left too much up to him. In a few moments they were inside on the king-sized bed, their clothes on the floor beside it. The full-length touch of a man turned Anna's skin electric, she wanted to yell at him to hurry up, to fill her up. His hand was between her legs and it was a fraction off but she tried to concentrate anyway on how good it felt. She shifted, hoping to throw Stoney in better position, but he took it as an invitation and quickly drove inside her.

Their bodies collided and the synchronization better familiarity would have provided eluded them. Anna wasn't excited anymore; now the offbeat rhythm was just making her sore. Her mind wandered and part of it saw Rand Ayres above her. Rand buried deep within but never speaking, she enjoying the initial stimulation and then losing it, thinking there ought to be more. But he never cared how she felt; he wanted nothing of her but that she should lie there, passive as dirt, and comply. When Rand stopped, she did not feel completed, filled up. She felt depleted. The more of him she took in, the more of her she lost.

"God, Anna, I can't—"

In a second Stoney thrust his pelvis toward her and she arched up to meet him and he cried out. She felt herself buck with him and thought she was ridiculous at best and a hypocrite at worst. Afterward he held her in the darkness for a long time. They didn't speak. Soon he fell asleep.

When his breathing was regular, Anna got out of bed and walked back out onto the balcony, stood naked at the railing and watched the ocean. The wind played across her, and the hair on her arms, as well as on her breasts, stood at attention. She imagined hands on the insides of her thighs and she closed her eyes and held on to the railing for support as they made their way up her legs. The hands belonged to a shirtless man working on a telephone pole they'd passed on their way to the beach. He had no face, only those massive hands reaching up inside her from behind. Faster, higher. Then Anna collapsed into a chair on the balcony, and for him, she eagerly spread her legs.

Six

TWO WEEKS LATER Essex fell apart again.

It was an overcast May morning, that first sultry hint of summer in the air, a too-dense closeness, the lethargy of August months in advance. Harriet Setzler arose at her usual time; tarrying in bed, even on days that felt exhausting at the outset, was not her custom. Clumping about her house, she could feel the change in the humidity. As though there weren't sufficient air to breathe, like being locked in a stuffy closet. No matter, she thought as she made her bed, there were things to be done. She stopped suddenly and rubbed her right shoulder, where arthritis plagued her. Then, slowly, she got dressed.

Before she finished dressing, she noticed the silent Seth Thomas clock on the mantel: she'd never forgotten to wind it before. What else might she forget now? Today, for some reason, felt old and worn out. Today she felt eighty-seven. Usually she felt only about fifty-five. As she aged, she bargained with herself: now that I'm fifty-five, I'll admit to feeling thirty; now that I'm in my eighties, I'll give way to my fifties. Fifty-five, however, was to be her last concession. She'd been alone already then, William gone and the children off pursuing jobs and marriages. At fifty-five she had made her peace with the solitary life. And at fifty-five Marian became the part of it which made the rest bearable.

Harriet crossed to the mantel and picked up the brass key and wound the chiming clock. Beneath her the small coal fireplace sat dank and dark and for a second she remembered when all the fireplaces in the house had to be lit at first light. Suddenly she smiled, her old face almost girlish. "William," she said aloud, turning back toward the mahogany double bed, "I don't know what it is about my fires but they always go out. I guess I don't build them right.'' After that, William got up first every morning; from then on when Harriet arose, the house had lost its nighttime chill. Until he'd fallen ill, William had kept the cold at bay. For just a little while someone had taken care of her.

Oh but he was a handsome man. Harriet looked at her favorite photograph of her husband on her night table. A rakish man in a three-piece black suit with a silk bow tie, a white scarf around his neck, and a felt fedora cocked low over the right side of his forehead, gazed back at her; he was standing in front of a brand new shiny Ford automobile (circa 1934); one leg was propped up on the running board, and his hand holding a lighted cigarette was resting on his knee. To her, he was still the best-looking man she'd ever seen—no man ever had bluer eyes or softer, finer hair across his forehead. Yet she had loved him most for his kindness.

Lingering between past and present, Harriet ran her eyes over the rest of the room. She hadn't changed anything since he died. She felt comfortable surrounded by the talismans of the past, the old-fashioned cherry dressing table with its three-panel mirror, Depression furniture, stained as dark as the times. Only one of Elizabeth's paintings hung in here, in Harriet's bedroom. It was the only canvas she could tolerate in a room where she was at a disadvantage, surrendering herself to sleep before it every night. She stared above the mantel at the small painting, her favorite of them all. It was the study of a lone young woman drifting on a river in a wooden boat; she wore a dress and apron of the previous century, her hair caught in a long plait down her back, and her boat had slowed to a stop in a grassy marsh thick with reeds. Her head was bowed low under a cloudy, barely discernible moon, pale white against the sea-green of both sky and water. It was as if the woman awaited the return of someone who would pilot her lonely boat homeward.

The old woman turned away. What was wrong with her this morning? She shook her head at her dalliance and headed for the kitchen. After she got her coffee going, she walked toward the front door to retrieve the newspaper. At the front door she hesitated for a second, stared at the locks which guarded her from the town she loved. She turned the locks, opened the door, gazed outside. Nothing moved, even the birds were subdued by the humid gauze outdoors. It was silly, Harriet decided, this fear, all these locks, no one going out after dark. If she took her dead bolts off, everyone else would too. They always did what she did—sooner or later. That's what she'd do: she wouldn't be intimidated like this any longer, she'd call Stoney and tell him to come back over here and take the fool things off her door, they looked plumb ridiculous anyway.

Through her screen door Harriet surveyed the morning. The mugginess would dissipate by noon, she decided. She looked around for the newspaper, squinted, and remembered it was time she had her glasses checked. Then she spotted the paper by the front gate. She opened the door and stepped over the threshold. Abruptly she stumbled, in a flash she saw herself in a wheelchair with a broken hip. She steadied herself by grabbing the doorjam and sighed with relief that she was still upright; then she gazed at her feet. Something lay in front of her door. She stared. It looked like . . . no, surely not. Then she smelled blood.

Marian Davis told no one what she found on her front porch that morning. Instead, she dressed rapidly and sped off to school as usual. All day she ignored the talk she heard in the hallways and in the teachers' lounge. But she was glad when the afternoon was over and she was driving back home. When she turned onto her block and could see her house, she spied Harriet Setzler sitting on the park bench at the far end of her porch. Oftentimes when she arrived home at the end of the day, she found Harriet sitting there waiting for her.

The younger woman smiled as she walked up her front steps. She saw the familiar plate covered with a tea towel on the bench beside Harriet, breathed in the aroma emanating from it. The octogenarian did not believe a diet of mostly salad was survivable; if Marian wouldn't cook for herself, someone had to. At least once a week during the school year Harriet brought Marian a hot dinner at night, enough food for three people. If the irony of the habit ever occurred to the older woman, it went unremarked.

The white-haired woman greeted Marian. "I was frying up some chicken, thought you might want some. Had some corn and butter beans, couldn't eat it all myself. Made some lime pies yesterday too."

Marian thanked Harriet for the food. She was inordinately fond of the other woman's lime pies. As small as cupcakes and rolled from scratch crust, they were notoriously popular in Essex. At any social gathering they constituted Harriet's personal signature; no one else made them because she guarded the recipe like a state secret. Marian was the only person in town who knew the secret ingredient was medicinal brandy.

"Smells good," Marian added. "Come on in and eat with me."

"Oh I couldn't. You know I never eat supper."

The dark woman nodded. It was true, Harriet never did sit down to an evening meal. But she ate enough leftovers from her noon meal, standing at her kitchen window in the late afternoon watching people come home from work, to make up for it. It was also true that, despite repeated invitations, Harriet had never once eaten a meal at Marian's house.

"I guess you heard about the town meeting tonight," Harriet said. "Pieces of that poor animal were found all over the neighborhood, almost like a warning. It was a goat. They found the carcass in the alley. The wretched creature had been stabbed to death." Harriet's voice rose nervously. "Just like Sarah. Some people say it's a voodoo thing. I don't know about that but it does look like whoever's doing this isn't gone. Just this morning I was thinking we were being silly, these locks and all." She caught her breath. "Anyhow, we went to Leland this morning, a bunch of us, and demanded he do something. You're going to the meeting, aren't you?"

"I don't think so." Marian tapped her briefcase. "I've got so many papers to grade. You know how it is this close to June." She looked out at the street. "Sure is warm today."

"There was something on your porch too, wasn't there?" Harriet didn't wait for a reply. "I wonder why it was mostly us over here."

When Marian still didn't respond, Harriet looked at her, but suddenly the old lady saw a little girl named Alma, a skinny little child standing on a stool so she could reach the oven, a huge white apron draped around her waist twice, swallowing her like a sheet. That was the first day her mother brought her to the house, to begin teaching her to cook. Lonnie left only a year or two later, and Harriet saw that day clearly too. Alma in a dirty white sack dress with the hem half ripped out, no shoes, telltale signs of tears on her cheeks, looking just a little hungry. Standing at the back door, dawn breaking behind her, that tiny voice just a squeak, "My mama be gone."

Harriet took the child inside and got a rag and wiped her face, took out a Mason jar and gave Alma a glass of milk, then sat her down in a kitchen chair. "Alma, tell me what happened." The child mumbled something and then she started to cry. Tears rushed down her cheeks onto the soiled dress. Harriet patted the child's shoulders. "Now, now, Alma. You're a big girl. You cry like that and people will think you're a baby." Alma cried even harder. Her shoulders shook and she wailed pitifully, laying her head down on the wood tabletop. Finally Harriet couldn't help herself; she reached out and took the little girl in her arms. Lonnie had run off, had left this child alone? With no father, no kin? Harriet shook her head. Nowadays Lonnie was almost as wild as Crazy Susie, who was always walking down the street talking to herself as though someone were there.

The white woman gazed down at the child's beige tear-streaked face. What should she do about her? She couldn't take Alma to the county; there was no home for colored orphans, they'd just turn her over to the state, who would send her off to an orphanage miles away. Again Harriet patted the child absently. She was such a good worker, Alma was. Finally exhausted, the girl fell asleep, one small hand curled around Harriet's thumb. Harriet stared at the child. She had such a cute face. Intelligence in her eyes too, you could see it, she was smarter than most of them. Alma just might amount to something. Harriet noticed the way the child cushioned her head with one hand. The woman smiled. Her daughter had done the same thing—the exact same way.

She couldn't keep her.

No, of course not. What would people think?

In a moment Harriet led the exhausted child back to the sleeping porch and turned down one of the single beds. Lying down gratefully, Alma grabbed the pillow like a favorite toy, and Harriet pulled the spread up over her and tucked her in. Then the large woman stood beside the bed in the morning light until the girl slept.

However, when Alma awoke six hours later, Harriet had recovered herself. She would send Alma to Aunt Posey. You didn't adopt brown skin, no matter how much you might want to.

But you could buy it.

A much-older Harriet, whose inconsistencies eluded her, who never realized this was precisely what she did later, refocused and stared at the grown woman she was so proud of. All those years after William and the children were gone had not been nearly so lonely as they could have been. The children came home a lot in those days and Marian was there and it was like they all belonged together. When her children left, the house grew quieter, but not silent. Silence didn't set in until Marian left, the last to go. It would be so nice to have her in the house again. Caught in the web of the past, Harriet said without thinking, "We're both alone, you and me. With all this going on." The elderly woman looked down at the floor. "You get nervous, my back room's still there. You come over and sleep in it anytime you want."

Marian gaped at Harriet, as she remembered how, years ago, she'd prayed Harriet would move her into the back room for good. Then she would have been sure she was loved as a daughter. But it never happened.

"I'm fine right here," she said.

Neither said anything for a moment. Then Harriet stood up. "Well, I best be going, don't want to be late for the meeting."

Gripping the plate of fried chicken like a mountain ledge, Marian watched the old woman move slowly off the porch. She saw Harriet teaching her to read, wheeling out a shiny blue bicycle one Christmas, fitting that white wedding dress. Come back, she wanted to cry. Please come back. Sit down at my table just once. Just once *accept* me.

But Harriet rumbled down the sidewalk like a tired dinosaur who senses, but never understands, that his kind are disappearing. Marian watched the twilight swallow the old woman. When Harriet was safely inside her door, Marian turned around, bit back the tears, and walked into her own house.

Social strata in Essex consisted of five levels and that evening representatives of all five (as well as one or two others that didn't much count) crowded into the town hall auditorium. The first level included the town leaders, Heyward Rutherford and Bill Jenkins and the two preachers and those who ran the downtown businesses; they sat largely in the front rows. Behind them gathered the elderly widows who lived in the older part of town and the families, like the Wilsons, who resided near them. Farther back sat couples from other parts of town and from Willowbrook subdivision; they tended to be younger, more affluent, college educated; many worked outside Essex, at the hospital and the community college in Ashboro, or were managers at the Nissan factory or at the Savannah River power plant. In the very last stationary wooden chairs, sitting together in a knot, were blacks like Amos Tumley who lived along the railroad tracks and on the outskirts of town. Even more removed were the people who stood along the hospital green walls, many of whom had been late in arriving, the small farmers from outside town and the poor whites and blacks who occupied pockets of poverty all over the county.

The air was stuffy and the room, designed for less than a hundred, bulged with humanity. Harriet Setzler, who considered herself a town leader, sat prominently in the front row. On the small stage, flanked by the American and the South Carolina flags, stood Heyward Rutherford and Jim Leland, the latter looking ill at ease. No one knew exactly how to proceed; there hadn't been a town meeting in years. In a moment Heyward Rutherford rapped on the wooden podium in front of him (a gift from the Wallermans in honor of their son killed in Vietnam) and leaned toward the audience. He wore a gray pin-striped suit, his silver hair slicked back from his forehead, the diamond ring on his right pinky finger reflecting the overhead light in its prism.

He called the meeting to order: "Now if we can just settle down, we'll get started. Let's begin tonight by remembering something. This is one great town. I know you're all upset by what's been going on—I am too. And let me assure you we're going to do something about it. The state law enforcement folks told me this morning that an agent will be here in three days. What happened this morning may have nothing to do with Sarah's murder, it could have even been a school-boy prank. But whether it's related or not, we're going to get this situation cleared up. Pronto. In the meantime let's try to keep our heads and stay calm."

Heyward paused and a woman in the fourth row stood up. Elsie Fenton said, "Begging your pardon, Heyward. But how can you be sure Sarah's killer won't kill somebody else before you find him? This morning sure looked like a warning to me. I think we need a curfew at night."

"I don't know about that," the town council president said. Sarah's store was almost his now and he wanted to get a crew in there to tear it down as soon as possible. A curfew might be inconvenient.

Then a man toward the rear of the auditorium raised his hand. "What bothers me about a curfew is our kids. It'll scare the children even more if we suddenly start telling them they have to be in before dark. Lots of them stay out late in the spring to play."

Watching from his seat somewhere in the middle, Stoney tried to imagine Essex under curfew. It was unthinkable. Besides, what sense did a curfew make with only one man to enforce it? A man who generally avoided hazardous duty, at that.

Finally Jim Leland moved closer to the podium. "I don't think a curfew will make much difference myself," he said. "A guy who kills somebody is not gonna care." Several people threw up their hands in exasperation and he added hastily, "We're making headway on finding him. We have some ideas. It's just a matter of time before we'll have the evidence we need."

The audience whispered among themselves. One man standing along the wall shook his head and muttered, "Ain't nobody gonna do nothing."

"What are people like me supposed to do 'til you get your evidence?" demanded a black woman in a wheelchair in the middle of the aisle at the back. She brushed at the perspiration on her upper lip. "How do I protect myself?"

"This used to be such a super town." A woman of twenty-eight stood up; she wore tailored navy slacks and a white button-down shirt. "Essex has always been a wonderful place to live, safe and peaceful. Now everything's changed. Every time my son goes out the door now, I wonder if he'll be okay, I have to force myself to let him go."

"You can't even go out for the paper without finding parts of a dead animal everywhere," chimed another voice, high-pitched and nervous.

Heyward Rutherford put up his right hand to try to restore order but a heavy woman in electric green polyester pants popped up and superceded him. "Whoever killed Sarah was sick," she cried. "A psycho! And anybody cuts up a goat is also sick. What else will a sicko like that do?"

Several people jumped up. "We need protection."

"Somebody's gotta do something."

Jim Leland stepped in front of the podium and called out, "Please, just calm down."

The crowd ignored him. "What we need is a real police department."

No one knew who said it but suddenly the room grew quiet again. Jim Leland folded his arms across his chest, impervious, but Heyward Rutherford beat on the podium. "Is this doing us any good? Is it?"

Now the crowd grew almost penitent, might have stayed that way had it not been for one voice. "I'll tell ya who done it," lazed a man in overalls who was chewing tobacco and standing at the rear of the auditorium. "We all know who it was. I ain't afraid to say so neither. It's that woman out to the swamp. They're all the time cutting up animals in that voodoo stuff. Oughta be a law against it. Got laws for everything else.''

Jim Leland rallied. ''There's no question but that Sarah was killed by a man,'' he said with a certain smug satisfaction. ''It was in the papers, the evidence, and you all know it.''

Marynell Pittman, a small scrawny woman standing on the right side of the auditorium with three children in tow, shook her head at the police chief and shouted, ''It's that woman. You best listen to us. She walked right by my yard once, years ago, and she said somethin' under her breath and ever since won't nothin' grow on the spot. Nothin'. Grass, flowers, even weeds— don't make no difference.''

Stoney gazed in the direction of the voice. Marynell Pittman was probably only twenty-five but she looked twice that; she and her fatherless children lived in a dilapidated farmhouse out near the swamps.

''That has no bearing on the case,'' Jim insisted from the podium, his eyes now appealing to Heyward for help. ''Maum Chrish may be odd, but we have no reason to suspect she's involved in this.''

''What about the way she acted at the funeral?'' The new voice was barely audible; shaky, it came from a white-haired woman near Harriet Setzler. ''That certainly was strange, her coming to Sarah's service and all. Why'd she jump out a window afterward?''

A history teacher from the high school, a black man in his fifties, stood up. ''That's an African superstition. The first person to leave a funeral will be the next to have one.''

''Yeah, why was she at the funeral at all if she didn't know something about Sarah? Everybody knows they cut up goats and chickens in voodoo.''

The last speaker remained in her seat but then the bank manager, a thin man in a camel sportcoat, stood up. ''Aren't we getting a little ridiculous? Voodoo?''

Several people nearby nodded in agreement, but most of the crowd paid no attention. Stoney gazed around him. Heads were together all over the room. They had lit on Maum Chrish now like hungry buzzards; only the blacks, who had said very little all evening but who didn't much care for the strange swamp woman either, sat in uneasy silence. Maum was not ''one of us'' to anyone. But she was what everyone needed—someone to blame it on, someone so far removed from themselves that even a brutal murder could be explained by her difference.

Stoney's eyes moved across the familiar faces. Right now he studied strangers.

In a second he got up and walked toward the back of the auditorium. The room was too stuffy, he needed air. He was almost to the open back door when he noticed someone standing in the hallway, just out of the light. Behind Stoney the town's paranoia rose another decibel. And in front of him, watching the crowd, Leonard Hansen was laughing his head off.

Anna did not attend the town meeting. Instead, she drove toward the outskirts of town, her black camera bag on the car seat beside her. It was the perfect time of evening for shots of the swamp, misty and blue-gray with humidity. What she really wanted, still, was a photograph of Maum Chrish. And this time she was determined to get one.

She was a little nervous about going to the swamp so close to dark, particularly with what was going on, but she never considered turning around. She felt drawn out here almost against her will. Within a few miles, the forest vegetation thickened along the roadside and she sat up straighter behind the wheel. Every spooky tree was a totem pole, a subliminal warning signal. She rolled down her window and warm air rushed against the back of her neck like the hot breath of a stranger. She rolled the window back up. As she entered the thickest woods, she reached down and ran her hand across her cotton slacks. Inside the fabric her thighs were clammy and she moved them apart. Nerves.

After a few more miles she slowed down, then stopped the car and parked near the pathway that led into the brush. Slinging her camera bag over her shoulder, she got out and checked her watch. She'd have about an hour before dark. Entering the woods, she pushed past the vines and overgrown bushes, moved in and out among them, slowly at first and then more rapidly as she gained confidence. The live oaks here were older than those in town; their rumpled roots lay spread out on top of the ground like a hand covered with sores.

As Anna passed deeper into the woods, sweat pooled between her breasts and ran down the inside of her blouse. All around her a heavy silence lay close to the ground, save for the soft, rhythmic motion of the black water against the swamp bank. Anna paused for a second and unbuttoned the top button of her shirt for more air. The shadows were long but it was still so warm in here. She leaned against a crepe myrtle tree, then suddenly stiffened. A sound. Somewhere far off. A dull thud over and over again. Like someone beating a drum. Then it stopped. Again Anna began walking through the increasingly dense underbrush. A thorny limb raked across her arm and she winced. It bled profusely for a moment and she wiped at it with her hand, then cleaned her hand on the moss that carpeted the ground at her feet.

Then she halted a second time. That sound again. It *was* a drum. Several drums. The beat intensified, hit hard in rapid succession.

Anna shivered. In a second the drums broke off abruptly. She started forward again. She had only gone five or six feet when she heard them once more. This time a single drumbeat, in cadence. She hesitated, it stopped again. She stared around her. Go home, her better sense admonished. Now. She gripped her camera bag tighter. She was almost there. She started walking again and the drum started again too, as if it were keeping time with her footsteps. And in a few moments she broke into a run and didn't stop until she reached the clearing where Maum Chrish lived.

No one was there. Anna leaned against a tree, breathing hard, and listened. The drum had stopped. She looked around, again took in the smoldering fire between the house and garden, the unlit candles around the decorated trees, the ship model suspended from the porch beam. All very silent.

"Anyone here?" she called, all but swallowing her words. She cleared her throat. "Uh . . . Maum Chrish?"

Her words hung in the empty air.

The house was a two-room rectangle, one room behind the other, each with a door leading outside. Atop it sat a pitched roof and below was a small covered porch with a rickety railing around it. Anna walked up the steps slowly. "Hello? Anybody home?"

Again no answer. The front door was standing wide open, as though someone had left in a hurry. I should leave, Anna thought, but she didn't turn around. Instead, dropping her camera bag on the porch, she walked inside the house. There was almost nothing in the long narrow front room. A bare wood floor, unpainted wood walls, and in the center of the room a square wooden post that rose to the ceiling. Set into a pedestal adorned with triangles, the post's entire length was painted with a bright spiral design resembling two intertwined snakes. A braided leather whip also hung on a nail on one side of it. On the floor was a geometric design, almost heraldic, the post rising from the exact center of it. Sprinkled along the floor diagram were bits of flour, in one spot, and sand in another. Then Anna noticed the table alongside the wall opposite her. Covered with a white cloth, it supported various clay pots and two rows of unfamiliar tools and implements made of iron. Then she saw the knives. Five of them, lined up side by side. Was there something to the rumors about Maum Chrish? Anna swallowed hard, jerked around to check the doorway.

She was still alone. Sweat gathered under the waistband of her slacks, and her pulse danced against her wrist. Above her head four flags hung from the four corners of the room, small red-and-white flags similar to those on ships. There were also several drawings on the wall across from her and she walked over to inspect them. Unlike the diagrams on the post, the first drawing was representational, a crude portrait of a human being with words in a strange language painted beside both hands, on either side of the hips, above the head, at the feet. Topping the male head, which reminded Anna of childhood pictures of Jesus, was a smaller drawing of another man with long hair. It was labeled "Kether." To either side of him were the words "Chokmah" and "Binah," the three words linked by straight lines to form a triangle. Below the entire figure, which resembled a family tree, was printed "Sephiroth."

Anna paused and stared at the doorway again. No sound, nobody. She moved to the next wall. Off by themselves on this surface were three small symbols, letters of an alphabet unknown to Anna; they were identified ALEPH, MIM, SHIN and were followed by a long column of similar symbols, each with a number beside it. The last two drawings here were humans. An androgynous figure in the lotus position, then a graphic portrait of a couple in obvious sexual congress. The erect penis was poised on the bank of the woman's vagina, in the act of entering. Anna stood frozen in front of the picture. The man was moving toward the woman, yet the woman was clearly the aggressor. Her face glowed with satisfaction, with the power of her sexual energy. Uncomfortable, Anna turned and walked toward the other room of the cabin, then she stopped again. In a moment she recrossed to the last drawing. The look on the woman's face. She'd seen it before. Exactly that expression. In the photographs in her locked desk drawer.

Backing away from the wall, Anna kept her eyes on the couple. She was hot as hell, there were no windows in the room, and she had the oddest, insane desire to take her clothes off and lie down on the cool wood floor and—

Something moved. Something outside.

Anna froze, sucked in her breath. She gawked at the front door. How would she explain herself? She stole quickly into the back room of the house, found a small bed and a table and a chair and some books. She crouched and waited, listened again. Several minutes passed. No sound, nothing. Everything was still again.

Stealthily Anna tiptoed back to the front of the cabin, crept to the front door. Had someone followed her? She was dripping with sweat now. Why had she ever come here? Taking deep breaths, she tried to calm down, find her courage. Then, slowly, she leaned out the doorway and peered around. She didn't see anything. The shadows were nearly complete now, it was late, time to get the hell out of here. She shivered again. Just get the bag and go, forget the pictures. Gingerly she stepped out onto the porch and looked down for her camera bag.

It was gone.

She stared out at the darkening night. She scanned the porch again. She gazed down the steps and saw, beyond them, footprints in the soft dirt. Hers leading toward the house. And a bigger set, leading away.

Her mouth was so dry she couldn't swallow. Her legs trembled. Someone had been here. And had taken her camera. Darkness settled deeper across the clearing every minute, sealing her inside it like the final drop of a coffin lid. Was someone still out there?

An owl in a nearby tree moaned suddenly and Anna nearly jumped over the porch railing. She counted to ten, took a deep breath, and plunged into the darkness.

Stoney had said nothing to Leonard Hansen and when he returned to the town hall doorway, Leonard was gone. Inside, little had changed. Jim and Heyward were still trying to placate those who blamed Maum Chrish for Sarah's murder. At least six people were on their feet arguing with the two men on stage.

Bill Jenkins was leaving as Stoney reentered. Stoney rolled his eyes as they passed. "Had enough?"

"Gotta take a leak. Run tomorrow at six?"

"If we can make curfew," Stoney said sarcastically. Then he walked back toward his seat.

"Enough already," Heyward was shouting. "Everyone,

please! This is pointless. We don't have any proof that Maum Chrish is guilty, and that's the end of that for tonight.''

"We got proof all right."

A man stepped out of a group lounging around the side door of the auditorium. Maynell Pittman's former consort, an auto mechanic named Ricky, strode down the perimeter of the room toward the stage. He was a muscled, swaggering man in jeans and a T-shirt that read MECHANICS FILL IT ALL THE WAY UP. When he got to the front, he said to Heyward Rutherford, "Me and some boys been checking 'round her place." He hopped onto the stage and everyone saw the Mason jar in his hand. He set it down on the podium. "Check this out," he snickered. "Know what that is?"

Jim picked up the jar. Inside was a filmy white liquid.

The muscled figure grinned. "Got any doubt, take a whiff. Enough joy juice in there to put ya into orbit. Found that in her cabin. Now whad'ya 'spose she needed that for?"

A cry passed around the room like a banner. Most of the women stared pointedly at the floor. A few people jumped to their feet. "There's your proof, Leland. She killed Sarah and put that on her."

"She ought to be arrested. We won't need any curfew if you put her in jail."

"Jim, you gotta go get that woman!"

Jim Leland stood on stage, embarrassed, dumbfounded, as the ranting and raving reached a feverish pitch. Stoney looked on either side of him. The town had turned into a mob. He got up and marched out of the auditorium, along with several others whose faces indicated similar disgust. Stoney lingered outside until Heyward disbanded the meeting. People came out shaking their heads and went home, and Stoney noticed how most clung to their own particular group tonight; the social order that usually intersected so easily was stratifying before his eyes.

Finally Jim Leland emerged from the auditorium and Stoney took him aside for a moment. "Jim, you think Maum Chrish did it?"

The other man gave Stoney a quizzical look. "Hell, I don't know what to believe. I can't ignore this." He nodded toward the jar in his hand. "I'll have to send this over to the lab, make sure that's what it is. I mean, do any of us really know what goes on out there?"

The policeman sighed inwardly. Those swamps gave him the creeps. He had no desire to confront voodoo-practicing black people. Who were said to use large knives to skin animals. "You ever hear about that case over in Rhett Cemetery in Beaufort? This old guy was in the cemetery one night, it sits right there on the water, and he was looking for firewood and he found a grave disturbed and all this voodoo stuff around it—curses written out on pieces of paper, hex dolls hanging in the live oaks."

"Aw come on." Stoney shook his head.

"No, it's fact. Documented. Case was never solved. They got a court order to exhume the body, where the grave had been partially dug up, and they found the corpse's head cut off. It was gone. They called in that guy from Frogmore who was supposed to know everything under the sun about voodoo. Even he couldn't figure it out and less than a month after he was called in he died too. Got pneumonia."

"What about J. T. Turner?" Stoney asked, changing the subject. "Have you talked to him again? Did you know he wears a heavy gold chain that seems new? Does he look like a guy with extra money for jewelry?"

Jim's eyes widened. "How do you know that? You think he's come into money lately, like from hocking silverware?"

"I thought maybe the chain was Sarah's but Mrs. Setzler doesn't remember whether Sarah owned a gold chain. I talked to Turner when I bought some gas in Ashton. But look, he's a drifter down on his luck, right? Suppose, like he says, he just landed in town that night and Sarah saw him and offered him a hot meal—I was talking to Jenkins the other day about how she used to do that. Turner had a good chance to look around her house, see what was in it, maybe he even spotted the silver. Maybe he came back late that night. She woke up and found him and he panicked, he's nervous as a cat anyway."

The police chief considered the scenario. "But what about the semen? A burglar who messed up would want to get out of there quick, wouldn't hang around to—get the picture?"

Stoney slapped his thigh with irritation. "I know. That doesn't make sense to me either." He looked down the street; nearly everyone was gone now and it stood empty and silent. "This town will never recover until we catch who did this. An arrest is the only thing that will calm everybody down."

"Something'll turn up soon," Jim said as he started toward his car.

For a moment Stoney regarded him doubtfully, then he called, "Wait a minute, Jim." When the police chief turned around,

Stoney asked, "Did you tell Leonard Hansen to check around town late at night? Several weeks ago?"

The other man squinted in thought. "Yeah, as a matter of fact, I guess I did say something about that, about how it'd be a good idea for someone to check on things. I've been meaning to get around to doing it myself. It was Leonard's idea, actually. He thought it might reassure some folks. Why?"

"Oh nothing really. I saw him near Harriet Setzler's the night I found the footprint. Did you look at that footprint, by the way?"

Jim nodded. "It wasn't enough to go on, Stoney. Couldn't even tell how long it was. Well, I'll be seeing you."

Stoney said good night and started for home, strolling down the street alone in the darkness and wondering if he should be concerned for his life. He had never considered himself particularly brave but he could not, despite what had happened, summon up the heart to be afraid of Essex.

When Stoney got home, Anna was sitting at the kitchen table with a bourbon and water in front of her. They ate ham sandwiches for dinner and she washed hers down with a second drink while he got a beer. She seemed unusually nervous to him, preoccupied. He told her about the town meeting, about the hysteria. Then he asked what she had done all evening.

"Not much," she lied. She was still so jumpy she didn't want to talk about the swamp. Or about the theft of her favorite Nikon.

In a second Stoney got up and walked into the living room, with Silas trailing at his heels. Momentarily the Temptations began to belt "My Girl" throughout the house and Anna smiled. Stoney always played music, at top volume, when he was troubled. Many times it was something moody and psychedelic, like old Yes albums. Beach music was different; it reminded them both of college. Then Stoney appeared at the door, swooped over to Anna and took her hand, pulled her to her feet and shagged toward her, singing at the top of his lungs: "I guess you'd s-s-say, what can make me feel this way?" Dancing always drove Silas crazy and the retriever jumped up beside them, doing his own jig. Stoney grinned and reached out and grabbed one of the dog's paws with his free hand and held it for a second. "I got all the riches one man can claim." Then he dropped the dog's paw and joined both hands to Anna's and they twirled, crossing their arms behind their heads. "Look what two old fogies can still do," he laughed above the music.

"Old what? Speak for yourself, McFarland."

They danced in the kitchen for an hour, stopping only for Stoney to put on new records. They played every Motown album they had—Temptations, Miracles, Tams, Marvin Gaye. Silas gave up and eventually lay down and watched them with seasoned patience. Finally Stoney and Anna flopped down at the kitchen table, sweating, panting, out of breath. They had always danced together well, anticipating each other step for step. Though they did not realize it until later, one thing they both always liked about dancing together was that they could never do so and think at the same time. Dancing was reacting, responding. Physically.

After a moment Stoney got up from the table and ambled over to the refrigerator for another beer. He was still humming "Ain't Too Proud to Beg" when he abruptly remembered that Marvin Gaye had been shot to death by his own father. With his back still to Anna, Stoney said as he opened the beer bottle, his voice now quiet and deadly serious, "Anna, I know I shouldn't say this, I never thought I would say anything like this—but if anyone ever hurt you, I swear to God I'd kill him."

For a second she didn't say anything. Children of the late sixties, she and Stoney shared a hatred of violence that was near fanatical. Still, she was certain he meant what he said. In fact, his stark passion rendered their untested moral stance obsolete, and when she looked at him she was strangely attracted to the raw emotion in his eyes.

Seven

I N AN UNAIR-CONDITIONED building in the South, the last few weeks of school quiver like an exposed nerve. Teenagers throw spitballs, shout, tap their feet, stare out the window, beg for freedom. Desperation rings in their shrill voices: if they don't get out *now*, they are going to die. Marian Davis, slumped at her desk on a Friday afternoon, stared morosely at her charges. The only quiet students were a tall white boy and the slim black girl he always sat beside; even today their heads were together. Marian gazed at the couple; she admired their defiance even as the sight of them unnerved her. Abruptly she looked at her watch. If the bell didn't ring soon, it was entirely possible someone might leave by way of the second-floor windows. Why didn't it ring?

Outside Marian's door Seth Von Hocke and his friend Donny, who had walked over from the grammar school to meet Seth's brother Bryan, were wondering the same thing. Seth stood on tiptoe to see through the glass pane at the top of the classroom door. He wished he was tall like Donny.

Donny whistled under his breath. "Bryan's got that black teacher for English."

"He likes Miss Davis. He says she's the best teacher in the whole school."

Donny turned around. "My daddy says she's funny-acting. That even her own people don't like her 'cause she acts so white all the time. Daddy says if I get her when I get to high school, he's gonna have me transferred."

Seth stared at his friend. He often envied Donny his parents. If Donny got in trouble, his folks always took his side and got him out of it. Seth sighed. When he got in trouble, it was always *his* fault. He even got sent to his room for calling that lady in

the swamps a witch. He couldn't say nothing about nobody
without getting into trouble. He'd get in trouble for that too. Bad
grammar—whatever that was—was another thing his parents
hated. Maybe he'd give up talking. Seth leaned against the door
again and peeked inside. He thought Miss Davis was pretty but
he'd never tell Donny that. A heck of a lot prettier than the
swamp lady, that was for sure. Sometimes he still dreamed about
that night. Still saw that girl and her . . . tits. He grinned. He'd
probably get sent to his room for a year for saying that. Tits.
Tits. *Big Mother Tits.*

"Donny, you remember when we snuck out?"

The taller boy nodded. "You see 'em too?"

"See who?"

Donny rolled his eyes, tapped softly on the door. "They're
in there. The guy and the black girl."

"Where?"

"Over in the corner, sittin' side by side."

Seth peered into the room again. They were. Bryan must
know the black girl. For a second Seth thought about the rest of
that night. "Donny, you tell anybody 'bout us being out there?"

The other boy's eyes widened. "Heck no. That was the night
Mrs. Roth got killed. I ain't tellin' nobody nothin' and you
better not either."

"My mama said that lady might be arrested. Maum Chrish."

"So?"

"We were there. She wasn't in town that night."

"We left, dummy. She coulda come into town after we left.
I bet she did. My daddy says she done it. They found semen in
her house."

"What's that?"

Donny laughed. "Boy, are you dumb. Don't you know nothing'? It's that white stuff comes outta you."

The other boy was silent. No, he didn't know anything. Nobody ever told him a single thing. The first time his got big, his
mother acted like he'd wet the bed. Bryan told him not to make
such a big deal about it anymore, he especially shouldn't holler
about it from the bathroom when the Lutheran churchwomen
were having their circle meeting in the living room. That was
all Bryan said. Seth sighed. Nobody told him what he was supposed to *do* about it. His father had grinned when his mother
whispered about it later, then his father just went back to reading
the paper. They had a million suggestions about what should
come out of his mouth but not one tip about his body. They were

into talk. They definitely didn't do what the girl and guy did in the woods. His parents probably just exchanged correct grammar. Maybe they got him by accidentally using that thing they kept calling the double negative.

The door burst open suddenly and three dozen teenagers streamed out. Seth and Donny were jostled by the crowd, then spotted Bryan. The older boy disdainfully waved for them to come on.

Inside her empty classroom Marian Davis put her head down on her desk and inhaled summer. Just two more weeks. After a moment she leaned up on one elbow and surveyed the room, the poster of Stratford hanging at half-mast, the pictures of Richard Wright and Walt Whitman yellowed with chalk dust, lost books and crumpled notebook paper scattered underneath the desks. She loved the classroom like this, silent and expectant. She even loved the smell of learning, the mustiness of the old mildewed cloth-covered classics she kept on a shelf at the rear of the room, the pine wax used on the worn plank floors, even the stale sweaty smells of teenagers—half stolen cigarette and half cheap cologne. She stretched back in her chair luxuriously. For her, the daily exchange of ideas here was almost sensual.

The door opened again and the math teacher from across the hall poked her curly auburn head inside the room. "Can you believe this week is finally over?" the other woman asked. "Think we'll make it to the end?"

Marian laughed and the math teacher asked her several questions about the Career Day program the following week. Then the visitor changed the subject: "I hear that SLED agent got here this morning. Talk is he and Leland are going to arrest Maum Chrish." A half-beat pause. "Guess I'd better get back to my room. Don't suppose you'd like to grade some math tests, would you?"

Marian's smile was playful. "I don't guess the fact I haven't had a math course since my freshman year in college will be a problem?"

"Honey, on some of these papers, you'll be an expert." The math teacher headed for the door. "You get too bored you come right on over."

Marian waved as her colleague left and then rose to collect her books and straighten her desk blotter. She looked around the room one more time. Soon it would be turned over to the janitors and the painters. She ran her hand across the empty desktop, the burnished oak warm beneath her touch. For some reason she felt like she was saying farewell. As much as she always looked forward to it, there was something sad about the end of school, something haunting . . . in the sudden, abandoned silence.

Someone rapped on the door and Marian looked up to see Anna McFarland through the panes of glass. Anna hesitated for a second, instinctively sensed she'd caught Marian at a reflective moment. When Anna entered, Marian's hand still rested on the desk and Anna noticed the light from the window framing it on both sides and thought of the photograph it would make. Then she said, "I was hoping I'd catch you."

"Hi," said Marian. "What brings you over here?" She and Anna had spoken only once since their lunch.

"I mounted some pictures to use at Career Day. I put them in the AV room along with the other stuff."

"You're going all out this year," Marian said. "I know the kids will enjoy it."

"I hope so." Anna stared at the books stacked on Marian's desk. "Are you leaving?"

Before Marian could answer, the door opened again and in paced the nervous assistant principal, who wanted to know what time the Career Day program would begin and did anyone check on that fellow from Beaufort who was supposed to come up and talk about marine biology? Marian assured the administrator that everything was done; she patted him on the arm as they crossed back to her door. He looked relieved, thanked Marian, and left. Anna had observed Marian's interaction with many people during last year's program, and she admired the other woman's ease with people. Marian's self-possession fascinated her. In all the places Anna felt pointed and prickly, Marian was draped in silk.

When Marian returned to her desk she said to Anna, "I'm afraid the man's going to have a coronary over Career Day."

Anna giggled. "Well, I know why they put you in charge. You're the calmest person involved."

"Then I've got all of you fooled." Marian looked down at her books. "Did you come by for something specific?"

"Actually I did."

Anna claimed a school desk across from Marian. "I went back out there. To where Maum Chrish lives. Marian, there's something very strange going on out there. I mean, her living room has nothing in it but this tall post with snake designs painted all over it. It sits on a pedestal decorated with triangles."

The black woman stared at the white. "You visited her?"

"Not exactly." Anna paused, then said. "She wasn't there, the door was open."

Marian stared at the other woman for a second. Trespassing. What wouldn't she do for a picture? "Those are religious symbols. The post is a *poteau-mitan*. Sort of like an altar, I believe. A religious axis. According to a book I once read, the vertical post is set into a horizontal base to form a cross, in order to achieve a perfect—or magic—square. The serpent on the post is the god Danbhalah, whose power is derived from the square. The area around the post is called the *oum'phor*, the temple. Usually there's at least one room off of it where initiates wait. It's called a tomb, because the believer must 'die' before being reborn in the belief."

Marian was silent for a moment. "Is this why you came by? To ask about Maum Chrish?"

"No. Well, yeah, sort of."

"Why me? You figured one black woman was as good as another for explaining mumbo jumbo?"

"No," Anna stumbled. "I mean, I am interested in it. But that's not all."

"Then why did you stop by?" Marian crossed her arms over her chest. "Do you realize that every time I see you, all you want to talk about is my being black? Less than a week ago we were discussing Career Day on the phone and you started in on how black photographers are making great strides in the field."

"I'm just curious about the voudou stuff," Anna said defensively. "I think it's interesting."

"You do, huh?" Marian's voice was hollow. "Sure, black folk wisdom makes perfect sense. If you want to ruin someone, just bury an oil lamp containing lime juice and the gall bladder of an ox outside his house. Works every time. Is that what you want to know about? That the kind of thing you're interested in?"

Anna was silent. Then she said, "I didn't mean to offend you."

Marian leaned across her desk. "Look, Anna. I'm not an authority on all things black. I don't want to be. And if we're ever going to be friends, we're going to have to get beyond my color."

"I don't think of you as black."

"Then how come that's all you want to talk about? Why don't you ask me how I feel about being childless? What I fear about growing old? Whether I like macaroni or fettuccine? How come those things don't come up?" When Anna didn't respond, Marian added, "You've sought me out to demonstrate what an enlightened liberal you are. Haven't you?"

"That's not fair. I've always been open-minded. I despise bigots like Harriet Setzler."

"Did you ever hold a black child's head while she vomited, then clean her up and put her to bed in your house? Or did you—in the safety of your nice Atlanta suburb—make an intellectual decision to love black people? Harriet went against her times, you just went along with yours. Which is harder to do?"

Anna stood up. "I don't need this." She stalked to the door of the classroom, paused in front of it, and said, "Maybe you don't have all your own problems about race tied up as neatly as you think."

After the door slammed behind Anna, Marian got up and gathered her books for the second time that day and made her way out to the parking lot. She climbed behind the wheel of her restored, low-slung Opel GT sportscar and soon she was flying down the state road that led out of town, toward the sea. At a sharp curve she downshifted, gunned the accelerator, watched the tach climb as she went back to fourth gear. She enjoyed the momentum of the changing gears, the whine of the engine, the rush of speed against her face. She didn't like Japanese cars; for someone who truly enjoyed driving, they were too quiet, almost prim. You could not be reckless in a car that purred, and sometimes Marian was deliberately reckless. In driving, as in sex, she gave herself up with abandon. Behind the wheel she palmed her destiny like an apple. She wiped her brow and reached toward a box of Kleenex on the console. She was sweating profusely. Maybe she had a summer cold, all the kids came down with something right before school got out. She patted her upper lip with a white tissue. In the rearview mirror her wide mahogany eyes mocked her: they were dilated, like someone on pure adrenalin.

She didn't know why she was going out here.

Various shanty houses began to appear on her right, set back from the road among the cavernous trees that protected them from the sun. A stray pig wandered across the road and Marian swerved to miss it. In front of one of the shacks barefoot children stared at the German car and one small girl in a pink dress two sizes too small lifted her hand in a mirthless wave. Marian waved back. How did they survive? Her people, of course, for the shanty dwellers were almost all black, blacks who kept to themselves and rarely came into town or had anything to do with Essex. What did they do out here day after day? Why didn't they get up and leave, start over, go someplace else where it'd be better for them, where they'd have a chance? Why stay here and rot? They could leave, they had that right. Just like her mother.

Marian swallowed, stomped on the accelerator, and felt the car shoot out from under her. She knew she was driving too fast. Soon she came to a place where the woods thickened and she pulled off onto the shoulder of the road. She knew the spot well, even though she hadn't been there in many years. She got out of the car and headed into the woods. At first the shade of the oaks was comforting; it blocked the piercing sun. But the closer she came to the black water, the more menacing the trees became. She began to feel chilled, anemic, as if living creatures could not be sustained by so little light. Around her, however, was proof to the contrary. The sweetness of the wild magnolias assaulted her senses and she resented them. They had no right to flourish here.

Ahead of her, spanning an inlet, was an old wooden bridge; it was so badly rotted that the far end disappeared into the river. Back then only people who hunted and fished had known where it was. Now no one did; even Maum Chrish lived several miles away. Marian looked beyond the bridge, into the woods on the other side. Nothing else had changed, nothing was different.

She stopped. Why had she come out here? She hadn't thought about this place, or what happened here, for many years. No, it was impossible. One thing couldn't have anything to do with the other. It was a coincidence, it had to be.

Marian closed her eyes, willed herself not to remember. Then she turned and strode back through the woods. She tore open her car door, revved the engine as if being pursued, and flew back to town at eighty miles an hour. Stopping sharply at Harriet's house, she ran up the steps and pounded on the door. Please be home, she begged silently. Please.

When the old lady came to the door, Marian almost threw her arms around her. Gratefully she slipped inside that safe living room and settled down comfortably on the well-worn sofa. Her heart ceased pounding, she unclenched her right fist. Idly she and Harriet talked about the last days of school. Marian answered questions she barely heard, described a day she could scarcely recall. All the while huddling against the familiar overstuffed furniture like a sick child. Harriet reminisced about her own teaching days. About what it was like to have to build a coal fire before you could even call the roll. About taking her lunch in a steel pail just like the children did. About the boy she'd taught who delivered the war telegrams and how she'd heard his bell outside her house the day the news came about her own son.

"We negotiated life with the only thing we had—firmness of mind. If you were poor, you were poor, but you didn't have to act poor. If you were uneducated, you could fix it, and you would if you had the will and some self-respect. If you were hurt, you turned that hurt into strength by maintaining an outer harmony at all times. You did not close out the world, but you let it see only what you wanted it to see."

Marian stared at Harriet. Then she noticed sunlight from an open window sparkling through the venetian blinds; one slat of light illuminated the diamond ring on Harriet's pinky finger, a round European-cut stone set in gold filigree. The older woman had two diamonds; the other, larger and square-cut, she wore with her wedding ring. People said the smaller ring had been Elizabeth's engagement ring. Marian gazed through the dining room doorway, at the fire painting above the mantel. Black or white, the Southern penchant for flailing oneself with the past went as unchecked as the heat.

The old sofa felt hard and lumpy all of a sudden, the room too cold and well preserved, too staunch, too well defended. Marian sat away from the back of the sofa and said, "I heard what happened at the town meeting. The kids say they're going to arrest Maum Chrish."

Harriet nodded.

"Do you know her?" Marian asked. "Have you ever talked to her?"

The older woman looked startled. "Why, no." A pause. "Have you?"

"No. I don't remember her from when I was a kid. When did she come to Essex?"

Harriet got up and went over to the piano, began dusting off the keys with a corner of her apron. "I think maybe it was when you were up to Columbia. I don't guess anyone much remembers now."

Harriet was still wiping off the piano keys when the doorbell rang. Both she and Marian looked up. "Wonder who that is," the old lady said as she crossed to the door and opened it cautiously.

On the other side of the screen stood Stoney McFarland. He smiled. "How are you, Mrs. Setzler? You busy?"

The white-haired woman pushed open the door and Stoney walked in. He saw Marian and nodded, "Not much longer now, I guess."

The black woman stared at him. "What?"

"Doesn't school get out soon?"

Marian smiled faintly. "Yes it does. I almost forgot."

Stoney, still standing, turned to Harriet. "I came by to ask you something sort of odd. About Leonard Hansen."

"Why would you be asking me about him?"

"It was something Jenkins—Bill Jenkins—said. About how all these kids stayed with Sarah from time to time. He said Leonard was one of them. I thought you might know about that, living across the street and all."

Abruptly Marian jumped up. "I've got to get home." She sailed across the room toward the door. At it she stopped and looked back at Harriet for a moment, then she waved and hurried out.

Stoney said, "I didn't mean to run Marian off."

Harriet still had her eyes on the door. In a second she faced Stoney again. "I don't know much about Leonard anymore. How come you're interested in him in particular?"

Stoney avoided her probing gray eyes. "I keep wondering if Sarah's kindheartedness is what got her killed. Her inviting strangers home to dinner all the time, taking in runaway kids, all that."

"You think Leonard killed Sarah?" The old lady eyed Stoney carefully, not missing a beat.

"Well, no, not exactly, I was just thinking about people who had something to do with Sarah." He stopped, drew a deep breath.

"Leonard was a bad sort as a boy," Harriet said. "But he's been nothing but polite and aboveboard since he came back."

"But suppose he's really no different? I mean, do you think the Leonard who grew up here could have killed somebody?"

Harriet walked back over to the piano and resumed her dusting. "I haven't the faintest idea," she said. But her hands, Stoney noticed, were unsteady.

"You do think so, don't you?"

"You're putting words in my mouth," the old lady snapped. "Sarah was my dearest friend. If I knew who did this awful thing to her, don't you think I'd tell absolutely everyone?" She stared at the piano again. "What about that man who was here that night? What about that insane woman in the swamps?"

Stoney shrugged. "There doesn't seem to be any real evidence against J. T. Turner. Nor any motive other than robbery. Nothing that was taken has surfaced yet. Maum Chrish—I don't know, she doesn't have any motive either." He hesitated, then asked, "Just for the sake of argument, do you remember when Leonard lived with Sarah? Did they get along?"

The elderly woman shook her head. "That was so long ago, and he only stayed a short while. As I recall, he was just out of the service when he came back, maybe he was planning to settle down here again even though his folks had moved on. But he didn't stay long. Sarah needed someone to do her heavy work and she thought somebody should help Leonard. But it just didn't work out."

"What happened? Why did Leonard finally leave?"

Harriet was silent for a second, then she said, "He took things. Money. He was still awfully young then, apparently he hadn't completely straightened out yet. Sarah finally asked him to leave. To get a place of his own, and a real job. He left town after that."

"Was he angry when Sarah made him leave?"

The white-haired lady shook her head. "I don't rightly know."

Stoney thought for a moment, then asked, "Bill Jenkins said Leonard's father *made* him join the Marines. Do you know why?"

"The boy was one handful too much." Harriet looked down. She thought about another boy who had been the same way. She looked up again. "What made you start thinking about Leonard?"

"Nothing that adds up to anything," Stoney admitted. "I'm grabbing at straws, I guess."

After Stoney left Harriet Setzler's house, he walked toward town. Crossing the street, he passed the empty lot where he'd practiced pitching a baseball with Monkey. The middle-aged black man had rigged up a plywood backboard for Stoney with a metal pie pan tacked to it to perfect his aim. When Stoney came by, Monkey would stop digging in Harriet's garden and come over and watch the boy throw the ball, would clap and cheer at a good curve, then kneel down and give advice about the angle of the wrist. Because of Monkey, Stoney had planned to become a professional baseball player, until he broke his arm in two places in high school.

He paused and stared at the vacant field, its grass nearly knee-high. Why would anyone call a grown man, a man Stoney remembered as proud and intelligent, by such a derogatory nickname? All over town right now people were ready to throw another black, with the unlikely name of Maum Chrish, in jail on unproven charges, and it occurred to Stoney—but briefly now—to wonder if the Essex he had known as a child was a mythical Camelot he'd invented.

Did one thing have anything to do with the other? The question echoed in Marian's ears like a sonic boom as she hurried through her front door. Nothing was exactly the same, it was years and years ago, and there was only that one thing—which no one on earth knew about, not even Harriet—that was similar. The black woman squeezed her eyes shut. For years she had kept the humiliation, the degradation, at bay. Should she tell someone about that, about all of it, on the off chance that it might be related? Probably it wasn't, probably it was just one of those coincidences in life. As long as there was no danger to anyone (And there wasn't, was there? She couldn't think of any. No one even knew she'd told Harriet, and Sarah Roth hadn't been involved at all), there was no reason to come forward. What did she really know anyway?

God, it was time to leave Essex. She'd been thinking about leaving for a year. Maybe she'd stayed on this last year to test herself. But with Sarah's death so much had changed.

Marian slipped off her damp dress and changed into shorts and a T-shirt. Suddenly her house felt oppressive. She stuffed her keys in her pocket and went out the door again. On the street she walked toward the outskirts of Aiken Avenue. In a few blocks the squarish white and pastel houses began to disappear and were replaced with rectangular wooden shacks. The dirt yards had grass now but it was sparse and unkempt. Most houses had been painted white a decade ago, but the walls were blistered and peeling. In the middle of the street two small black children, a boy and a girl about six or seven, threw a basketball back and forth; beyond them a larger boy straddled a BMX bicycle. There were at least five or six dogs around but no chickens anymore, and glass had been added to the windows, most of which were now choked with large box fans.

Marian stood for a second in front of the house in which she'd been born. A shrunken black woman who was almost blind sat in a rocker on the porch. Sadie Thompkins, who now lived in the house, had been a contemporary of Aunt Posey's and was one of the people who had been most helpful to Marian in her quest to learn about her mother. Marian often came to see the old woman, brought her cookies or a cake from time to time. Even Harriet Setzler remembered how much Sadie liked sweets; Harriet would give Marian a batch of lime pies and say, "Now if you can't eat all that, maybe old Sadie would like some."

Marian walked up toward the house. "Sadie, it's me, Marian, how you doing?"

"Oh, I'm all right." The elderly woman lifted a thin, veined arm; it was no thicker than a child's pogo stick.

Sadie was as much a fixture in this neighborhood as Harriet Setzler was in hers. A number of years before, Sadie had shocked everyone by adopting a child that a teenage girl down the street hadn't wanted. Everybody in the shacks laughed about the sixty-year-old adopting a toddler: running after that child would kill her for sure. But Sadie said this way she'd have somebody to take care of her later on. As it happened, though, the adopted girl left town at sixteen and had come back to see Sadie only once. Which Sadie always explained diplomatically, "I'm guessing it was too little too late."

Sadie had a large face, an old face. Each passing year had left its mark upon it, her history now visibly measured out by the crusted layers of her skin. Deep gorges around her eyes dissolved into concentric furrows fanning out across her cheeks. And underneath her chin hung pendulous folds of loose flesh. She looked ancient yet venerable, like an important historic monument.

"I recall me something about your mama, her, yesterday."

Marian smiled. Sadie was almost the only black left in Essex who occasionally lapsed into Gullah. "What did you remember?"

"She binnah standin' on the porch, her, mebbe in a dream, and she crack 'er teet, her."

"What did she say?" Marian asked gently. Many people assumed Sadie was senile now.

"Tek foot een 'er han' en lean fuh home."

Marian's eyes widened. She walked up the stairs toward the old woman. "Sadie, what do you mean, she's gone home?" When the other woman didn't answer, just closed her eyes, Marian reached out and touched her shoulder. "Sadie? Sadie, you okay?"

Finally Sadie opened her eyes again. "Aunt Posey's girl Diamond send me a pie, you wan some?"

Her mind must be wandering. Marian declined the pie but walked into the cabin and back to the kitchen to cut a piece for the older woman. The covered pie plate sat on top of a white metal table and Marian found a knife and reached into the cupboard for a small plate. As in her own day, none of the plates or stainless steel silverware matched, just bits and pieces gathered here and there. She always felt strangely disconnected from the surroundings in this house, as though she had left them so long ago they barely meant anything to her now. In a few moments she took the piece of pie back out onto the porch.

"Sadie, does Diamond come check on you every day?"

The old lady nodded. "Most 'bout. 'Fore Miz Sarah got kilt, anyways." Sadie picked up the wedge of pie with her fingers and began nibbling at it. "She be wearing that rock you give her."

"Who?"

"Lonnie, her."

"Sadie, you dreamed that."

But all the way home Marian thought about the rock anyway. She was five when she found it. Digging in the yard one day. A large flat piece of granite with two veins of white quartz running through it which intersected to form a misshapened cross. That afternoon she showed it to her mama and her mama said probably it was a holy rock, it would protect Alma from evil. Two days later her mother came home dragging, her eyes red from crying. Miz Harriet had scolded her for not polishing the silver good enough and had called her down in front of the preacher and the preacher's wife, who were visiting at the time. It was one thing to fuss if she hadn't done her work right, it was another to say those things in front of the preacher. Watching her mama that night, Alma had tried to think of something to make the older woman feel better. So in the middle of the night she got up from her cot and took her holy rock and slipped it under her mama's pillow. The next morning Lonnie found it there and tried to give it back, but Alma wouldn't take it. Finally the mother put her arms around the child and said, "I'll put me a string on it and wear it whenever people don't treat me fair. It'll protect me."

And she had done just that, had worn that rock around her

neck like jewelry. What made Sadie remember that rock? Marian wondered. Even she had almost forgotten it.

The first time the man walked by the house the next day, Anna didn't think anything of it. She was sweeping the front porch when an unfamiliar man in his late twenties, rotund and erratic, sauntered by and stared at her without a greeting. A few hours later, while she was dusting the bookshelves in the living room, she saw him again. This time he paused in front of the house and studied it, gazed at the mailbox with Stoney's name painted on it. Anna crossed to the window. Was he casing the joint? When the man saw her staring out at him, he turned and scrambled down the street. She licked her lips. Not the most uptown guy she'd ever seen. Feeling ridiculous, she went to the front door and locked it.

She hated cleaning house so she waited until it got unbearable and, having waited so long, she usually had to spend an entire day at it. By late afternoon she'd finished downstairs and was steering the vacuum cleaner around the upstairs bedrooms, stopping every now and then to answer the phone. When she finally finished the vacuuming, she flopped down on the bed in the guest room. She was hot and sweaty; small crescents of water had gathered under her breasts and spotted her red T-shirt. She lay there for a few minutes resting, warm and languorous. In a moment she closed her eyes. For days an insatiable physical craving had been her constant companion. Christ, was it true what they said about women in their thirties?

Like yesterday. After she'd taken a shower, she had just stood in front of the mirror in the bathroom looking at herself. Slowly, she realized that the sight of her own body (defects and all) turned her on. The curve of her hip when she touched it in the night turned her on. The smell of roses blooming all over town turned her on. She and Stoney had not made love since that night at the beach and she told him none of these things, nor that she sometimes deliberately stayed in bed after he left for work in the morning. To have told him any of this would have been too threatening, a confession of need.

Then she heard the door. Downstairs Stoney was walking inside the kitchen. She jumped up and went out and met him in the hall. "Hi. Where've you been?"

He leaned over and kissed her. She looked frazzled to him. Kind of sexy too, as a matter of fact. "I drove out into the sticks and then I went over to see Harriet Setzler again. How'd you know I wasn't at work?''

"Sumter Brownlow called twice. Wanted to know if I knew where you were. I felt like I was talking to your truant officer.''

"Sorry about that.''

They started down the stairs. "What's for supper?''

"Stir-fry.'' At the bottom of the stairs Anna added, "The last time he called, Stoney, he sounded, I don't know, threatening or something. He said the head of the department in Columbia wanted to talk to you. I got the feeling you were in for an official reprimand. Why's that?''

Stoney sighed irritably. "Oh, Sump's uptight because I've left the office a few times lately. To check on things about Sarah.''

In the kitchen Anna took celery and green pepper out of the refrigerator and began to dice them on the wood chopping block. She looked over at Stoney and wondered how he managed to get the bottom of his slacks so dirty. "Are they really going to arrest Maum Chrish?''

Stoney poured his wife a glass of white wine. "I don't know. I don't think she did it, though.''

Despite her scary experience in the swamps the last time, Anna was also inclined to give the black woman the benefit of the doubt, given the way the town was ganging up on her. Then she thought about her argument with Marian, speaking of getting falsely accused. Too bad, it would have been nice to have had at least one friend in Essex.

"I went out there today, Anna.''

She looked up. "Out where?''

"To the swamps. I found her cabin, it's way back in the middle of nowhere, I'm glad I asked somebody before I went.'' Stoney went over and began mixing himself a martini.

Anna was quiet for a second. Then, "What happened?''

"Nothing. She was sitting on her front steps. She didn't act crazy, I mean, she wasn't threatening or anything. I asked her some questions but she didn't say one word, just stared at me. Finally I left.'' Stoney took his drink back over to the kitchen table and sat down.

Anna was still staring at him. She had not told him of either of her trips to the swamps and she did not do so now.

"I just had to see her for myself,'' he went on. "But the more I think about it, the more convinced I am that whoever did this planned it. She doesn't seem coherent enough to plan anything, it's like she's in some world all her own; she's weird for sure, but she doesn't seem aggressive enough to be a killer." He paused. "Afterward I went to see Mrs. Setzler to ask her about Leonard Hansen."

"What about Leonard Hansen?"

"Sort of a hunch." He crossed to the back door and peered outside to see if Silas had come home yet. Anna went back to chopping the vegetables and Stoney wandered over to the counter and picked up a celery stick and bit into it. "I keep wondering if maybe Leonard killed Sarah."

Anna turned around, knife in hand. "We are talking about that guy who beat you up, aren't we?"

Stoney nodded. "Which doesn't make me unique. Leonard beat up nearly everybody in Essex when he was kid."

"What makes you think he had something to do with the murder?"

"Nothing that sounds like much. He once lived with Sarah and stole money from her. And he was laughing at the town meeting, like he was getting off on the town's hysteria."

Anna opened the cabinet door and took some onions out of the bin underneath the sink. "*That* makes you think he's guilty?"

"Well, what if he hasn't changed like everyone thinks? What if he's still mean as a snake?"

"Stoney, don't get mad—but aren't you a little prejudiced when it comes to him?"

"Because I got into a fight with him once? For crying out loud." Stoney paused, then added, "Oh, I get it—the guy had a hard life so that excuses anything he does. How come when somebody's a miserable human being it's never his fault anymore? It's his parents, poverty, something else. What happened to individual accountability?"

"What's the difference between blaming Leonard because he's a redneck and blaming Maum Chrish because she's black?"

"I'm not doing that," Stoney said vehemently. His drink hit the counter and sloshed over.

For a few minutes neither spoke. Anna took the strips of chicken breast out of the refrigerator and sprinkled Cajun seasoning on them. She looked up after a minute. "It's just— sometimes I think you don't really care exactly who's blamed for Sarah's murder. All you want is for things to go back to the way they were before. You're losing your perspective."

Stoney eyed his wife somberly. "You're wrong. If that were true, I'd be all over Maum Chrish like everyone else."

He went over to the back door and whistled for Silas. In a

second the retriever came careening around the side of the house. Stoney opened the door and the dog bounded inside and Stoney knelt down to greet him. "Hiya, boy. How's tricks?" Then Silas ran over to Anna and aimed his nose at the food smells on the kitchen counter. Finally Stoney said, still staring out at the back yard, "I'm not sure you understand what I feel, Anna. There's a small town in almost everyone, a core inside us that needs familiarity and safety. I know you don't like it here but I don't see how you can be indifferent, so coolly analytical, about this." He hesitated, then added, "The rug has been pulled out from under this town. If people aren't safe here, then there is no safety. There are no safe harbors left anywhere."

Anna wiped her hands and walked over to him. "I'm sorry, Stoney. I don't mean to be insensitive, I know how much this has upset you." She slipped her arms around him from behind and leaned against him as though to put the breadth of his shoulders between her and the chaos outside the door. And inside her. "I almost wish the state would fire you. Then maybe we could leave, put Sarah's murder and everything else behind us." She stared out at the live oaks dripping with Spanish moss. "Even the trees here have an onus on their backs."

He pulled away from her, walked out the door into the back yard. She followed, leaving a whimpering Silas inside the storm door. "Stoney?"

His eyes were determined when he turned around. "Anna, you agreed to come here. Now that things are tough you're suggesting we run away, turn our backs. I can't do that. If you love me, you shouldn't want me to do that." He walked over and leaned against a tree in the twilight. "I guess some of us never get over being Southern—we love the place too damn much or we hate it too damn much." He turned to her again. "Have you ever touched Spanish moss?" He reached up above his head and extracted a single strand of the mysterious air plant. "It only looks gray and spooky and forbidding from a distance; actually it's green and soft and smells of mint."

With the stringlike moss draped across his palm, he gazed at Anna again. "Makes a lot of difference how close you're willing to get."

Harriet Setzler put down the telephone receiver and stared around her breakfast room. Nearly eight o'clock. She'd been talking to her oldest son Bill who lived in Denver. All her children were so scattered now, in Colorado and California and

New Hampshire, that they got home only rarely. Her daughter came once a year, and Harriet kept up with her grandchildren through the mail. Billy was her favorite of her two sons, however; he always reminded Harriet of William, with his now rounded belly, his twinkling blue eyes, his short stocky frame, and that soft gentlemanly laugh. Not like Johnny at all.

For days she'd thought of little else but Johnny, ever since Stoney McFarland had stood in her living room talking about Leonard Hansen. It was Stoney's shoulders—how wide and firm they were. Johnny had held himself exactly like that in his uniform, as though his back were braced with steel. Even as a child he'd had a man's shoulders, shoulders that should have borne the foolishness of the world well. But hadn't. She'd first noticed their strength at his father's funeral. How old was he then? Fifteen? Eighteen? It was hard to remember now. But everyone was there, the entire town. She had stood just in front of the family tombstone in her best black dress. Alone. The children remained a step or two behind, the minister on the other side of the grave. She had refused to have chairs at the service. She was not about to seek—or provide—comfort on the day William left. She could hear all the voices whispering behind her now. The snickers. Respectfully hushed but still there.

The grave was open and now they knew where William would lie.

Johnny stood apart from everyone, on the far right beside his mother's grave, like a sentry on duty, back straight as a ramrod in his first black suit. Between him and his stepmother loomed the empty space, where no grave had yet been dug, and he stared at it incredulously. His father was over on the far left, in the spot he'd purchased for his second wife. The minister made the sign of the cross and the men hoisted the coffin up with leather straps and began to lower it. The children drew near, huddled at Harriet's back.

Except Johnny. Johnny stood by his real mother and watched. When everyone left the cemetery, he was still standing at the foot of his mother's grave.

Was it five years later that the battles began? When he'd stumble into the house with a bottle in hand, startling the dogs and crashing around so loudly half the block could hear. One night, as usual, Harriet got up and went into the dining room to tell him to quiet down. That if he wanted to drink himself to death he would not do it in this house. Only this time she found him sitting at the dining table, his arms outstretched, his hands gripping the butt of his father's shotgun. With the barrel aimed at his chest.

"Leave me alone," he growled, so drunk his eyes didn't focus. "One more step and I'll do it." His voice was bitter. "I'm not taking orders from you. You are not my mother, you do not tell me what to do."

She retreated and no shots were fired that night. Later, she sent him into the Army. Much like Joseph Hansen would do. The service would straighten Johnny out, stop the drinking. There was no war then. But Johnny never came home again. Because later, there was.

April of 1944 was the kissing cousin of the April Sarah Roth was killed. Almost in defiance of the war in Europe, it was dramatically lush. The prickly yellowish grass, doormat of so many bootsoles, soon stood as erect as hundreds of tiny wooden soldiers dressed in evergreen. Gardens came alive almost overnight, and suddenly all the houses sparkled diamond white under the expansive sun. That was the same spring the streets were paved. On the day the workmen arrived with their trucks and asphalt, everyone camped on their porches to watch. The ladies, Harriet and Sarah among them, shelled butterbeans or cracked and picked out pecans, sitting there nearly all day. And when the concrete post reading AIKEN AVENUE finally went in the ground, they all gathered around it and cheered. They had, after all, been waiting a long time for an address. Essex, and Aiken Avenue in particular, had finally arrived.

But so had the War.

One Saturday that April, Harriet Setzler, thinner and her dark hair only slightly ribboned with gray, stayed in her kitchen making lime pies almost all day for the church picnic on Sunday. She had opened the windows over the white ceramic sink and the fluttering breeze inflated the curtains and dispersed the baking smells all over the house. Her daughter Betty loved it when the house smelled like that; the girl, who was quite a good cook herself, would be home from college for Easter next week. Harriet deposited the new pies on the wooden table in the center of the room to cool and then she sat down to rest a spell, picked up the flimsy Air Mail envelope lying beside the pies. Johnny had never made his T's right. His letters were always addressed to "Dear Family" even though no one was left at home but his stepmother. But he did seem changed. He wrote with a new sense of responsibility; apparently he was a man now, the Army

had been the right solution. Abruptly Harriet pressed the envelope to her cheek and wondered how far away from South Carolina France was. She would send him some cookies this week.

Harriet looked up for a second. From somewhere she heard
a strange noise, like a bell. In a moment she got up and went
into the breakfast room and came back with a piece of paper
and a fountain pen. She sat back down and began to write:
"Dear son. I received your last letter and I am very glad you
are still at the same base. I hope you will be there for a while
as I am sending you a pair of shoes. I know you said the Army
gave you shoes, but I was afraid they might not fit as well as
these I'm sending. We are all fine. I heard from Billy this week
and your sister is coming home next weekend."

The middle-aged woman looked up from her letter. That
funny sound again, somewhere outside. She gazed back down
at her letter and saw she'd inadvertently left a huge ink blot
where she'd stopped. She balled the letter up and walked over
to the sink to stare outdoors. This wasn't what she wanted to
say to Johnny, she didn't know how to say what she wanted to
say. She wasn't sorry she'd sent him in the Army but she did
worry; she was proud of his distinguished service, the bronze
star, but was he being careful over there? She wanted to ask if
he was still drinking. Had he finally forgiven her? Harriet was
pondering these things when she saw a young boy outside the
window whizz by on a red bicycle; he nearly knocked over one
of the Loadholt's setting hens, which had escaped into the street.
She heard that bell again as the boy disappeared.

Harriet walked through her house toward the front porch.
Across the street Sarah's door was open and the other woman,
that red hair glowing in the sunlight, was beating a small carpet
against her front porch post. Dust was flying everywhere. Harriet had more than once suggested to her friend that beating
carpets was a chore best done on the back porch where no one
could see it.

Sarah called to Harriet, "Come on over and help!"

"No thanks. You're raising enough dust for all of us." Harriet
moved down her front steps (they were wood then, not brick)
and stared around her garden to see what was blooming.

"How 'bout some coffee, Harriet? I made ladyfingers this
morning. I'd like to send some to Henry but I know they'd just
fall apart."

Harriet declined the coffee but she did cross the street to ask
Sarah, "Did you hear a bell or something this morning?"

Sarah looked down. "It's the Wallerman boy, on that bicycle they got for him to deliver the War Department telegrams. The bicycle has a bell on it. There are more and more telegrams these days so they needed him to get around quicker—what with the war in France and all." Sarah stopped sharply, remembering where Johnny Setzler was.

"I think it's disgraceful," Harriet said.

"What is?"

"Putting that boy on a bicycle with a bell. Like he's in a parade or something. Don't you see, Sarah? Every time we hear that sound we'll know another boy's dead. That bell's a death rattle."

When Harriet went back across the street, she paused for a second on her porch. The early climbing roses were already blooming. How odd. They also needed pruning, they were roaming everywhere, wild and crazy. On the porch she got her pruning shears from behind the metal glider and went back down to the trellis. The sun had receded now and the sky lay blanketed with a gray cotton. Soon a light rain began falling. Harriet pruned anyway, snipped away excess branches. Like butter on a hot griddle, the raindrops skittered across the velvety blossoms in front of her. With each drop the half-opened buds spread wider and wider, almost as if they were advancing toward Harriet from a distance, growing larger as they got closer.

"Prring—prring—prriiing."

The woman with the scissors looked up. She didn't see anything. The sound of the bell was distant, he must be somewhere across town. She turned back to the trellis as the rain came down harder. Then she noticed the yellow petals all over the ground at her feet. The new buds she'd just admired had fallen victim to the vicious rain.

Later that afternoon the day turned almost wintry again. Harriet closed her windows and sat down in her living room to knit. She was going to send Johnny a sweater for his birthday. As the afternoon wore on, she got up and built a fire in the fireplace; the air had turned positively cold. She looked out the front window and saw that nearly all the new buds on the climbing roses were ruined. It was her fault they'd bloomed this early. She had overfertilized them. Harriet threw more coal on the fire and settled back down again.

In a few minutes she got up to wind the mantel clock. Then she sat back down again, measured out the sweater sleeve she was working on against her arm. Yes, she thought, it would need about five inches more.

"Priinnnng."

Harriet dropped the sleeve. That infernal bell. She would speak to someone about it tomorrow. It was unnerving, even when it was miles away. The rain increased to a steady drumbeat on the tin roof above her, like stick pins cascading into a metal bucket. Harriet went over and poked the fire.

"Prring—prring."

Shouldn't that child go home in the rain? Where is he? Whose house? Harriet laid down her knitting and crossed to her front window, wondering why she was tiptoeing. Outside she saw nothing. She almost laughed aloud with relief. It was only the rain. She went back over to the sofa and picked up Johnny's sweater again.

"Prring—prrinng—prrrinnnng."

Harriet froze. It was close now. Bob Loadholt?

"Prring—prring—prriiing—prrrinnng."

Harriet scrambled to the window again. She saw nothing but the rain. That, and Sarah's face across the street, framed by her own window. The two women stared at each other.

"Prrriiinggg—priiinnnnnggggg."

The flash of red rounded the corner. Sarah saw it. Harriet saw it. The bicycle halted in the wet street between the two houses. "Let it be Sarah's boy," Harriet prayed under her breath. "Please, Lord. Not Johnny."

"Prrriiiinnnnggggg."

The boy, an angel of death barely ten years old and encased in an oilcloth slicker, climbed off the bicycle. He turned. And walked up Harriet's steps.

A year later he stopped at Sarah's. Neither woman ever mentioned that first telegram in the rain, what both had wished as each stared hysterically at her best friend. But Harriet always believed that she might be responsible for both deaths. She always felt she owed Sarah a restitution no lime pies could ever make good. So years later, when Sarah did something that reminded them both of that day, Harriet kept quiet about her disapproval. That one time she acquiesced, against her nature, to the Southern dictum which forbids saying exactly what you think.

Abruptly Harriet picked up the telephone receiver again. This time she dialed Marian's number. She couldn't afford another mistake. But she put the receiver down before Marian answered. Marian didn't know what she had done years ago—afterward.

That Harriet had not entirely kept her word. But it was so long ago, it couldn't mean anything now. Abruptly Harriet got up and went to her front door and checked the locks. That crazy woman in the swamps must be guilty.

Eight

W HEN LOU BROCKHURST arrived in town, Essex
breathed a sigh of relief. We could stop worrying. This man would give us answers, would put our town back
together again. Even though he wasn't the typical law enforcement type, he emanated a quiet, understated confidence that was
far more convincing in Essex than overwrought zeal. Most agents
of SLED, the State Law Enforcement Division, were burly
strapping fellows, former athletes and student body presidents.
Brockhurst, at barely five feet with a slight limp left over from
a childhood bout with polio, didn't *look* remotely capable of
overwhelming the bad guys. He also smiled too much, a crooked
grin that challenged no one and put everyone at ease. His fellow
agents continually wondered, we heard later, how a guy like
that managed to maintain the best arrest record in the whole
state.

The criminal mind had long been Brockhurst's hobby. After
finishing college, he tried to become a SLED agent but didn't
meet the height requirement, so he landed a job with a Charleston newspaper and worked himself into the police beat, a dead
end studiously avoided by most novice reporters. Not Lou
Brockhurst. He sat at the city desk day after day with one ear
tuned to the police radio, always poised to strike out for the city
lockup or for the police commissioner's office. He won awards
for his crime reporting but often forgot to go to the banquets to
collect them. If a robbery or murder had taken place that day,
he couldn't be bothered. Most people didn't know what to make
of such a kind, self-deprecating man who thrived on violence
and crime. Even in college Brockhurst had been pegged the All-
American "nice guy." Coeds who didn't trust the men they
dated always went to Lou for advice. He was someone few ever

had a complaint against, much less a grudge. Now he lived in a world inhabited by pushers and thieves and murderers—but he was equally comfortable with doctors, housewives, and farmers. He was still, quintessentially, a nice guy.

And hated it.

Close friends said it was a woman who had made him a cop and a forty-two-year-old bachelor. In his senior year in college the incredible had happened to him: the most beautiful girl on campus fell for him. She reminded Lou of a delicate china doll, this wispy golden only-child of wealthy elderly parents, this flaxen-haired miniature with enormous aquamarine eyes and a wide sensual mouth. She changed Lou's life. Her perfection made him bold. He began to do things he'd never done before, go places he'd never gone before, his diminutive size and slight handicap compensated when she walked beside him. He planned a career in advertising, worked out with weights and grew huskier, stronger, proud.

So he gave her a ring and a spring wedding was planned, right before graduation. All was right with the world. Until she changed her mind.

One morning, without warning or explanation, the beautiful girl got a yen to see an old beau who'd just come back from Vietnam with a chest full of medals. The only man who'd ever left *her*. And in the space of one hour, sixty interminable minutes, thirty-six hundred eternal seconds, Lou Brockhurst was cut down to size again. He didn't protest her abandonment, didn't call her dirty names or crash her wedding (to which she personally invited all her old boyfriends); no, he accepted her betrayal stoically, as he'd accepted his size, his limp, his life. But he did not recover. In that one year when he was twenty-one, his entire life was cast.

Upon graduation from college he tried to join the Army. He was turned down. He wanted to become an air marshall but was refused there too. His height and his limp automatically disqualified him with the law enforcement agencies to which he applied. Later he set his sights on becoming an undercover narcotics agent. Over and over again he was put off. In the meantime his reputation as the best crime reporter in Charleston grew. For years he detailed exploits he secretly admired. Those guys didn't ''take'' anything. Time passed. Then a miracle occurred. By now Lou Brockhurst knew enough important people in South Carolina law enforcement that a position just happened to open up for a short guy with a limp.

The man who arrived in Essex had close-cropped black hair, alert green eyes, and a swarthy complexion undercut by a bridge of freckles spanning his nose. Broad and muscled through the chest, his shoulders dwarfed his small frame and skinny legs, his khaki slacks always hiked up in the back because his limp stemmed from a deformity in his right hip. He used no crutch or cane, just walked slowly, dragging the stiff shorter leg slightly. When stationary he always stood at military attention, his chest thrown forward, his legs spread far enough apart that they appeared evenly matched.

"I'm sorry, I just don't agree," he told Jim Leland, facing the police chief across his desk in the Essex Town Hall. "I don't for a minute believe one old woman killed another old woman and then dumped sperm all over her."

Jim Leland regarded the other man with skepticism. This was a big-city cop? The town could think what it liked but Brockhurst didn't look capable of solving anything to him, much less a violent murder. This fellow looked like he ought to be in some school somewhere teaching kids or something. Damn those state bureaucrats. If Sarah Roth had been killed in Charleston or Spartanburg, they'd have sent someone else. Brockhurst was second string, no question.

"I've gone over the material evidence with the Ashton County sheriff," Brockhurst said. He eyed Jim Leland and added, "Of course, if we'd been called to the scene, it would have been much better. Nothing replaces what you can find right after the murder. As it is, we have only the photos and the paperwork to go on. Next time I'd get in touch with our people right away."

Who the hell did this shrimp think he was? Jim nodded. "So who do you think did it?" Let the smart ass answer that.

Brockhurst leaned back in his chair, tapped the file folder he was holding against his good knee. "Well, I had some blowups made of the victim. There were no hesitation marks, so suicide is out."

Jim laughed out loud. "Suicide?"

"It's not that uncommon, especially among the elderly; it's the first thing we try to rule out. You'll find shallow cuts, the initial stabs the victim made while working up his courage to kill himself." Brockhurst paused and looked back at the folder. "By the way, I didn't see the results here from the DNA semen test."

Jim was quiet for a second. "We couldn't have a test run. See, the county coroner was a good friend of Sarah's family.

When he took her over to the hospital for the autopsy, he was so upset he cleaned her up; he wasn't thinking straight and he rinsed off the body. When Ed Hammond got there to do the autopsy, it was too late to do anything about it.''

"You mean to tell me the evidence was destroyed?"

The police chief shook his head. "I'm afraid so. Like I was telling you, though, the whole town is convinced it's this black woman who lives in the swamp."

"You've questioned her, I gather?"

"No, not just yet." Jim didn't look Brockhurst in the eye. "See, there's been so much to take care of here, what with how stirred up everybody's been. This is a one-man office. Buck Henry—he's the county sheriff—did go out there but he never could find her. I thought you guys would want to be in on her questioning, anyway."

"I'll want to see her right away, of course," Brockhurst said. "But what bothers me about her is the statistical improbability: over 95 percent of all sex murders, and this one certainly has sexual overtones, are committed by men." He paused, then went on, "The massive facial injuries are our strongest lead. Usually that means the victim and the attacker knew each other. An act of revenge, for example, almost always involves facial injuries. However, none of this constitutes real evidence."

Jim looked annoyed. What did it matter then?

The SLED agent went on, "I approach a case by trying to understand the psychology, especially when there's so little physical evidence. A man who masturbates after killing a woman is likely a man who masks his insecurity about sex with exaggerated machismo—that's my guess, anyway. He really feels threatened by sex, by women; sometimes he will feel his sexual responses are a power women have over him against his will. Power is what the whole thing is about anyway, or so our crime psychiatrist is always telling me. Many rapists actually hate women. Some will later attack that part of the woman which sets her apart as feminine—her breasts or vagina, for example. That's the story behind cases of mutilation. He'll think: she controlled me with these, now I've taken them away from her."

"That's crazy," Jim sputtered. "Mrs. Roth was seventy-six years old and a widow. She wasn't having sex with anybody."

"That may be. But I feel like a sex offender could be involved." Brockhurst opened the folder on his lap. "The guy would probably have a record of minor violations—Peeping Tom, obscene phone calls, breaking and entering. The excitement for the perpetrator is often the ritual he goes through, what he said, what he did, being in the victim's home. I once worked a rape case where the rapist always wanted the husband in the house and always had a leisurely cup of coffee afterward in the kitchen. The act—of whatever nature—is least important. Everything leading up to the crime is more exciting to him. Stalking the victim, entering the house, that kind of thing. Anyone around here with a history of minor offenses, including sex offenses?''

"No," Jim said. "You think it's some kind of psycho?"

Lou Brockhurst stared at the other man. "That depends on your definition of psychotic. But no, I don't think so." The SLED agent looked back down at the folder. "I would guess our man is in his mid-twenties to mid-thirties. It might be a guy who's never exhibited violent behavior before. If he is psychotic, it's possible he's lived a perfectly normal life up until now. Some psychotics do, then they abruptly reach a crisis point and they explode." Brockhurst's voice was quiet and serious. "The problem is—once the guy's exploded, it's usually not long until he kills again."

"You keep saying *he*," Jim argued. "According to our doctor, Sarah wasn't technically raped. This black woman in the swamp had a jar of semen in her house. She showed up at Sarah's funeral and acted very odd. She is certifiably looney, all you gotta do is look at her. Then there was the goat who was cut up, scaring people to death. Voodooists sacrifice animals, use knives to kill them, I'm told. None of this means anything to you?" Jim stopped. It occurred to him more and more lately how much simpler things would be if Maum Chrish did prove to be guilty.

"It's a convincing circumstantial case, yes, and I sure intend to check her out. I'm planning to do the same to J. T. Turner. Was this Maum Chrish ever seen with the victim, did they know each other?"

Jim nodded negatively. "Not that we know of."

Brockhurst stood up. "Let me make a few calls and then we'll pay Maum Chrish a visit." He walked to the door, his good leg leading the way. "After that I want to talk to Turner. Oh, also"—he turned around—"I'll need to speak to the fellow who found the victim. What's his name? McFarland?"

Career Day at Essex High, held later than usual this year to accommodate an almost-famous marine biologist from Beaufort, was almost over. Marian Davis stood at the rear door of the cafeteria. In front of her, teenagers lounged at conference tables as Anna McFarland walked among them holding matted black-and-white photo enlargements. Anna was electric when she talked about her work; her face glowed and her eyes radiated pure energy. She and Marian had not spoken, except perfunctorily, since that afternoon in Marian's classroom, but Marian found herself listening intently anyway.

"Actually I think Walker Evans was the best distillation we've had yet of the work of Jacob Riis and Lewis Hine," Anna was saying, concluding her review of the history of photography. "That is, in giving us truth without too much sentiment. We now call it the documentary style and Evans' pictures of the Depression set the modern standard for it."

Next Anna talked about what constituted bad photography. She held up pictures of a barn, a cemetery, a white clapboard church. "There is no story in these. A great photo has vision, a good one has a concept, a poor one has neither. An old barn can be interesting but that doesn't necessarily make it a meaningful concept, much less a vision. And it certainly doesn't make it art."

When Anna finished, several students raised their hands and asked practical questions; Anna advised them to study composition and to spend more money on a good lens and a good tripod than on the camera body. The questions tapered off and Marian went to the front of the room, thanked all the speakers, and dismissed the program. Knots of students formed around the adults whose careers interested them and Marian noticed two students a few feet away hanging on to Anna's every word. The taller girl was a college-bound senior; she was the oldest daughter of the most affluent black family in Essex. She was leaning toward Anna, a small Canon camera in her hand, asking if she needed a larger format like a Hasselblad. Anna talked to the black girl enthusiastically, while the other student, Marynell Pittman's younger sister, stood beside them silently.

Marian ached for Amy Pittman. Who would give her a camera? Who would even notice she was interested in anything? And of course, Anna was talking almost exclusively to the other girl. Marian frowned. Anna tended her liberal reputation more fervently than Harriet did her garden.

The marine biologist stopped Marian, to say goodbye, and when she turned back around, she didn't see Anna and the two girls. Then she spotted Anna and Amy over by a window. Anna was taking her expensive Leica out of a camera bag. She held it toward the girl, who seemed afraid to touch it. Anna put the camera into Amy's hands. "Try it. Look through the lens. Get the feel of it. Come on, fire a few shots out the window." Then Marian heard Anna tell Amy the story of Dorothea Lang, whose impoverished background had not prevented her from becoming a famous photographer. Soon Amy was giggling as she looked through the Leica's lens.

In fifteen minutes everyone was gone and the cafeteria was empty, save for Marian and Anna, who was packing up her equipment. She didn't notice Marian until the other woman stood in front of her.

"You were terrific," Marian said. "I know Amy appreciated the attention."

"I liked her." Anna tied her portfolio shut and picked it up. "Well, I'll see you."

She was almost to the door when Marian's voice stopped her. "Anna, wait."

Marian walked toward Anna. When they stood within touching distance, Marian said, "Thanks again." She paused and added, "You know, if you're still interested, I've got a book about African voudou I'd be happy to lend you. Why don't you come by and get it sometime?"

Anna studied Marian's mahogany eyes for a second. Then she smiled.

Lou Brockhurst and Jim Leland stood in front of Maum Chrish's cabin and stared at each other helplessly. The large black woman on the porch glared down at them, impassive as a statue. The policemen had been there for half an hour and still Maum Chrish had said nothing which made sense.

"Ma'am, we have to know where you were the night Sarah Rothenbarger was killed," Jim repeated, his voice as monotonous as a child reciting memory work. "That was April 12th." A pause. "I don't think you realize the position you're in. I suggest you cooperate this time. That'll make it easier on everyone, including you."

The dark woman opened her mouth. "It came the night of the Dark Satellite," she intoned, her clear musical voice filling the clearing. "Not evil, but the absence of light, statis, the failure to ascend. When the fire of heaven and the water of earth mix without the air to reconcile, the absence of their mediator."

Lou Brockhurst studied Maum Chrish closely. Maybe she was crazy and maybe she wasn't. One thing was interesting, which had apparently eluded everyone else. This was not an uneducated woman. She hadn't been in this swamp forever.

Maum Chrish spoke again: "Who walked the night of the Dark Satellite will be felled. Will descend to a place, fouled, filled with countless forms like beasts. There will unfold scenes of infamy but this one cannot be with it now. The lack of a physical body is a tormenting viper. This one is forever tantalized, constantly seeks that which can never be attained now. Punishment by the sin."

Jim Leland shook his head and muttered under his breath, "She's a fruitcake." He cleared his throat, said more loudly, "Once again, ma'am, can you tell us where you were the night of April 12th? Why did you attend Sarah Roth's funeral, did you know her? How often do you and—your people—kill goats? Can you tell us why a jar of male semen has been found in your house?"

The woman said nothing. Brockhurst turned and looked in the direction Maum Chrish was staring. A murky mist shrouded the swamps, an extension of the overcast skies above. Something moved in the woods and instinctively he felt for his revolver. Then something else moved, on the other side of the clearing this time. Brockhurst squinted. A black man wearing nothing but a pair of white shorts stepped out of the dark thicket and moved slowly toward the house. On the other side of the river a black woman wearing a long white caftan also stepped forward. Leland was talking about Maum Chrish but Brockhurst kept his eyes on the two black people moving toward them. Trouble? In a second he saw two more blacks step out of the woods; they were wearing red, both males, boys of eighteen or so, who also edged slowly toward the cabin, keeping a ritualistic distance between the other blacks dressed in white. Brockhurst tapped Jim on the shoulder and nodded toward the yard below them. Jim's eyes widened as he saw the four black people advancing.

Maum Chrish was still peering into the woods and Brockhurst had the eeriest feeling that she had summoned these people. The man and woman in white reached the edge of the shack and stood at separate corners of it like military sentries, backs perfectly straight, eyes distant and noncommittal. As Brockhurst and Jim watched, the young men dressed in red crossed behind the older blacks and took their places at the other two corners of the house, affecting the same posture.

"They're guarding her," Brockhurst said in a terse whisper. "At least I think they are. But they don't have weapons."

Jim Leland, who had grown up around tales of voodoo, shivered. "They may not need any."

Brockhurst counted to twenty, and waited. Nothing. The four people at the four corners of the house remained immobile. He took a deep breath finally, withdrew a document from inside his coat pocket, and turned back to Maum Chrish. "This is a search warrant, ma'am. It gives us permission to search your home." Sweat rolled down Brockhurst's temples. He did not like being outnumbered. "If you won't cooperate with us, we have no alternative but to exercise it."

The SLED agent nodded at Jim and started up the wooden steps. When Jim didn't follow, Brockhurst pivoted and frowned at the other man until Jim moved forward.

Maum Chrish shrank back against the doorway of her cabin. "Sacred," she hissed. She spread her arms wide. "The cemetery, the crossroads, and Grans Bwa, there will happen."

Brockhurst said, "Stand aside, please."

The black woman didn't budge. This time her voice was low, murderous. "*Oum'phor* sacred."

Both men surveyed the corners of the cabin. None of the blacks had moved. Abruptly Brockhurst jerked around, angled full-circle. Out beyond the house more black people were now standing in the yard, mostly women and children, some in rags, some in white cloth, just standing there staring. Where did they all come from? Even the children were motionless, silent effigies called upon to witness the moment. Brockhurst perspired harder and recalled the case in Rhett Cemetery in Beaufort. He stared into the faces of the women and children; none of them contained anger or aggression. It was a psychological scare tactic, he decided. And a damn good one.

"Take her arm," he ordered Jim. Brockhurst grabbed the other arm and together they physically forced Maum Chrish away from the door of her house. The black woman walked down the steps and was immediately encircled by the women and children.

The white men entered the cabin. For a few minutes neither said anything, just gaped at the post, the floor designs, the drawings on the walls. Then they heard footsteps. Jim looked up in terror and Brockhurst tensed. The two men in white marched inside the front door. They separated, then went and stood in the two front corners of the room. In a second the men in red entered the room by way of the back door and took up their posts in the rear two corners.

"Jesus Christ," Jim whispered. "I don't like how they're watching us."

Jim and the SLED agent stood close together near the post in the center of the room. "I thought maybe it was just talk about her and voodoo," Jim added sotto voce. Brockhurst walked over to one side of the room. The Essex police chief followed quickly, one eye cocked on the teenager in the corner. The Columbia detective stopped at each drawing and examined it. At one set of symbols his right eyebrow shot up. He lingered there for a moment. Then the white men moved in unison to the table on the other side of the room.

Brockhurst stared at the collection of knives. He touched the only knife that was serrated on one side, with a seven-inch blade. "Why would a woman keep a hunting knife like this?"

"To butcher animals—like chickens and goats," Jim said. "The serrated side will saw through small animal bones."

"We need to take this in," Brockhurst added. He walked over to the man in the front right corner of the room, the oldest of the blacks in the house, and explained that he needed to confiscate the knife for evidence, that it would be returned later if the suspicion about Maum Chrish proved groundless, that it would be well taken care of in the meantime. Jim waited for the black man to make Brockhurst disappear or turn him into a toad, but the sentry merely inclined his head ever so slightly, as though he understood and accepted the policeman's explanation. Brockhurst crossed back to Jim and slipped the knife in a clear plastic bag. Then he went into the back room of the cabin, Jim shadowing, and searched the bed and an old trunk that contained nothing but white pieces of cloth. There was no sign of Sarah Roth's silver, nor anything else taken the night of the murder. Finally Brockhurst sat down on the rope bed and said, "Not much here."

In a few seconds they walked back into the front room and Brockhurst deliberately crossed to the opposite wall and stood looking at it for a moment. Jim stared at the black people in the corners and wondered if he and Brockhurst would yet be hexed. Or worse. When Brockhurst nodded, they went back outside and looked around. The yard was empty now; even Maum Chrish was gone. Brockhurst paused for a moment and stared into the burning fire near the edge of the swamp, glancing back at the house from time to time. The live oaks around it stood like tenacious centurions whose armies had fled; only they remained behind to guard this enclave.

Walking back through the woods toward the car, Brockhurst asked the Essex police chief, "Sarah Roth was really Sarah Rothenbarger, right? She was Jewish?"

"Yeah. People dropped the end of her name years back."

Brockhurst came to a stop and gazed at the other man. "Answer me something: why would a black woman who practices voodoo have the Hebrew alphabet on her wall?"

It wasn't until Stoney tried to tell Lou Brockhurst about finding Sarah Roth's body that he realized he had no conscious memory of that night. Even in the Ashton sheriff's report Stoney's statement was garbled, nearly incoherent, and his attempts to recount that night for the Columbia detective were even worse. Stoney talked at length about the phone call from Harriet Setzler, his walk to Sarah's house in the moonlight, finding Sarah's front door locked and the back door open. But once he stepped over the threshold he went blank; he could remember almost nothing upon entering Sarah's house. "I opened the door and went in and . . ."

"And what?" Lou Brockhurst, seated behind Jim Leland's desk in the police chief's absence, leaned forward. "What did you see first?"

Stoney's eyes were fixed on a distant planet. He blinked. "I don't know. I found her."

"Right away? Or after a while? Did you notice anything, hear anything?"

The engineer held up his palms uselessly. "I don't remember."

"Good God, man, you must remember something. She was on her bed covered with blood. You couldn't forget that."

Stoney closed his eyes. There was the door, the back door of Sarah's house; he saw the doorknob, saw himself turn it, saw his reflection, the moon behind him, in the window panes of the door as it opened. Then—darkness. Nothing. Like a "Twilight Zone" episode, in which someone steps over the boundary of a different world. Nothing there. No blood, no dead woman, no smell, nothing. He looked back at Brockhurst. "I don't understand it, but I just can't seem to remember."

The SLED agent took out a pack of chewing gum and stared at Stoney as he unwrapped a stick. "You ever see a murder victim before?"

"When I was real young, once. In D.C. An old drunk some-one had rolled: they hit him on the head and left him in a ditch."

"Do you remember that?"

"Vividly."

When Stoney refused his offer, Brockhurst put the pack of chewing gum back in his shirt pocket. "Sometimes the mind will block these things out. It'll probably come back to you. What I'd like to do—"

The door opened and in waltzed Heyward Rutherford. He crossed to Brockhurst and put out his hand. "I'm Heyward Rutherford, president of the Essex Town Council. I just wanted to welcome you to town. You need anything, you let me know. I'll see that it gets done. It's great to have you here and we'll sure be glad when this whole thing is settled."

Brockhurst got to his feet during the obviously rehearsed speech and took Heyward's proffered hand. "That's very kind of you. I'll be glad when the case is cleared up too."

Heyward said hello to Stoney, then turned back to Brock-hurst. "Jim tells me you questioned Maum Chrish. Any the-ories about her yet?"

"It's a little early to start speculating about anyone," the SLED agent said. "I prefer not to discuss suspects until I'm sure of my facts. When that happens, there'll be an arrest. You can count on that."

The taller man clapped the detective on the back. "Well, good to have you here. Let us know if you need anything."

After Heyward left, Brockhurst sat back down and said to Stoney, "Nice fellow. Sure is eager to help."

"That's Heyward all right. Eager. He *is* Real Estate around here. I hear he's buying Sarah's store, seems he's wanted it for a long time."

Brockhurst looked up. "That so?" He surveyed Stoney's face, wondered if the other man was trying to tell him something. Stoney's face was inscrutable. All the same, Brockhurst de-cided, it was worth checking into later.

Stoney again tried to remember what he had seen at Sarah's house the night of the murder and Brockhurst egged him on by reading the Ashton sheriff's report aloud. They were halfway through it when someone else knocked on the door. "This is a busy place," Brockhurst said. He called out louder, "Come on in."

The door opened and Jim Leland walked in followed by Leonard Hansen. Jim waved at Brockhurst, whom he liked better since the trip to the swamps. "Thought you two might want some coffee." He set two steaming Styrofoam cups down on the desk. Then he introduced Brockhurst and Leonard.

Brockhurst stood and shook hands a second time. Leonard Hansen had unforgettable eyes, he thought, almost purple, the right one a deeper shade than the left. His face was broad and flat, with bushy eyebrows and a large nose. Above his upper lip was a slight split, remnant of either an uncorrected harelip or some childhood injury, and it gave his face a slight vulnerability that stood in sharp contrast to his small, cruel mouth. Altogether, though, he had the Elvis-style brutishness women always loved.

Leonard pumped Brockhurst's hand. "Nice to have you in town. You need any help, I'm pretty used to handling a gun, being in the Marines and all."

Stoney studied Leonard carefully. The other man looked perfectly sincere. He and Brockhurst talked about the firearms used in Vietnam for a moment, while Jim fumbled through his desk looking for something. Once or twice Leonard glanced at Stoney, as though trying to include him in the conversation. When Jim finally found the document he was searching for, he said he'd be back in a second and left the room again.

"Don't wanna keep you," Leonard concluded, his eyes on the Columbia detective. "But if you need anything, just give a yell. I'm around all hours." He nodded at Stoney, brushing his blond hair out of his eyes. "How's it going, McFarland?"

"Okay, Leonard."

When Leonard left, Brockhurst eyed Stoney thoughtfully. "This is a very helpful town, 'though I don't expect to have to form a posse." A silence. "He work for the town too?"

"No. He did live with Sarah once, by the way."

"He lived with the dead woman? How old is he?"

"It wasn't like that." Stoney smiled. "It was years ago, when he got out of the service. His parents had moved away from town and he came back here and Sarah took him in for a while. He didn't have a job and she had a real soft spot for those down on their luck. But it seems Leonard stole some money from her before it was over."

"How do you know that?" Brockhurst sat forward; most small-towners didn't gossip about their own to the law—unless there was a good reason for it. After Stoney explained, Brockhurst said, "Sarah Roth's penchant for taking in stray people really bothers me. Anybody could have killed her."

Stoney agreed and rose to leave. That the murder had been a random incident by a stranger Sarah befriended truly made more sense than Leonard or Heyward, if you discounted the goat incident. No stranger would stay around town to play tricks to make Maum Chrish look guilty. Unless, of course, the town was right and Maum Chrish really was the killer and the dead animal was her own handiwork. Stoney sighed. He had also told Brockhurst about J. T. Turner's proclivity for jewelry and the SLED agent would be questioning him in a day or two. Sometimes the nervous stranger did seem the most likely answer.

Out on the street Stoney headed toward his office. Near the post office he saw Leonard Hansen again, leaning against the brick wall talking to a woman Stoney didn't know very well. Stoney was almost past them when Leonard called out, "So what'd you think of the big-city detective?"

The woman smiled at both men and headed for her car. Stoney stopped and faced Leonard. If this was a man who'd committed murder, he sure was cool. "I think he'll find out who killed Sarah and lock him up."

Leonard's eyes flickered. "Him. So you don't buy the swamp woman theory?"

"Do you?"

"Naw, not really."

"Who do you think did it, Leonard? I mean, you stayed with Sarah for that time way back, you know how she was about asking strange people home for dinner. Think maybe that had something to do with it?"

Leonard leaned in closer, his voice conspiratorial. "You know, I really don't. I think it was somebody here in town. Somebody with a score to settle. That's what I think." Leonard smiled. "I better get going. See ya later."

Stoney stared as the other man walked off. It couldn't be Leonard, nobody had balls like that. Stoney started for his office again, thinking about a summer day over twenty years before. . . .

It started at the McCloskey pond. A game of ducks and drakes. Everyone else eliminated, only Stoney and Lenny Hansen left in. The kids usually let Lenny win, they knew what happened when he lost. But today everyone stood around shouting at Stoney, "Get 'im, Stone. Beat 'im." Lenny pitched a flat rock across the pond; it bounced across the surface but then fell out of sight a few feet from the opposite shore. The tall blond kid rocked back on his heels, turned to Stoney, and sneered,

"Beat that." Stoney walked over to the edge of the pond. Once or twice he'd thrown stones that actually jumped across the water and landed on the other side. He took aim at the opposite bank, leaned in, and sent his rock sailing. Cheers rose as the stone tap-danced on the flat surface of the water—boink-boink-boink-boink—and then came to rest with a final plop. On the other bank.

Stoney never knew what hit him. It came from behind, an elbow around his neck pulling him backward, a hard fist flying into the small of his back. Then he was pinned to the ground, straddled by a heavier body. Over and over again a fist slammed into his jaw, slapped at his head, as someone shouted at him, "You Yankee prick." Another fist to the face and blood gushed from Stoney's nose, he could taste it in his mouth. What was that hard thing? A tooth?

Stoney reared up as hard as he could, arms flailing, legs kicking. The weight riding his stomach overpowered him again. A fist slammed into his belly. Enough already! Suddenly Stoney arched his back and took Lenny by surprise, managed to connect with the larger boy's right shoulder. Lenny sat back. The blow had barely grazed him but he had a surprised look on his face. He hadn't expected Stoney to fight back.

Defiance galvanized the troops. The other boys had been standing back but now they rushed forward and surrounded the two on the ground. "Kill him, Stoney!"

"Yeah, show him. Hit *him* for a change."

Lenny glared at the group and that was Stoney's second advantage as the smaller, lighter man. Hesitation made them equals, if only for a moment. Stoney scrambled from underneath Lenny and wriggled free. Lenny caught Stoney by the legs and threw him back down on the ground. Stoney punched Lenny in the nose and blood splattered all over them both. *"You prick!"* Lenny yelled, his eyes glazed. He grabbed a rock from the pile on the ground and slammed it into Stoney's chest as hard as he could. Then Stoney blacked out.

For several days after the Career Day program, Anna had sequestered herself in her studio. She had an assignment on Daufuskie Island due to a Savannah advertising agency soon, but it was old work she studied as she leaned over her desk. Spread out in front of her, in five rows, lay all of her favorite photographs. Street scenes in D.C., sunsets and sunrises on the Potomac, inaugurations and senators whispering to each other in the halls of the Capitol, the black men hawking oysters in the Lexington Market in Baltimore, a Chinese man touching Abe's foot respectfully at the Lincoln Memorial one winter dawn, the old Agnew pictures and the anti-abortion picketers outside the gates of the White House with their miniature coffins, Stoney in a white T-shirt with huge headphones over his ears crooning to himself beside the stereo in their Georgetown apartment, her father in front of his house in Phoenix a month before his heart attack.

Her own voice echoed in her brain: "A great photo has vision, a good one has a concept, a poor one has neither."

She looked at the more recent pictures. The successive study of a live oak as evening shadows moved across it, the herons feeding in the marshes near Hilton Head, the cornfield she'd shot from a water tower to replicate its endlessness, the women under helmet hair dryers through the plate glass window of the Essex beauty shop. Only the last one interested her at all. Anna leaned back in her chair and sighed, closing her eyes. Maybe she was too devoted to Walker Evans' long lens—to its distance. If only she could photograph what she felt these days—you could use the camera to expose or enhance but you should not use it just to record. The camera should deepen experience, reality. She got up and walked into the kitchen and looked out at the back yard. For several minutes she studied the live oaks. Sturdy, strong, suspicious, stunted. They mimicked human nature. Concept become vision. Anna blinked and for a second she saw Maum Chrish in the trunk of a live oak. At the oddest moments, when she was daydreaming or just staring into space, the image of the riverbank would crawl in front of her eyes and she'd see the naked woman singing to the skies, follow again the erotic pull of the couple on the wall of the cabin. But she had not been out there again. She was afraid now. Perhaps of more than whoever took her camera.

Anna had almost abandoned photography once. But who would she be without a camera, she asked Stoney. "I don't want you to quit," he said. "But I think it's a mistake to cling to a profession because you think it defines you. You assume that what makes you special, what makes you interesting, is your work as a photographer. I don't. You were special first. The camera only added to the picture."

He was so wise, but he'd been wrong. He had been talking about himself, even if he didn't realize it. Anna walked back in her studio and stared down at her best pictures. She had always defined herself through them. It was far easier.

Depressed, she walked back into the kitchen and got her keys and headed out to the Subaru. The next hour she spent at the ancient Piggly Wiggly downtown. When her groceries were in the trunk, she started up her car and pulled away from the curb, not at all anxious to get back home to the pictures on her desk. To avoid them, she turned onto Aiken Avenue at the fire hall and drove past the telephone company and the water tower. A few minutes later she stopped in the unlikeliest place of all for her—Harriet Setzler's house.

Harriet's eyebrows kissed her hairline when she saw who was standing on the other side of her door. Anna, unsure, mouthed something about the azaleas around the McCloskey house dying, how Stoney said the other woman would know how to save them. Harriet gazed at Anna for a second. So, Mrs. High-and-Mighty wasn't too proud to come begging when she needed something, huh? Well, no one would ever say Harriet Youmans Setzler was rude to a neighbor. No matter who the neighbor was.

Presently Harriet took Anna on a tour of her garden and pointed out at great length how well *her* azaleas were doing. Anna nodded her head in agreement; the yard was spectacular. "Your flowers really are wonderful," Anna said. "I don't understand gardening, I guess. We never had to do any in Washington. What I mean is, you can work so hard on it and yet if it doesn't rain or gets too hot, it'll all die anyway. No matter what you do."

The older woman looked at Anna as though at a child who had yet to learn self-discipline. "You must be patient, diligent. I enjoy working out here. I'm more at home in my yard than anywhere else," she said, glancing up at her house. "I like to see beautiful things grow up around me. You might say"—she paused for a second—"it's an art. You put everything in the right place and tend it carefully. My garden belongs to me. When I got married, there was nothing here but grass. Now there's this. And I created it all myself." Harriet reached down and broke a dead stem off a gardenia bush. "We do need rain though." Then, "I had to start from scratch twice."

Anna was staring at the old lady. Behind her was a huge live oak. Impulsively Anna asked, "Mrs. Setzler, could I take your picture sometime?"

"My picture?"

"Yes. I'm a photographer, you know. I'd really like to some-time, out here, with the live oak behind you just like this."

"Oh I don't know." Harriet was actually thinking which dress and hat to wear. "Maybe, if it means that much to you."

Anna smiled. "I'll call you and bring my camera over one day." She had almost forgotten the azaleas now. "What was it you were saying about having to start your garden twice?"

"They ruined it," Harriet exclaimed sharply. "Stoney never told you about the trouble we had with the Nigras? Oh I guess he wasn't here then but I thought certain he knew about it."

Can I photograph that too? Anna wondered. Can I get her pronunciation of that word on film? Nigra? She voiced Stoney's wisdom on the subject absently: "There wasn't any racial trouble in Essex, I thought."

"That's not so." The old lady put her hands on her hips. "We had our share of bad days for a while. When those outside people came in and stirred everybody up. About changing the schools over. I've always gotten along with every color in this town but I'm not one to pretend even now: I was against it from the beginning. Anyway, one night a group of them got liquored up and came in my yard and hacked off every shrub, every flower, every bush." Harriet trembled, remembering. "Most of the small plants died; even those that lived didn't bloom for two or three years afterward."

That hardly sounded like racial trouble to Anna. Maybe an extreme response to Harriet Setzler's basic personality, but not much more. "You didn't have real riots here?"

"No, nothing like that. Course there's always been that question about ole Monkey. Black man, worked for me a long time. Those outside people got hold of him and got him all steamed up and the coloreds went along with it, listened to him, made him their leader in a way. Then one day Monkey just up and disappeared. Nobody ever saw him again, nobody has since. After he was gone, things settled down; the coloreds went about their business like before. He was the starch in their sheets."

"Are you implying what I think?" Anna's eyes were wide. "That someone got rid of him?"

"All I know is we never saw Monkey again. Last time anyone ever saw him, he was arguing with a group of white men down-town about being served in the diner. Next day he was gone." Harriet's voice quavered slightly. "He never said goodbye to his family and his things were still in his house."

"You think he was killed?"

Despite Anna's urging, Harriet would say no more. She took Anna around to the back of her house, to the toolshed where she kept the fertilizer she put on her azaleas, a concoction she mixed up herself. She gave Anna some of it in a plastic garbage bag. "Try that," she said. "It oughta perk them up, even in this heat." Anna, holding the pungent bag at arm's length, thanked the old lady and they walked back around to her car.

"I better get my groceries home before everything spoils," Anna said then. She thanked Harriet again and got in her car. The older woman walked up her steps slowly and went over to sit in her porch swing. As Anna started her car, Harriet was scanning her yard protectively and against the backdrop of the bountiful, fecund property, she looked for a moment like a feudal lord, powerful and secure. Anna focused on the other woman, using her eye as lens. But as she drove away, she took the lens off. Her naked eye looked back and caught a glimpse of old eyes. Old eyes unveiled. Old eyes looking down the street, wondering what would disappear next. And for just an instant—despite herself—Anna felt for the lonely despot bereft of all her retainers.

It was the first day of June and that night was hot, thick, and heavy; smells and sensation hung long and low like gorilla arms. The groceries were safely consigned to the pantry and Anna and Stoney sat at the trestle table in their kitchen. She picked at her salad and from time to time smoothed a hand across the polyurethaned beech tabletop; it was as cool and slick to the touch as chilled apple skin. The back door was open as well as the windows, and outside the coming night descended on the yard with clouds of violet steam. Anna yearned to go over and stand at the back door alone, to give in to that dark warm air rather than fight it, to let it take her. Every so often Stoney said something about the music wafting into the kitchen from the living room stereo. Anna agreed vaguely to whatever he said, without hearing, and watched him. He wore a yellow chambray shirt, bright and loose, tucked into white jeans and he was already tan; his arms below his rolled shirtsleeves were the color of honey and she liked their strength, how the thick muscles rode the length of his forearm.

He moved his arm suddenly and grinned and beat out the rhythm from the other room on the table. Music had always been a ballast in their relationship and tonight Stoney had selected a recording of Louis Armstrong and his Hot Seven playing the blues in the late twenties, without orchestration, just the naked lowdown exhilaration of the jazz instruments. "It's hard to believe," Stoney said suddenly, "that the blues consisted of only three chords in a twelve-measure frame—God, what they did with those three chords." He stopped and listened to the New Orleans–inspired trumpet solo. The raw and searing sound took flight again until they both sat still listening, held captive in its emotional power, dinner all but forgotten.

Our relationship is like music, Anna thought. It sounds so good but the chords beneath the harmonic structure may be flawed after all. She was about to suggest as much when Stoney picked up his glass of wine and said, "Let's go listen in the living room." He got up and turned away, beating out the rhythm against his leg with his hand.

By the time Anna joined him, he had changed the record, was sitting on the floor beside the stereo reading the back of an album cover. She was about to say something again, about what she was feeling about them, when he laid the album cover down and said, "I keep thinking about the other day, about Leonard Hansen and Heyward Rutherford both showing up to meet Lou Brockhurst. I know it doesn't add up, but I still think Leonard may have killed Sarah. Despite what he said to me on the street— the guy's so damn brazen."

Sitting on the floor, leaning back against the sofa, Anna wanted to scream. She was sick of Sarah Roth's murder, sick of the town of Essex, sick of Stoney's incessant obsession about both, sick of all of it, sick of being here, of feeling so . . .

"It's just a matter of proving it," Stoney was saying.

She wondered if he knew why she'd put the Indian rug beneath them in this exact spot, whether he could smell the gardenias blooming across the street, why he needed music and murder to express his emotions.

"But why do you have to prove it? That SLED agent is here, can't you just leave it up to him?"

He gazed at her over the rim of his wineglass. "This time, Anna, I have to *do* something—instead of just letting things happen." He thought for a moment about what his father once said to him: You just coast along, son, and you are never going to have much of a life if you keep it up. The argument, that sleeting winter day in Virginia, had been about Stoney's college plans: the boy wanted to go to a jock university and major in physical education, become a coach or trainer or sportswriter now that professional baseball was out. The father wanted the child to take life more seriously: a man couldn't play games for a living. He also wanted his son close to home where he could keep an eye on him. And Stoney loved his father, so his father won.

"Stoney, Sarah Roth's murder really has nothing to do with you." Anna's voice was tired. Would he talk so eagerly about the things that did have to do with him, with them?

The music ended and without it the room lost altitude like a damaged plane. Anna knew she should stop but she went on anyway, "Isn't Leonard Hansen just a scapegoat? Someone you can blame for the fact Essex really isn't the paradise you remember?"

He glared at her. "I need more wine." He got up and walked out of the room.

Anna followed him. He was at the counter pouring more wine in his glass. Couldn't he sense she needed him to be with her tonight, not trying to repair this damn town? "You're all wrong about Essex, you always have been. Did you know that during the sixties a black man working for desegragation here was probably murdered? A man they called *Monkey*!"

Stoney flinched. He jerked around. "What?"

"Harriet Setzler more or less said a black man was killed here during the Civil Rights movement."

Stoney's lips trembled and his voice was flat, came out one word at a time. "Monkey was *killed*?"

"The last time the guy was ever seen, he was arguing with some white men, over whether he could be served in that horrible diner downtown. You always said there was no racial trouble here and I guess there wasn't—not after they murdered the first black man with guts enough to speak up."

Stoney grabbed Anna by the shoulders. *"Why are you doing this?"* He released her abruptly, turned away, and leaned over the kitchen counter. "My God. No wonder no one talks about him anymore."

"I didn't know you knew him." Anna stared at Stoney, then her eyes narrowed. "Oh no—he was the baseball guy? I didn't realize."

Stoney whipped back around. "Would it have made any difference?" He stared at Anna with black ice in his eyes. "Since when did you ever yield your fucking principles for the sake of not hurting someone?"

He turned and slammed out the back door. She went after him as far as the storm door, leaned against it, and watched him stalk down the sidewalk toward the pond. Spanish moss loomed low over his head at the end of the concrete path and he reached out and angrily pushed it aside, yanked a strand of it loose, and threw it on the ground behind him. Then Anna couldn't see him anymore, he disappeared among the live oaks. Had she finally pushed him away for good?

The tears were hot on her face. When had she realized theirs wasn't the perfect marriage, when had she drawn back— literally, physically—almost as if to say, well, this can't possibly be my fault? The alternative, the truth, had been too painful. Admit that intellectual compatibility had failed them? Acknowledge that she had only trusted him with the safe stuff: her ideas and opinions. Never with her weaknesses, her frailties, her deepest fears.

Abruptly she remembered once when they were making love, years and years ago. They had spent the evening with friends and after the other couple had left, she and Stoney stayed up until two in the morning arguing in good humor about abstract expressionism. Then they fell into bed and made love as they usually did in those days, very simply, some foreplay, mission- ary or her on top, mutual orgasm or close, sleep. That night, however, she lay awake a long time afterward. All that intellect, the sex, their obvious love for each other, and still something was missing. She yearned to roll over against him and tell him how she sometimes worried she preferred being on top too much, her fear that she needed to be in control of sex to enjoy it, that she could relax only in a position Rand Ayres had never used. She was neurotic, yes? She ached to have Stoney reassure her— as she felt certain he would—that she wasn't sick, that she didn't need to emasculate men, that sometimes the apparatus worked better one way than another, and why worry about such a good thing anyway? She could tell him so much, but she could not tell him this. And this was far more important.

They did not talk about Essex any more that night. Rather, Stoney stayed outside until long after Anna went upstairs, alone, to bed.

Nine

STONEY STOOD ON the porch of Sarah Roth's house and stared at the FOR SALE sign. Sarah's cousin had finally accepted Heyward Rutherford's offer on the store, but no one seemed interested in the old house. Stoney gazed around at the paint peeling on the floorboards and the cobwebs hanging in the eaves like decorative scrollwork. The house smelled of abandonment and decay.

He turned and looked out at the street. It was the hottest June he could ever remember. Every day dawned hazy and overcast, no brilliant South Carolina sun, no cutouts of dancing light dappling the old trees. Just a heavy dull grayness which covered the town like a tent. By afternoon people grew paralyzed, as lethargic as sleepwalkers. Breathing, speaking, lifting a hand in greeting, simply took too much effort. At four or five o'clock everyone looked to the skies. Surely a thunderstorm would come, would cleanse the humidity, end this pollution. The drama would actually begin: the sky would darken and roar, white flashes would stiletto tree limbs, bushes would claw at each other in the hot wind. Any minute the rain would fall. People waited, prayed for release. *Soon.* Then—suddenly—silence. No more thunder, no lightning, no movement, nothing. Trees very still again. No rain, only the hot dry stillness once more.

Stoney walked back down the steps and followed the sidewalk to the curb, looked both ways, and then retraced his path to the porch. Sweating, he sat down on the steps. Why couldn't he remember that night? He closed his eyes. He visualized the front of Sarah's house, the back door, the doorknob. Then . . . nothing. Darkness, nothing else. His memory was as impotent as the rainclouds.

Of course he should be at work. Sumter Brownlow had probably called out the Thought Police by now. Stoney smirked. The old man had been certain a phone call from a hotshot in Columbia would make the wayward boy "shape up." Brownlow was so much like his own father, a master of the art of well-intended coercion. What he had taken from his father, though, he would not take from anyone else. In fact, he wanted to punch Brownlow in the nose.

Thinking suddenly of fistfights, Stoney reached down and rubbed his stomach. On impulse he pulled his shirt up and stared at a small scar on his stomach. Leonard Hansen's handiwork.

When he came to beside the McCloskey pond, the fight was over and the other boys were gone. It was quiet and all Stoney could see was the sunshine filtering through the live oaks above his head. God he hurt. His chest ached, his head throbbed, blood was still oozing from his nose. But his stomach was the worst. It felt like he'd been split open. He tried to sit up but he was woozy and fell backward onto the ground again. Gingerly he reached out for the middle of his shirt. He pulled it up and felt his belly. It hurt so bad. His fingers touched raw flesh and he cried out. Damn! Several inches above his navel, a hole. He propped himself up and, clamping his teeth together, yanked his shirt off to get a better look. A hole the size of a dime, ringed with black, had been burned into his flesh with a cigarette.

Had Leonard left his mark on everyone he beat up?

Suppose Leonard had just come to Sarah's house to steal. He knew the house, it would be safer than breaking into a strange place. He stole from Sarah once before; he knows that Depression-reared old people still don't put much stock in banks and often keep large amounts of cash on hand. Yet, if he'd come to steal, why wasn't the house trashed, torn up like it would be if someone was looking for valuables? Why would a guy with a good job at Nissan resort to stealing anyway? Maybe he got in and things didn't go as planned, she woke up and found him and he panicked and killed her, then realized what he'd done and got out of there as fast as he could. Leaving three hundred dollars in a bureau drawer and stopping to jerk off on the way out.

Right.

In a second Stoney circled around to the back of Sarah Roth's house. He came to a stop on the stone path that led to the back door, pulled a Swiss Army knife out of his pocket, and opened the largest blade. He crouched, hunched his shoulders, and looked around wildly. He closed his eyes. I've just killed a woman. I'm breathing hard, I'm jumpy as hell, it got outta hand,

I don't know what came over me but she's dead and I gotta get out of here. *Fast.* Stoney looked left and right, then darted around the house keeping to the path, the knife in his right hand. He stopped in the shadows of the front yard, out of the moonlight. Across the street was Harriet Setzler's house, the vacant lot, the Loadholts farther down. I've killed her, it's the middle of the night, I have the knife still on me, I'm fucking scared now, I just meant to rob the old bag. I gotta get rid of this stuff. Gotta ditch the knife. Have I wiped the blood off?

"Stoney!"

He froze, saw an elderly woman on the sidewalk, and automatically lowered the knife. "Hello, Mrs. Fenton, I'm sorry if I scared you."

"You've been over here at Sarah's every day this week. What are you doing with that knife? I don't mind telling you, you're acting peculiar."

Stoney almost grinned, thinking about Elsie Fenton's eccentric refusal to accept daylight saving time. He pocketed the knife. "I know it looks a little funny. I'm trying to figure out how it happened."

The gray-haired matron folded her confident arms across her chest. "That woman came into town and broke in Sarah's house and robbed her and then killed her and put that stuff on the body to cover her tracks. That's how it happened. And we'll all be better off when she's locked up."

Stoney knew Elsie Fenton was only mouthing the general consensus of the town. He babbled some excuse about work and was about to leave, when he noticed the smug satisfaction in her eyes, her assurance that she was right about Maum Chrish. It was a look he had seen, without really acknowledging it, all his life. It meant: we don't say it these days but we all know "one of them" can't be trusted. It was a visual password shared even by enlightened Southerners, sometimes without their realizing it. No one confronted it, so it never really went away.

"But why?" Stoney asked, staring at the woman who lived beside Marian Davis. Did Elsie Fenton secretly include Marian in "one of them"? "Why would Maum Chrish kill Sarah? She's never hurt anybody before. Is it just because she's black?"

Elsie Fenton looked as though she'd been slapped. "You have no cause to speak to me that way, Stoney McFarland. I knew your grandmother, and I know your parents taught you better than that."

The older woman marched off and Stoney turned back to

Sarah's house, wishing for the first time that he and Anna had just stayed in Washington. Traffic and pollution and noise were almost easy to contend with—when compared to the subterranean precepts of a small Southern town.

While Anna McFarland was avoiding the swamps these days, Seth Von Hocke was not. This was the summer he would always remember, that brief page of childhood wherein he explored the world totally independent of the known and the understood. For every child there is this season of genesis, when the patterns of personal evolution are etched onto the psyche in a secret code the adult spends a lifetime trying to unscramble. So Seth ran and jumped and swam and swirled in the full energy of his own consciousness. Still young enough to be attracted to difference rather then repelled, he was making love to the exotic, roiling in that which went beyond the known confines of his world.

Almost every day he tied his bamboo fishing pole to the back of his bicycle and pedaled down the swamp road. He always stopped in the same spot, unstrapped his pole and his can of worms, and disappeared into the woods. The daylight swamps no longer frightened him, and he knew the best fishing was where the water barely moved. So he would settle down by the black water, within sight of her shack. His first visit had been to test himself, to assure himself of his courage now that he was almost a teenager. Most days now he'd munch on an apple and lie on the moist riverbank almost carelessly, staring up at the tree-framed sunlight.

The first time she had appeared she acted like he wasn't even there, she didn't yell at him to leave or anything. Sometimes he didn't see her at all. Once or twice, though, even when she saw him sitting there, she came out of her house and lifted off her robelike dress and dove naked into the dark river. Now it wasn't any big deal. When she climbed out of the water, sometimes she would kneel in front of the fire and sing or pray. Later she'd put on another robe, this one always white, and put something on the spit over the fire. Soon he'd smell sizzling fish; she had two lines that stayed in the water all the time. Occasionally she'd motion him over to eat. They rarely spoke. Seth liked that. With most old people you had to talk, you felt weird around them if you didn't say something, but not with her.

This morning's sun was a brilliant ball of hot wax almost dripping onto the live oaks, the fickle sun that these days was frequently mummified with haze before ten o'clock. Inside the shelter of the trees, where Seth set his pole down and baited his hook, it was cool and protected. He leaned against a tree and threw his line in, looking around for her briefly. He fished for a while. Everyone in town was afraid of her now, even Donny, who kept asking where Seth was going every day. Seth grinned. He enjoyed doing something that scared Donny.

In a few minutes Seth heard her behind him and he turned around. She sat down on the ground and waved him over. He propped his pole between two stones on the riverbank and walked toward her. She was sitting on the ground and had the cards spread out in front of her. Seth gazed at them. He loved it when she played with the cards; they were so bright and interesting, not like any playing cards he'd ever seen before. He even liked the unfamiliar words under the pictures that she'd taught him in one of their rare verbal exchanges—Hieroplant and Magus were his favorites. And Lust. When he asked her to explain it, she didn't act the least bit embarrassed, just said it straight out like it was nothing at all.

Maum Chrish dealt several of the cards, placing them side by side in three rows. She frowned and gathered them up again and reshuffled. The same card resurfaced at the end. Seth didn't like the look on her face when she saw it. He no longer feared the great black woman, but he did respect her. She dealt again. The same card appeared. Seth looked at it and asked what it meant but she put her finger to her lips and reshuffled. When the same card turned up again, he studied it. It had a big eye on its top and what looked like flames of a fire at the bottom. "The tower," she said finally, her singsong voice very low. "The New Aeon."

Maum Chrish got up and went back inside her cabin. Soon Seth heard her singing, although it really sounded more like a moan. Some days she was more interesting than others. About a week ago, she had unnerved Seth to the point that he stayed away for several days. He had come out late in the afternoon for a change, and there'd been some other people there, cinnamon brown girls in white dresses and red scarves and this old black man who just sat and beat a drum all afternoon. When Seth first arrived, they were in a circle around the fire and this huge drawing had been made in front of the fire with sand and they were sorta dancing around it. When they saw him, the girls looked worried but Maum Chrish shook her head, like she was saying he was okay, and then the girls just went back to dancing.

Ignoring the gathering, Seth sat down on the riverbank and baited his hook and threw in his line, but out the corner of his eye he watched the girls—he noticed there were now some guys dancing too. But you could tell Maum Chrish was in charge. The drum was getting louder and louder; two men produced similar drums and knelt down beside the fire and were helping the old guy with the drumming. Maum Chrish was talking, staring into the fire, but Seth couldn't understand a word she said. Suddenly the extra drums stopped. Next a sharp beat sounded on only the old man's drum. Maum Chrish started shaking, her whole body swaying and trembling, like a snake was crawling up her spine; she cried out and crouched low and all the others watched her, even the young goat tied up by the house.

Abruptly Maum Chrish shot up again and whirled around the clearing, reaching out to the others with her hands. Everybody got excited when she touched their hands. She moved faster and faster, turned and dipped and sailed back and forth. Then— suddenly—she stepped through the fire. Seth cringed, but the black woman didn't cry out. Soon the others handed her bags of food and she ate as though starved. Then she whirled around some more while everyone danced and called out to her. In a moment the old drummer stopped, went over and got the goat, and led the animal into the clearing. Everyone quietly gathered around it. Seth saw Maum Chrish lean over the goat, speaking to it softly and petting it. She raised her right hand. The other people moved in closer. And the knife descended.

Seth heard the cry of the goat as he ran toward his bike. The next day he waited to see if parts of the animal would appear on anyone's doorstep. When nothing unusual happened, he decided he'd go back out to the swamps again. Nothing like that had happened again. It was like today. He lay on the damp grass after Maum Chrish took the cards away and he fished, but Maum Chrish didn't reappear and he didn't catch anything. Sometimes she came out of her house and just sat on the steps and read books all day. But even when she wasn't friendly, he liked being here. Nothing was expected of him; it was like being invisible. Sometimes he wondered if the black girl and white guy would ever come out here again, but he never saw them. Of course, he always went home before dark; he was very careful about that.

An hour later Seth picked up his pole and headed back home. On his way out to the road he noticed another set of tire tracks besides his. Made by a 10-speed with smaller tires. Sorta like that fancy Raleigh Donny had.

* * *

Things did not add up to Lou Brockhurst. He had talked to dozens of people now, and still nothing made sense. An elderly woman reportedly liked by everyone had been brutally murdered and there was no motive, no suspect, and no murder weapon. There was a guy who'd wanted her store, a guy who'd stolen from her when he was a kid, a guy who was in the right place at the right time, and who knew how many bums who'd been invited home for a hot meal? And that wasn't even counting all the migrant workers passing through here on their way to Florida. Yet the whole town believed the murderer was an elderly black woman, a trifle off the beam, who had killed for no reason other than voodoo maliciousness. Brockhurst sighed and glanced surreptitiously at the portly man in his twenties who was sitting across from him sweating profusely. The detective wanted J. T. Turner to sit a few more minutes, so he turned his attention back to Maum Chrish.

He didn't buy this voodoo nonsense; if the woman was into human sacrifice for cult reasons, she and her people wouldn't have left the body behind. Yet why did she have the Hebrew alphabet on her wall, wasn't that just too much of a coincidence? (If the town knew about that, they'd really be ready to march her off to a hanging tree.) Had Maum Chrish and Sarah Rothenbarger known each other, had there been something between them that ultimately resulted in murder? Brockhurst had questioned every neighbor who lived near the victim. He reached down and flipped open the small spiral notebook resting on his knee, unconsciously massaging his aching right foot. He'd talked to Elsie Fenton, Harriet Setzler, Mr. and Mrs. Loadholt, Douglas Kendall, the schoolteacher Marian Davis. Brockhurst paused, staring at the last name. Good-looking black woman living there with all those ancient white people, odd. He shook his head again. Not one of them, though, had known of any connection between Maum Chrish and the victim, not one of them had seen or heard anything that night (except Harriet Setzler, whose memory was suspect at best). Not one of them knew of any grudges against the dead woman.

Brockhurst rubbed his eyes. He hated cases in small towns; either the locals talked too much and said nothing or they just said nothing. Could be five or six minidramas going on and they were so tight nobody'd say a word. Scared as they might be, that code was sacred. You might hate 'em worse than taxes, but in this part of the world you didn't criticize your kin or your neighbors in public. Especially to the law. Which made Stoney

McFarland rather unusual. That man had obviously been trying to tell him something without saying it straight out. As a result, yesterday Brockhurst had hung around the only restaurant in town, a diner really, until Heyward Rutherford showed up for lunch and the two men had had a long chat. The town council president was a pompous son of a bitch, Brockhurst had decided, but no killer.

For a moment Brockhurst studied J. T. Turner, then cleared his throat. "Mr. Turner, I'm going to ask you again. Did you know Sarah Rothenbarger? Did you ever meet her?"

The sullen, fat man shook his head no, his guarded eyes furtively searching the corners of the room. He was being detained in an examining room of the Ashton County Law Enforcement Center, a bare eight-by-twelve rectangle of space containing only a wooden table and four chairs.

"Can you tell me, then, why you had to be brought in under restraint? Why you tried to run away from the two officers who picked you up?"

Silence. Then, "I told 'em all I know before. I didn't kill nobody."

Brockhurst stood up. He and Turner were both short and he wanted to loom over the other man. "Why were you afraid of talking to me?"

Nothing. But the round hulking shoulders twitched.

The SLED agent took out a pack of chewing gum, selected just the right stick, and drew it out deliberately. "If you wanted to look guilty, you sure did a good job." He paused a half-beat and added, "Obviously you wanted to avoid being questioned again. Afraid you'd forget your story?"

Turner's eyes narrowed and he seemed about to protest; then he stopped and said in a low guttural twang, "I ain't done nothin'."

Brockhurst sat back down. He let Turner sit a few more minutes. He wanted the questioning of the suspect to drag on, and he kept his voice deliberately controlled, deadly serious, throughout. "You know, someone saw you in Essex. Before this murder. That other time you were there."

"Who seen me?"

Turner's eyes were wide open now. The detective added quickly, "When you were there before, somebody saw you. Saw you talking to Sarah Rothenbarger."

Turner jumped to his feet. "I ain't never talked to her."

"But you *were* in Essex before. Weren't you?"

"I—" Turner stared around him for an avenue of escape.

"What were you doing there? Did you break in somewhere?" Silence.

"You heard about her, didn't you? About how she took in drifters and gave them a meal. You remembered it, didn't you? And when you went back, you set out for an easy mark. An old lady who'd *let* you in the house. *Didn't you?*"

"I wanna lawyer," Turner snarled.

The Columbia policeman let out a long sigh. He'd almost had him. Damn. Oh well. That Turner had waived his rights this long had been too good to be true. But at least he'd got this much. Hell of a good hunch, if he did say so himself. He knew who Turner was now. This was a guy who made a living hitting small towns, picking up car stereos and family silver, moving on to the next town before an investigation even got under way. The family silver ended up in an antique store five states away. (He had to have a car somewhere.) Probably the sucker hadn't meant to kill her. He'd gone back to Essex the second time because he remembered her—an easy mark, had to have money because she owned a store. But it got away from him this time. He screwed up. Then he holed up like an animal, probably ditched the loot and the knife. But why stick around to be caught?

Three hours later, after a court-appointed attorney had been secured for Turner, Brockhurst questioned the suspect again. But this time, under advice, Turner said almost nothing. Brockhurst spoke with Sheriff Buck Henry and they agreed they could detain Turner for a few days, despite the howling of his attorney, but not for very long—they had to find hard evidence soon or he'd walk again. Meanwhile, the Ashton sheriff gave Brockhurst a copy of the rap sheet detailing Turner's petty theft conviction in Georgia.

Back at his motel that evening, Brockhurst showered and changed his clothes and then drove out to Fairfield Plantation for dinner. The cool Federal mansion was soothing and Brockhurst eagerly took on a thick New York strip as he watched the sun set over the Salkehatchie River and its attendant acres of pine trees. As he ate, though, the case continued to tug at him, like a child at his sleeve wanting everything explained. Walking back to his state car an hour later, he concluded that it was only a matter of time before the pieces fell into place. J. T. Turner was a guy who would break. Easily. And at this point, Turner looked like the surest bet. Just a little more time. Maybe the murder that had shaken this quiet town had come from the outside in the form of J. T. Turner. Or maybe it hadn't. Brockhurst was pleased with his interrogation of Turner today—but the jury would be out a little longer yet.

Although the relaxing meal had refreshed him, the long drive back to Essex ruined his mood. He was always edgy until a case was perfectly clear to him. There were no lights along the two-lane road and the live oaks crouched above him like vultures, each branch reaching out a tentacled claw. He smiled at his imagination, next thing he'd be believing in ghosts and hex dolls, but he drove faster nonetheless. He agreed with those who found this part of South Carolina rather sinister—it was a far cry from the sloping foothills of the Up Country where he'd been raised, or from the open white beaches of the coastline. This interior of swamps and history, of sated cities and moldering small towns, was a chasm between the piedmont and the coast; it looked like quicksand on maps, a dangerous bog from which some never emerged.

So far, this June had not been the best summer vacation for Marian Davis. Something was out of sync, off balance. One hot midnight she lay back against the pillows of her bed and stared at the four walls. Perhaps she should plan a trip, spend the rest of the summer in Charleston. She should definitely decide whether to break her teaching contract for next year. It was summer, she could read, landscape her garden, go to New York and see some shows, she could do anything. Except she had no desire to do any of it.

This damn murder. She got up and crossed to her window and looked through the miniblinds. She wished it were over with. She wished they would find the killer and be done with it. She wished it would rain. She wished people like Anna McFarland and Lou Brockhurst would stop asking so many questions. She wished she could run away and never come back here.

She gazed back out at the street again. This time she noticed something. Moving. On the sidewalk. A shadow? Instinctively she froze. Who would be out there in the middle of the night? From this window she had only a partial view of the sidewalk but she was certain someone was standing in front of her house, just out of view.

Marian grabbed the wand and twisted the blinds shut. She stood trembling for a second, thinking; then she flew down the hall. In her living room, without turning on a light, she twisted open the blinds in her front window.

The sidewalk was empty.

Had she imagined it? Chiding herself for being silly, Marian strode back down the hall to her bedroom and climbed back into bed. She turned off her bedside light. Abruptly she got up, crossed to the window, and moved a slat of the blinds to see outside. Nothing. The shadow was gone.

She eased into bed and gazed across the room at the picture of Alma. She wished she had a picture of her mother, some tangible symbol that Lonnie Davis had lived and given birth to her. But of course there were no pictures because Lonnie had feared cameras, had believed the old superstition that a camera steals a portion of the soul. Harriet had tried to take a picture of Lonnie behind the Thanksgiving turkey the first year Alma helped with the meal, and Lonnie had threatened to quit on the spot, said she wouldn't even serve the meal if Miz Harriet made her do it. Harriet had relented, the meal had gone as planned, and there was no old black-and-white snapshot of a cleaning woman turned cook for a special occasion. On second thought, maybe that was just as well.

When Marian finally slept, she had erratic scene dreams that flashed by like projected slides, in such rapid succession she hadn't time to register one fully before another appeared. She had the feeling she had been assaulted but she wasn't sure and several times during the night she instinctively, unknowingly, reached between her breasts. Their soft fullness reassured her; still asleep, she rested her hand between them, as though her touch had the power to heal old wounds.

The next morning Marian was exhausted and she decided to spend the day outside, working on the unkempt garden behind her house. Which is where Anna McFarland found her shortly before eleven in the morning. Anna first knocked on the front door, then started down the driveway, checking for Marian's car. It was in its usual place, so Anna followed the driveway to the back yard. The black woman, in halter top and shorts, was on her knees amid a profusion of wild growth. The yard looked like a child's drawing, meaningful in intent but unmindful of symmetry. Nothing was contained within the boundaries once assigned it. Flowers leaned way out of brick borders, overgrown shrubs sagged, and unruly mounds of grass hunched up here and there like independent city-states.

"There you are," Anna called out, and waved. Marian's back yard surprised her. Everything else about the schoolteacher was so orderly. Obviously Marian had been outside for a while; the waistband of her shorts was soaking wet, and her halter was also damp.

Marian looked up and smiled. Anna wore a blindingly white shift of Egyptian cotton, embroidered around the V-neck, unbelted for a change, loose-flowing. Suddenly she reminded Marian of a woodland sprite, one of Shakespeare's nymphs, all that dark wild hair and swirling white cloth.

"I tried the bell," Anna said. "Thought maybe I'd missed you."

"Last night I decided I had to do something about this yard. I've never cared much about gardening, but this is such a mess I've either got to revive it or lay it to rest."

Anna knelt in the grass across from the other woman. "I was wondering if your offer's still good, about borrowing that book?" When Marian assured her it was, Anna added, "How can you stand to be outside on a day like this? Stoney says I don't sweat enough. That if I did, the heat wouldn't bother me so much. He actually goes running in this weather."

"Sweat does cool you off." Marian leaned over and attacked several weeds with a small trowel, winking at Anna out of the corner of her eye. "Besides, it's sexy. You know that."

Anna looked nonplussed. "You must be enjoying your vacation."

Marian's eyes widened slightly. Was Anna one of those women who didn't talk about sex or did she suspect something? "It's nice, all right. What are you up to these days?"

"I've been trying to plan a photo assignment on Daufuskie Island, it's for an ad agency in Savannah. They've been hired by International Paper to promote the island." Anna didn't mention that she was going to have to shoot the assignment without her favorite Nikon.

"Sounds challenging. I guess you know a lot of people are pretty upset about development over there." Marian sat back on her heels, sweat pouring off her forehead. "God, it is hot." She laid her trowel down. "You want a sandwich? Maybe a gin and tonic? I know it's early but a little quinine might be nice in this heat."

A half hour later they were sprawled on the floor of Marian's cool living room, with its wicker and tropical plants so reminiscent of Key West. The Degas prints and some female nudes, by an artist Anna didn't recognize, adorned the walls. She almost giggled when she saw them, imagining Harriet Setzler's reaction, having no idea that Harriet had never been inside the room. All the fabrics were light and natural and Anna was struck by how simple the lines of the furniture were, how sleek yet soft the room was. It was as compelling, in its own way, as Maum Chrish's strange cabin. Marian talked about Daufuskie and they nibbled on turkey sandwiches and welcomed the breeze from the ceiling fan above their heads. After her first gin, Anna was mellow and the hum of the fan seemed to fuse to her brain and beat out syncopated time like a drum. Marian was sitting, cross-legged, on the carpet across from Anna, her back against the sofa, her arm flung casually across it. Studying her, Anna imagined Marian in soft-focus through a gelled lens, in a provocative, languorous pose.

They talked about Career Day and the murder investigation and about this and that. Finally Marian got up and disappeared down the hall and returned with a hardback book which she dropped on the floor beside Anna. "That'll explain a lot of what you're interested in, I think." She sat back down and picked up her glass again. "What it doesn't cover, I can probably fill in. My mother was really into folk beliefs—I guess that's why I took all those courses. Maybe that's why it sometimes gets to me."

Anna wondered if she was going to anger Marian again but she asked anyway, "Will this book explain why Maum Chrish would have a jar of semen?"

"Maybe not. But I can hazard a guess. Seminal fluids are thought to be ethereal by some mystics. To suppress natural sexuality is to do spiritual and physical harm to oneself—it can create violent discord. She probably uses it in rituals, the way they use flour or cornmeal or sacrificed animals. As an offering to the gods. It's the source of potency, new life."

"I see. Do *you* believe suppressing sexuality can be harmful?" Anna asked abruptly.

"Not if you're fifteen." Marian smiled and set her glass down. Then, noticing the intent look in Anna's eyes, she said, "I guess I do. Don't you?"

The room was very still, except for the whirring of the ceiling fan. Anna thought about her recent frantic desire for Stoney, about her lack of desire for him too, and about her inability to deal with either. "I think it's hard not to."

The other woman was silent for a second. Marian wasn't sure how much she wanted to say. "I think the South tries to turn all its women into whores or eunuchs. Personally I'd rather be a whore."

Anna turned shocked eyes on her companion. "Don't you think sex is often just a power game—with women always the losers?"

"Maybe so, but power is so self-defeating in love. It's addictive. For women to be freely sensual creatures, we have to learn how to surrender our need to control everything. Which we inherited from our mothers, no question—'don't let your guard down, look before you leap, watch what you're doing.' Our grandmothers, yours more than mine, gained control of their lives through their minds. They had no voice in their choices or circumstances or even the disposition of their sexuality. They lay in marital beds and were often raped by brutish husbands taking their conjugal rights or by white masters—and they kept themselves intact through mental control. I will feel nothing. Sacrificing sensuality for the sake of control. And in the end still losing. Do we want to go on doing that?"

Marian sat forward and added, "During the height of feminism, we weren't supposed to even think about sex, we acted like these bodies—with their very real needs—didn't exist in order to get people to recognize that we had minds. On the other hand, it was also suddenly okay for us to sleep around like men, to have one-night stands just to prove we could do it without emotion. The sexual revolution and feminism were like two old cats squaring off against each other. I'm glad things have moved beyond that, that now we can fully accept that we're human beings who need love—and sex. Which still isn't easy, of course, given all the propaganda we've been fed along the way."

Anna was dying to ask Marian why she didn't date anyone, but she was hesitant to say any more. "I guess I'd better be going," she said. Then she looked the other woman in the eye. "I admire your—openness."

Marian gazed at Anna. "Actually, that was someone else's doing. It was a love affair totally without manipulation or guilt or possessiveness. Too perfect to last, I suppose. Sometimes I think women need to pass sexual confidence along to each other, where it's easier to be flat-out honest. Most of us have been hurt at least once by sex, by the way someone used it against us."

Anna picked up the voudou book and stood up. "Thanks for lunch." At the door she smiled at Marian and added, "You know, you ought to stop putting that straightening shit on your hair. I like it curly, like it is now."

Marian was silent for a half beat, then burst out laughing.

"Spoken exactly like the woman who first set foot in this town and made her mark by telling Harriet to go to hell."

The other woman flushed. "We must have been here too long, she's actually beginning to grow on me. I'm even going to do her portrait. I want to try to shoot Maum Chrish again too, but I'm a little spooked since the last time I went out there. You wouldn't want to go along by any chance, would you?"

"I don't know," the other woman began. Then she saw Anna's chin drop and she changed her mind. "Okay, yeah. Sure. Beats cleaning the yard up. You call me."

Ten

OR A MAN who wasn't passionate about his profession, Stoney McFarland usually excelled at it anyway. Ironically, he often did such a good job that he was offered promotions he didn't want. In every job he'd ever had, he had moved up faster than most, and he was accustomed to being considered a valuable asset. Thus, he was unprepared for being virtually fired.

Each year state employees were subject to an annual review, but this year, with the death of Sarah uppermost in his mind, Stoney did not even notice that Sumter Brownlow failed to go over his annual review with him. Nor did Brownlow mention his trip to Columbia, where his own annual review was conducted each summer and Stoney's was discussed and turned in.

Instead, Stoney sat at his desk on a Tuesday morning opening his mail as usual. Brownlow had gone to meet with several fee appraisers who would be hired to help with the new project in the swamps. Absently Stoney ripped open several letters and scanned their contents, threw two away, and placed two others on top of his desk for filing. He picked up the next letter and gazed for a second at the official state seal. Used to regular communication from Central Office, he slit open the envelope and drew out the single sheet of bond paper. The message was short:

This is to inform you of your temporary
suspension from state service, owing to your last annual
review. Please call this office at your earliest
convenience to arrange an interview to discuss your
employment with the State of South Carolina.

Stoney stared at the letter in his hand. What? He read it again, more carefully this time. His annual review had apparently been so negative he had to appear in Columbia to appeal it. He threw the letter down on his desk and thought for a moment. Then he jumped up. Brownlow. Who didn't even show him the goddamn evaluation. Just wrote it up like a sneak and sent it off. Stoney marched over to the other man's desk, reached out for a drawer. Where was it? State employees always got a copy. Stoney jerked open the bottom desk drawer, catching a splinter in his thumb. He winced, then stopped short. No. He was not going to rifle another man's desk. Even if the man was Brownlow.

Turning around, Stoney went back over to his own desk and reread the letter. He was relieved of his duties until he talked to Brownlow's supervisor in Columbia. Jesus. How had he let this happen? What was wrong with him? He closed his eyes: for a second he and Anna were sitting on the steps of the McCloskey house begging someone to buy it so they didn't have to go to jail. They lived on his income and banked her more unreliable one; you could do that in Essex, where even air was cheaper than it was in D.C. They had some savings. He opened his eyes. This wasn't the end of the world. He would go to Columbia, explain things. What the hell had Brownlow said about him? That he had left the office several times? That was reason to be suspended? Was there always going to be someone checking up on him like a frigging spy?

He stood up. Was he supposed to clear out his desk or what? Stoney walked over to the window. He was not about to give Brownlow that satisfaction. Instead, he went back over and picked up the phone and called the Columbia number on the state letterhead. The earliest appointment he could get was for a week later. After that he sat back down and waited for Brownlow to reappear. It was almost lunchtime. Was the other man going to stay in the swamps all day? Stoney looked at the envelope from Columbia. Postmarked a week ago. Had Brownlow intercepted the letter, recognized what it was, and waited to put it on Stoney's desk when he knew he'd be out of the office? Stoney stood up again. It was just the sort of thing that man would do. Momentarily Stoney remembered all the contentious landowners Brownlow had sent him to deal with, the condemnation proceedings Brownlow had initiated but asked Stoney to carry out. The man was a weasel.

Stoney walked back over to Brownlow's desk and stood there for a moment. Nobody should have to work for a coward. He stared at the desktop, at a framed snapshot of Brownlow and the governor. Abruptly he picked up the picture and threw it in the trash can. He could still hear the crash of the breaking glass as he walked out of the office, empty-handed.

Outside, he decided to go see Jim Leland. Already the day was steamy and by the time Stoney reached the town hall, the back of his white cotton shirt was soaked. It was cooler in Jim Leland's office. As usual, the Essex police chief was sitting with his feet propped up on his desk, reading a newspaper.

Jim lowered his feet when he saw Stoney in the doorway. "Hey there. What brings you out on such a hot day?"

Stoney walked into the room. "I was wondering if Brockhurst got anything out of J. T. Turner."

The police chief looked blank. "What about Turner?"

Stoney's voice was querulous. "Wasn't Brockhurst going to question him yesterday?"

"Oh, yeah, he sure was."

"And?"

"And what?"

"What did Brockhurst find out, for crying out loud? Did Turner tell him anything?"

Jim Leland sat up straighter. "I don't know, Stoney. Brockhurst hasn't been in yet."

"It's almost noon."

"I can tell time."

Stoney swiveled and headed for the door, then stopped and turned back around. "When do you think he'll be by? Maybe we should give him a call."

Jim slapped his paper down on his desk. "I'm not the man's keeper. He'll be here when he gets here." A long pause. "Maybe you ought to let us handle this."

"From what I can see, nobody's handling anything."

Jim flushed. "Look here, Stoney. I don't need this. Just because you spent a little time here as a kid doesn't give you the right to come back and start ordering everybody around."

Stoney strode toward the policeman. "Essex has a right to efficient law enforcement. And I'm as much a part of this town as anybody else."

The other man was on his feet. "No you're not. You think you are but you're not. You were a nice city kid that used to come visit. Then you came back all grown up and what'd you do—you bought that fancy McCloskey place and you brought along your flashy wife who's thumbed her nose at absolutely ev-

erything here. Now you've taken on Sarah's death like she was
your mother or something. You're not the prodigal son, you
never were.''

Stunned, as much by Jim's vehemence as by what he had said,
Stoney turned and slammed out of the office. They thought he
was interfering? They thought he and Anna bought the Mc-
Closkey house to show off? For these people he'd damn near
lost his job?

He crossed the Main Street triangle and stumbled onto the
unkempt green mall on the other side and careened down the
railroad tracks. Someone called out to him from the road but
he didn't even turn around. Then he broke into a run alongside
the tracks, dashed across them just as he had as a boy—timing it
so he'd just make it before the oncoming train sounded its whistle.
On the other side of the tracks, where the blacks lived, he leaned
against a live oak and breathed hard. He looked back toward
downtown, surveyed where he'd just been from this side of the
tracks. They would arrest Maum Chrish and try her and convict
her and put her in jail for life and smile their smug little smiles.
Sumter Brownlow would approve. And that would be that.

Abruptly Stoney noticed the white spire of the library building several blocks away. Instinctively he started toward it.

Every Southern town has its haunted Victorian mansion and
Essex was no exception. Ours was our library now. The house
stood three stories tall, all white clapboard and gingerbread
brackets, a ten-foot-wide wraparound porch encircling three
sides of the first floor. Rising from the gabled roof above it was
also the only widow's walk in Essex, built by the house's original
owner, a railroad man who'd always wanted to go to sea. Legend
had it that, on full moon nights, various 1860s ancestors of the
house's original owner could be seen leaping off the widow's
walk into space, white apparitions flailing windward to escape
Sherman's flames. That the library house was built *after* the
Civil War didn't bother anyone a bit.

The Southern sun of summer bathes us in an unhurried pool
of inevitability. Stare into its yellow eye long enough and you
can believe anything. A house with a widow's walk fifty miles
from the ocean, a beauty shop named for a woman named for a
city in Italy, Civil War ghosts who've got the wrong house, and
people who accept the ghosts but aren't bothered by untidy geography or history, these are webs spun by an inherited suspension of disbelief. Historical fact, reality, truth, slide across us

like rain; to us, they were organic and so we nourish them, add a nutrient here and there, so new things will grow. The fact is, if you can secede from your country and shoot at your cousin from Connecticut, a ghost is downright reasonable.

Stoney climbed the steep brick steps of the library, stared at the ten-foot oak door flanked on both sides by bay windows. He opened the heavy door and slipped inside. On both sides of him were large airy rooms with twenty-foot ceilings, oak floors with burnished mahogany woodwork, heavy burgundy drapes hanging at the floor-to-ceiling casement windows. Along each wall painted white bookcases reached to the ceiling; wooden ladders stood nearby for the top shelves. Here and there by a window sat an old upholstered armchair for reading. In one of them Stoney had curled up with Man Friday and David Copperfield on rainy summer mornings. The smell of the place made his head swim. The pine wax used on the wood floors, the mildew of dusty clothbound books, the oniony new-mown grass floating through the open windows. And that eerie silence—the echo of his leather heels against the polished wood floor, the crackle of yellowed pages against a human hand, the endless columns of dizzying black ink spread out before him like a magic carpet.

He breathed in the aroma of the past and found it soothing. Anna sometimes said he yearned to be a child again and perhaps he did. The library was empty at the moment, having just opened, and he walked down the hall toward the rear of the building. At the end of the hall rose a massive curved staircase with a carved mahogany bannister. Ever since Stoney could remember, the staircase had been cordoned off with a velvet rope and a sign reading DANGER. Like every other child in Essex, he had believed something nefarious lurked at the top of those stairs. No one Stoney knew as a child had ever been up there. Some of the other boys said Harriet Setzler murdered children who talked too much in the library and then carried their bodies up there and walled them in. Others said there were caskets at the top, where the Civil War ghosts slept when the moon wasn't full.

"You still think there are dead people up there?"

Stoney jumped. He whirled around to face Harriet Setzler. The old lady wore a tailored blue suit and held a stack of books.

"Scared you, did I? That's what you get for sneaking around. You know, children still try to go up there."

"What *is* up there?"

"Nothing. The town never had enough money to renovate

the upstairs. It's unsafe—the floors are half rotted. Like I used to tell you, you might fall through the ceiling and crack your skull open.''

"I don't remember your saying that."

"You probably liked the ghost story better. Not that any Lutheran should be believing in such nonsense."

Stoney gazed up the stairs. "Looks like in all this time somebody would have fixed the floors."

Harriet didn't say anything for a second. "Go on up if you like. Just be careful."

His eyes were still on the staircase. "No," he said quietly. "Not now."

As Harriet went in the front room to reshelve the books she carried, Stoney wondered what would happen to the library when she died; she had run it, for virtually no salary, for over twenty years. In a few moments Harriet walked back to the office at the rear of the building, and Stoney followed her. Once a kitchen, the office now contained an antiquated card catalog and racks of magazines and several oak reading tables, as well as the rolltop desk Harriet used to organize all library business.

"I hear that Columbia detective is talking to everybody in town," she said, standing behind her desk staring at the circulation card in the back of a frail copy of *Jane Eyre*. "He seems like a competent man."

Suddenly Stoney was tired of talking about Sarah Roth's murder. "I'm sure he is."

"You still suspicious of Leonard Hansen?"

Stoney looked up abruptly. Actually he hadn't thought much about Leonard in the last few days. Maybe he just couldn't stand the guy and was grasping at straws like Anna said. Nobody else suspected him.

"Will that detective be talking to him too?" Harriet Setzler's face was still glued to a book.

"I don't know. Why?"

"I'm just curious. He's talking to all the rest of us."

"And you think he ought to talk to Leonard? Did you tell Brockhurst that?" A pause. Then Stoney asked, "Mrs. Setzler, do you know something about Leonard?"

Harriet thought about promises. Her voice was vague and innocent. "Whatever do you mean?"

Stoney marched toward the elderly woman. "Maybe Anna's right. If anybody in this town ever told the truth, just once, maybe we'd know who did this. I'd think you—of all people—wouldn't hide behind convention or fear of public disapproval.''

Across the desk Harriet Setzler stared levelly at Stoney. She was red in the face, but she also respected Stoney for doing exactly what she would do in the same circumstances. She took a deep breath. ''I don't have any proof, but I can't get it out of my mind.''

''Can't get what out of your mind?''

Harriet closed her eyes, begged forgiveness for the small lie. At least it wasn't a broken promise. ''A few weeks before Sarah was killed, I saw the Hansen boy—late one night—just standing in front of Sarah's house. It was real late. He was watching the house.''

Stoney leaned toward the older woman. ''Mrs. Setzler, are you sure?''

''Absolutely.''

The Low Country of South Carolina is a land where earth is just barely holding its own against water. Beaches overburdened by the development of the New South erode and are shorn up again with long armies of granite boulders; swamps are drained and then filled in to become farmland, only to flood once more. Near every river bogs form, mysterious and implacable pockets of muck and slime, and along the coastal shoreline, marshes thick with reeds and grasses eat into the pie-shaped wedge of hard firmament. Small rivers lead to larger rivers which drain off into sounds, and through these, small ligaments of earth are continually washed out to sea.

A swamp and a marsh are not the same thing. Marshes lie along the coast with the ease and indolence of sunbathers. They are open expanses, home to sawgrass and sedge and cattail, where only working boats in search of oyster and shrimp break the horizon. A marsh lets a human breathe, look outward, plan ahead, see into the distance. It has nothing of the crowding, the thick incestuous entanglement of a swamp. The swamp quivers with the weight of trees and darkness and secrets. Cypress and tupelo, black gum and juniper and palmetto, live oak in its tattered shawl of Spanish moss. Vines that encircle a tree again and again until they disappear into the black caul of water like limbs sucked up by quicksand. Alligators, mosquitoes grown fat and mean, crumbling tombstones of those bought and sold like cattle. And absolute crystal silence, its edge as sharp as cut glass. Always inwardness, the omnipresent danger of seeing down too far.

These breed in swamps.

Literally, the Coosawhatchie Swamp near Essex was a fresh-water square ten miles across made up of the spongy land situated between the Coosawhatchie and the Salkhatchie rivers, small waterways that paralleled each other and drained off into Laurel Bay and St. Helena Sound on either side of the town of Beaufort, miles away. The end of the swamp nearest Essex, more inland, looked much as it had in colonial days, a remote prehensile world of water. This was Indian country once, home to dozens of small tribes with names like Chickasaw and Ye-massee, whose history the victorious Englishmen of the Indian Wars did not see fit to preserve. Today only the rivers and towns bear the names of the native Americans of the Low Country, who used marsh grass and palmetto leaves to thatch their huts and who traced their lineage through their women. After the demise of the rice plantations a century later, scattered groups of black people—many freed slaves—replaced the Indians along the Coosawhatchie. Their descendants, including a small girl in an ill-fitting pink dress whom Marian once passed on the swamp road, frequently turn up arrowheads and clay pipes in the soaked earth where they eke out an existence bleaker than any red man ever knew.

Today, when Anna stopped along the swamp road where she'd parked before, Marian suggested they go on down a little farther, where the road had more shoulder. Anna was so glad for Marian's company it didn't even occur to her to wonder how the other woman knew the swamps so well. Safely parked, they had to backtrack slightly and recross a concrete bridge where the road spanned the river. While they were on the bridge, a mammoth flatbed truck suddenly roared onto it and they were pinned along the railing on the other side of the truck. Massive tree trunks, severed and on the way to market, whizzed past on the truck and the bridge trembled under their weight. Instinctively Marian reached out and threw her arm in front of Anna, like a mother protecting a child. When the truck disappeared down the road, the black woman walked to the end of the bridge and took a dirt path Anna had never noticed before. They followed it for several hundred yards. Even though only Anna knew where they were headed, in here, Marian seemed in charge. Several times Marian turned to look behind her. At first Anna thought Marian was checking to make sure she wasn't lagging behind but then she saw that Marian was actually checking behind both of them, as though she expected someone else to be following. In a few minutes they came to a small inlet; mosquitoes hovered over the water, buzzing and skittering. As the women quickly skirted the inlet, Anna recognized where they were. It was near here that she scraped her arm the night of the town meeting. She saw the tree limb, still dangling by a slender sliver of bark. Below the damaged limb a small circle had been drawn in the damp dirt and a candle stood in its center.

Marian saw it too. "Sacred ground," she said. "Human blood fell there, I bet."

Shivering, Anna repositioned her camera bag on her shoulder and stared at the other woman. "How do you know that?"

"I just do." Why did this place remind her so much of her mother? Marian closed her eyes for a moment, thought about all those old circles in the dirt yard in town. When she would fall and cut herself, her mother would draw a ring around the spot. To preserve where her blood had gone back to the earth. Later Lonnie would plant flowers around the spot, to mark it for good.

A bird squawked nearby and Marian jumped. She always expected someone to be here.

Anna was staring at her curiously when Marian asked, "Which way to her house?"

They walked on through the woods, Anna in the lead now. Nervously she kept her eyes on the ground, ever mindful of snakes. It was going to be all right today, she told herself; there were no drums, no sign of anyone else. She told Marian in whispers about her other camera being stolen the last time. "I should have told you before. I guess I was afraid you wouldn't come along. I don't think I had the guts to come back by myself."

"Thanks a lot. Now if the bogeyman gets you, he'll get both of us, right?"

At the clearing they hesitated. Marian was nervous too—just being in the swamps could do that. She looked at the tall cypress trees and she could feel their vines snaking up inside her body, winding around her internal organs, choking the life from her lips. She wished she'd stayed home, left well enough alone.

Finally Anna approached Maum Chrish's cabin and called out, "Hello? Anybody home?"

Silence. Anna turned back and looked at Marian; then Anna

squared her shoulders and brazenly climbed the rickety stairs. Marian watched, admiring her chutzpah.

"Maum Chrish?" Anna called again. "Could I talk to you for a minute?"

But Maum Chrish was nowhere to be found. Anna and Marian strolled around the yard, took in the smoldering fire, walked around the garden and the adorned live oaks, looked into the woods on both sides of the house. Finally Anna unpacked her camera gear and took some shots of the yard and the outside of the house. Marian wandered around idly, unaware that some of the photographs were actually of her.

Then Anna asked, "Want to see inside? She leaves the door open. Come on."

Anna was on the porch before Marian could respond. There Anna grew more cautious. She poked her head inside the door, then withdrew again. "It's okay. Nobody's here."

Curious, Marian joined Anna on the porch and followed her inside the cabin. She gazed in awe at the interior, the decorated *poteau-mitan* with its carved triangle, the drawings on the walls, the *vèvè* design outlined on the floor with chalk. If her knowledge of voudou was right, a ceremony had recently taken place. Otherwise the *vèvè* would have been erased. While Anna shot more film, Marian walked around the room. She stopped at the Sephiroth drawing. For a moment she studied it. This had nothing to do with voudou. Some of the words were Hebrew. My God, was it true? Had some fanatics out here killed Sarah Roth?

Anna was shooting pictures of the interior of the room, of the objects on the table. She didn't notice that one of the knives was missing since Lou Brockhurst's visit, but the sight of them rattled her again. Several times she took various shots of Marian against the decorated walls. By now Marian realized Anna was photographing her and she wondered, in a brief homage to her mother, whether shards of her soul would be left behind on the floor of Maum Chrish's house when they left. Marian paid little attention to Anna; instead, she inspected the room, more and more mystified by the conflicting symbols she kept noticing. She half suspected she and Anna might be in real danger, invading the sanctity of what amounted to a cult temple. Several times she caught Anna's eyes and knew Anna was wondering the same thing. Once they both stopped in front of the sexual drawing. It was so explicit that both women immediately looked down.

"Now there's a woman who knows what she wants," Marian said at last, lightly.

Anna laughed. Was Marian always so at ease about sex?

Marian crossed to look at the bottles and jars on the other side of the room. "What's in there?" she asked, nodding at the rear doorway.

"Sort of a bedroom."

The black woman entered the adjoining room. Maum Chrish, she saw, lived simply, meagerly. Almost a reverence about her simplicity, very Thoreauvian. Neat, clean. Not the hallmark of a crazy person at all. Today the swamp woman seemed less and less the primitive throwback to the Dark Ages. Her life here looked like a deliberate choice. Maum Chrish *lived* whatever it was she believed, which was more than you could say for most people. Did she also kill Sarah?

Beside the rope bed was a tattered Bible. Jewish words, voudou, now a Bible? Marian walked over and picked the book up. A place was marked in Genesis with a long string, a stone dangling from it. Absently Marian palmed the worn stone, glanced at it. She gazed at it several moments. Then, abruptly, she held it up, looked at it closer. Granite. A vein through it. Dark. Turn it one way and it almost looks like a . . .

Marian ran into the other room, grabbed Anna by the arm, and held the rock up. "Have you ever seen this before?"

Anna shook her head. "What is it?"

"Have you ever seen her wear it?"

"Marian, I've only seen her here once. And she was naked."

"Naked?" Marian said the word like she didn't know what it meant. Then, "Did she have a birthmark on the top of her left thigh?"

"Why?"

"Did she?"

"I don't know. I couldn't see her that well."

Marian held the rock up, as though to get more light on it. Her hand shook violently and she babbled to herself aloud, "Could it be the same rock? All this time, right here. Out here? And no one told me? Do they know?"

"Marian, what is it?"

They left abruptly, at Marian's insistence. The black woman did not say a word all the way home.

When Lou Brockhurst told Jim Leland he wanted to question Leonard Hansen, the Essex police chief immediately objected.

"That's crazy. Leonard even came and offered to help me after Sarah was killed."

"Which would make a great cover."

Later the two men drove out to the country in the detective's state-owned midsize Chrysler. They turned off the Charleston highway onto a dirt road, passed endless acres of tall corn stalks, then rows of soybeans nesting in the sandy soil baked an impotent beige by the rainless summer. Once in a while an old house or a trailer appeared, set back from the road amid a graveyard of rusted automobile parts and odd pieces of battered furniture, including an ancient green sofa whose yellowed innards poked out like an exploded Thanksgiving turkey. Some farmland outside Essex had been overtaken by weeds and brambles, the fences down in more places than they were up, and now and then the two men spotted an abandoned church or a collapsed barn, one of which still had a huge red tin COKE sign attached to its side.

"What did Stoney say again?" Jim asked. "Mrs. Setzler saw Leonard outside Sarah's house several nights before she was killed?"

Brockhurst nodded, carefully negotiating the deep ruts in the unpaved road.

"But what does that prove? How come Mrs. Setzler didn't say anything before?"

"Hansen a friend of yours?"

Jim looked out the window beside him. "Not exactly. But I don't have it in for him like Stoney does. Those two got into a real row once when they were kids. If you want my opinion, Stoney McFarland has lost his good sense over all this."

Lou Brockhurst drove on. He wondered if Jim Leland, a slight man who clearly avoided confrontations, might be the tiniest bit afraid of the man they were going to see. "Well, it won't hurt to talk to him."

"I thought you were pretty sold on Turner," Jim said.

"I'm sold on nothing until I've got proof in my hands." Brockhurst turned to Jim. "I don't want to mention what McFarland said, I don't want to tip Hansen off until I get a chance to talk to some other people, see if anyone else saw him near Sarah Rothenbarger's house anytime."

Jim nodded and they pulled up in front of Leonard's house. It was a frame structure, a one-story cube, with a front porch that spanned its entire front width. The foundation was mountain stone and there was a basement which no doubt had once also functioned as a root cellar. The lapboard siding was newly painted and gleamed white under the broiling sun; the pitched roof was also covered with new asphalt shingles. But the chimney leaned precariously and several of the top bricks were missing or loose, and two window frames in the front wall were rotted. Approaching the building, Brockhurst noticed that the eaves were also rotting; three small holes admitted air into the bloodstream of the house. Part of the old guttering, rusted and bent, lay on the ground nearby but no new system was yet in place. This was clearly a house in which the renovation was, almost grudgingly, slow and untidy.

Before the two men reached the porch, Leonard pushed open the front door and called out to them. He was wearing paint-splotched jeans below a bare chest, an electric drill in his hands. He put the drill down in a folding aluminum chair on the porch and wiped his hands on his jeans. "How's it going, Leland." Then he looked at Brockhurst. "What brings y'all out here?"

Jim stared at the ground. Brockhurst, who thought it odd that the television was blaring away inside while someone used a power drill, smiled and said, "I got to thinking about your offer to help. I've talked to so many people in town about the murder. I thought it might help to talk to someone who doesn't live in Essex, that it might give me a fresh perspective."

Leonard sat down on his steps. "Be glad to tell you anything I know. Though Jim'll tell ya I spend most of my time right here. Trying to fix this place up so I can sell it."

"Understand it used to be your family place." Brockhurst propped his good leg up on the bottom step and leaned his elbow on it. "Nice and quiet out here."

Leonard laughed. "Is that. Me, I'll be glad to get back to a city."

Brockhurst smiled. "Mr. Hansen, I've asked everyone else so I may as well ask you too—what can you tell me about the dead woman? I need to know everything I can about her. Her life is really the best clue to the identity of the murderer."

"Afraid I can't help you much there."

"But you did live with her once, I understand, so you knew her quite well at one time." Leonard shot Brockhurst a quick look and the SLED agent surveyed those odd violet eyes carefully, looking for a sign that Leonard didn't want to talk about this. There was none. "Could you tell me about that?"

Leonard looked over at Jim. "He'll tell ya how Sarah loved to help people out. I had just got out of the service and I came on back home to see a few buddies. I wanted to have a little fun before I settled down to working. Saw Mrs. Roth on the street one day and she said, when did I get back to town? I told her. We talked a bit about what all I'd done in the Marines, and she said why didn't I come have a bite of lunch with her. So I did and while I was there she asked me would I be getting a job and I said I'd probably be moving on. Anyway, happened she needed her cellar cleaned out and would I be interested in doing it? I didn't really need the cash, still had lots of my back pay, but she was *some* cook. So she had me stay awhile and I helped her fix up some things 'round her house. She was a real nice old lady.''

Brockhurst thought the speech had a rehearsed feel to it.

"And you left later on?''

Leonard smiled deprecatingly. "Well, I was still pretty fresh then, I didn't exactly want to spend my whole life with an old lady who was like a mother—if you get my meaning.'' The lanky man stretched his legs out in front of him. "Mrs. Roth and I sorta had an argument too. She was getting up in years, you know, even then. And one day she gives me up some money and tells me to get her some stuff from the grocery store and I did, but when I got back with the groceries and gave her the change, she swore up and down how some money was missing from her pocketbook. I reminded her of the money she gave me for the groceries; she said how that wasn't the money she was talking about at all. Anyways, no way could I make her understand that she'd spent the money she said I took. I had plenty of money, like I said. But she got real mad and I got right fed up. So I decided to clear out.''

Jim added, "Sarah could be like that sometimes. She'd get something in her head, no way you could talk her out of it. Two or three of us told her in the last few years she shouldn't be taking strangers home—especially those migrant pickers—and she didn't pay us one bit of attention. Which is probably how she got killed.''

Brockhurst continued to study Leonard. "What was your relationship with Mrs. Rothenbarger when you came back to town?''

Leonard stared at the detective. "You gonna ask me where I was that night too?'' Then the blond man turned to Jim. "Is this an official call?''

"Oh no, Leonard,'' Jim said quickly. "I told Agent Brockhurst all about how you volunteered to help right after Sarah was killed.''

Brockhurst wondered again if Jim Leland was afraid of Leonard Hansen. Or if he was trying to protect him for some reason. "It's all routine, Mr. Hansen," he said. "We've got a case with no clearcut suspect. I'm asking the same questions of everyone."

"Of Stoney McFarland too? He was right there with her."

Jim rolled his eyes. This was getting crazier by the minute. Next thing they would be grilling Heyward. Or maybe Harriet Setzler herself.

Brockhurst said, "But if you'd killed a woman, would you then immediately report it to the authorities?"

"Can't say." Leonard leaned back against the steps, his face bland. "I never killed anyone. But it might be a good way to fool people. As for me and Mrs. Roth, we were friendly enough although I didn't see much of her, living way out here. We weren't pals; I don't think she ever believed I didn't steal that money or ever forgave me for it."

"And the night she was killed?"

Leonard thought for a moment. "Oh yeah. I was over in Belton, helping a buddy work on his car. Ricky Gibson. You can call him."

Brockhurst took down the name and the phone number. Then he realized he hadn't mentioned the date of the murder. Either Leonard Hansen had a good memory or he'd formulated his alibi earlier.

"You married, Mr. Hansen?"

Leonard's eyes widened; he ran his fingers through his hair, as though considering what the question meant. "Was once. Why?"

"Just wondered."

Jim grinned abruptly. "Leonard was a hell of a ladies man in school, don't let him kid you." Then the police chief changed the subject. "You do any hunting anymore, Leonard? Lordy, your daddy really could shoot."

"Yeah, he could." Leonard hesitated for a moment and Brockhurst thought he noticed a change in the other man's eyes. "Naw, I don't have time to hunt anymore."

In a few minutes Brockhurst and Jim left, thanking Leonard for his time. When the two policemen were back in the car, Jim said, "I don't get it. When are you going to ask him about what Mrs. Setzler said?"

"I'm not sure. If he turns out to be a genuine suspect, I don't want him to know about it until I'm ready. He'll be a lot more forthcoming *before* he knows he's being seriously questioned.''

''So you agree with Stoney—you think Leonard might have done it? But why?''

''No, as a matter of fact, I don't agree. I want to talk to McFarland, but right now my gut instinct is no—Hansen's too open and nobody's open unless they're very sure they aren't involved or else very stupid. And I don't think he's stupid. He could be that cocky, I suppose—so positive he won't screw up and give himself away. But I still think the best bet is J. T. Turner. He's a guy who's turned on by breaking into houses. And sometime before that night I think he met Sarah Rothenbarger.''

Relieved somehow, Jim settled comfortably against the car seat for the ride back to town.

Anna and Stoney's twelfth wedding anniversary was that Saturday. They had always enjoyed celebrating special occasions, particularly their anniversary. On their wedding night they had drunk Dom Perignon for the very first time, as they had continued to do for several years afterward on their anniversary, until Anna quit working full-time and they could no longer afford eighty-dollar champagne. But they still nearly always went out to dinner, always bought each other special gifts, always drank out of the same sterling goblets used at their wedding. It was one of their few concessions to tradition. Even when their marriage lost its original ardor, they always kept up the ritual of their anniversary as though nothing between them had ever changed.

They had been very distant for weeks now, ever since the night Anna told Stoney about Monkey. A vital thread that always connected them, despite problems, had snapped that night. Sometimes she thought about having an affair. It wasn't that she wanted to be free of Stoney; she didn't, she had never stopped loving him. But she wanted to be breathless again, she wanted that cherished illusion back—that she would not only love a man for life but be in love with him for life too. She wanted the passion back too. Somewhere along the way she and Stoney had forgotten how to communicate without words, and now even the words piled up into mountains of misunderstanding. She had to fix it or leave him. She refused to accept less. Women who settled—or gave up like her mother—always turned bitter in the end.

But she wanted it to come easily.

They didn't go out on their anniversary this year. It would have meant driving all the way over to Fairfield Plantation and the drive home late at night, after cocktails and a good bottle of wine, was long and arduous. They would stay home, grill out under the trees. Anna would have preferred a weekend in Savannah or Charleston, but given their edginess with each other lately, she didn't even suggest a trip. But she did buy the only bottle of Dom Perignon that could be found within fifty miles.

Stoney came down for dinner in his tux coat and bow tie and cutoffs. Anna turned around, champagne bottle in hand, and saw him and laughed out loud. They just stood there laughing for a few minutes; it seemed like the best, the only, laugh they'd shared in months. After he fixed them a drink, he changed again and they went outside and broiled filets on the grill—a treat, since they rarely ate red meat anymore.

Silas stood at attention by the charcoal kettle grill and stretched his long nose to inhale the sizzling aroma. Stoney, wielding a pancake flipper, reached down to pet him. "Don't even think about it."

Anna watched them, martini in hand, her rayon slacks and shimmery matching blue top already damp in the humid evening air. "What's been our best anniversary?"

Stoney didn't hesitate. "The day I came home two years ago and you had this fat little puppy tied up to the porch post so he wouldn't fall off and kill himself." He looked at Anna for a moment. "I always wanted a dog like this and I always wanted someone to give him to me. I loved it. Until two weeks later when he lifted his leg on my golf clubs."

"Yeah, then you wanted to give him away, as I recall." She stared silently at the pond. "My favorite was our first. That French place in Georgetown. That waiter who was so friendly. You asked him if we could take the menu home, since it was our first anniversary, remember? The menu was gorgeous, it looked like a real etching. And he shook his head sadly and said they weren't allowed to give them away. Then as we left you slipped him this huge tip because he'd been so nice. We were going out the door when he suddenly opened it behind us and there he was with the menu in his hand. He put his finger to his lips and winked and just handed it to us."

"I remember," Stoney said. "You framed it and put it on

the kitchen wall in Baltimore.'' He paused, then started laughing.

''What?''

He laughed harder. Then he said, choking, ''I was thinking about our worst anniversary.''

Anna rolled her eyes. ''The Outer Banks. Gotta be.'' She giggled. ''I'd almost forgotten that. God. We were camping in that godforsaken place outside Nags Head—and it was a 110 degrees in the shade, not to mention inside our nylon pup tent. We had to stay off the beach because we got so sunburned the first day, so we just got in the car and rode around with the air-conditioning on. All damn afternoon.''

''And remember dinner? We went to that seafood restaurant at five o'clock to get out of the heat and we got there so early they weren't even serving yet but they said we could order a drink''—Stoney gasped, laughing so hard his eyes watered—''but we only had enough money for dinner so we had to sit there drinking water until they started serving.''

''It was so awful! And when we went back to the campground, the elderly woman at the next campsite had been taken to the hospital for heatstroke. I just couldn't believe it. So then we went down to sit in the surf to drink our champagne and a wave knocked the goddamn bottle over!''

Stoney was hugging his side. ''You know, it's a wonder we ever celebrated another anniversary.'' Wiping his eyes, he walked over and kissed Anna. ''You're a hell of a good sport.''

Despite the heat that night, they ate dinner in the back yard, at the picnic table covered with Anna's grandmother's Irish linen tablecloth. Shadows fell finally and the air cooled a little but it was really too hot to eat outside and even Silas got tired and stopped begging and lay down in the grass. Stoney and Anna talked desultorily, tried several topics that all eventually fizzled out and left them wanting more. Several times Stoney started to tell Anna about his suspension. Like a crazy man, he kept leaving the house these days like he was going to work and then riding around all day. Maybe he'd just do that until it was time to go to Columbia, then tell Anna about it when it was all over. When he was reinstated. He knew Anna would take the suspension in stride, but somehow he just couldn't tell her about it now. He couldn't talk to her about that or about the murder, and he couldn't think about anything else and so he grew quieter and quieter throughout the evening.

When the heat got too bad, they finally went inside, taking the champagne into the living room in an ice bucket. Stoney put on some music—Anna's favorite Bach—and they poured the Dom Perignon into the silver goblets and sat on the floor, leaning back against the sofa. Stoney gave Anna her anniversary gift and she gasped when she opened it. He was a man who always gave her nice gifts but over the years the gifts had become both less extravagant and less personal. She held up the royal blue silk nightgown and matching robe, the gown slit far up the right thigh and deeply plunged at the neckline. The soft material felt like liquid pearls.

"Stoney, it's beautiful. It's so—elegant. I can't remember the last time you gave me something so lovely." She thought for a moment about her first Christmas with him, about the red leather jacket he had given her. She had grown up without lavish gifts—her mother had always provided the necessities, but single parents could rarely manage luxuries. Out of style now and even a little tight, that red coat was still hanging in the back of Anna's closet.

Stoney opened his gift and laughed. He held up the paisley silk pajamas from the same store in Savannah where he'd bought Anna's gown and robe. "We must be two people in need of a lot of sleep." He lifted his champagne glass and touched the rim of hers. "So. Want to put on our gifts and meet upstairs?"

"Do you?" Why didn't she just say yes? Why did it feel like she was being put on the spot, being required to make a decision.

"I asked you first. Would you rather just stay put?"

"What do you want to do?" She waited for him to commit.

"Whatever you do."

She didn't want to be a power broker. She wanted him to bend her over and just kiss her until it rendered her incapable of thought.

He wanted to give her choices, since that seemed important to her. Inside he could feel how badly he wanted her, needed her, needed her touch, but he could not make himself say that he needed her. If she needed him, she would say so, wouldn't she?

She waited. If he wanted her, he would do something. Wouldn't he?

After long seasons of self-protection, neither would risk being the only partner desperate for change. And so they both went to sleep that night—only to sleep—in silk that had somehow lost its luminescence.

Eleven

WHEN ANNA STARTED packing for her trip to Savannah, she had no idea she was embarking on a journey of seduction. She moved back and forth from the bedroom closet to the soft-sided nylon suitcase spread open on the bed like an unmade sandwich, absently stuffing a pair of jeans and extra rolls of film in its deep pockets. She crossed to the oak dresser and pulled open a bottom drawer and withdrew a tank top and clean underwear; then she went back to the closet and glanced inside at the hanging rows of clothes, her eyes fingering each item tentatively. Anna never felt secure when packing for a trip; she was always sure she would leave behind the one thing she would need most. About to pull the folding closet door shut, she abruptly noticed a black lace gown hanging at the very back, behind the bulk of the clothes, right next to the new silk gown Stoney had given her for their anniversary. He had also given her the black nightgown, on their second anniversary. She had kept it all this time, although she rarely wore it now. Black lace had not solved their problems. But she took the nightgown out of the closet and put it in her suitcase. What the hell, she might as well wear it sometime.

She was still packing when the doorbell rang. Half-asleep in the kitchen, Silas growled and Anna walked over to the bedroom window and peered out at the street. No car. In a moment she went out in the hall and down the stairs and opened the door.

Marian Davis stood on the other side of the storm door. "Hi," the black woman said. "You busy?"

Anna shook her head. "Not really. Packing. You know, to go to Savannah. I shot those Daufuskie pictures last week. My meeting at the ad agency is so late this afternoon I'm staying overnight."

Marian nodded as Anna waved her inside and asked what she had been doing all week.

"Not much." Anna was leading the way to the kitchen when Marian stopped suddenly. "Anna, can I talk to you?"

The other woman turned around. "Sure. What's up?"

Marian paced into the living room with Anna following. "It's about that day we went to see Maum Chrish," Marian said. Her voice wavered and she stopped and took a deep breath. "I discovered something out there and I've got to tell somebody." She gazed down at the carpet beneath her feet. "Most people will think I'm crazy."

Anna crossed and laid her hand on Marian's arm. "What's going on?"

"You know I came back to Essex to look for my mother?" When Anna nodded, Marian added, "I think I've found her."

Anna's eyes widened. "She's come back?"

"She's been back. God knows how long."

Anna frowned. "I don't understand."

"She's been here all the time." Marian sat down on the sofa and told Anna about the granite amulet she had once given her mother. Anna sat down too, listened quietly.

"Suddenly I remember so many things I'd practically forgotten—how superstitious she was, how esoteric and mystical, how tall. I was so busy turning my back on everything I didn't see what was sitting right in front of me."

Anna stared. "You're losing me."

"It's her. Maum Chrish."

"Maum Chrish?" Anna said slowly.

Marian held out her hands. "Don't you see? She's my mother."

"What?"

Suddenly Marian smiled, clapped her hands together. "Now that I've said it out loud, to someone else, it's so real. I've found her."

Anna started to raise several disturbing doubts but then Marian ran on again, her voice high and excited, "I know it sounds crazy. How could I have been here for five years and not found her before, just ten miles down the road? How come nobody else knew, and if they did know, why didn't they tell me? I thought about all that, I've thought about nothing else all week. It's incredible, but it's got to be true. I've been here all this time but I don't think I ever laid eyes on her until Sarah's funeral.

Very few people in town ever see her, she keeps to herself so much. It's been decades since she left. She looks different now, just like I do. I don't think she knows who I am at all. Or she would have come to me or maybe"—Marian stopped abruptly—"maybe she can't, maybe she is out of touch with reality." A pause. "Oh, Anna, don't you see?" Marian reached over and took Anna's hands. "I've found her."

Despite her misgivings, Anna reached out and hugged Marian. "Have you told anybody else?"

"No. Not even Harriet. I wanted to tell you first. If it weren't for you, I wouldn't even know. If you hadn't kept asking me about her. If I hadn't gone with you that day."

"What will you do now?"

"I'm going to tell her who I am," Marian said, getting up. "I haven't been able to think clearly all week. But that's what I'm going to do. I'm going to tell her. Today."

Before Anna could say a word, Marian was in the hall, heading toward the front door. Anna followed her, called out cautiously, "Be careful."

Marian stopped and looked Anna squarely in the face. "You can't believe she's connected to Sarah's murder?"

"No." Anna swallowed. "What I mean is, she may not recognize you. She may not want to be found."

Marian shook her head. "I know. I've thought about that too. But I've got to tell her. No matter what happens, I've got to tell her I know who she is."

Five hours later and seventy-five miles away, Anna headed for the Savannah riverfront, and her room at the Hyatt, as late afternoon settled over the old Georgia city. She crossed to Lafayette Square and continued on Oglethorpe Avenue near Colonial Park Cemetery. The burial ground for Georgia's Jewish colonists made her think about Sarah Roth, a woman she'd hardly known but whose death was like the circles Stoney made skimming stones on the McCloskey pond. Wider and wider those circles grew, changing the surface of the water until the reflection of the live oaks churned and scattered—reforming later, albeit altered.

Ahead lay River Street in its cobbled expanse of gentrified restoration, a village of shops and bars and restaurants housed in restored cotton warehouses fronting the Savannah River. She padded along Factor's Walk, the iron maze of suspended stairs and walkways once trod by harried men bidding on cotton; then she climbed down the steep stone steps, worn slick in the middle, that led from Bay Street to the river. River Street itself, with its painted tavern signs jutting out above sidewalks paved with oyster shell tabby, was vividly alive this late afternoon with the sounds of shuffling shoppers and late lunchers or early drinkers. A mammoth ocean barge flying the Australian flag was making its way through the narrow channel fronting the street; beside it, a small red steam train whooshed down its tracks in the middle of the pedestrian street, carrying tourists from one end to the other. Anna usually enjoyed this carnival atmosphere but today it had little effect on her. She was too irritated about her meeting. Thinking of it, bristling, she walked all the way to the end of River Street. There she sat on a bench and snapped her portfolio open and thumbed through the glossy prints of Daufuskie Island. She thought these were perhaps the best photographs she had ever taken.

The voice of the ad agency president rang in her ears: "I'm not saying these aren't good, Anna. They are. But they're not right for the brochure. They aren't what we discussed six months ago when you asked for the assignment." The man in the pinpoint shirt regarded her as he might a confused child, then picked up one of the contact sheets. "I can't put my finger on it exactly. They're too . . . emotional, sentimental, something. They lack intellectual distance." The man hesitated again, still staring at the contact sheets. "There's also an exotic, almost erotic, quality here that I've never noticed in your work before. Like you didn't have control over your material." He turned and winked at Anna. "What *were* you thinking about out there? Not that I don't find it personally appealing, you understand. But our client's market is Yuppie families. Those condos weren't meant to be love nests."

Anna stared at the glossies again. There was something sensual in these pictures. Despite the commercial nature of the assignment, she'd deliberately emphasized the remoteness of the island, its primitive wildness. These photos were cousin to those she shot that day in the swamps with Marian. Frenzied pictures. Landscapes that were violent outbursts. As though she'd bypassed isolated light in favor of exposing its conjunction with matter. *Sentimental?* Who the hell did he think he was?

She put the photographs back in her portfolio and snapped the case shut. Then she barreled back down River Street so fast that she almost collided with a teenage boy in baggy jams. Next she passed an old man with a three-day-old beard, a suitcase in one hand and a carved walking cane in the other; he wore a T-shirt which read I CAME, I DRANK, I OFFENDED. At the first outdoor café on the street, Anna sat down under a multicolored umbrella and ordered a glass of chardonnay. Of course, if she wanted to make a living taking pictures, she couldn't afford to screw up big-ticket assignments. When her wine arrived, she turned to stare out at the river. Wavy sunlight lay across its surface like a gold racing stripe painted by a drunkard. Just across from Anna's café was a small concrete plaza built out over the river. Several tourists lolled comfortably on benches watching ships come in and out of the harbor. One man had his arms crossed and his loafered feet stuck out in front of him like long stickpins. He was so attractive she stared. Corporate type, a little roguish with long curly black hair, some Italian in there somewhere, Brooks Brothers suit worn with crafted careless-ness, silk tie loose, black eyes fastened directly on her.

She looked away. Glancing in the other direction, she studied the eighteenth-century wooden ship which had been converted into a floating restaurant, watched it rock back and forth. The wine, now her second glass, made her feel equally afloat. She uncrossed her legs, lifted her tie-dyed silk skirt slightly to feel the breeze, and signaled the waitress for another glass of wine. The heat and wine and frustration of her meeting crowded in behind her eyes and she leaned back in her chair, letting Savan-nah's languid slowness wiggle up between her sandaled toes like a fever, spreading itself along her calves and thighs.

"Want company?"

Brooks Brothers stood at full tilt, over six feet as lithe and winsome as a ballet dancer. He pulled out the chair opposite Anna and slid into it, his movements consistently graceful. He introduced himself, then said, "It's too nice a day to drink alone."

Anna smiled. He was incredibly beautiful, almost feminine. Gay? Even his eyelashes were long and silky. They talked for a few minutes about the continuing restoration of River Street; by tacit nonverbal agreement they didn't exchange backgrounds or vital statistics, almost as though they knew this was a one-reel movie. Like an adolescent on her first date, Anna flushed with the novelty of being alone with a strange man and suddenly remembered what a friend in D.C. had once said—"The best sex in the world is with a stranger." Anna had thought such a claim perfectly ridiculous, having slept with a few strangers in college. But now she wondered.

"The renovation's really coming along," he said, leaning over the table toward her. "I live right up there." He pointed above them, to the right. "They're converting the upper stories into lofts. Finally. Gives you a terrific view of the river and the marshes."

The musk of the river water combined with his aftershave and she breathed in both. A part of her still loved drama and mystery and men who embodied them. The stranger watched Anna intently and she knew that he was trying to decide when—and how.

"Another glass of wine? Upstairs?"

She looked at him for a long time and then, without thinking about it, she was walking down River Street beside him. They stopped at a building two blocks away, beside a service elevator marked RESIDENTS ONLY. His loft was a long open room with exposed brick walls and a stark white ceiling above heart pine flooring recently refinished. A brass and glass table with four cane chairs sat in the front bay window that overlooked Bay Street, while a papazan sofa surrounded by large throw pillows sat atop an Oriental carpet in the center of the room. At the other end, beneath the open windows that admitted the setting sun and the sounds of the river, was a king-sized brass bed. No kitchen at all.

He was behind her when he closed the door. "I wanted you the minute I saw you," he said quietly over her shoulder.

She turned around and looked at him. Where did men get such sexual confidence with women they didn't even know? She couldn't imagine herself saying anything like that to Stoney, to anyone. Even when it was true.

"Would you like more wine?"

"No." The only thing she wanted was for him to take his clothes off.

Obligingly, he moved toward her, smiling confidently. He did not kiss her, did not reach for the buttons on the front of her blouse. Instead, staring her in the eyes, he just leaned down and raised her skirt with practiced ease and slipped his hand beneath it.

All the way out to Maum Chrish's cabin, Marian thought about Anna. Inadvertently, Anna really was responsible for her finding her mother. What could she do for Anna? What could she do to make Anna feel more at home in Essex? Then, as the

woods thickened around her car, Marian thought only of her
mother.

What would she say to her? How should she put it?

Marian parked her car and plunged into the woods, too
excited to be nervous about the perennially dark interior. It
was hot and the dead brush under her feet crackled from the
lack of rain, as she passed several cypress trees and a row of
live oaks. She thought for a moment about the tree spirits of
the voudouists, which she had always dismissed as unenlightened. Trees were just trees, products of the nutrients in the
soil from which they sprang. The same soil into which dead
bodies were placed. Briefly Marian remembered her mother
saying she wanted to be buried in a pine box when she died—
and especially not in a concrete vault underground like
Mr. William. Abruptly Marian stared at a live oak in front
of her. The earth absorbed nutrients from everything placed
in it. Bodies decayed and became a nutrient, helping to produce new trees. A scientific fact. Thus, to the voudouist the
spirit of the dead resided in the tree their body nourished.
Lonnie had feared being trapped in a metal casket or concrete
vault, her spirit unable to get out. Who was to say this wasn't
as valid as Christians who were buried facing East in order
to see their Maker on Judgment Day?

When Marian reached the clearing, Maum Chrish was standing at the fire in front of her house, wearing a white caftan with
a white *agouéssan* scarf draped across it. Marian thought the
older woman looked as though she were waiting.

For a moment they stared at one another, neither woman
saying anything. Finally Marian approached the larger woman
and said, "I need to talk to you. I know who you are now."

"You are the one who's been sent."

The voice was not familiar to Marian but she could scarcely
recall her mother's voice anymore; this, however, was the most
mellifluous sound she'd ever heard issue from inside anyone.

"I'm Alma."

Maum Chrish did not say anything, just looked at Marian as
though memorizing her.

"Don't you recognize me? Don't you know me? Alma. Your
daughter."

"You are the one who's come."

Marian's eyes filled with tears. "Please," she cried. "You
must remember me. You have to." She stared at the ground for
a second, then raised her head. "The rock. You have a rock.

With a cross on it. I gave it to you. I found it in the yard. In town. Remember?''

When Maum Chrish did not respond, Marian whirled around and ran toward the house. She took the steps two at a time, burst into the cabin, and scrambled into the bedroom. She shook the Bible and the rock on its string fell out and hit the floor. A small shard of granite broke off on impact but Marian didn't stop to pick up the extra piece; instead, she careened through the house and back down the steps. She held the broken stone in front of Maum Chrish. ''I gave you this. You said it was your good luck rock.'' Marian held the string wide and slipped the amulet over the older woman's neck.

Maum Chrish stood very tall and crossed herself on the fore-head, then crossed herself over her breast. Her hand made a cross on her left shoulder. She paused for a moment, then she cried *''Hévio-Zo,''* joyfully, crossing herself on her right shoulder. She stepped back and prayed fervently and Marian was suddenly sure the other woman prayed for someone's *gross bon ange*, the part of the soul irrevocably lost at death. Mesmerized, Marian watched and tried to understand. Then Maum Chrish walked over and touched Marian's forehead and sang aloud:

Ma'p di ou bonjou,
Papa Legba Ati Bon Katarouleau
ma'p di ou bonjou
Papa Loko Ati Dan Poun'goueh Ibo Loko
ma'p di ou bonjou,
Papa Danbhalah Wédo.

Maum Chrish stopped and took off her *agouéssan* scarf and draped it across Marian's chest and right shoulder, knotting it at the opposite hip. And Marian realized the older woman was singing the voudou initiation ceremony.

Marian became a child again. Maum Chrish led her inside the cabin and around the room, speaking to her in whispers as they passed each symbol on the walls of the house. Together the two of them stood in front of the *poteau-mitan*, as Maum Chrish talked and Marian listened. From time to time Maum Chrish sprinkled water on the center post and once she left some rice at the crossroads of the *vévé* drawn in front of it. All the while the younger woman felt as though she moved in a dream, a somnambulant consciousness she had known only a few times in her life—during sex sometimes, when communication was so entirely physical and telepathic that hours were crammed into minutes and minutes loomed longer than years. Maum Chrish held Marian's hand and Marian was content with that; in the soothing hypnotism of the other woman's voice she didn't demand the answers she needed—why did you leave me, why are you living like this, why haven't you tried to find me, why does no one know who you are. Rather, Marian merely received what she was given, became a vessel of transfer.

Night had overtaken the swamps but Marian wasn't afraid: if anything, she felt inordinately peaceful as Maum Chrish led her outside again, back beside the fire. The older woman left her beside the fire and went to the edge of the river and leaned over the spot where Seth fished and she cupped her hands to capture river water. "*Manman Bagaille-là*. The water to Ilé in Africa," she said slowly, her back to Marian. "*Djo-là-pasée.*" Marian knew the water had been passed through. Maum Chrish turned around and crossed to the other woman, put her hands out, and framed Marian's face with them as the river water dripped down the younger woman's cheeks. An abrupt breeze blew between them; it crossed Marian's visage with force, migrated from the house to the river to the giant woman to Marian's forehead, an electric charge that made her flesh quiver. She stiffened, almost cried out. Finally she fell to her knees, covered her head with her hands to protect herself from both the power and the responsibility. She felt the current move through her until she jerked and cried out again, her hands on Maum Chrish's feet as the other willed the power complete, forced it into Marian's sacred regions, until it penetrated her cerebellum and took its place inside her consciousness.

In a moment Marian stood up again, shaky, disoriented. She focused her eyes several times, then she picked up a stick and walked beyond the fire and drew another symbolic *vèvè* in the loose dirt. Inside her hand another hand moved and when the drawing was completed, she stared down at the *vèvè* for Maum Chrish. Within it was a smaller design, derived from the larger but clearly distinct, and Marian knew—instantly—that it belonged to her. Her birthright and her inheritance.

It was almost dark by the time Lou Brockhurst left the Ashton County Law Enforcement Center. He had been there most of the afternoon—arguing the greater part of it. Shortly after lunch, when he got back from checking out Leonard Hansen's alibi for the night Sarah Rothenbarger was killed, he had questioned

J. T. Turner again—this time with the man's court-appointed attorney present. Ben Estes, who was so fresh out of law school his diploma probably wasn't framed yet, had obviously instructed his client not to open his mouth.

"Look, Turner, you've been caught ripping off people before. My guess is that's your career goal. You any good at it or do you always screw up and get caught?"

Nothing. The chubby little greaser didn't even look angry.

They sat in the same examination room, a windowless box, and the stench of the incarcerated man reminded Brockhurst of a drug case he'd once worked, dopers who'd lived in an abandoned farmhouse and didn't bathe for weeks or wash any clothes or even empty their garbage. Turner smelled just like that, a combination of filth and sweat so pungent it was worse than a day-old corpse. Brockhurst got up from the table and walked around behind it to clear his head and olfactory passages, wondering what the wet-behind-the-ears lawyer thought about his client's hygiene.

"You've admitted being in Essex before Sarah Rothenbarger was killed and—"

"Mr. Turner didn't quite understand when you asked him about that," the young attorney interposed. "He thought you were referring to the night of the murder. To me, quite honestly, your question almost sounded like entrapment."

Brockhurst smiled. "Mr. Turner didn't understand then, and now he's gone completely deaf and dumb. That the size of it?"

"He has explained his whereabouts the night of the murder and he's cooperated with the authorities on every count. You have no justification for holding him any longer."

The kid was right but Brockhurst ignored that fact for the moment. "But can Mr. Turner deliver anyone who can verify what time he left Essex that night or where he spent the remainder of that evening?" Brockhurst sat back down at the table. "Mr. Turner is a man with a record who happened to be in the right place at the right time and can't prove what he was doing there."

Turner shot Brockhurst a derisive look. Brockhurst saw it and stared back. "Easy to kill an old lady, I guess, hefty guy like you."

Turner opened his mouth but Ben Estes' hand on his arm stopped him. "Don't answer that." The attorney gazed at Brockhurst. "You're not going to get anywhere by badgering him."

And in the end Brockhurst didn't. Later Turner was released and Brockhurst watched him shuffle out of the lockup. When the suspect stepped outside and started down the road toward Ashboro, the detective moved to a window and continued to stare at him. Watching to see how Turner acted, what he did, upon being released. But the obese man did nothing unusual, so Brockhurst left his window perch and went into the file room to again study the post-mortem report on the dead woman, along with the initial statements given by Stoney McFarland and Ed Hammond. There had to be something everyone was overlooking. Something that would make the difference between seeing this case from the outside, as a detective, and seeing it from the inside, from the vantage point of the killer. Think like him, find him.

He sat down and studied the reports for another hour, chewing gum to keep from nervously biting his lips. After a while he looked up and rubbed his eyes, alone in the small room. He pushed the files on Sarah Rothenbarger away and thought about his interview that morning with Ricky Gibson, who ran a one-man auto repair garage in the small town of Belton some fifteen miles from Essex. White concrete building with two bays, odd parts of a Chevrolet engine spread all over the floor of one side like a jigsaw puzzle. Sixties Corvette parked outside, missing a door and fender, several VW bugs, and what looked like an old Army jeep.

Brockhurst found Ricky Gibson underneath the Corvette, in dark green workclothes smeared with oil and grease. The detective identified himself and saw the immediate antipathy in the other man's eyes. A guy who didn't like cops. "I wonder if you could tell me what you were doing on the night of April 12th."

"How come you wanna know?"

"I'm checking the whereabouts of various people that night. Strictly routine. But one of them claims to have been with you."

"Hansen, right? Yeah, he was here; he helps out once in a while for extra cash, good man with transmissions."

"Was anyone else here?"

Ricky Gibson put down his wrench. "No. Why?"

"What time did you two finish that night, what time did Mr. Hansen leave?"

"About midnight, I reckon. We worked late. We put a new muffler on this baby." Gibson indicated the Corvette.

Midnight, Brockhurst thought as he walked out of the law enforcement center. Sarah Rothenbarger was killed between eleven P.M. and one A.M. Around midnight Hansen was leaving Belton, presumably driving to the other side of Essex, where he lived. About midnight Turner was hitching a ride out of Essex and, failing to find one, walking toward Ashboro, finally stopping to sleep in an old barn. If Gibson was telling the truth, Hansen hardly had time to get to town and kill Sarah Rothenbarger before Stoney McFarland showed up. Turner, on the other hand, was already there at the right time.

Brockhurst got in the Chrysler and started back to Essex. He needed to question Maum Chrish again. Finally he turned on the radio to take his mind off the case. He fiddled with the dial and settled on a rock station. The DJ was talking about a "Blue Moon Party" along River Street in Savannah that night, how the second full moon in a month was so odd clairvoyants believed it portended change and upheaval. Brockhurst wondered, briefly, if he was going to need a clairvoyant to solve this case. He didn't really believe in them.

He was tired by the time he reached the Essex Motel, which sat forlornly along Route 321 and featured a string of one-story stucco cabins painted a garish yellow. In the center of the wagon train of rooms was a small office with a neon sign blinking VACANCY in its plate glass front window. Brockhurst noticed that the elderly manager had closed up and gone to bed. He maneuvered his car around the cracked blue swimming pool whose slightly stagnant water completed the general aroma of neglect. Better days clearly weren't expected here.

The only guest, Brockhurst climbed out of his car and headed for his room.

Anna did not drive back to Essex until the evening of the following day. She almost didn't go home then. Had there been anywhere else she truly wanted to go, she'd have just started driving. But ironically, the person she most wanted to see right now was in Essex. Who was also the person she least wanted to see. Stoney. Which was why she spent the entire morning having breakfast and idly looking around the shops on River Street. Putting off what she simultaneously desired and dreaded.

Anna's experience the night before had not exactly been a fait accompli. God, she couldn't even do cheating right.

She had stopped her stranger while he was going down on her. She still couldn't believe it. He was as seductive as a man who'd attended an exclusive finishing school for sex, the way he'd stop and raise his head to watch her face, to gauge what she felt, throwing his dark curls back carelessly as he watched her. There was no hesitancy in him, no awkwardness, no insecurity. He was born for what he was doing; he kept lifting her up to some high place (heaven?) and leaving her there so skillfully, just long enough for her to float back a little, so he could bring her back up again, make her go even higher than she'd believed possible. It should have been the experience of a lifetime, something to remember in odd moments, when making love to her husband or just feeling the sunlight on her face in a certain way or hearing the expression "Blue Moon."

It would have been too—if she hadn't stopped him so she wouldn't come. Suddenly she did not want to give him this, did not want to share herself with him. He was so suave she felt manipulated. She didn't want him to know what her face looked like. And so she suddenly pulled away, got up, and began getting dressed. At first her companion looked dazed, an erection the size of a submarine nestled between his legs. When she headed for the door, he began to call her names, all the coarse and vulgar epithets men have invented for women. Anna stood outside the door after she slammed it, leaning against it, listening to the curses. Hot tears ran down her face, not because of the derogatory names but because she knew she could never tell Stoney what she felt now. It called for an ancient word she would bear alone, something so unstylish people would laugh if she said it aloud—heartsick, maybe. She had broken something fragile inside which could never be fused into place again. Yet she had aborted the moment's pleasure on purpose: in her way she had finally paid back Rand Ayres.

By the time Anna pulled up in front of the McCloskey house, she had choked back the tears. Past and present. Tiredly she climbed out of the Subaru, the smell of unrequited sex still on her somehow in spite of her shower that morning, and walked up the sidewalk. Then she noticed that all the downstairs lights were on. She dreaded seeing Stoney. Would he be able to tell? (And worse—was this legitimate cheating, given that she didn't finish it?) At the back door Anna fumbled in her purse for the door key, gazed for a second at the pond and the live oaks. It had been so long since they'd sat out there, Stoney throwing stones in the water. Sarah Roth's murder had unleashed a madness none of them were safe from. Anna found her key and pushed it in the lock and turned the doorknob. The kitchen was blazing; the lights over both the sink and the stove were on. She knelt down to pet Silas. "Hi, boy. You leave on all these lights?"

She walked into the room. Beside the stove sat a full pot of soup, cold and untouched. Next to the pot was a bowl and a spoon. She turned around, called toward the hallway, "Stoney?"

When he didn't answer, she crossed to the hall and stared up the stairs. "Stoney, you home?"

No answer. Anna hurried up the staircase and checked all the rooms but there was no sign of him. Where would he be this time of night? She came back downstairs and recrossed to the kitchen to look for a note. There wasn't anything on the counter or on the refrigerator door. Obviously he'd left in a hurry, without eating the soup he'd warmed up for dinner. Finally Anna put her portfolio in her office and turned off some of the downstairs lights and locked the back door. Upstairs, she filled the bathtub with hot water. Thinking of Blanche DuBois and her hot baths in the hot summer, Anna slipped off her wrinkled dress and sank gratefully into the steaming, sudsy water. She lay there for a moment, her head cradled by the white ceramic ledge. Then she looked for her washcloth and saw that she'd left it on the sink across the room. So she soaped up her hands and took her right leg in her hands and washed it, enjoying the satiny feel of her own skin in the water. She washed her left leg the same way, ran her soapy fingers across her abdomen and over her breasts.

A half hour later Anna stood up and dried herself off, rubbing the towel between her legs with a longing left unquenched by the bizarre events in Savannah. She walked into the bedroom and glanced at the clock. Where was he? In a moment she pulled on a short gown, the silky fabric soft against her skin, and climbed into bed. The bed felt immense and she moved to the center of it and tried to go to sleep.

The hum of the cicadas outside the window throbbed in her ears and soon she got up again, thinking she'd close the window and turn on the air conditioner. What would it cost to put central air in this rambling old house? She stood at the window and breathed in the dense scent of midsummer, loam and fertilizer and narcissus and new-mown grass and ripening tomatoes. She grew warm at the window and the gown clung to her, already damp. That strange blue moon was still above her, outlining the trees around the pond with phosphorous. The live oaks glowed electric, overcharged, their thick hard trunks disappearing inside the soft folds of their leaved branches, which trembled and shuddered in the warm slow-moving wind.

Technically maybe she hadn't broken her marriage vows but

it was a moot point; she knew she would never be the same again. Anna looked back out the window. This place, this damn place. South Carolina always felt like the Mideast looked: hot, recondite, as dangerous as a black hole.

And intensely sexual.

Before she and Stoney had moved here, things had made sense between them. They were evenly matched intellectual companions. Good friends. Now they couldn't even talk. Now all she did was lie sweating in a stupor of caged lust. Anna turned around, looked at the clock again. Where on earth was he? She licked her lips. Tonight was beginning to remind her of the night Sarah Roth was killed.

She leaned out the window and breathed in the fragrant night air. Late summer roses were just opening up; soon the chrysanthemums would bloom, that last flower before winter. In the distance she heard thunder. Moving closer, it rolled across the sky and rattled the windowpanes. A flash of lightning, another crash of thunder, and she could hear Silas moving around downstairs as he usually did during a storm. More lightning, the wind pounded against the house. Maybe it would finally rain. She listened intently. But it stopped dead in a second. Another electrical storm, nothing more. Just like all the other nights.

Twelve

BY MIDNIGHT THE Essex Motel had become a blazing sideshow. The door to every room stood open with all the lights inside glaring garishly. At least ten people moved back and forth between the office and a particular room in the center of the motel, Jim Leland and Sheriff Buck Henry among them. The elderly motel manager, who looked more dazed than shocked, kept repeating his story to anyone who passed him on the sidewalk. How he didn't see or hear anything, he usually closed up about six or so and retired to the end room where he lived, how at about nine o'clock he went down to the office to get a book he'd left there, he loved reading those Mickey Spillane novels. Also he had to shut off the coffeepot in the office. Yes, he heard the detective's car pull in, he thought it was maybe seven or seven-thirty, wasn't even dark out yet. Anyhow, later when he went back to the office to get his book and do something about the coffeepot, the coffee was still hot so he decided to go ask Mr. Brockhurst if he wanted a cup. The detective was the only guest so far this summer. He knocked on the SLED agent's door, he knocked and knocked but nobody answered. So finally he got the pass key to see if the man was sick or something. Then he found him. "That nice young fella just a-laying there in a pool of blood."

Jim Leland, who had heard all the details already, nodded at the manager again and walked on down to Lou Brockhurst's room. The SLED agent's prone form still lay on the floor, now covered with a sleazy polyester bedspread. The lab team from Ashton County swarmed around the room like greedy buzzards, picking at the entrails of the carpet and the bed, dusting the furniture for prints, looking for anything they could take away. Outside, Sheriff Henry, who had finished going over the room, headed for Brockhurst's car and Jim turned to follow him, unconsciously tapping the pistol at his belt which he'd begun wearing regularly this spring. The cold-blooded murder of a police detective had made an impression on Jim that even the grotesque slaying of Sarah Rothenbarger had not. "This is too much," he had exclaimed to Stoney earlier. "A guy comes to town, a SLED agent no less, and he gets murdered like this is Chicago or New York City. Something's gonna be done about this—I swear it is."

Stoney didn't say anything. Jim had called him earlier that evening, after the motel manager had called the police chief. Jim hadn't been able to locate Ed Hammond so he'd telephoned Stoney in an attempt to find the medical examiner. Finally Ed had arrived and had examined the body and his initial conclusion was that Lou Brockhurst had been knocked unconscious before his throat was cut with the single slash of a knife. Hard to say what kind of knife yet. Except for the abrasion on the right temple and the one knife wound, there were almost no other marks on the body. Brockhurst had apparently been attacked upon entering the room and, judging from its condition, the struggle had only lasted a few seconds. Whatever hit Brockhurst must have belonged to the killer, because nothing in the room was small enough and heavy enough to have left such a bruise.

Stoney stood in the doorway of the room. Was J. T. Turner big enough to overpower Brockhurst? Was Leonard? Yeah, Leonard could easily have taken Brockhurst; the SLED agent did have a bad leg. But was Leonard stupid enough to kill a policeman? To invite that kind of investigation? For now, surely, something would be done about both murders. Hopefully before anyone else got hurt.

An hour later Stoney drove back to town, but instead of going home, he drove on to the town hall. Despite the late hour, it too was awash in light. Most of the activity, he saw as he entered the unlocked front door, was coming from inside the police chief's office. When Stoney got to the door marked CONSTABLE, he heard the ingratiating voice of Heyward Rutherford.

"This was a great town once. Now we've got *two* murders on our hands. *Two*. It's high time you started acting like you're a policeman. It's time you started doing your job. You can be a great man now if you just apply yourself."

Jim Leland, seated behind his desk, jumped up angrily.

"Heyward, would you quit saying that? I don't want to hear one more goddamn thing about how great everything is."

Heyward rose primly. "My point remains. You are responsible for cleaning this mess up."

Stoney walked in the room just as Jim shot back, "Heyward, maybe you oughta tell us how bad you wanted Sarah's store."

Everyone in the room looked up. Bill Jenkins, who was sitting on the other side of the room reading the report on Lou Brockhurst, stared at the two men, then glanced at Stoney and lifted his eyebrows slightly. They waited for Heyward to respond.

"You can't possibly *mean* what you're suggesting," the silver-haired town council president said to Jim slowly, weighing each syllable.

Bill Jenkins stood up. "Is there anything you wouldn't do for money?"

Heyward looked from Bill back to Jim and then turned to stare at Stoney. "Y'all think I could kill Sarah just to get the store?"

"Heyward, it's not that we—"

The older man cut Jim off. He stared again at each person in the room, one at a time. "What now? Treat every man in this town as a suspect, require everyone in Essex to provide an alibi, trust no one? Is this where we are now? I do have a lot of money, I am a wily negotiator, so of course I could kill Sarah with my bare hands?"

Heyward turned and stalked out. Jim Leland stared after him for a moment, then slammed his fist down on his desk. In a moment he opened a desk drawer and took a key out of an envelope. Crossing in front of Bill Jenkins, he strode to the gun cabinet on the other side of the room and unlocked it and drew out a Winchester shotgun. He pulled open a small drawer in the bottom of the gun cabinet and took out several shells, broke the barrel of the shotgun, loaded it, and then snapped it shut so hard the metal chamber rattled.

Stoney walked toward Jim. "What about J. T. Turner?"

Jim crossed back to his desk, the shotgun under his arm with the practiced ease of a hunter. "Buck called from Ashboro a few minutes ago. They went to pick him up but couldn't find him. Cleared out of that rooming house he was staying in this afternoon. Gone. APB being put out right now."

"Have you—" Stoney hesitated, then went on, "have you considered Leonard?"

Bill Jenkins looked up. "Are you serious?"

Jim turned and glared at Stoney. "Didn't you hear anything Heyward said at all?"

"Heyward and Leonard are two different people."

"Are they? Heyward's lived here forever. Leonard's been gone a few years. Just like you." Jim sighed. "Give me one hard reason to suspect Leonard, one shred of evidence."

When Stoney didn't respond, Jim said, "Leave Leonard alone then. Brockhurst questioned him and even he didn't find anything." Jim paused, then added, "Somebody's killing people around here, and it's scary how different the murders are—no pattern, nothing to go on. And right away you suspect people we've all known a long time—Heyward, Leonard. What about Maum Chrish?"

Jim headed toward the door. "I've got to go see about a warrant. Help yourselves to the coffee."

After he left, Stoney went over and poured himself a cup of coffee; maybe Jim and Heyward were right. Desperation was making them turn on each other. It was almost three now. Did Anna get home all right? Of course she did. Did he leave her a note? He had run out of the house in such a hurry when Jim called he couldn't remember. Anna would be okay; she was not afraid to be alone. He loved that in her, loved her strength and resilience. But he knew he should get on home; he was scheduled to meet with his supervisor in Columbia tomorrow at ten. His whole future might rest on that meeting and so it was imperative that he be alert, rested, clear-headed.

Bill Jenkins, who was still reading on the other side of the room, stood up and stretched. "You going home?"

"I should," Stoney said. "Anna's been out of town, I haven't even seen her since she got back." A pause. "Who's the warrant for?"

"One for Turner, one for Maum Chrish."

"He's really going to arrest her?" Stoney stared at Bill. "I never figured Leland for a bigot."

Jenkins rubbed his ample belly like he'd forgotten to eat dinner. "I don't think this has to do with the color of her skin, Stoney. She's really been a suspect all along. I think Leland's afraid he should have brought her in weeks ago, that maybe if he had Brockhurst wouldn't be dead."

"You really think she lay in wait at the motel, then overpowered a muscular man like Brockhurst and cut his throat?"

"She's not exactly frail herself. Did Jim tell you what Brockhurst discovered in her cabin?" Stoney shook his head and Bill continued, "He found a connection between Maum Chrish and Sarah—Jim just told me about it tonight. Apparently there's some writing all over the walls of her house and some of it happens to be the Jewish alphabet. You gotta admit, that's an odd coincidence."

"Yeah," Stoney agreed slowly, "it is."

"And you know Leonard's got an alibi, don't you? He was with Ricky Gibson the night Sarah was killed, Brockhurst checked it out."

"And Ricky Gibson just happened to show up at the town meeting with proof against Maum Chrish. How convenient."

"Look, I'm no fan of Leonard Hansen's. But you don't have anything even faintly resembling proof to connect him to either murder."

"That's true," Stoney admitted. He drank down the last of his coffee. "I should get home."

"Me too. I'll walk you out." They closed the door to Jim Leland's office and ambled down the hall and out into the predawn darkness. "Think we'll have enough energy to run this evening?"

"Better not count on me." Stoney paused, then asked, "How come you came back to Essex when you finished school?"

"To be your running partner maybe?" The heavier man expelled a tired chuckle. "We've been up all night, so now you want to know my life story? I don't know why I came back. My folks were here? Probably just to be ornery."

"Come again?"

"I refused to turn the place over to the Heyward Rutherfords and Harriet Setzlers—not to mention the Leonard Hansens—of the world. I wanted to be around to annoy them."

Bill waved and peeled off toward his newspaper van as Stoney approached his own Land Rover. Stoney got in and sat for a moment, rubbing his burning eyes. He drove home slowly, carefully watching the streets in front of him. Later, in the bedroom, he mumbled to Anna as he kissed her and fell instantly asleep with his clothes still on.

When Anna woke up the next morning, she could tell it was late by the angle of the sunlight streaming in the window. She reached to the other side of the bed and came up with only empty air. She got up and pulled on a terrycloth bathrobe and headed for the stairs to see if Stoney had let Silas out; if not, the dog was probably about to float away. When she got downstairs,

Silas was nowhere to be found. However, chaotic moving sounds emanated from the basement.

"Stoney?" She crossed to the open basement door on the other side of the kitchen.

"Yeah. Down here. Sorry if I woke you."

In a moment he stomped up the wood steps and put his arms around Anna and kissed her absently. "How was your trip?"

"Where were you all night?" Her tone was indignant and made her feel that much guiltier.

"At the motel, then at the town hall. I was too tired to talk about it last night." He turned to go back down into the basement. "I'll be up in a second."

She stared down the stairs, at his disheveled clothes. Then she went over to the counter to make coffee. While it was brewing she heard him throwing things around, and she wondered how long it would take to straighten out down there once he was finished. Something heavy hit the basement floor and she jumped. Then she went to the basement door and yelled downstairs, "Are you all right? What are you looking for?"

"Found it."

In a moment Stoney's head poked through the basement doorway again. "Did you put Silas out?" Anna asked, turning toward him. Then she stopped, gasped. "What are you doing with that?"

Stoney held the dusty Marlin rifle his parents had given him when he was a kid. He looked at Anna. "Lou Brockhurst was murdered last night."

"My God." She sat down at the table. "What happened?"

"He was attacked at the motel. It was different from Sarah; the weapon was a knife but it was cleaner, more professional." Stoney took the rifle and leaned it against the wall. "I want to show you how to use this."

"No, Stoney. I will not live with a loaded gun in the house. You can't want that either. I thought you hated that thing."

His voice trembled. "*Don't you see we have no choice?* Someone around here is killing people. I'm going to make damn sure the next victim isn't you—or me."

"This is so awful." She crossed to him. "We lived in a violent city for years, yet it never felt like this."

He put his arms around her. "We didn't know the people it happened to. We didn't really care."

Over a breakfast of coffee and toast, Anna asked questions about Brockhurst's murder and Maum Chrish's possible arrest.

Afterward Stoney went upstairs to shower and change. When he came back down in a pin-striped suit, she looked at him oddly. "What's with the suit?"

"I have to meet with some people from out of town," he said. "I'll probably be late."

He started for the back door. "Anna, keep the doors locked. Be careful."

Inside the Rover Stoney put the vehicle in gear, yawning slightly, and headed down Laurens Avenue toward town and the highway. But he veered off to the right at the main intersection and stopped at the town hall; he'd just duck inside for a second and see what was going on. A small knot of people had gathered outside; apparently the news about Brockhurst was spreading fast. Everyone was waiting to see what would happen now. Stoney skirted the group and was almost to the steps when a hand tugged at the back of his jacket. He turned around to face a large boy pushing a Raleigh bicycle. "Hey, Mr. McFarland, they arrested that crazy swamp woman yet?"

"No, Donny," Stoney said brusquely. Then he saw Seth Von Hocke, also standing beside a bike. "Hi, Seth."

Seth regarded Stoney with large, troubled eyes.

"They're gonna arrest her now, ain't that right?" Donny motioned toward the town hall. "I been telling Seth no way she'll get off now. Will they bring her back here?"

"I don't know," Stoney said.

Donny giggled, punched his smaller companion on the arm. "Seth wants to see her real bad. Dontcha, Seth?"

Seth flushed. He had given Donny his piggy bank, two years' worth of quarters, in return for silence about his visits to Maum Chrish.

Stoney nodded at the boys and walked inside the building. When he entered Jim Leland's office, the police chief was standing at the window looking down into the street. He was wearing a fresh khaki uniform but his face was haggard from lack of sleep and he didn't return Stoney's "good morning."

"I'm waiting for Buck Henry," Jim said. "We're on our way to get Maum Chrish." He tapped the legal document folded and tucked into his shirt pocket.

"Jim, you know what will happen." Stoney thought momentarily of Monkey. "Everybody's hysterical. Turner's gone, so they want her. She won't have a prayer in hell of getting a fair trial."

"Why do you care so much? What the hell does that old woman mean to you?"

"Why *don't* you care?"

"Because I know how things *are*. Because I'm smart enough not to argue with what I can't change." Silence. Then Jim turned back to Stoney. "But you aren't giving us—the town—much credit, you know. I'd think a man who made a point of coming back here would be willing to give Essex the benefit of the doubt. Maybe she'll be convicted—if it comes to that—simply because, in the best judgment of the jury, she's guilty. Is that impossible? You want me not to arrest a viable suspect because she might not get a fair shake? What if she did it? You'd have me endanger everyone on the chance some of them can't be impartial?"

"She didn't do it, Jim."

"Then prove who did."

When Stoney left, Jim looked back out the window. People were talking loudly now, gesturing, most looking up at the window where he stood. He closed his eyes for a second and wished he'd wake up doing something else for a living. Why couldn't he be a hunting guide out West like a fellow he'd met in the National Guard? Jim opened his eyes. But who the hell needed a guide around here? No, he'd stay a cop—only he never really thought of himself as a cop. Lou Brockhurst, limp and all, had been a cop. Jim's eyes narrowed. And nobody could be allowed to kill cops. Nobody.

He heard the sheriff's voice in the hall and picked up the shotgun and went out to meet the other man.

A few hours later Anna knocked on Marian's front door. There wasn't a soul on the tree-lined street and it was deathly quiet. Anna knocked again much louder.

Finally the door opened and Anna said, "Did you hear about Lou Brockhurst?"

Marian nodded, her eyes worried. Wearing a long purple caftan, she stepped back to let Anna into her living room. "Somebody called Harriet and she called me."

"Stoney thinks Brockhurst figured out who killed Sarah and the killer knew it." Anna hesitated. "They've got a warrant to arrest Maum Chrish."

"Stoney thinks she did it?"

"No. But Jim Leland does."

Marian closed her eyes and thought about her visit with her

mother two days before. This could not be happening. "But they talked about arresting her after the town meeting and they never did."

"It's different this time." Anna paused. "Did you go to see her? What happened?"

Marian could not talk about it yet, could not share her experience with Maum Chrish with anyone else. "It was—it was something I've been waiting for forever." The black woman's eyes looked distant, as though caught in another time.

Then Marian focused abruptly. "They can't arrest her, Anna. We have to *do* something. She couldn't kill anyone."

The sudden certainty in Marian's voice bolstered Anna's confidence. She said, "You and Stoney and I are the only people in town who believe that." Anna lowered her voice. "We could go out there. We could warn her. Tell her what's happening. At the very least she'd have time to think what to do, to make plans."

"She'd have time to get away," Marian finished. But where would she go? Could she let her mother leave after she'd just found her? Could she let her go to jail? Marian crossed to the window and stared in the direction of Harriet's house. She knew what Harriet would do. She turned to Anna. "This could be interpreted as obstruction of justice, you know."

"Justice? You know better than I do why they're going to arrest her. It doesn't have much to do with justice. It has to do with fear and hatred."

"I'll change my clothes."

Anna nodded and idly walked over to the window as Marian went down the hall. The sun was out, had finally pushed the interminable grayness of the past few weeks into hiding. When Marian reappeared, she was dressed in black slacks and a black T-shirt. Anna studied her for a moment. In the black clothes the honey-gold woman looked darker, more mysterious, more powerful. They barely spoke as they got in Marian's small car and headed out of town. Marian kept her eyes on the road, as the humid wind rushed across them like a warm tide. The more the sun hit both women the more they perspired, and soon the black cloth against Marian's back softened and clung to her skin.

She turned and noticed Anna looking at her. And they hurtled on down the highway.

Stoney was twenty miles outside town when he stopped at a roadside rest area and stared at the endless fields of corn. The stalks were brown on the edges, victims of the vicious drought. What had once been fertile farmland had now turned into an inhospitable environment, was killing itself from the bottom up. He gazed at his watch. He would never make his appointment on time. Begging for his job because of Sumter Brownlow's petty sniveling was demeaning anyway. In light of what was happening in Essex, it seemed downright inconsequential.

He took off his jacket, loosened his tie, and headed back to Essex. Ten miles short of town, he turned off onto a dirt road and followed it past some trailers and several crumbling barns until he pulled up in front of Leonard Hansen's house. Leonard's truck was gone, so Stoney got out and walked toward the house. Apparently Leonard was at work, which was what he'd hoped for. If Jim wouldn't search Leonard's house, he would. There had to be something in there which gave him away.

Unless of course he was wrong about Leonard.

By midafternoon the news of the second murder in Essex had run through town like a wild deer, then it loped out into the far reaches of the county. We hadn't truly recovered from Sarah's murder yet but time had passed, so we were resting more easily in our beds when someone upended them again. True, we didn't lose one of our own this time, someone we had known a long time, whose existence in that house on Aiken Avenue and in the store downtown was crucial to our memory of our own lives. No, our dismay wasn't so personal this time. But it was a whole lot scarier. One incidence of violence could be considered an aberration, a freak occurrence, but two. . . . And a SLED agent no less, a professional trained to be on guard?

Years later we would all remember the few days after Lou Brockhurst's murder as the time when Bill Jenkins published the most incredibly asinine editorial in the Essex *Telegraph*. All about some scientific study involving rats in a cage; seems the rodents got along fine until the scientist increased their number, crowded them up. Then the rats would invariably begin attacking each other. So the aggressive rats were taken out of the group and more docile ones were put in, but still some rats would turn on the others. When the scientist decreased the population, the aggression stopped. Every time. A lack of something (space, whatever) turned the least tolerant violent. Not one of us liked that editorial. We didn't give a damn why some rats attacked others, we just wanted murderers caught and locked up forever. We asked Bill what overpopulation had to do with a town where you were lucky if you saw five people on the street at one time. Bill said that if we were a larger town we'd have had more crime before this, that it was our size which had granted us immunity for so many years. We said, oh how reassuring, thank you very much indeed.

Theorists we needed about as much as we needed a hotter summer. What we needed was for this madness to stop. Now the man we'd trusted to accomplish this was dead. Obviously the killer wasn't a loony preying on old women. He (she?) hadn't stolen this time either. Nothing had been taken from Lou Brockhurst's room; his watch, gold class ring, even his wallet with over a hundred dollars in it was with his body. Brockhurst had not been killed with a hunting knife; instead, Ed would say later, it was probably a switchblade or a long thin kitchen knife. Was there one murderer in Essex or two? That question remained uppermost in our minds for days afterward and most of us finally decided it must be one person—who had killed Sarah and was afraid Brockhurst would find out, and so had to kill again for protection. Perfectly logical theory, assuming the killer was logical.

For some of us, J. T. Turner would have been the murderer of choice, but J. T. Turner could not be found. Anywhere. If he had been found, perhaps the events of the next few days might not have happened. It was Marynell Pittman who started talking about Maum Chrish again. About how big and strong the black woman looked, how she'd probably cut the throat of any number of God's animal creatures. Suddenly everybody was remembering the goat and what happened at Sarah's funeral. Then we heard that Jim Leland was going to arrest the swamp woman, and that fact virtually proved her guilt—when was the last time Jim Leland arrested anybody? Soon rumors clamored for attention like little boys trying to beat each other to the top of a hill. Leland must have found out something new about her, about Maum Chrish, and now they were bringing her in. Maybe now we'd get to the bottom of this. Maybe now—finally—it would end.

If only it'd been that simple.

The swamp lazed at the full height of its senses when Marian and Anna arrived there. Insects buzzed atop the black-green pools of water and the water's surface reflected the outlines of the trees above as well as the rounded shoulders of clouds floating overhead, all suffused with mesmerizing waterborne movement that transported both women instantly. Was the water moving—or did the clouds just make it appear so? Along the bank where they stood, red-passion wildflowers spilled over the edge like honey, and bees hovered at the open-faced yellow lilies which bloomed at the feet of giant oaks half-submerged in water. A monarch butterfly danced by, then rested in the green-yellow reeds that flapped back and forth in the water like bamboo windchimes.

Breaking a law or a taboo with someone invites a rare camaraderie and so the two women moved in harmonious unison. Their worlds had intersected at this corner of a shared nightmare that now eclipsed history. Right now they were not a black woman and a white woman whose ancestry had been bitterly entwined, right now they were compatriots. And so, with the sun behind them as they walked, their shadows fell into the water together and, refracted on its glassy surface, merged until one silhouette could barely be distinguished from the other.

"I'm afraid for her," Marian said suddenly.

Anna reached out and squeezed her friend's hand. "Don't worry, we'll find her first."

All her adult life Marian had prided herself on her loyalty, veracity, honesty. She knew she and Anna were interfering in an arrest and yet it felt perfectly sane to be doing so. The troublesome part was how easy it was—what else might she do if pushed far enough? Marian gazed over at Anna as they moved deeper into the woods. For Anna, it wasn't even blood, it was principle. She suspected both of them shared an unspoken belief—an irrational certainty that an incarcerated Maum Chrish would almost surely die.

When they got to the clearing, they ran up the steps of the cabin and looked through the open door. Marian called out, then strode into the room and crossed to the bedroom. When she returned, she said anxiously, "You think they've already come for her?"

"I don't know," Anna said. "Let's look outside." But she was worried about how quiet everything was. The swamp was too placid. As though what gave it its force, its power, was missing.

They searched the yard, skirted the garden which was verdant despite the drought and examined the fire that still smoldered in its usual place. Anna walked to the edge of the clearing, gazed into the dark water at her feet, and saw her face in a patch of sunlight on its surface. Marian looked beyond the woods on both sides of the house, wandered farther off down the river. As in her visit there with Maum Chrish, the more she walked along the river, walked away from the town, the younger she felt.

Then she stopped sharply, on the edge of a grassy knoll. Her eyes widened, riveted to the scene inside the stand of oaks. A white boy and a black girl whom she knew were obliviously making love. Marian started to turn around but then she saw Anna and put a finger to her lips. Thinking of Maum Chrish, Anna gazed inside the shelter of oaks. Transfixed, she watched the boy and girl for a moment. Then, still unseen, the two women backed away quietly.

Marian and Anna walked back to the far side of the cabin, out of earshot, and sat down in the grass along the bank of the river. Here the water rippled slightly, bubbled across the organic debris that had fallen from the trees, coming toward them, then retreating, as they sat in silence, their thoughts on the young couple. Both women were suddenly shy, afraid of speaking. Watching two people make love was almost as intimate as watching each other.

Finally Anna said, "I guess we should wait a little longer to see if she comes." Her eyes opened wide. "Maum Chrish. If she comes home."

Marian laughed out loud.

"You know what I meant."

They grew silent, linked now in a different way, as the swamp enclosed them in its lacy web.

"Think it's their first time?" Anna asked, surprised at her frankness. "I wish mine had been like that."

Marian looked over at her. "Think there's ever a great way the first time?"

"There are better ways and worse ways." Anna gazed at Marian. "What I mean is, I wish my first love had been something my own age. Another kid who cared about me." She stopped abruptly, looked out at the river, and then boiled over angrily, "I wish it hadn't been a slick older guy who got off on controlling women too young to know better." Above Anna the live oaks took on the sharp, unforgiving outlines of Atlanta maples. "First he made me emotionally dependent on him, then he seduced me, then he virtually blackmailed me into continuing the relationship. And I was crazy about him. Sometimes I think I'll never be free of him, that he's going to ruin the rest of my life too." Anna felt Marian's eyes on her and she looked up. "What is it?"

"I was raped my first time—not far from here."

For a long moment they looked at each other. "Oh my God, Marian," Anna said finally. "I'm sorry. Maybe I shouldn't have brought this up."

Marian held up her hand to fend off sympathy. "It's okay. What you said hit a chord. Blackmail." Marian paused and looked behind her, wishing Maum Chrish would show up. Then she turned back to Anna. "It was a white guy, about my age but bigger. I was only sixteen, living in Harriet's house, feeling more white than black. I started meeting him out here to get drunk, like kids do in high school. A white boy in a dry county could always get booze and for a while I became something of a tippler. Which I kept hidden from Harriet except once or twice when it got out of control, I knew Harriet wouldn't tolerate anybody drinking."

Marian was quiet for a second. "I'd been meeting him for a while and then he started—in my world we'd say 'messing' with me. I didn't pay much attention, I just liked getting tipsy; after a while it was pretty clear he really hated black people. Anyway, one night he was different—he'd had too much whiskey. He kept saying how I was asking for it." Marian rolled her eyes. "Don't you love that line? I gave him the bottle back and said I had to go home. He went into a tirade about how I wanted to get my 'filthy black hands all over his white dick'—so I started running." Marian swallowed, her eyes bereft of self-pity. "He tackled me from behind and it was all over in two horrible minutes."

"Jesus Christ."

No one spoke for a few seconds. Then Anna asked, "Did you tell anyone?"

Marian stared at her hands, at the tense knuckles covered with sweat. She got up and walked over to stand beside the river, her back to Anna. She didn't want to talk about the rest.

"You didn't tell anybody?"

Marian whirled around. "Anna, he did it four times. Who was going to believe four times was rape? Who was going to believe a black girl over a white boy?"

"He raped you *four* times?"

Marian threw her head back. *"See?* Even you don't believe it. You think I must have let him do it, don't you? *Don't you?"*

Anna was on her feet too. "Marian—"

"Admit it. It wasn't rape. *Was it?"*

Anna grabbed Marian and shook her. "Stop it! I wouldn't think that. You know I wouldn't."

Marian pulled away, turned her back on Anna again.

"Let me tell you something," Anna cried. "I didn't know we were telling the whole truth, almost no one ever does. I got used over and over again, Rand Ayres treated me like a puppet. He'd call and there I'd be—legs open, ready to believe whatever he told me. You know why?" Anna's voice trembled, rose sharply. "It wasn't just because I loved him, it was also because I loved getting laid. I loved doing it. But I was scared of being a bad girl. He said he loved me, so I could screw him. And I did, no matter what he did to me. I'm not sure I ever really enjoyed it, but I got off on thinking someone like him wanted me—I was trained since birth to think I was nothing without a man. Rand manipulated me sexually, I knew he was doing it and I let him do it; somehow it gave me a perverted sense of self-worth."

When Marian responded, her voice was thick and twisted, "You were the victim in a power game, Anna; that makes all of us irrational. Take my case. He hated niggers, he even told me that once, but he just had to have one. We were easier to get. Later—after the first time—I got so I felt masochistic revenge in seeing his eyes so full of lust for the very thing he hated. By then, I had no choice anyway. After a while I began to think I was as sick as he was." The black woman took a deep breath but her voice broke when she continued, "What I hate most is why I kept giving in. I took something from Harriet's house once, just once, in anger, a sterling comb that belonged to Mr. William and just sat in a drawer, people always said a black would steal if given half the chance and so I did, I gave the comb to him to sell to get booze—this was before he raped me the first time—and he recognized the initials on it and knew where it came from. He didn't sell it, he kept it. After he raped me, he told me if I told anyone, he'd take the comb to Harriet and tell her what I'd done. That I'd stolen from her. I knew she'd throw me out. She was kind to me but stern—she did not tolerate those who lied or cheated or stole. I would be orphaned a second time."

"What finally happened?"

"I gave him what he wanted. Until one night he went too far—humiliated me beyond words, beat me up. I planned to run away. But then his family suddenly moved out of town."

They were both silent again. Marian glanced back at Maum

Chrish's shack. "I always thought none of that would have happened if I'd had my mother. You think that sort of thing when you're young." She hesitated, briefly remembering her afternoon this past week with Maum Chrish. Then she stood up. "Where is she? God, I hope we haven't come out here on a wild-goose chase. Too little too late." The last words made her think suddenly of Sadie Thompkins. The only person in town who had recognized Lonnie Davis.

"Let's wait a little longer," Anna said. "Maybe she'll show up. If we can't find her, they can't either."

Marian smiled at Anna. "You know, when I first met you, I didn't like you very much. You're probably going to hit me, but I think Essex has been good for you. When you came here, you were one of those people who go around sampling things without any of it ever affecting them. They touch without feeling, eat without tasting, listen without hearing. They 'see' everything with intellectual detachment. But you've changed."

Anna laughed. "Well, I certainly don't feel new and improved. In fact, I don't understand why I do things anymore or what they mean. I think I want one thing but then I get close to it and that doesn't seem to be what I want at all. You're about the only person I can talk to these days."

"Why's that?" Marian was thinking about Stoney, whom she deemed one of the good men of the world.

"I guess because between us there are no expectations, no danger of misreadings."

Misreadings? What she doesn't know, Marian thought. Again she glanced at Maum Chrish's cabin, hoping for a sign of the older woman.

Anna was gazing at Marian apologetically, as though begging off for a coming impertinence. "Did being raped affect you later? You know, in other relationships?"

"Maybe a bit in the beginning," Marian said. "Not anymore."

"I guess what I'm saying is—you seem so comfortable with yourself, about who you are, about sex too."

Now the black woman laughed abruptly. "You mean I look like I've taken responsibility for my own orgasms?"

Anna giggled. "What?"

"Didn't you see *Tootsie*? Remember the scene where the girl says that to Dustin Hoffman?"

"Not really. But it should be that way, don't you think? I mean, I remember my first real affair after Rand, I always felt like I was having to put on a performance so the guy would feel like a great lover—as if my sexuality and everything connected to it belonged to him.'' Out of loyalty, Anna did not mention Stoney's name.

Marian took a deep breath. ''But when you start saying my orgasms are mine, I do it all, that's a power trip too. Sex is no good unless everyone gets beyond ego. If you're going to be that distant from the person you're making love to, you might as well just have sex by yourself. Don't you think? It's like when you always wait for the other person to make the move. Playing the indifferent gatekeeper—a biological role we've inevitably ended up with—is an exercise of power too.''

In a second Marian added, ''I've thought about this for a long time and a lot of it really is biology, I think—men are programmed to breed indiscriminately, but women are programmed to be more careful about it. After all, it has far greater consequences for the female. So she becomes gatekeeper, deciding when is the best time. That's an exercise of power over him, which stems in large part from her biological as well as her emotional nature, and he resents it. We're keeping him from getting what he wants. So over the years men have invented ways to exert their own sexual power over us, to pay us back. The most obvious power he uses is rape—I'll take what you won't give. There's economic power—I'll support you but you must sleep with me regularly. Or psychological power—you should be a good mother and stay home with your children rather than forging a career. Or, if you don't give me what I want often enough, I'll find another woman who will.''

Anna was quiet for a long time. ''Well, what do you do to get around all that?'' Had she and Stoney unconsciously fallen into their own role-playing?

''Anna, I don't have all the answers. I'm just now getting the questions straight.''

''Well, what is it that makes your relationships work now?''

''I don't think that will help you.''

''How do you know?''

Marian sighed. She looked down at the river for a moment, then turned back to Anna and said slowly, ''Because now all my lovers are women.''

Anna went completely dumb.

''No one else in Essex knows this, of course,'' Marian added. ''I might lose my job if anyone did. There's someone I see in

Charleston. I wasn't planning to tell you but I can't be dishonest."

Finally Anna found her voice. "I had no idea."

"I know. It's a pretty invisible thing in this part of the world. I don't tell many people."

"I don't know what to say." Anna paused, then asked, "Is it different, the power thing I mean?"

Marian looked over at Anna. "You really want to know?"

"Yeah, I do."

The black woman smiled a long slow smile that began at her mouth and rose to her cheeks like a blush. "Now I understand why you and Stoney are right together." When Anna looked startled, Marian went on, "Stoney probably doesn't remember this but one night when I was drinking out in the swamps, I got picked up later by the sheriff who brought me back to Harriet's in the middle of the night, threatening to throw me in jail. It was a real scene and Stoney saw the whole thing, the sheriff woke up half the neighborhood. The next day some of the kids who heard about it started calling me names on the sidewalk and Stoney came along and strutted up to me like a good friend and said, 'Hiya, Marian, whatcha doin'?' Not one word about what he'd seen the night before."

"Marian, you know it doesn't make any difference to me."

"I know a lot of people say that."

Anna put her hand on Marian's arm and stared levelly at her. "But I mean it." Then Anna turned to gaze at Maum Chrish's cabin. "It's getting late. What do you think we should do?"

They walked back over to the clearing and rechecked the woods on either side of the house; then they met again at the front porch.

"Anna, I'm scared. I'm afraid they've either found her or else she got wind of it and has already taken off. What if she doesn't come back? I've got to know where she is."

Anna didn't answer. They sat down on the porch steps and waited another hour. Marian went inside the cabin at one point and sat cross-legged on the floor, her eyes closed. When she came back out, she said, "Let's go. We're not going to find her here."

"How do you know? How can you be sure she won't just suddenly show up?"

"I just know. I feel it. Come on."

Together they walked back into the woods.

Thirteen

Harriet Setzler was in the dressing room at Winona's Hat Shoppe when she heard about it. Winona's was Harriet's favorite store in Essex besides Sarah's (which was now all boarded up pending Heyward Rutherford's disposal of it). Harriet trusted Winona's plate glass windows and red brick walls (it was once a gas station) and the heavy oak door whose bell still jingled when it was opened. Whenever Harriet entered Winona's, she saw it as it had looked thirty years before—the narrow front room bisected by an aisle down the middle with bouquets of hats clustered around wooden dressing tables on either side. Winter felts with grosgrain ribbons, spring straws fussy with veils and flowers, cloche and pillbox and wide-brim perched on treelike stands to the ceiling, like bridesmaids staggered by height on the church steps after a wedding. Here, to Winona's, William had brought Harriet every season. He would stand in a corner and nod at the hats he liked as she tried them on.

These days the front room sported only one hat display; Harriet kept hoping hats truly would come back in style but she was about the only woman in Essex doing anything to aid the cause. Thus, most of the floor space in the long narrow room was given over to dresses and suits. Harriet passed the eight-foot oak counter with its ancient cash register and spoke to Winona's granddaughter, a thin severe woman of thirty. Who didn't have the slightest idea how to fit a bra, Harriet thought to herself, moving into the back room of the store. She checked to make sure she was alone, crossed to the budget dresses, and selected three of them after shaking her head at most on the rack. Then she headed toward the makeshift dressing rooms jutting out against one wall, flimsy curtains across their fronts, and sighed for the days when Winona herself came to the house with an armload of dresses for Harriet to consider.

Mildred Stokes and her grown daughter Milly were in the curtained cubicle next to Harriet and Harriet wondered how in the world the two plump females got in that small space at the same time. Hanging her own dresses up in the dressing room, Harriet heard the elder woman ask her daughter, "Did you hear they arrested Sarah's killer? That swamp woman?"

"No, Mama. News never seems to get out our way."

"Picked her up not two hours ago, that's what Jimmy at the gas station said. Wonder why she did it. She always seemed harmless enough, what I saw of her anyhow. Course you can never tell with them. That Ella what worked for us so long, I know she took one of my silver teaspoons."

"If she was stealing, how come you kept her so long?"

"Oh Milly, now you know Ella's right fine. She was with us a long time, I wouldn't hesitate to recommend her to anyone. I just wish she'd bring back my silver teaspoon."

"Mama, maybe you lost that teaspoon. Put it in the disposal or something. What would Ella want with one teaspoon anyway?"

"Ella *took* my teaspoon. It's a fact."

The younger woman sighed as she struggled to get out of a dress that was too small. "Mama, you think I'm too fat?"

"Fat? You're not fat. Just big-boned. Sturdy. All the Stokes women are like that. Why, Aunt Pearl was at least . . ."

Harriet, having tried on two of her dresses, rejected them all and left in the middle of the history of the Stokes clan. Outside she heaved open the door to her ancient Buick and climbed inside and drove toward home. Once on Aiken Avenue she stopped at Marian's house. She knocked and waited, then she walked to the end of the porch and peered into the driveway looking for Marian's car. When it was clear Marian wasn't home, Harriet sat down on the porch bench anyway. It felt better to sit there than to go home alone.

She had been worried about so many things in the last day or two. Ever since that policeman was killed. She gazed down the street and ached for Sarah, for her old friend, for someone to talk to who remembered everything she remembered. That was so important sometimes, just to know you weren't the only person who remembered certain things. Solo memories were too painful, like widowhood. If Sarah were here, Harriet would tell her how concerned she was about Marian right now. About how odd Marian had looked all week, how she kept going off somewhere alone and coming back with a dazed expression on her face—preoccupied with something she would not share. She even looked different—was wearing those big floppy dresses all the time, like the ones Nigra women used to wear to clean in. Her hair was funny too, like she had forgotten an appointment at the beauty shop. This was so unlike Marian, and Harriet knew that when a woman couldn't be bothered with her appearance, she was in serious trouble.

Ever since Sarah died, Harriet had felt she had to protect Marian. But this second murder made it even harder. She could not protect Marian and still do what she felt she ought to do. It wasn't for herself she worried but for Marian. Harriet knew she ought to do what was best, safest, what might protect Marian most in the long run, but *this time*—she felt like she had to do what Marian wanted. She remembered a time when she hadn't done what Marian wanted; she also remembered Sadie Thompkins' ''too little too late.'' Nonetheless, right now nothing would keep Harriet from trying to make it up to her unacknowledged adopted child.

When Anna got home from the swamps later that same day, she found Stoney in the back yard washing the cars. Naked to the waist, he was standing beside the soaped-up Subaru aiming the hose at it. Under the still bright sunlight, the spray of water arced between the two of them and for a moment Anna gazed at him through it, seeing him almost as she might if she didn't know him. From a distance he was just an outline, a man with powerful shoulders and the taut stomach of an athlete; then, as she drew nearer, he took on more dimension, filled out. As he moved back and forth around the car, she could see the bones in his wrist, the hamstrings in the back of his thighs, the slight creases around his eyes. For once, she just stood watching him, not expecting or anticipating anything.

Finally he saw her and called out above the noise of the hose and for a second Anna, so sweaty from the afternoon with Marian in the humid swamps, wanted to jump in the hose spray like a kid. The harsh sun beat down unrelentingly and the water was a welcome respite, so she stepped into the edge of it deliberately as he finished rinsing the car. Then he turned the water off.

Sweat and water running down his bare chest, he looked across the car at her. ''They did it, Anna. They arrested Maum

Chrish. Didn't even have to go out to the swamps, they found her walking along the highway outside town. Like she knew, like she was coming in on her own. She didn't say a word, Jim said, didn't protest or put up a fight or anything. Just went with them. She's locked up in Ashboro. I went over there this afternoon—she was already processed so I went in and asked her if I could help. I don't think she understands what's happening.''

It occurred to Anna that she and Stoney had both spent the afternoon trying to do the same thing—only separately. Why was that? ''Surely there's something we can do.''

At the sound of a mockingbird Stoney glanced behind him, a helpless look in his eyes. Why hadn't he found anything at Leonard's house besides porn magazines? ''I'm not sure there is, except maybe find her a lawyer. There's to be a hearing in a few days. The town is convinced she's guilty and they're going to crucify her. I feel surrounded by hate.''

Anna started to say something but the lost look on his face stopped her. She couldn't think of any words that would help. As he leaned over to dip his sponge back into the bucket filled with sudsy water, Anna came up behind him and slipped her arms around his waist. Without speaking, without asking why he was home in the middle of the day or why they never understood each other anymore, she just held him around the middle, rubbing circles on his stomach with her right hand. Neither said a word. He stood still as her fingers trailed along the waistband of his jogging shorts, and between the sunlight above and the cold water on their skin, they both shivered with the juxtaposed sensations. In a moment Stoney turned back around, smiling but not really aware. ''We haven't had a chance to talk for days, have we?'' Then he kissed Anna quickly.

She opened her lips beneath his mouth and felt his surprise as she slid her tongue inside his mouth insistently, demanding, needing, her arms around his neck pulling him closer until the heat between them grew so potent that she drew back and said, ''I don't want to talk.''

She turned and pulled him by the hand toward the back door. She didn't stop until they were in the cool living room with its bay windows wide open. Wet, they knelt atop the Indian carpet. Her tongue was inside his mouth as she slowly undressed herself and reached out for him with a passion that had finally announced itself at the door.

Later, at twilight, the swamp lay like a sleeping snake coiled up in the darkness. Seth Von Hocke stood in the clearing in front of Maum Chrish's house, and for a second he remembered how scared he had been the first time he'd ever come here with Donny. That was the first time he'd ever seen Maum Chrish. Now the place was scarier without her here.

The fire near the garden had burned down low and the boy dropped to his knees and stirred it back up, threw on several pieces of kindling until the blaze was holding its own again. He didn't know why, but she never let the fire go out. In its revived light his strained face stood out in relief, like a medieval fresco of beggar children. After a few moments he got too hot by the fire and he walked over to the cabin. He'd never been inside. He tiptoed to the front door and peeked in. There was a tall pole in the center of the room and a table but not much else. Didn' look like the work of the devil to him.

That's what they were saying in town. That she was a witch. That she gave up without a fight because she was guilty. That she'd get the gas chamber and never hurt anyone again. Seth stood in the doorway and thought about going on inside the house. Then he changed his mind. Instead, he pulled the seldom-used wood door shut and walked back down the steps.

In his ears he could still hear Donny's mother: "Seth honey, what's wrong with a boy like you, going out there to that old nigger's place all the time? Don't you know she killed two people? You're lucky she didn't cut you up for some devil worship."

Seth knew it was probably a sin but he thought Donny's mother was just a little dumb. And he didn't like how she called Maum Chrish a "nigger" either. Donny had told everyone about Seth's visits to the swamp—despite the piggy bank, the other boy had not kept his word. Now most of the guys were always giving Seth a hard time about having a "thing" for an old black lady.

Eventually his brother had heard about it and his brother had told his parents. His father was red in the face when Seth came home that day: "Young man, you are not to go out there again. Ever. Whatever you've been doing out there, it isn't healthy; a boy your age should be with his friends, not hanging around an old recluse. You stay away from that woman—we don't know her."

The boy sat down by the fire. Every one of them made his time with Maum Chrish sound so—wrong or dirty or something. *And* he was grounded, wasn't supposed to ride his bicycle for the next four weeks. A month. If his parents discovered he'd sneaked it out here this afternoon anyway, they'd probably take it away for good. Maybe he should run away. To Chicago or New Orleans or someplace like that. Only he felt most comfortable right here, with her. Now everybody said she killed people. That she was evil. Seth thought for a second about when Maum Chrish took her clothes off in front of him and dove in the river. He knew if he told anyone about that, there would really be trouble.

Abruptly he kicked sand on the fire, deliberately aiming his sneaker at the new pieces of kindling until he'd knocked them aside. Over and over again he attacked the burning center, knocking the wood askew, stamping on the embers, burning his shoes in the process. He kicked and kicked, his face red, tears running down his scorched cheeks. Finally the fire was out, dead.

Two nights later Judge Harry Thompson yawned at midnight and looked out the window of his dusty study in Ashboro at the clipped yard below. Sometimes he wasn't exactly sure how he'd become a judge. Accident? Fate? About six years after he had begun practicing law in South Carolina, a district attorney he knew put him up for the judgeship rather suddenly, without explanation. At the time Harry Thompson had been something of a young hotshot in these parts and, flattered, he'd pursued the judgeship as though it'd been his idea to begin with. It was only later that he realized that the district attorney had finally rid himself, very effectively, of his most skillful opponent.

To date he'd sat on the bench for over fifteen years, and now he was a lot less flattered by the position. What it took to be a good judge was an uncanny ability to always see both sides of an issue. That much was good; he could do that. He nearly always felt sympathy for the defense and the prosecution, unless a case was obviously one-sided or the attorneys were untalented. But the trouble was—if you empathized so well with both sides, how the hell did you determine who was right?

You guessed.

It was such an inexact profession it kept him awake nights. Sometimes he lay in bed and wondered about cases he'd heard ten years before. His wife of twenty-five years would sigh out loud, to let him know his tossing and turning was keeping her awake. Sure hadn't been anything else going on in that bed for some time to keep a body awake. But he'd pat her rump and mumble something and she'd go back to sleep. Then he'd try the case again in his head. More quietly. One time he made a

list of thirteen cases from the past ten years he was certain he'd
ruled on incorrectly. He felt like he was totaling up his sins so
he'd have an organized list when he got to heaven.

Provided he got there at all, what with all the screw-ups. Like
his very first case, an Ashboro black woman accused of knifing
her husband. When the couple was brought before him, it was
clear the husband beat the wife regularly. The jury sided with
the husband, though, who was still bandaged and had lost part
of his right pinky finger. Then the judge of the century stepped
in and commuted her sentence, let the woman go instead of
incarcerating her. The joys of parole would be hers, thanks to
him. The trial ended. But that night her husband killed her with
a two-by-four.

It was the black-white cases that made his skin crawl. The
judge turned away from the window and looked down at the
arrest report on the woman known only as Maum Chrish. Lord
help—a defendant with a slave name. The whole town of Essex
would probably be at the preliminary hearing. Did he do the
right thing to call an open hearing, or would it just stir those
folks up even more? They wanted a trial. However, he simply
did not see enough evidence to impanel a grand jury now, which
was making him about as popular as Judas Iscariot in that small
town down the road.

Judge Thompson closed his eyes. It was not going to be a
routine hearing. No, it was going to be a packed house. Hot as
hell too. Nothing like a crowd of paranoid people all bunched
up, angry and sweating to death. Often he envied the Japanese
justice system—the severe and irreversible penalties inscribed
for serious crimes. It was one of the oldest civilizations in the
world and one with almost no violence. Was it possible your
civilization had to be millions of years old before it truly lost its
barbarity? If so, was America as old as the Europeans who
founded it—or just as old as itself?

Fourteen

MAUM CHRISH DIDN'T hang her head.

"If I hear one more outburst like that, I'll clear this room! I will. I told all of you at the outset, this is only a preliminary hearing. All we're trying to do today is decide whether to impanel a grand jury or not. This ain't no trial and you ain't witnesses." Judge Harry Thompson cleared his throat and mopped sweat off his face with a balled-up handkerchief. Then he gazed around at the crowd below him. "Everyone just simmer down. I deliberately called an open hearing so you could see that something's being done. I know two murders are scary, hell, one's scary enough. But you're gonna have to be quiet so we can get on with it."

To the magistrate's left sat the tall black woman, the object of the day's inquiry, imperious in posture with her chiseled, masculine features. Maum Chrish wore a floor-length white caftan and her head was wrapped in a white cotton turban. Beside her was her court-appointed attorney, Ben Estes, the recent law school graduate who had also taken on J. T. Turner earlier. The young lawyer looked at his client for a second, then gazed down at his best pin-striped suit and picked invisible lint off the left sleeve. On the other side of the conference table, serving here as the judge's bench, slouched a district attorney for the state of South Carolina, a sway-backed man of forty-five whose navy tie was spotted with ketchup. Despite his appearance, however, Emmett Atkins was a skilled prosecutor with many convictions to his credit.

Owing to the incendiary nature of the case, the preliminary hearing was being conducted like an informal trial; evidence would be presented by both the prosecution and the defense but without benefit of cross-examination and without a jury present.

235

They were meeting in the largest conference room of the Ashton County courthouse (Judge Thompson had deliberately not used the courtroom—it would have permitted even more spectators); a long oak table sat raised on a dias at the back of the room, framed from behind by three Palladian windows which overlooked the street outside. Two smaller tables on either side of the raised platform functioned as defense and prosecution enclaves. Beyond the smaller tables were rows of folding metal chairs. Each was filled. Nearly all of Essex had turned out, but no one looked comfortable. From the oldest to the youngest, from the best dressed to the dowdiest, people perched precariously on the edge of their seats, as though unsure of where or with whom they should sit.

For the first hour and a half Emmett Atkins had presented the state's case against Maum Chrish. Photographs of Sarah Rothenbarger's body were entered into the record, along with a statement by Mr. Gabriel McFarland and the post-mortem report completed by the Ashton County Medical Examiner, Dr. Edward Hammond. The district attorney, in his unpressed tan summer suit, then stopped in mid-sentence and looked up at the judge. "If you'd like any of these witnesses to testify, they are all present."

Judge Thompson waived testimony of the crime statistics. "I see no need for that here."

Now the district attorney began to build a case on the basis of Maum Chrish's eccentricities. When he spoke of the dissected goat, the crowd murmured to itself, remembering.

Emmett Atkins rose to his full six feet and rocked back and forth in his scuffed loafers, appealing visually to the audience. "Those of us who live around here, we know odd things go on in those swamps. We've accepted that. We mind our own business and let others live in peace. We've always pretty much ignored what goes on out there. But"—the attorney paused for emphasis—"when someone comes into town and commits murder, then—then it becomes our responsibility to do something about it."

He turned back to the judge. "Those of us in law enforcement hear every day about some new cult that's sprung up, that perpetuates atrocities in the name of a mystical religion. Detective Lou Brockhurst knew this too. In a way these cults have become legitimized by what is currently being called the New Age. My own daughter brought home a rock the other day—which she bought in a crystal store in Charleston—and she expects it to tell her what to major in when she gets to college.'' Here and there a chuckle erupted among the spectators, and the district attorney turned in the appropriate direction and smiled.

Knowing he had the audience on his side, Emmett Atkins walked toward the crowd, nodded to them as he would a jury. ''It's a well-known fact that some voodoo ceremonies involve the killing of goats, sheep, chickens, all kinds of animals. These beasts are skinned and the blood is saved for use in rituals, just as certain other body fluids are used—which I'll get to later on. But for now, consider this—a woman who routinely kills animals with a knife has only to go one step further to do the same to a human being. I submit to you—and the state will prove—that Maum Chrish murdered Sarah Rothenbarger as part of the ritual of her cult.''

''Damn straight!''

It was a single voice and it was impossible to tell where it had come from. Judge Thompson pounded on his tabletop anyway. A single voice in court rarely stayed single. Then the magistrate said to the DA, ''Evidence is what we need, counselor.'' The judge also eyeballed the defense attorney, visually admonishing him to defend his client. Eyes forward again, Judge Thompson added, ''The court is willing to stipulate, based on the photographs entered, that the defendant practices a religion unknown to most of us. But that, as you know, is not the issue. That's a civil right. Murder is the issue. Let's get on with it, please.''

The district attorney walked back over to the prosecution table and picked up a photograph. ''This is the photograph you mentioned, Your Honor.'' The prosecutor faced the crowd again, flashed the picture many of them had now heard about. ''On the walls of Maum Chrish's home are several drawings and various kinds of writing. It was the discovery of what some of these symbols mean, the state will contend later, that led to the murder of State Law Enforcement Agent Lou Brockhurst, who was the first person to understand them.'' When the defense attorney stood up suddenly, the district attorney turned to the judge. ''I know that's a separate case, Your Honor.''

The judge looked at both attorneys simultaneously. ''This is not a trial. Please proceed, but keep to the case at hand.''

The defense lawyer, looking crestfallen, sat down again and the prosecutor continued, ''Sarah Rothenbarger, as you all know, was Jewish. Indeed, she was the only Jewish person in the town of Essex. Maum Chrish, on the other hand, is a black woman who seems to practice some form of voodoo. Yet on the walls of her cabin''—the lawyer tapped the photograph he still held—''what do we find but the Jewish alphabet.''

The front row leaned forward to see the photograph better.

''There was clearly a connection between Sarah Rothenbarger and Maum Chrish,'' Emmett Atkins concluded. ''A connection that resulted in murder.''

''This is like a witch trial,'' Stoney whispered to Anna. ''It's like something out of the thirties.''

His wife didn't respond. She was too angry with him to discuss anything. Instead, she focused on the photograph the district attorney was holding. She had been inside that cabin any number of times but she hadn't recognized any Jewish alphabet. Of course, that was about the last thing on earth she would have expected to find there. What did Marian think about this? Searching the room, Anna's eyes fell on the back of Marian's neck; Marian was sitting five rows ahead of Stoney and Anna. Two rows behind Marian loomed Harriet Setzler, replete with wide-brim hat. Twice Anna noticed the old lady turn and stare at Marian. Then Anna looked at Maum Chrish. The black woman's face was oddly untouched by what was going on. Anna's eyes moved in an arc from Maum Chrish to Marian and then back to the older black woman. They were both tall, but Marian's face was full and wide where Maum Chrish's was long and lean. Of course, Maum Chrish was older and had no doubt had a much harder life. Did Marian realize she herself had probably had an easier life *because* her mother left her? Again Anna studied the back of Marian's head; the other woman didn't take her eyes off Maum Chrish. But Maum Chrish wasn't looking back. Rather, she was staring ahead vacantly, as though her consciousness had shifted to another astral plane. Why didn't she look at Marian—my God, Marian was begging her to.

In a moment Anna got up, nodded at Stoney, and pointed at the back door of the room. She walked down the aisle and out the door and toward the restroom. Inside it, she wiped her forehead with a damp paper towel. It was so hot in this building. Or was it just her? Then she went back out into the hall and walked over to the pay telephone near the water cooler.

Back inside the conference room, the district attorney was talking about the ''physical evidence,'' by which Stoney gathered he meant the semen found on Sarah Roth's body. ''It's a well-known fact,'' the prosecutor continued, ''that certain

occulists attach mystical properties to various body fluids besides blood. I refer now specifically to semen." He smiled apologetically at the women in the audience. "Sexual fluids were
accorded magical status in many primitive cultures. They were,
for example, sometimes applied to new crops in ancient Greece
and Egypt as a talisman of fertility—to help ensure a good
yield."

Judge Thompson raised the index finger of his right hand.
"The point, counselor?"

Stoney turned around and stared at the back door of the conference room and wondered what Anna was doing. She'd been
gone a long time. He sighed imperceptibly. He had to tell her
about his job soon; this charade (she assumed he was taking
annual leave to attend the hearing) could not go on any longer.
He had to tell her that, after failing to appear for his appointment
in Columbia, he had sent his supervisor a letter requesting an
indefinite leave, that if such leave couldn't be granted he was
herewith tendering his resignation. He had to tell Anna he had
quit his job because Essex was more important right now. Even
to him, it sounded absolutely insane, the act of an irresponsible
child. Yet he felt better about it than almost anything he had
done in years.

But he could not tell Anna right now. She had been so un-
predictable this week. First she comes on to him out of the
blue—that afternoon on the living room floor was incredible, he
had never known her to be so uninhibited, even now it made
him smile, he had always wanted a woman he could talk to who
was also that sexy (every man really did, even those who married the woman their mother liked or the woman who had the
best looks, they all got divorced because what they really wanted
was a good friend who liked to do it like crazy). That afternoon
Anna had been everything he'd imagined when they were first
married; afterward, they had lain there naked for hours talking
about Maum Chrish, about crime and punishment, about what
made some people hurt others. Then—four days later—suddenly
it was like it had never happened; if anything, his wife was more
remote than ever before.

Abruptly Stoney looked around him again. He thought he'd
seen Leonard Hansen earlier. When he wasn't thinking about
Anna, Stoney kept going over his invasion of Leonard's house.
It had yielded absolutely nothing. Leonard was redoing his
house. Leonard liked naked women. Hardly a breakthrough.
Put him right up there with almost every man in town. Again

Stoney turned and stared at the back of the room. He didn't see Leonard anywhere now. Once more Stoney wondered if he could be wrong about Leonard. He just didn't like the guy—but that was no reason to accuse him of murder. Make that two murders. True, Leonard still struck Stoney as basically unchanged from the Lenny of twenty years ago—but even that didn't make him a criminal. Did Leonard know Stoney suspected him? Had anyone seen the Rover outside his house that day?

Up front the district attorney was still going on about the existence of semen on Sarah's body. He finally ended with, "Now I ask you, what better way to disguise a murder committed by a woman than to leave semen on the body? This is the only possible explanation for why Sarah Roth was not raped. Her attacker was female."

Stoney got up and headed out the room to see what was keeping Anna. When he opened the door into the hall, he saw her on the phone. Probably with that lawyer friend of hers in D.C. Stoney smiled; one thing he loved about Anna was how she never gave up. They hadn't been able to get the guy by phone all week but Anna was still calling, was still hoping he could put them in touch with someone in South Carolina who would provide Maum Chrish with free, but more efficient, legal services. Stoney waved at his wife and headed toward the men's room. As he was about to open the door, though, he saw a man leaning against the opposite wall, lighted cigarette in his hand, his eyes on Anna. Leonard Hansen didn't even notice Stoney; Leonard just kept staring straight at Anna.

Stoney never went in the men's room. Instead, he went over and stood beside Anna until she hung up the phone. Then he took her arm and Leonard smiled at them as they crossed back to the conference room door.

Back in their seats, Anna whispered, "Stoney, let go, you're hurting my arm."

He looked down at where he'd gripped her forearm. Vigorously he massaged the red imprint left by his thumb. "Sorry."

She gazed at him. "What's wrong?"

He shivered despite the heat but didn't tell her what he'd just realized. That if Leonard Hansen ever did want to get him, he would not come at him directly.

Harriet Setzler tried not to listen when they talked about the semen. The things they said in public nowadays. No worse than what you could hear on your own television set, though. All her life she had tried to keep distasteful subjects at bay. Decent women did not think about some things. Thank the Lord William had not been the kind of man to make an issue of—of things. Harriet regarded Maum Chrish silently. The black woman sat up tall like Cleopatra on her barge. Harriet almost smiled despite herself; the old thing was tough as nails. A lunatic, of course, but tough all the same. Harriet rather admired the way Maum Chrish kept her own counsel. Sometimes if you pretended things didn't exist, they didn't. Maybe that old woman knew that.

A sudden shift nearby startled Harriet and she turned to see Stoney and Anna take their seats again. Then she faced forward once more, and just beneath the rim of her hat she studied Marian, who was hunched over, staring at Maum Chrish as though trying to figure something out. Harriet was still so worried about Marian. She looked so—wild, uncontrolled. The old lady had bequeathed her own precision and dignity to Marian, had tried to make her forthright and unflappable. She wanted Marian to be able to look back someday and think, I've made only a few mistakes. Just a few. Which was a lot more than most could say.

Harriet swallowed. Except, the ones she herself had made were such big ones. And they kept coming around again and again.

Marian seethed with loathing when the prosecutor began shaking his finger at Maum Chrish. In fact, Marian couldn't remember hating a white man so badly since she was a teenager being routinely raped by one. She wanted to get up and march to the front of the room and slap that man's face, slap him silly, until he shut up, until he stopped badgering her mother.

"This woman has refused to answer our questions," Emmett Atkins was saying. "She cannot account for her whereabouts on the night of the murder; indeed, she hasn't attempted to. She cannot even prove who she is. It is unlikely Maum Chrish is her real name, yet she will not tell us what her real name is. Nor does she possess any legal identification."

Should I stand up and identify her? Marian wondered. Will it hurt or help her to be rendered more concrete? Marian looked around the room; Jordan Taylor had said he would try to get by, that he was too busy to take the case himself but he would try to find someone who would, that he would definitely find someone before the case went to trial—which, at this point, certainly seemed likely. Marian had been to the Ashton County lockup every day but Maum Chrish had not spoken since being incarcerated. Finally, frustrated, Marian had driven out to the cabin to get her mother's Bible as well as the granite amulet. "Wear it in court," she told Maum Chrish. "You always said it would protect you."

But she didn't have it on. Marian stared at her mother. Why hadn't she worn it? Why wouldn't she talk—especially now—about why she'd come back, why she'd chosen to live in the swamps, why she'd left all those years ago. What if they didn't have much more time together? What if Maum Chrish was convicted and they locked her away forever? That just couldn't happen. Jordan would have to see to it. They'd all have to do whatever it took. Again, she stared up at her mother. She searched the other's long face for the slightest sign of recognition, familiarity, acknowledgment. None was forthcoming. "You are the one who's come," the older woman had said that first afternoon when Marian approached her. But that was all she'd ever said. Why didn't she say more? Was she simply incapable of dealing with reality anymore?

In a dramatic flourish the district attorney suddenly brandished a plastic bag containing a pewter-colored knife. "This knife," he announced with an orator's cadence, "is no ordinary knife. It's a hunting knife. Seven inches long. This serrated edge"—he held the weapon up so everyone could see it—"will cut through small trees. A knife like this is useful in skinning game. A knife like this leaves a jagged wound on whatever it cuts. A jagged wound is easily identifiable. Such wounds were found on the body of Sarah Rothenbarger. And this knife"—the prosecutor paused, his face flushed—"was found in the home of Maum Chrish."

Marian felt faint with the heat. She got up and walked outside to get some air.

Behind her, Emmett Atkins laid the knife back down, folded his hands together as in prayer, looking first at the judge and then at the spectators. "For the protection of this community, the state contends that the woman known as Maum Chrish should be tried for the murder of Sarah Rothenbarger."

The noise began slowly. Just a clap of the hands, then another, then another. Soon the room shook with applause, people were on their feet, nodding, calling out to one another. It was going well, wasn't it?

Stoney McFarland sat silently while Anna looked around for

Marian. And Judge Thompson, picking up his gavel, reached under his robe for his antacid tablets.

Marian sat on the front steps of the courthouse and her hands shook so badly she longed for the cigarettes she'd given up six years ago. She even looked down the street for a store that might have a vending machine. Hardware store, another county office building, ice cream parlor, small Chevy dealership. Nothing that might sell smokes.

It was worse than she'd ever expected. Her identification of Maum Chrish was not going to be enough.

"The day mebbe come," her mama had once told her, sitting there on the wood steps staring at the swept yard, "when you gonna have to choose up sides. Don't choose iffen you don't hafta. But when that day come, and you gotta, just choose and don't look back."

Suddenly Marian laughed aloud as she also remembered a strange trip she'd once taken with Harriet. When Harriet's brother was still alive and owned a farm in Orangeburg. Harriet was always trying to help him out, whether he wanted her help or not. She would save watermelon seeds and dry them on newspapers on the back porch to give to him to plant new watermelon crops—even though he told her a dozen times those weren't the right kind of seeds to plant, you had to buy seeds from the feed store, you needed seeds specially prepared for planting. In those days Harriet still kept a milk cow in the back yard and it had had a calf and suddenly one day she decided to take the calf to her brother. In the back seat of her car. She made Marian help her drag the bench seat out of the back of the car and put down newspapers, then force the hundred-pound calf through the door. Marian had been mortified; Harriet was really going to drive that animal fifty miles in the back seat of a car? Worse, Harriet expected her to go along? Sure thing, there they went down the highway, no air-conditioning in the car on that hot summer day as they slowed down to pass through small towns, people on the street stopping dead in their tracks to stare at this woman and a colored gal driving a calf somewhere. The car really smelled now (the calf was nervous and did more every time they went through a town). All this to take a calf to a man who didn't even want it. The day got hotter, the calf got more agitated, more people stared and laughed, and the miles got longer and longer—and Harriet was pleased as punch. She sat up tall and haughty and waved to people as though there was something unfortunate about the fact they weren't chauffeuring farm animals cross-country today.

Even when verging on lunacy, both of her mothers had always been women of fearless action.

Out of the corner of her eye, Marian spied a small boy on a bicycle peddling furiously toward the courthouse. Seth Von Hocke, Bryan's younger brother.

Seth parked his bicycle and strode up the courthouse steps. He wondered if his mother had discovered him gone yet. If she knew he'd taken his bike despite being grounded.

When he passed Marian she called out, "You're Bryan's brother Seth, aren't you?"

Seth nodded. "He's in your class."

Marian thought the boy was rather young for court proceedings. "You're a long way from home."

"I wanted to see the trial."

"It's not a trial. Only a hearing."

"Will they put her in jail for good?"

So the little white boy had pedaled all the way over here to see an old nigger sent up the river, that it? Marian's jaw stiffened. "They may. You come to give 'em a hand?"

"Pardon?"

"You want them to send Maum Chrish away, don't you?"

Seth's eyes widened. "No ma'am." He turned and looked up at the courthouse door. His legs felt weak. If he told the people inside what he knew, his parents probably wouldn't let him play football next year. His mother didn't like sports anyway. And the kids would laugh, would call him a wimp. Donny would call him a nigger-lover.

The boy walked past Marian and on up the stairs. Maybe he was a nigger-lover.

Marian turned and watched him go. Something about the set of his thin shoulders impressed her.

When defense attorney Ben Estes began to speak, timidly, leaning toward the judge as if that might aid his case, Jim Leland stretched back in his chair and relaxed. All that stuff about voodoo made him nervous and he was glad it was over with. Ever since he was a kid, those swamps had given him the willies. He now hunted only in dryland woods, the shady stands of pine where the bucks fed; other guys could have all the lowland game there was. Only once had he been on a lowland hunt, a huge organized affair near the Dismal Swamp in Virginia which Heyward Rutherford had talked him into five years back. Everybody hunted in teams. Two teams got on opposite sides of the swamp and marched toward each other, with two other teams to the right and left. The four groups advanced and trapped the deer between them and everyone shot at once. The animals had nowhere to go. Five or six would go down at a time, the teams split the take. It was the worst hunting trip Jim had ever taken; the whole time he'd privately rooted for the deer.

He looked around the crowded room. The district attorney had won the crowd, no doubt about it. Now Ben Estes was saying how the case was circumstantial, no eyewitnesses or fingerprints or even any fibers to tie Maum Chrish to the scene; he even hinted that racial prejudice might be at work here. Who the hell will ever know if she really did it? Jim thought. Personally he would just be damn glad when the whole mess was over. She probably was guilty. A nut case gone off the deep end.

The Essex policeman felt sweat trickling down the back of his khaki uniform. Hot as blazes. You'd think a county as big as Ashton could afford decent air-conditioning. Every time the cotton-picking thing came on, it sounded like a plane passing by overhead. He kept expecting the windows to rattle. In a moment Jim shifted to let the back of his shirt breathe, and looked around behind him. Leonard Hansen was just coming in the back door of the conference room. For a moment the blond man stood staring at the group, then fixed his eyes on Stoney and Anna McFarland. Jim watched Leonard for several seconds until he noticed Jim and, nodding slightly, sat down.

Jim stared idly at the judge's bench and wondered, only briefly, if there was any way Stoney was right about Leonard. Then, abruptly, Jim felt a tap on his shoulder and looked to his right. Buck Henry was standing in the aisle motioning to him and Jim got up and followed the larger man out into the hall where the Ashton sheriff whispered, "Got a call a few minutes ago. Trooper near Beaufort stopped a guy for speeding, noticed the guy looked familiar. Thinks it might have been Turner. While he was tracing the license, the guy took off. Turns out the car was stolen."

Ben Estes' pin-striped suit, a Brooks Brothers clone with just a shade too much polyester in it to be convincing, was damp and wilted by the time the twenty-eight-year-old finished his impassioned textbook speech about innocent-until-proven-guilty. He looked out at the crowd, searching for a friendly face. "It's unfortunate that once you are arrested for a crime, most people think you're guilty. Arrest is *not* evidence of guilt any more than the practice of an unusual religion is. Some people think Mormons are odd, other people think of Unitarians are suspicious. But we don't go around accusing them of murder on that basis. When you get right down to it, Catholics can sound like proponents of cannibalism; in their communion service they believe they are actually drinking Christ's blood. Do we arrest them for it? Of course not."

Judge Thompson almost chuckled. The boy was learning.

The defense attorney continued, "We live in a country where by law people are assumed innocent until *proven guilty*. Lately this valuable premise is being eroded on countless fronts. Pick up your newspaper any day and you can see how many businesses in this country no longer believe in that concept—they want to test their prospective job applicants for drugs up front, they refuse to take an individual's word anymore, they want proof. Some companies even want to give lie detector tests—or written tests that simulate the lie detector—to determine if the applicant has ever lied or stolen office supplies on a previous job. In other words, in these instances, there is no presumption of innocence anymore. In corporate America, people are being assumed *guilty*.

"That is precisely how the district attorney would have you judge Maum Chrish; he insists that because of her religious beliefs she should prove she is innocent. Which is a violation of her constitutional rights. A court of law *is* still governed by our Constitution. It is the responsibility of the prosecution in this case to prove 'probable cause' for Maum Chrish to have killed Sarah Rothenbarger. And they haven't done that. They have told us Maum Chrish is odd, that she lives oddly. But that is not against the law. They have told us she owns a knife, had a jar of semen in her house. But that is not against the law. They have told us the Jewish alphabet is written on the walls of her house. Is that against the law? Is that a conclusive basis for a criminal indictment?"

Even Emmett Atkins looked a little worried now, and Marian was openly smiling.

But inexperience reared its soft unprotected head and, inspired by his own eloquence, Ben Estes suddenly added, "Maum Chrish *is* different. That is not a crime. As a professor of mine used to say, in order to protect the best of us, we must also protect the worst of us.''

Judge Thompson grimaced.

A man in the back of the room stood up and shouted, "Okay, sonny, protect us. Put her in jail."

Laughter rippled across the room. "Yeah," agreed several others before the judge got his gavel in place. "Jail is where the worst of us belong."

Ben Estes looked confused. "That's not what I meant," he stammered.

Seth Von Hocke, standing against the back wall, opened his mouth to say something. But no sound came out.

The judge rapped on his desk and the crowd grew quieter but not contained. Chairs were moved, legs crossed and uncrossed, feet tapped. The room swayed with undercurrents. The magistrate motioned the two lawyers forward and whispered to them for a moment, then they returned to their seats. After they sat down again, Judge Thompson turned to Maum Chrish. "Ma'am, do you understand that you have been arrested for the murder of Sarah Rothenbarger? Do you have anything to say?"

The judge paused. The crowd waited.

"Ma'am, I must insist that you respond to my question. Do you understand that you stand accused of having killed Sarah Rothenbarger on April 12th of this year?"

Maum Chrish looked at the judge briefly and he had the uncanny feeling she had actually passed through him. Physically. It was crazy. He felt suddenly lightheaded, not uncomfortable, just uncertain of things that should be certain. Like how far away from the desk his chair was, how long it would take him to pick up the gavel again if he had to do so. He swallowed, tried to clear his head, looked at the prosecutor momentarily and then at the defense table.

In a second Judge Thompson turned back to Maum Chrish, stared at her intently. "Please, can't you tell us anything that will shed some light on this accusation?"

"She's looney, Harry. Maybe she can't talk."

The judge felt his fist hit the table before he realized he'd even raised his arm. "Silence!" Then he added, to no one in particular, "I guess we'll need a competency evaluation."

The crowd grew restless. "She did it, she won't even deny it," yelled a man in the corner. The adults clamored so loudly they never heard the high childish voice announce from the back of the room, "She can so talk."

"Maum Chrish," the judge tried again, "won't you please speak in your own behalf?"

Marian, who had been listening outside the door, suddenly walked back in. All the way down the aisle she kept her eyes on Maum Chrish. If ever you're going to acknowledge me, do it now, she demanded with her eyes. Give me a reason to do this. Please.

When she reached her own seat, Marian didn't stop; instead, she continued on down the aisle until she stood at the front of the room, just below the judge's bench. Now everyone had noticed her and instinctively they'd stopped whispering. The prosecutor and the defense lawyer both looked up expectantly, as did Judge Thompson.

Marian, however, kept her eyes steadfastly on Maum Chrish. She waited for a sign that she now knew would never come. Then she opened her mouth and said, "Maum Chrish did not kill Sarah. I was with her the night Sarah died."

All over the room mouths flew open like pneumatic doors. Blap-blap-blap-blap.

"What would Marian be doing with *her*?"

"If Marian knew something about this, how come she didn't say something before?"

"Why you reckon Marian's doing this?"

"Got me. Why would she have anything to do with those people in the swamp anyway? Marian's always been so—so different."

Harriet Setzler stared at Marian but the old lady didn't say a word.

Stoney McFarland turned to Anna, just looked at her for a moment, then asked under his breath, "Do you know anything about this?"

Seth Von Hocke, in the back, knew Marian was lying but he was relieved all the same.

And Marynell Pittman, eyes shooting daggers, jumped up and screeched, "Them kind'll say anything to cover each other, won't they?"

Judge Thompson had been on his feet for five minutes trying to restore order. Now he was in front of the raised oak table, facing the spectators, and his face was flushed with irritation. "I said, that's enough! Those of you who cannot be quiet will be asked to leave. I won't hesitate to have you ejected. *Do you understand?*''

The symphony of the crowd subsided into disparate notes.

The judge turned in Marian's direction. Looking into his eyes, Marian knew exactly what he would ask. And she knew she would have to tell him; otherwise, her alibi for Maum Chrish would not be believed. Behind her sat the townspeople she had known all her life, whose respect had come to symbolize stability and accomplishment to her. She turned and let her eyes rest on Harriet.

Then she faced forward again, her back to the town. She didn't wait for the judge. "Your Honor, my name is Marian Davis, I teach English at Essex High School."

"And you know Maum Chrish? You can identify her?"

"Yes sir, I can."

The prosecutor got to his feet. "I object to this soap opera staging. If this woman has something to reveal, might we not hear it in chambers first?"

Turning, the magistrate frowned at the district attorney. "No. We're going to hear her out right now." Judge Thompson swiveled and stared down at Marian again. "Please tell us what you know."

Marian said loudly and clearly, "Maum Chrish's real name is Lonnie Davis. She's my mother."

A hundred voices erupted like lava and grew heavier and hotter, until Judge Thompson saw it was useless to try to restore order. Even people who had no particular enmity against Maum Chrish felt cheated of the catharsis they needed. For Maum Chrish to have been the murderer would have worked so easily, would have made so much sense, and we needed it, this easy restoration of reason. Most of us never hated Maum Chrish. But her esoteric existence in the swamps made us nervous and so we weren't above using her. If any of us had thought about it, we might have reasoned rather glibly that she had put herself in the way of being used. She could have come into town and said hello once in a while, right? She could have hung a cross from her rafter instead of a tribute to a moon goddess, couldn't she? Was it really so bad to sacrifice one crazy swamp woman—she'd probably eat better in jail anyway—if it put everyone else at peace?

In the end, though, the preliminary hearing was adjourned for the day, to resume the following morning to hear Marian

Davis testify. So we all slowly filed out, got in our cars, and drove back to Essex, not as vindicated as we'd expected to be, more confused than anything, almost all of us questioning how the hell Maum Chrish could be Marian's mother (they all did look a little alike to some of us, even though we didn't admit it in public anymore), and why the hell Marian hadn't brought all this up before, and what on earth she was doing out in the swamps—mother or no—in the middle of the April night Sarah was killed. Marian was one of us, and not one of us would have set foot in that hellhole in the middle of any night.

So we trudged back to town and that evening we once more examined our door locks and stared out at the sidewalk, wondering who might have killed Sarah and that detective if Maum Chrish hadn't. We were angry too. Marian had cheated us, she who always seemed one of us. Now she'd gone somewhere out of reach. Taking with her the solution we needed.

Stoney and Anna stayed behind to see Marian after the hearing was over. Marian spoke with the judge for a few minutes; then she walked with Maum Chrish and Buck Henry over to the police car that would take the older woman back to the Ashton jail. Marian opened the car door for Maum Chrish and leaned inside to say something to her before she closed the door again. Then Stoney and Anna joined Marian and the three of them crossed to Marian's car, not saying much of anything, just walking along together.

All the way home Anna worried about what Marian was doing. Why didn't it occur to anyone else that Marian might be mistaken, that Maum Chrish might not really be her mother after all? Maybe Marian wanted to find her mother so badly she couldn't see the facts—that she and the other woman didn't look enough alike, that Maum Chrish had yet to avow their relationship, that no one else in town had recognized the black woman as Lonnie Davis except a half-blind senile woman. Did this occur to anyone else? Anna didn't think so. Everyone else seemed to think Marian would never align herself with the crazy swamp woman unless she had incontrovertible proof that they were blood. Only blood would make Marian stand against the town, right?

Stoney was silent during most of the ride back to the McCloskey house. Never our house, Anna thought abruptly, as they pulled into the driveway. Never our home. They got out of the Subaru and walked around to the back door which, when

opened, admitted a rambunctious Silas who did his welcome
dance and then sailed into the yard and picked up a stick and
scrambled back to Stoney to have it thrown. The man indulged
the dog and then he and Anna went inside. In the kitchen Stoney,
who still had his mind on Leonard Hansen, said suddenly,
"Anna, I want to show you how to use my rifle tonight."

"Not now, okay? I need to run over to Marian's." Anna went
upstairs to wash her face and change into shorts. In fifteen minutes she came back downstairs and found Stoney leaning into
the window frames in the kitchen. "What are you doing?"

"Checking the locks."

She stopped still. "You're scaring me."

He straightened up. "Sorry. I've just been meaning to check
them, that's all." He looked down; he still couldn't stop thinking
about Leonard. Then he looked at Anna. "Want something to
eat when you get back?"

"You're going to fix dinner?"

He smiled. "I'm going to find an appropriate complement to
a very large bottle of wine. We'll call it dinner."

As Anna left, Stoney insisted she take Silas with her. "But
it's not even dark," she sputtered.

"Anna, please, just do it."

The look in his eyes frightened her far more than his checking
locks and so she clipped the leash to the golden retriever without
comment and she and Silas started walking down Laurens Avenue. Anna wasn't sure what she was going to say to Marian
but she was convinced she should talk to her. Someone had to
make her admit that Maum Chrish might not really be her
mother. Someone had to make her see that committing per-
jury—and Anna had no doubt she was lying to alibi Maum
Chrish—was very serious. Anna sighed and yanked on the dog's
leash. "Heel, Silas." Then she looked up at the cloudy sky. If
only it would rain.

Anna found Marian on her front porch reading her mail.

"Hey," Anna called, "mind if I bring this bear up there?"

Marian smiled and waved them up. When Anna and Silas
reached her, Marian leaned down to pet Silas but the dog craned
his neck to sniff a basket sitting on the bench beside her.

"Is there food in there?" Anna asked. "This dog can smell
edibles ten blocks away."

Marian nodded. "It was here when I got home. Harriet must
have brought it over."

Anna thought Harriet should have stayed after the hearing to see Marian, but she offered no comment. Instead, she ordered Silas to lie down and then she sat down beside Marian. "That was something, today."

"Yeah. I hope tomorrow they'll let her go."

But at what cost, Anna wondered. She looked at Marian and saw the deep shining purpose in the other woman's eyes. She finally had what she'd always needed. Anna looked away. Can I tell her it's not real? I've got to. Somebody's got to. She's my friend, I have a responsibility to tell her, I'd want someone to tell me. I can't let her do something that might hurt her.

"You know, Anna, I never had a day like this in my whole life." Marian laughed abruptly, a high girlish laugh that was unlike her. Then she reached over and impulsively hugged Anna.

Anna smiled woodenly. To suggest that Maum Chrish was not her mother was going to tear her apart. The truth was that Marian would probably never find her mother.

"I know she's going to be all right now," Marian was saying. "Tomorrow will make it all right."

And you could go to jail for it, a voice rang in Anna's head. She looked at Marian and again noticed the peaceful look in the other woman's eyes. Tell her, a voice admonished. Now.

"Marian, I have to tell you something. I don't know how to say this, exactly—"

"Just say it."

"I wish this were easier."

"After everything we've talked about lately, what can't we say to each other?"

"It's about Maum Chrish."

Marian's eyes changed instantly. "What about my mother?"

"Well, it's . . . it's . . ." Anna stopped and looked at her friend for a long time. Then she said, "I was proud of you today."

Marian's eyes widened and she looked at Anna intently. Finally she said, her voice tremulous, "Thanks, Anna. I knew you'd understand."

Stoney was staring into the half-empty refrigerator when the phone rang and Bill Jenkins suggested an unscheduled jog. Something in Bill's voice implied he had news so Stoney agreed to meet him at the entrance gates to Willowbrook. When Stoney got there, Bill was waiting and they started running down the Savannah highway, away from town, starting slow, pacing themselves. Jenkins had lost ten pounds in the last month and was now a more spirited runner. After they had cleared the first mile, Stoney asked the other man, "So what gives?"

"Whad'ya mean?"

"You never call me to run out of the blue. You know something?"

"You should have been a reporter."

"So you *do* know something."

"I know Diane is making spaghetti for dinner and I'll never keep the ten pounds off if I don't sweat before pasta."

"Would you quit screwing around?" Stoney glanced at the other man out of the corner of his eye. "You love being the Washington *Post* of Essex, don't you?"

"Yep."

"Sooo?"

Bill Jenkins slowed down. "They spotted Turner."

"You're kidding." Stoney all but came to a stop. "Where?"

"In Beaufort. That close. Driving a stolen car. He got away, though."

"Damn," Stoney said. "So maybe he did do it. Maybe he really did kill Brockhurst."

"And Sarah."

Stoney wiped sweat off his forehead. "Maybe the same person didn't kill both of them."

"Aw come on, McFarland. We haven't had a murderer in our midst in a hundred years and now suddenly we got two of them at once?"

They picked up their pace again, at Stoney's insistence. He wanted to get his exercise in too. "So what did you think of the hearing?"

"Nice piece of melodrama."

"Meaning?"

"Meaning it's pretty farfetched. About Marian Davis and Maum Chrish. But hell, I don't remember her mother. Do you?"

"No," Stoney admitted. "But Marian wouldn't lie; it must be true."

"I think when we get Turner back here, we'll get some real answers. He took off when the cop stopped him. Brockhurst gave him some pretty tough grilling, Jim told me."

"Yeah? He didn't seem like the type who could take much of that." Stoney pointed toward a dirt road to the left and the two men turned onto it. They jogged in silence for a few minutes, then Stoney asked, "Did you see the post-mortem on both Sarah and Brockhurst?"

"Yeah, why?"

"Anything similar at all?"

"No. If there had been, I'd have put it in the paper. Two very distinctly different murders—the only thing in common was a knife."

"Yeah, but Brockhurst wasn't all cut up like Sarah," Stoney said as much to himself as to the other man. "That would make you think Sarah's murder was an act of revenge—didn't Brockhurst say something about that?"

"I don't know. Two new SLED agents are scheduled to come down soon, Jim says. To investigate both murders. I gather they're waiting to see what happens with Maum Chrish." Bill Jenkins slowed down again. "Hell, I'm not gonna eat that much spaghetti."

Stoney slowed down also and the two fell into a companionable trot. The skies above them looked like rain and the humidity plastered their running shorts to their legs.

"Makes sense though," Bill said, "what you said about Sarah and revenge. Odd too about how Sarah had those tiny little marks all in a row."

"What?"

"It was in Ed's autopsy report. Most of the wounds were very deep, big things. But on Sarah's arm were several small cuts in a row, almost a pattern, superficial cuts, maybe made with a razor, the report said. Nothing like that at all on Brockhurst."

"Maybe he was leaving his signature," Stoney said half in jest. Then he stopped suddenly and instinctively rubbed the stomach scar beneath his T-shirt. "Jesus."

Bill looked at Stoney. "What's wrong?"

"He likes to mark his victims." Stoney sped up. "Are you sure there weren't any marks on Brockhurst?"

"Positive. Why?"

"Did you ever get in a fight with Leonard Hansen when you were growing up?"

"Does a dog have fleas? Most of us got over it."

"Did he—leave any kind of mark on you?"

"What are you talking about?"

"Cigarette burn?"

"No, nothing. Hell, it was thirty years ago."

Stoney thought for a second. "Did you fight back?"

"What?"

"Did you?" Stoney looked apologetic. "Look, most guys didn't. But it might be important. Did you?"

"Shit no. He broke bones when you did. If you want me to feel like a coward about it this late in life, I'm afraid it won't wash."

"That's it," Stoney exclaimed. "He hated anyone who fought back. I did and somehow Sarah did too, but Brockhurst didn't."

Bill Jenkins laughed aloud. "You *are* crazy. That's sheer speculation. You don't have one damn thing on Leonard that isn't just in your head."

Except for the way he was looking at my wife this morning. Stoney looked up abruptly. "I gotta go." And he turned and started for home, leaving Bill staring after him.

In the end Stoney did not show Anna how to use his rifle that night, thanks largely to Silas. After Anna returned from Marian's, she left Silas outside and he wandered off for an hour and managed to get into someone's garbage before coming home smelling of spoiled chicken livers. "Oh yuk," Anna cried when she bent down to pet him at the back door. "Silas, you big glutton, what have you been into?"

When Stoney came home, she was just beginning to wash the dog. The retriever, who was totally enamored of swimming in any stagnant pond he could find, was not fond of bathing. Stoney had once bought a large galvanized tub for the chore but Silas made it very clear, after two attempts, that he would not submit to the indignity of climbing inside it in order to be assaulted with soap and water. Now he would agree to a bath only by standing on the concrete sidewalk in the back yard while someone hosed him down, soaped him up, and then hosed him off again. After which he invariably rolled in the grass to get the water off, arriving at the back door later looking doused with organic confetti. However, a dog covered with dead grass was far preferable to one reeking of rotten chicken.

When Stoney arrived, he stared at the malodorous dog and gave Anna a quick kiss as he reached for the other sponge in the soapy bucket by her side. "Hey," she teased, "is that any way to kiss the woman you're hot for? If washing the dog turns out to be anything like washing the cars was the other day, we're going to be pretty tired by bedtime."

Still thinking about Leonard Hansen, Stoney just nodded vaguely and began washing the dog. He did not pick up on her cue; he wasn't sure what it meant or how he should respond to it. Sudden changes always made him uneasy.

Anna stared at him for a second, then turned the water on full blast, mumbling under her breath.

By the time Stoney and Anna finished washing Silas, taking their own showers (always a requirement after washing an eighty-five-pound dog) and having a dinner of leftover tuna salad, some Gouda cheese, and half a loaf of French bread, along with an excellent Savignon Blanc, they were both so sleepy they went upstairs and fell gratefully into bed. Before they went to sleep, Stoney mentioned that he was going to take the day off again tomorrow to attend the rest of Maum Chrish's hearing.

The next day the hearing room was less crowded than the day before. Maum Chrish was up front again, with the same serene, distant look on her face. The two lawyers, both of whom were quieter than the day before, looked ill at ease and spent most of their time scribbling furiously on legal pads. Marian sat in the front row, waiting to be called to testify. Judge Thompson again asked Maum Chrish to speak in her own behalf which she—again—did not do. After which, the judge called Marian forward. The oath was administered by the clerk-stenographer and Marian took the seat to the left of the judge.

"Since this is a hearing," the magistrate explained, looking out at the sea of faces beyond him, "I have the option of questioning the witness myself. Either attorney may interrupt at any time, as long as neither does so frivolously."

Marian took a deep breath, looked at Maum Chrish on the other side of the judge for a moment, and then out at the crowd. She knew instinctively that Harriet had not come today. But Anna and Stoney had.

"Ms. Davis, could you tell us how you came to discover that Maum Chrish is your mother and how you happened to be with her on the night Sarah Rothenbarger was killed?" The judge smiled at Marian briefly. "Take your time. The floor is yours."

For fifteen minutes Marian explained how she had come back to Essex to look for her mother over five years ago. She detailed her conversations with people in Essex, how she had even once hired a private detective from Savannah who had had no luck tracking down Lonnie Davis. How Marian had virtually given up when she noticed Maum Chrish in town one day. "I have no idea what it was. But I was just drawn to the image of her, I guess. I remember—later on—standing at the window of the church after Sarah's funeral, the window Maum Chrish climbed out of, and I had that same feeling then. Of course I was beginning to suspect who she was by then.''

It was part fact, part fiction.

Marian described her conversation with Sadie Thompkins, her first visit to the swamps, her inspection of Maum Chrish's cabin, and her eventual discovery of the amulet she had given her mother as a child. (All of these events, however, she placed in an earlier time frame, and she omitted Anna's involvement.) How she finally confronted the older woman and had received confirmation that she was right, that the older woman really was her parent.

The prosecutor stood up irritably. "Your Honor, we don't dispute whether or not Ms. Davis is related to the accused. It doesn't matter to us. What we do question is the convenient alibi she's suddenly provided for her."

Seth Von Hocke again sat on the back row of the conference room. He had lied and told his mother he was going to Donny's; he was lucky to have thumbed a ride with the Jamersons or he'd have had to walk the whole way, since his bike was now locked up in the storage building behind his house. He didn't particularly like defying his parents, but he just had to be here. He felt like he had to be present in case the schoolteacher needed help. In case she couldn't do it. Weird how it was really wrong, what she was saying, but seemed right. And anyway, if she didn't do it, then he'd have to tell everyone how he and Donny were there that night.

Marian was talking again. More about how she'd begun to believe Maum Chrish was her mother and had gone out to the swamps to get proof before confronting her, how she went out there several times and just spied on the other woman, to see what she could find out, only often Maum Chrish was not at her house. How on the night Sarah was killed, she couldn't sleep so she had driven out there to see Maum Chrish again, she was determined to talk to her, she got out there and this time Maum Chrish was home, was there in her cabin, alone, shortly past midnight.

"This is preposterous," Emmett Atkins shouted, rising to his feet. "We are to believe Ms. Davis just happened to go spying on Maum Chrish in the middle of the night Sarah Rothenbarger just happened to be murdered? We are to believe a woman alone was not afraid to go into those swamps at night?"

"If you're not afraid of racist rumors about voudou," Marian countered, "why would you be afraid of the swamps?" She looked around the room. "What is there to be afraid of out there—snakes? Or is it black people who believe something different, is that the danger?" Marian turned to the judge. "The funniest thing is, Maum Chrish doesn't strictly believe in voudou."

Audible disbelief made its way around the room. Marynell Pittman snorted loudly.

Marian looked at Judge Thompson. "What I mean is, I think she practices voudou to scare people so they will stay away and leave her alone. The drawings on her walls indicate an interest in many different beliefs—astrology, tarot cards, Christianity, cabbalism."

"What?" Judge Thompson squinted. "I'm not sure I know what the last one is."

"Your Honor, since discovering Maum Chrish is my mother, I've tried to research everything on the walls of her cabin. The Hebrew alphabet is there, yes—but I don't think it necessarily has anything to do with Sarah Roth. A long time ago some Jews were also mystics. In the Jewish Cabbala, the alphabet can be used to divine, to ascertain spiritual meaning. Perhaps Sarah and Maum Chrish did share this sometime—they were both outcasts in a way, it must have been lonely to be the only Jewish person in town. And that might explain why Maum Chrish showed up at Sarah's funeral, because the two of them had this in common."

The prosecutor got to his feet again. "It truly is remarkable," he said to Marian, "how you have the answers for everything."

"Yeah," someone shouted from the gallery. "That's a fact."

The judge looked up, ready to grab his gavel again, when Marian's voice took over in its stead.

"I think what makes everyone fear Maum Chrish," she said, staring at the assemblage in the folding chairs, "is not how backward she seems. It's not even her color. It's how progressive she is. Because she apparently believes in many philosophies, because in her mind differences must complement rather than divide, we call her crazy. Maybe she reminds us of our own shortcomings."

Marian stopped and stared across the room at Maum Chrish. "Who is it that decides one set of beliefs is backward superstition while another is enlightened truth? Freemasons put a triangle on their lodges to represent the Christian trinity; voudouists put a triangle on the center-post altar in their temples to represent their trinity." She turned and gazed at the townspeople.

"We accept one without thinking—and we fear the other without thinking. Why can't we accept both?" Then Marian stopped; she looked at the judge and added quietly, "That's all I have to say. I was there. She didn't kill Sarah."

Judge Thompson thought for a moment and then said to Marian, "May I ask why you didn't come forward sooner?"

"I didn't think it was necessary until now."

"You are positive you were with Maum Chrish on the night of April 12th and that you did not see her leave her house?"

"Yes, I'm sure."

"Then I will take your testimony under advisement." The judge looked over at the two lawyers. "Even though this is only a preliminary hearing, in view of this development, I feel I should offer you the opportunity to cross if you wish."

Ben Estes declined. However, Emmett Atkins got to his feet at once. "Ms. Davis, do you have any documented proof that Maum Chrish is your relative—blood tests, old photographs, birth certificate, anything like that?"

"No."

"Was anyone else aware of your nocturnal visits to her house, of the relationship you were allegedly forging with her?"

"I didn't think it was anyone else's business." Marian gazed at Anna for a moment.

The prosecutor resumed, "You say you got to her cabin shortly past midnight on April 12th. What time did you leave?"

Unprepared, Marian answered, "I don't know exactly."

"Can't you at least estimate how long you were there?"

"An hour, maybe a little longer."

"So you left a little after one in the morning?" When Marian nodded, the district attorney said, "You must answer out loud, please."

"Yes, I think I left about one or a little after."

"You drove all the way out there in the middle of the night to stay for one hour, is that correct? All because you couldn't sleep?"

"Yes."

"Would you say that's normal for you? Erratic behavior like that?"

"No, of course not."

"Could any of your testimony be construed as the action of an intelligent, educated teacher—spying on someone who is supposedly her mother, telling no one about her, allowing her to be arrested without coming forward until the last moment?'' Emmett Atkins turned his eyes on the spectators rhetorically.

The judge intervened. "Counselor, the witness is not on trial."

The prosecutor shrugged. "No more questions at this time."

"Then I'll see both attorneys in my chambers," the magistrate concluded. "We stand in recess for now."

Marian got up and stepped down from the dais, prepared to go back to her seat. But before she left, she crossed to Maum Chrish and bent down and touched the older woman on the cheek. And for just an instant she saw something move in those old eyes. Then Marian walked back down the aisle. But she didn't stop at her seat; rather, she moved on toward the rear door of the room, her gait slow and tired, as though she were exhausted by the weight of the old skin being sloughed off. She moved alone, a woman who took on a deeper hue as she moved into the shadows at the back of the room. At the door she hesitated, stood very tall and thought for a moment about Harriet.

She reached for the doorknob, but a small hand shot out in front of her and opened the door for her. Marian looked down at Seth, then she walked through the door.

When Marian got back to Essex, she drove straight to Harriet's, got out of her car, and walked up the steps and rang the bell. Harriet opened the door, her eyes uncertain. "I sure could use your help in my garden," Marian said. "Could you come over this afternoon?"

Harriet looked down, quickly blinked her eyes. "I think I can spare the time today. Let me get on a housedress and I'll be down directly."

They worked together in the dirt all afternoon, Harriet giving orders and Marian heeding those she truly thought were sensible, about what to plant where and how to fertilize it. Together the two women turned up a lot of earth under that perpetually hazy sky. They spoke of nothing else but growing things. When it was finally dusk, Harriet got up to go home, her cotton housedress black with Low Country dirt. For a moment Marian almost asked her to stay to dinner but then, in the end, she didn't. Instead, she stood in her driveway and waved as the old lady walked home.

Later Marian took a long bath and climbed, naked and aching all over, into bed. She closed her eyes tiredly, wanted only to sleep even though it was not completely dark out yet. But the white walls of the room were too bright and aggressive, and she lay there restless and strained.

A few minutes later the phone rang and she picked it up to hear Stoney McFarland's voice. "Maum Chrish was released about an hour ago; the judge dismissed the whole case. Bill Jenkins just called and he said Emmett Atkins really put up a fight but Judge Thompson didn't agree." Stoney paused. He still wondered why Marian had not said anything about Maum Chrish before, but he didn't think this was the time to ask about it. "Anna says she'll see you tomorrow. If you need anything, we're here."

Marian held the receiver for a few minutes after Stoney hung up. Then she placed a call to Charleston and talked for a few minutes. After which she got up and closed all the blinds in the room and drew the drapes. The sweet darkness settled in around her and soon she slept.

Fifteen

WHEN IT WAS all said and done, Maum Chrish's hearing would be stuffed into the spare closet of our memory, whereas the drought that both preceded and followed her arrest would remain uppermost. Before she was incarcerated, we lived on hints of rain—the impotent electrical storms that made our hearts race with anticipation. We dallied wildly in the assumption that the drought was bound to end soon. But after Maum Chrish was released, and certainly no one who attends the Lutheran or Baptist churches would ever suggest she had a hand in this, the electrical storms stopped. Day after day after day we had nothing but statis. Either a dull gray sky or an unrelenting sun pressing down like a hot iron on flowers and trees. The regiment sitting in front of the Piggly Wiggly said they had never known the sun to shine so long into the evening; two fellows claimed it didn't set until after ten at night one time in August but of course we didn't believe them. Anybody who sat in front of the grocery store all day that summer, bottle or no, probably had heatstroke.

The lawns all over town died first; green faded into a sickly yellow and then slowly dissolved into a brittle brown. At first everyone tried to water the grass but, as Harriet maintained, no water out of a spigot could take the place of natural rain. Then the state bureaucrats issued advisories about water usage, asking people not to water their lawns. Most everyone in Essex complied except Elsie Fenton, who thought this was another Communist plot like daylight saving time. All the flowers withered, the shrubs didn't shoot up, we lost our homegrown vegetables, even the trees drooped after a while. Several small pine trees died. And beyond our borders even worse disaster: the marshes along the coast were so dessicated the snowy egrets were starving, the lakes were so low boaters could only put in at certain points, the corn and soybean crops were almost totally gone (thank God, the peaches were in before it got so serious, South Carolina without peaches would have been entirely too much to bear), wells all over the state were going dry, and generally speaking everyone was pissed off but good.

Beginning that first week after Maum Chrish was released, when the drought intensified, people in Essex went around with a thirsty look on their faces. Maum Chrish herself went back to her shack in the swamp and that was the last most of us thought about her. Marian spent many afternoons out there, afternoons in which Maum Chrish received her much as she had received Seth. (Poor Seth was barely allowed out of his house these days, what with being grounded.) After a while Marian gave up asking the other woman for answers; little by little, like Seth for whom it was easier, Marian learned merely to accept what was given to her. Which was quite a lot really. Under Maum Chrish's tutelage, Marian learned how to sit very still in the woods in naked absorption, how to be where she was and yet at the same time not be there, how to escape beyond herself, how to return to herself when need be. She made friends with her African kra-soul. She met other blacks who came to visit Maum Chrish, listened to their tales and stories, and watched them dance. Invigorated, she went home every evening to work, after the heat of the day evaporated, in the garden she and Harriet were building in her back yard—despite the odds of its surviving the summer. Almost every day they worked in Marian's yard together for an hour or two; almost every day Marian moved directly from one world to another without the discordancy that doing so had once caused her. Harriet asked no questions about Maum Chrish or the swamps and Marian offered no confidences; they just built a garden together in the middle of a drought.

It was almost as if the town, in the week after Maum Chrish went home again, took time off from the murders that had ripped our lives apart. Certainly it occurred to some of us that whoever had killed Sarah and Lou Brockhurst was still out there. It occurred to Stoney McFarland quite a lot. But much of that week, Stoney spent in other pursuits. He went to Columbia, saw his supervisor, and was reinstated in his job, a reprimand being attached to his permanent employment files. His first bad-conduct report ever. Two days later he returned to his office on Main Street, and Sumter Brownlow, certain the junior engineer had learned his lesson, welcomed him back enthusiastically; the workload while Stoney was gone had just about done the older man in. Within a few days Stoney was settled back in again but he approached his work a little differently now—when he thought Sumter Brownlow was pushing too hard, he didn't joke back, he just told the other man straight out to stop badgering him. Then, one night when Stoney and Anna were listening to a Mystic Moods record featuring the sound of thunderstorms, Stoney finally told his wife about being suspended.

"I like that you stood up to Brownlow, that old tyrant," was all she said.

Anna spent a lot of time thinking about Stoney that week. It occurred to her now that perhaps she and Stoney would never get back the passion they had let slip away from them. When they were younger, he had often hinted he wished she were more sexually aggressive. That felt like another order then, another performance she was supposed to give for his benefit, and so she had rarely taken the lead. Now, she had—that afternoon she washed the cars. Yet afterward Stoney had just let it drop. She had hoped things would be different; when he came home from work, instead of that perfunctory kiss, she had hoped to be met by a lover. She wanted seduction back in their everyday lives. She had tried but he had not held up his end.

It was wonderful to get to your midthirties and finally see how you'd screwed up your life—now that there was nothing you could do about it. Reading Henry Miller and Norman Mailer hadn't helped. Nor had her mother. On the night before Anna's marriage, her mother had given her one piece of unsolicited advice: "Never say no twice in a row if you want to keep him." Even now Anna could remember her mother's cold eyes. Is that why her father left? The advice infuriated Anna—all those *s* words came back: surrender, submission, subjugation. Afraid that she might end up as passionless as her mother, Anna plunged into her first years with Stoney with gusto—only to have the words, the times, her experiences with Rand show up later like a resurrected Grim Reaper. She had matured on the cusp of an era when women didn't give themselves, they gave in. Thus, denial in her adult life became self-assertion and she had ruined her marriage, sexually, by turning down a man she had always been attracted to.

Two weeks after Maum Chrish was released, Leonard Hansen's house was set on fire. It happened on a Wednesday. At seven in the evening Anna was working in her darkroom, developing the two rolls of film she had finally shot the day before of Harriet Setzler. She heard the car pull up in front of the house. Stoney was in the back yard, lying in the Pawley's Island hammock reading a book by Gabriel García Márquez, Silas curled into a ball of sleep on the grass beneath the hammock. Every so often the book slipped from Stoney's fingers and he dozed too; he was worn out from working on six different projects this week.

The visitor was Bill Jenkins, who told Stoney about the fire at Leonard's house. Apparently someone had broken into the house, burglarized it, then set fire to it. Leonard got home just as the burglar was running away; the guy had been on foot and Leonard said it was a short fat guy with black hair. Now volunteers were needed to search for him.

In a few minutes Stoney left with Bill Jenkins but not before telling Anna, "Lock up tight and keep Silas in. I'll be back as soon as I can."

Driving out into the country as darkness fell, Bill and Stoney were quiet most of the way, both noting the parched farmland with its ruined cornfields. The county had been lucky so far; without rain there would be more fires, forest fires. Stoney tried to remember if he had ever seen the land outside Essex look so ugly, so arid and lifeless. Sometimes now he got the feeling that before this summer was over, something even more terrible was destined to happen, that after it nothing—and none of them— would ever be the same again.

When they were almost to Leonard's house, Bill said, "I guess this shoots your theory about Leonard."

Stoney didn't say anything.

When they reached Leonard's house, the two Essex fire department trucks were pulling away but there were still at least eight cars parked around the small structure. The acrid air smelled of charred wood. Buck Henry was there with one of his deputies; several men from Essex were also milling about, stopping to talk to Jim Leland on the front porch. Most of the men walked down and got in their cars before Bill and Stoney reached the porch. Leonard's house was fairly intact, although there was a large gaping hole in the roof and the leaning chimney was singed black. The fire, Stoney guessed, had been started in the living room and had got no further before it was extinguished. Leonard would be able to salvage the house, even though he'd lost quite a bit of his new roof.

Jim looked up as Bill and Stoney came up the stairs. "Thanks for coming, you two. I need somebody to ride down Chapel's Ferry Road and look for him.''

"You think it's Turner?" Stoney asked.

Jim looked tired, like a man asked to perform a task outstripping his talents. "I think maybe it's always been Turner. The guy's got something against us, against the town. Leonard said he never even saw him before, there was absolutely no reason for Turner to break in here, except it's way out where nobody passes by much.''

Bill looked around. "Where's Leonard?"

"He went with Ricky Gibson to check around the highway." Jim nodded at his own car in the yard below. "You better take one of those shotguns from the office. In case you do find him. He's killed two people."

"I don't understand why he would do this," Stoney said. Then he added, "Anna and all those women are alone in town, Jim. You think he might go back there?"

"Not without one of us seeing him. But I'll drive back in myself later on, just to be sure everything's okay."

Now Bill turned to Jim. "Could Turner be some sort of psycho?''

"Brockhurst didn't think so," Jim said. "Brockhurst thought he made a living hitting small towns, stealing, then moving on. In fact, Brockhurst tricked Turner into admitting he'd been in Essex once before, had broken into a house here, I think. It was Brockhurst's theory that Turner had met Sarah then, maybe she took him home for dinner like she loved to do, and he remembered her house and when he came this way again he just decided to go there. Only Sarah made a fuss—which Harriet Setzler heard—and Turner got edgy and killed her. That's my conclusion too. Remember, Sarah could be right feisty.''

"But why all this other?" Stoney asked. "Why didn't he just leave after that?''

Jim shrugged his thin shoulders. "He—Brockhurst—figured Turner stayed around to avoid looking guilty. I mean, the natural thing to think is the guy would get the hell out of town if he did it, right? Maybe Turner heard about what Maum Chrish did at the funeral, he decides to make her look guilty, gets an old goat and carves him up and scares the town to frigging death, makes it look like that old woman did the whole thing. Only Brockhurst isn't convinced and Turner knows that—so he kills Brockhurst too.''

"But after that he wouldn't come back here. Unless he's either very crazy or very stupid.'' Stoney stared out at the yard; true, Turner had never seemed particularly bright. "Why—after killing a policeman—would he still be here breaking into houses? And the fire—that just draws attention. Did Brockhurst know if he'd ever set a fire before?''

Jim shook his head. "If the guy's crazy, Brockhurst said he might just blow up at some point, freak out—maybe we can't expect what he does to make sense. It looks to me like he's intentionally terrorizing the town. Maybe he's getting off on that.'' The police chief shook his head. "Can we talk about this later? Will you two search around Chapel's Ferry Road? If we wait too long, he's gonna get away.''

In a moment Stoney and Bill got back in Bill's van and took off down the darkening two-lane road.

Harriet Setzler had not set foot in Stoney and Anna's house since the week they moved in, when Anna was so rude to her, so it was with a certain misgiving that she climbed the steps to the McCloskey monster (as she privately referred to the house) about half an hour after Stoney left with Bill Jenkins. The old lady didn't like the house. She vividly remembered that upstart McCloskey with his shiny new money (rumor was his daddy was a carpetbagger). The man just sashayed into town one day, with his fancy horseless carriage and his gold-tipped cane, and plopped his behind down on this piece of land and proceeded to build the gaudiest house in town. William said they should treat the McCloskeys just like anybody else, but Harriet never listened. White trash dressed up with money was still white trash.

At the front door, Harriet almost turned around and retook the steps in the encroaching darkness. She wasn't quite sure why she was here, but she knocked on the door anyway.

Anna opened the door with a look of surprise. "Hello, Mrs. Setzler.''

The younger woman was a little annoyed; she was busy in her darkroom and she preferred that visitors call first. She studied Harriet's face. The old woman's hair was splayed across her head in unruly tangles and she was wearing a faded cotton housedress instead of her usual sleek jersey. Her shoulders were still held imperially but it was a forced stance today, as though she herself had stopped believing in her own invincibility.

"Is Stoney home?'' Harriet asked. "I heard something about a fire out at that Hansen boy's place. Elsie said that J. T. Turner was running around loose somewhere, that now they think he killed Sarah and that detective.''

"Stoney and Bill Jenkins just went out there," Anna said. Again she noticed Harriet's uncharacteristic nervousness. "Would you like to come in for a minute?"

"Oh no, I need to be getting back home." But Harriet didn't move. Instead, she waited for Anna to insist she stay.

Anna didn't.

Finally Harriet, thinking that despite taking the pictures the other day, Anna was still the rudest woman she'd ever met, added, "Well, tell Stoney to come by when he has a minute. I need to tell him something."

Again Anna noticed the desperate look in Harriet's eyes. Under other circumstances it would have appealed to the photographer in her, the interesting way the eyes fought the fear that threatened to overwhelm them, but right now she was worried the old lady might collapse on her porch. "Mrs. Setzler, would you like some tea or coffee?" she heard herself ask, feeling idiotic, trying like everyone else in Essex to feed whatever ailed anyone.

"No, no. . . ." Harriet trailed off. Her eyes receded into her head and her mind moved back to another time. A young Marian standing there on the front porch, her dress ripped, her face contorted with dirt and tears, blood on her left shoulder where the dress had been torn and on her right leg too. As though someone had hit her and dragged her down to the ground. Marian's mouth open but no words coming out, her eyes rolling back in her head like she'd lost her senses, her hair filthy dirty and stuck to her head with sweat, the smell of liquor, the smell of something else too, something vaguely familiar but not pleasant. The girl crying, then trying to talk, asking Harriet to keep something from happening again. Harriet patting her shoulder, the pitiful dress falling off to expose Marian's tiny brown breast from time to time and Harriet daintily pushing the dress back up to cover the girl.

Harriet said abruptly, "I shouldn't have told her. It's all my fault."

Anna stared at the elderly woman. "Pardon?"

"I shouldn't have told her," Harriet insisted. "She was never able to let things be, we were alike that way. I should have known what would happen in the long run."

God, Anna thought, she's losing it. This time Anna insisted Harriet come in and she finally did. Anna led the way to the kitchen, kept Silas from mauling Harriet, and got the octogenarian installed at the kitchen table. Then Anna left to rescue her prints, of Harriet ironically, from the developer in the darkroom. Back in the kitchen again, she put some water on to boil.

While Anna was getting mugs out of the cabinet above her head, Harriet said, "Someone was in my yard last night. I woke up and I heard him. Walking around. Just like before. And just like the night Sarah died."

Anna swallowed, turned around to the old lady. "Are you sure? Could you tell who it was?"

"I'm not certain. I thought I knew but now I'm not sure. All I know is, he keeps coming back to my house."

Anna didn't say anything. But before she poured the tea, she went back into the living room and double-checked the lock on the front door.

Stoney and Bill rode slowly down Chapel's Ferry Road, so named for a long-since-abandoned Baptist church. No one remembered how the ferry part figured in the naming of the road in the twenties; there wasn't even a wooden bridge along it. It was just one of dozens of potholed backroads radiating from the three highways which bisected the rural countryside northwest of Essex. Along it stood a few small farms and one large spread owned by the Fenwicks; that farm, consisting of a thousand acres, had been in the Fenwick family for nearly a century. As Stoney and Bill turned into its long driveway (actually a short private road), they passed fenced pastures where cattle grazed and eventually came alongside a small oblong frame building with a pitched roof—it had once been the farm store from which the Fenwick farmhands purchased their supplies each week. Beyond it, some distance away, stood two barns surrounded by various pieces of farm machinery, including two large John Deere tractors. The white house was a modest two-story Cape Cod with dormers and to its rear was the one-story flat-roofed frame grandchildren's house with its walls of bunk beds for when all the Fenwick kids visited at the same time.

Stoney and Bill climbed up the steep front steps and knocked on the door they both knew was unlocked. Martha Fenwick, who had run the huge farm for the last forty years after her husband died of a heart attack, was not well but her sixty-year-old unmarried son, Tex, who lived with her, came to the door. Always smiling, an avid bird-watcher, Tex now oversaw the farm's operation, often from his motorized golf cart, for his mother. He had been out in the fields this afternoon, praying for rain if you wanted to know the truth, but he hadn't seen a thing, didn't Stoney and Bill want to come in?

Stoney and Bill didn't stay but told Tex Fenwick to keep an eye out for anything unusual; the dimunitive man pressed them with flashlights and some fresh vegetables and a bottle of bourbon before they left. Stoney and Bill rode farther down Chapel's Ferry Road and stopped at several dilapidated barns; cautiously they shone the flashlights into various leaning structures but they didn't find anyone inside or see any sign that anyone had been near them recently. They did manage, however, to surprise a nesting barn owl who flapped suddenly and took off in a huff, scaring both men so badly they opened the bottle of liquor when they got back in the van.

"We're not exactly the kind of guys who should be out looking for killers," Bill said, twisting the top off the bottle and tipping it back. He drank deeply, then coughed and laughed. "Next we'll be whizzing along the side of the road and going to cock fights."

They rode on slowly, stopping from time to time for Stoney to get out and shine one of the flashlights into a vacant field. When he got back in the van after doing so a third time, he said, "You know, we are never going to find him this way. If he's even out here."

Bill put the van in gear. "Where else could he be if he's on foot?"

"Doesn't this strike you as just a little weird?" Stoney stared out the window at the night-shadowed field on their right. "I mean, how many guys break into a house—planning to get away on foot?"

"Meaning what?"

"Maybe Leonard set the house on fire himself." Stoney began to sweat now that he'd said it; he was glad he had left his rifle in town, with Anna. He would show her how to use it when he got home tonight. "I mean, what better way to make yourself look innocent—than to become one of the victims?"

"I swear, McFarland, you're just not gonna be happy until that man confesses, are you? Tell me this—if you were renovating a house to sell it, and you'd just put a new roof on, would you set the fucking thing on fire?"

Stoney sighed. Then he said, "But did anybody else see Turner?"

"Yeah, a cop in Beaufort. Just over a week ago. Which is

proof that the guy's still around. Driving a stolen car. Not exactly a hallmark of innocence.''

"Then how come he's on foot now? Nobody's found that car.''

Bill handed the bourbon bottle to Stoney. "Here. You need this worse than I do. Maybe he hid the car.'' Then Bill said more seriously, ''I really think you're wrong about Leonard. I remember the shit he used to pull. But I don't think he did this.''

For once I hope to hell you're right, Stoney thought, thinking again about Anna.

Now Harriet was talking about teaching school. Anna stared across the kitchen table at the old lady and poured more tea into Harriet's mug and wondered if she'd ever stop talking. It was after eleven and Anna was so sleepy she was having trouble looking interested.

"And on my very first day, don't you know, in those children marched and they knew I was a new teacher. Green—oh I was so green. I could tell, though, that there was some mischief in the air but I pretended not to notice. I told them to take their seats and I sent around a piece of paper—we never had class rolls then, half the children in the county didn't even come to school—and I said for them to sign their names on that paper. I waited and waited. Seems like it took a long time. The paper went around the room and then I collected it. I saw some of them tittering. I took the roll up to the front of the room, right by the old coal stove, and I began reading it out loud, calling the names. 'George Washington,' I said. 'Jefferson Davis, Betsy Ross, Thomas Jefferson, Madame Curie, Babe Ruth,' and on and on I went. Not one child in that room signed his real name.''

Anna smiled. To have been a fly on the wall. "What'd you do? How'd you get their real names?''

"I didn't even ask. I started the history lesson, I let each famous person in the room tell me about his life and accomplishments. Some of those children didn't look a bit happy about that. I called them by those names all year long, even when I knew better. I graduated some of the most famous people in America from that school.''

Anna giggled. God, she probably did. For a second Anna stared at Harriet. She really was funny sometimes.

Then Harriet's face tightened. "If only I hadn't told her,'' she said, losing time again.

Concern unfolded across Anna's face like a map. "Told who?"

Harriet stared across the room, into a distance Anna didn't see. "Why, Sarah of course. I've been thinking about it all day. I told her and she did what she thought was right. And now all this has happened and I keep wondering what it means."

"You told Mrs. Roth about what?"

"I was shocked, outraged. That such a thing could happen to such a sweet child. And I just told her one day, while I was mulling over what to do. I didn't think about it, like I usually think over things. We were doing the spring cleaning, I recollect. I just had it on my mind and I blurted it out and there it was. I never thought she would do anything about it. I never thought it could mean anything all these years later. But now—" Harriet stopped, then finished tersely, "I think she believed I wouldn't do anything about it. Because of Marian." She faltered. "Marian's . . . color."

Anna gawked at Harriet in genuine alarm. The older lady was rocking back and forth, looking at the floor as though she saw someone in it. Anna gazed up at the clock. Shouldn't Stoney be home by now? What was he doing out there? Was he okay? Should she call a doctor for Harriet? Anna was about to get up to go to the phone to call Marian when she remembered Marian was in Charleston. That was why Harriet had come here. Should she call Ed Hammond, have him check the old lady out?

Harriet was still mumbling, "I shouldn't have told her. She went to him and he marched him downtown. Later she said if you couldn't accept a person knowing all the things about them, then what good was it? She said she was responsible and she had to do what she could. I told her, don't ever tell him, don't you ever tell him, Sarah."

Anna swallowed. Something about this was beginning to make sense. "Mrs. Setzler, are you all right? Who are you talking about?"

The old woman halted somewhere between past and present. "I can't help but think she told him later and for some reason he killed her because of it."

Anna grabbed Harriet's hands, to stop them from shaking. "Sarah told *who*? Tell me, for God's sake."

Harriet went mute, just rocked back and forth.

"Mrs. Setzler, who do you mean?"

Harriet still stared vacantly, as though she'd forgotten what they were talking about. Sensing that the moment was lost, Anna finally said, "It's okay, really. Everything's fine." Which clearly wasn't the case at all. She hesitated, then asked, "Listen—could you stay the night? Stoney's not back yet and I'm sorta nervous. Do you think you could stay?" Anna heard herself begging; she could hardly believe her own voice. But she couldn't send Harriet home alone, this disoriented, with a very real murderer wandering around out there somewhere. "We have a nice guest room upstairs."

The old lady looked up, totally recovered herself. "Oh I don't know, I need to be at home, there are things that need looking after."

The eyes and the words didn't match. This time Anna said, "I really would appreciate it if you could stay. I feel sorta anxious without Stoney here—with all this going on."

"Well, if it'll make you feel better, certainly I'll stay."

Anna got up and rinsed out the teapot, wondering what on earth Harriet's ravings really meant. One thing was certain—the woman was frightened by something in the past, and by whoever she thought she saw in her yard the night before. As Anna and Harriet walked up the stairs slowly, Anna said, "There's a half-bath off the guest room with clean towels already in there. If you need anything else, just let me know."

"Oh I won't need a thing, dear. I'll have to get up real early and go check on my house." She said it as though the house might disappear in her absence.

"Well, I appreciate your staying." It wasn't entirely a lie. Harriet's ravings *had* made her nervous. She told the older lady good night and turned back into the hall. Who was Harriet Setzler so afraid of? On impulse Anna went back downstairs and checked all the windows and door locks again. In the kitchen she noticed the dusty Marlin rifle still leaning against the basement door. Of course, she didn't remember where Stoney put the ammunition and she didn't even know how to load the damn thing. But its presence in the room was somehow reassuring all the same.

At midnight Anna was lying in bed, trying to read but unable to concentrate, thanks to Harriet's thunderous snoring down the hall. About every fifteen minutes Anna turned and looked at the clock radio, and at least every half hour she got up and either stared out the window at the street or went in the bathroom for a drink of water. Where was Stoney? What was happening out there? Why didn't he call and at least let her know everything was okay? Again she crossed to the window and gazed down below her. Stoney was out there somewhere looking for a man who had killed two people. Who had also now set fire to a house. To Leonard Hansen's house, the man Stoney believed might actually be the killer. No wonder the world didn't make sense. Anna had seen J. T. Turner only once, that afternoon a month or two ago when he kept walking by the McCloskey house. He gave her the creeps. Leonard Hansen she'd seen quite a few times but she never liked the way he looked at her either, his insidiously invasive smile. It was a look she'd seen before, in the eyes of other men, men on the street in D.C. or passing by in cars; its purpose was to let a woman know that if they ever wanted something from her, they would just take it. This man she'd defended to Stoney?

Outside the window the new full moon was misted over, its surface enclosed in a translucent filmy caul. Anna glanced down the street; from this window she could see all the way to the corner and she watched the silvery moonlight caress the tops of the live oaks, the concrete sidewalks, the clean lines of the bungalows with their clipped flower gardens and porch swings. In this light the town was almost pretty, drought and all. To her back, down the hall, Anna heard Harriet snort and turn over. She was almost glad to have the old lady in the house. What had Harriet meant though? Did she know about Marian being raped all those years ago (but Marian said she didn't tell anyone) and what did that have to do with Sarah Roth anyway?

Abruptly Anna heard a car outside the window; it pierced the stillness like a baby's wail. Then she saw headlights and she strained against the windowscreen looking for Stoney's Rover. But the vehicle stopped short of the house, just out of sight. The headlights went dark and a car door opened. The door sounded too heavy and Anna's heart plummeted: it wasn't Stoney. Besides, Stoney would park in the driveway. Anna licked her lips, whirled around to look back at the clock. It was so late. Who would be moving around the neighborhood this time of night? She turned and doused the bedside lamp and leaned out the window farther. Footsteps. On the sidewalk in front of the house. Anna froze. Whoever it was, was coming toward her.

Suddenly he was on the porch. The floorboards squeaked. He was walking back and forth on the porch, going toward one end and then turning around and crossing to the other end. Why didn't he just ring the bell? Unless . . . Then the footsteps changed—he was going back down the steps. She thought she heard the car start up again. No. She was wrong. He was on the sidewalk again. Muted footsteps now, thrump-thrump-thrump. He was walking through the yard.

He was going around to the back door.

Anna grabbed her bathrobe and tied it around her waist. He was going to try the back door. She waited a few moments, to make sure it wasn't Stoney, to make sure he didn't just let himself in the kitchen. Five minutes passed. No door opened, no familiar voice called hello. Where the hell was Silas? Why wasn't he barking? Anna strode across the room and picked up the phone and flipped through the local phonebook and dialed Jim Leland's number. One ring, two, three, four. She hung up the phone. This was stupid. Jim Leland was out there with Stoney.

And somebody else was on the back porch.

Then Silas barked. Anna could hear the retriever running back and forth in the kitchen. She took a deep breath, wondered what it would take to wake Harriet Setzler. Then Silas was still for a second and Anna heard the storm door rattle outside the kitchen. *Do something.* Silas barked again, it sounded like the dog was jumping against the back door. Didn't Silas faze him at all? Wasn't he worried about the noise? Anna's hands were clammy and she couldn't breathe, so she leaned over and took another deep breath. He wasn't going to kill another old lady. Not in this house. He wasn't going to kill anybody in this house. *No sir.* She scrambled over to the other side of the room and opened the bedroom door. The rifle was in the kitchen; he didn't know it wasn't loaded. She had to get to it before he did.

Down the hall Harriet snored on, blissfully unaware. Softly Anna crept to the head of the stairs and stopped and listened. When Harriet breathed in, Anna could hear the wall clock in the kitchen ticking. Silas was still moving around too, growling low and serious. Anna padded down the staircase. She had reached the middle of it when Silas suddenly yelped again and began to jump around the back door, scratching at it. Whoever was on the back porch was also moving around, outside the kitchen door. He was going to come in the back door. The same way he did at Sarah Roth's. Anna shivered and plunged on down the stairs, biting her lips, holding on to the bannister with a desperate grip.

At the bottom of the stairs she felt her way toward the kitchen. He was still moving around on the back porch. First she heard him at one end, then at the other. She stole across the kitchen floor, ordered Silas down under her breath, wiped her right hand on her cotton bathrobe to get the sweat off, and then reached for the rifle leaning against the wall. She lifted the gun to her chest, held it like a baseball bat. Then she swallowed and walked toward the back door, Silas scooting around behind her trying to get the feel of the new game. Through the sheer curtains at the top of the door, Anna could see the outline of a man.

If he saw the gun before he got in, maybe he'd take off. That was her only hope. Her plan—pull the curtain back, surprise him, hold the gun up where he could see it. If he broke the door in, Silas would rush him and maybe she could get upstairs again and lock herself and Harriet in and they could yell out a window.

But would anybody hear them?

Anna held the rifle out lengthwise and inched toward the back door. He was still there on the porch, very close. He was walking toward the door. Oh God. What if it doesn't work? Anna threw her head back and held the rifle up, put her finger on the trigger. She stood squarely in front of the door. She looked over at the light switch beside it. Flick the light on, push the curtain aside, crouch down so all he can see is the gun. Maybe he'll think it's a man holding it. A man with bullets.

Nothing but the piece of glass between them. Silas beside her, Anna closed her eyes and held the rifle higher. Her arm shot out, fingers on the light switch. *Now.* Everything went bright. She brushed the curtain aside, dropped down, shoved the metal barrel against the window.

"Get out!"

A body thudded to the floor. "Shit."

Dead silence.

Then, timidly, a voice. "Mrs. McFarland? Would you put that gun *down*? It's Jim Leland."

Anna collapsed against the door and the rifle fell onto the floor. She laughed hysterically, then sobbed, "What are you doing scaring me to death like that?"

Slowly Jim peeped over the bottom part of the door. He checked to make sure the gun was gone. Then he stood up. "I came by to see if you were all right. To tell you Stoney'll be a while."

Anna flung the door open and Silas rushed out to sniff Jim. "You scared me half to death," Anna cried. "Why didn't you come to the front door?"

"I thought you'd be asleep and I didn't want to wake you. I was looking in the windows to see if there was a light on, if you were still up." Jim looked exasperated. "I never thought I'd get shot at."

"It's not loaded," Anna exclaimed, her voice tired. "I don't even know how to load the damn thing."

Jim reached down and picked up the rifle, pulled the bolt back, and examined the chamber. "If you don't mind my saying so, there's nothing more dangerous than a gun in the hands of someone who doesn't know how to use it."

"I totally agree. But two people in this town are dead. And my husband has been out all night looking for the guy who did it."

"I know. We're all a bit on edge." Jim put the gun back down and looked at Anna. "I'm sorry, Mrs. McFarland. You gave me quite a scare is all."

"I'm sorry too," Anna said. "Thanks for coming by. And do call me Anna." She pointed upstairs. "Harriet Setzler's here, in case you go by there and her house looks deserted. Is Stoney okay? Did you find Turner?"

Jim patted Silas on the head, wondered if the retriever would be any good at duck hunting. "Stoney's fine; he and Bill are together, they're like Mutt and Jeff, those two. No luck on finding Turner when I left but maybe something's turned up by now. We'll find him. Then maybe this whole thing will finally be over."

"I sure hope so," Anna said.

"Well, I better be going." Jim yawned. "You get some sleep now. Stoney'll be along soon."

Anna walked him toward the back door. "Thanks again. Really did scare me when I first heard you on the front porch," she laughed.

The police chief stopped dead. "I wasn't on your front porch. I parked in the driveway and came immediately around the back to see if any lights were on."

"You didn't park on the street."

"No."

"Did you see another car out there?"

"I saw some headlights when I turned down the street but the car pulled away by the time I stopped." Jim hesitated. "I wasn't going to say anything but to tell you the truth, that's sorta why I stopped. Did you see who that was?"

Anna stared at her hands, willed them not to shake. "No. But I heard him on the front porch."

Jim patted her on the shoulder reassuringly. "I'll check outside for a while. Lock up behind me."

Until Stoney came home two hours later, Anna sat in her living room, wide-eyed and awake, listening to Jim Leland's off-key whistling on the porch steps.

Sixteen

THE NEXT MORNING Harriet was relieved to get back to her own house. Everything seemed much saner in daylight. She had breakfast with Stoney and Anna (they really shouldn't give that dog scraps from the table) and heard about how J. T. Turner had not been found. She heard, too, how Jim Leland had come around (no one said exactly why) and had scared Anna out of a year's growth—Jim Leland showing up to act like a policeman *finally* and she had missed the whole thing. Later, when Harriet got back home shortly after nine in the morning, she felt revived. She was comfortable now, in her own house; all that worry last night was for nothing. This was where she belonged and she wasn't going to leave this house again— no matter how much Anna McFarland needed company. She was always glad to help a neighbor but this being away from her house was too much to ask. Your house needed you, you needed it; it just didn't do to be separated from it for too long. William's aura (which wasn't what Harriet called it but was nonetheless how she recognized it) still lived in this house and she needed that aura in order to breathe herself. When the aura left, when William was finally gone from the house, she knew she'd be gone too.

She spent the morning cleaning. Marian was due back from Charleston late that night and maybe she'd like to come over tomorrow for some lunch. Despite state regulations, Harriet had been religiously watering Marian's new garden in the black woman's absence and she was excited for Marian to see how the new plants had taken hold. Wasn't just anyone who could make things grow in the middle of a drought. Marian would be pleased. Sometimes Harriet wondered about that woman in the swamps, about what Marian thought about her. Except for being

279

so tall, Maum Chrish sure didn't look much like Lonnie but it had been a long time since Lonnie left. What did Marian do out there with her all day? Sometimes the thought that the swamp woman really was Lonnie, was Marian's real mother, brought Harriet up short and she wanted to drive out there and find her and tell her to go away. Wasn't it enough in life to be usurped by one dead woman, now she had to play second fiddle to a resurrected one?

In the middle of her vacuuming, Harriet abruptly stopped and looked out the window at the bright sunshine. Then, without putting the vacuum up or finishing the living room carpet, she suddenly threw open the front door and rushed down the steps and stumped down the street to Marian's house and crossed to the back yard to check on the garden. She sighed with relief. The new roses looked good, no sign of bugs. The azaleas were taking hold, the caladiums were flourishing (would Marian remember to dig up the bulbs in the fall, well if Marian didn't, she would just have to come over and do it for her). And that border of monkey grass was going to be beautiful in another few weeks. Harriet walked in and out among the flowers and the shrubs, surveying her handiwork. Yes, Marian was going to like this. Then the old woman looked up at the skies, wishing for rain. Bet a swamp woman couldn't grow a garden like this.

In a few minutes Harriet went home again, finished her housecleaning, and put the vacuum cleaner back in the pantry closet in the kitchen. Later that afternoon she rolled out pie crust dough to make a batch of lime pies so she'd have some tomorrow when Marian was home again. Harriet was going to take some to Anna McFarland too. Kneading the dough, Harriet thought about Anna. The younger woman had apparently been quite shaken last night—hearing about that fire, that J. T. Turner was back in town. Harriet paused for a second. She was fed up with being afraid. Of everyone in this whole town being afraid. Maybe what happened all those years ago did matter and maybe it didn't—but she was going to talk to Marian about it and no matter what Marian said, Harriet decided suddenly, she was going to go to Jim Leland and tell him a few coincidental things that bothered her. She would not keep silent anymore, there was no reason to. She would tell Marian the truth, that she had not kept her word, and if Marian deserted her in favor of her real mother, she would learn to live with that too.

When Harriet had her lime pies in the oven, she untied her apron and walked into her dining room. She stared for a long time at the painting over the fireplace, of the forest fire. And what she saw in it, this time, was an old friend in a fedora.

Harriet went to bed that evening contented. And when—hours and hours later—she woke up to an odd smell, it was William she thought of first.

Stoney and Anna were lying in bed talking about Leonard Hansen's house. It was almost midnight. The fire of the night before had been troubling Stoney all day long. It did apparently exonerate Leonard in the two murders. Stoney certainly had no "proof" to the contrary, no reason to think otherwise. Then, when Anna told him about J. T. Turner spying on the McCloskey house months ago, he was even more convinced. Maybe he was singling Leonard out because, as Bill put it, Leonard was the kind of Southerner he didn't like.

So who had been wandering around the McCloskey house last night scaring Anna half to death?

"Why didn't you tell me about Turner earlier?" Stoney asked. "You could have been in danger."

"Stoney, I didn't know who he was. You didn't exactly tell me about going to Ashboro to talk to him. I thought you were hung up on Leonard Hansen."

"Eventually I was. I am. Until last night I would have sworn to it. I just wish we'd seen Turner. I'd feel a hell of a lot better if I could just understand why he's doing this."

"I'm not sure the why makes any difference."

Stoney pushed his pillow up. "What do you mean?"

"Killing someone is so beyond our concept of being human— yours and mine, at least—that I'm not sure any explanation of motive ever makes it understandable. That's what horrifies us, I think—it can never be rendered reasonable. Or undone. Only on television, in movies, is murder made to seem reasonable. Because you're encouraged not to care, to pass over the reality of it for the sake of entertainment, for the sake of knowing who did it and why. Much more attention is focused on the killer's motivation than on the effect his acts have on others, on those close to the victim. Media trivializes violence by trying to make it a game—with a neatly tied-up conclusion. When in fact it really isn't neat. It isn't understandable. It's sad and cruel and very scary."

Stoney looked at Anna for a second. It was the first time she'd talked about how she felt about the Essex murders. Christ, what if someone had hurt her last night? He tried to sound light. "You're pretty smart, you know."

She yawned. "Pretty sleepy too." She reached up and turned off the bedside lamp. "I keep thinking about Harriet Setzler."

"Why?" Stoney refocused in the darkness, punched his pillow fatter the way he liked it.

"I told you, she was talking so crazy last night. I really thought maybe she was—you know, going a little batty. She was so upset about something she told Sarah and how she felt it might be the reason Sarah was killed."

"What did she tell Sarah?"

"I don't know exactly. She kept talking about somebody she called 'him' but she never did say who she meant." Anna paused, thinking about whoever had raped Marian years ago. And moved away afterward.

"You should have said something about this earlier. I'll go talk to Mrs. Setzler tomorrow, this might be important."

"She seemed okay this morning. And when I tried to bring this up, she ignored me. God, she snores. She's kind of funny, though, last night she told me all about when she first started teaching."

Eyes closed, Stoney reached out and patted his wife on the leg. "Imagine you and Harriet, chums."

Anna slapped the covers beside Stoney. "Would you quit that? All I mean is, she's . . . she can be . . . interesting."

"You like her."

"I do not like her. I think she's a character."

"You like her." Stoney settled into his pillow and closed his eyes.

Anna stared across the room. Then she said, "If you'd just seen how upset she was. I mean, all about how she shouldn't have told Sarah and Sarah went to 'him' and then Sarah felt sorry for 'him.' I was really worried she was going to faint."

Stoney didn't answer. When Anna looked over at him, he was breathing rhythmically, one arm tucked under his pillow. Sound asleep. Anna watched him for a moment. She still loved the way he looked, that soft thick hair, the fragile cheekbones, those strong shoulders. She turned over and tried to go to sleep. It felt like one of those nights when no amount of saying to herself— "go to sleep now"—was going to work. She thought about Marian for a moment, how odd it was to have met such an unconventional friend here of all places. Who would have believed that a woman who had given up men would turn out to be more honest about sex than anyone? Abruptly Anna remembered a conversation she once had with Stoney, wherein he suggested that many men wouldn't be as upset about their wives having an affair with another woman as they would be about another man.

"That's absurd," Anna had sputtered. Were they driving down M Street? She couldn't remember. "God! That's just another male condescension. Of course they don't feel as threatened—after all, the other woman doesn't have a mighty penis, does she? And that's what's important in sex, right?"

"Anna, I didn't say *I* feel that way. I just think some guys do."

Being a feminist was much easier if you weren't living with a man. Invariably when their conversations wandered into sex and gender, she attacked men and he defended them. Over time their bed became a political battleground. Love became war, precisely because they were so honest, and then the war stopped. No winners. Anna tried to think about other things and finally she drifted off but she still felt uneasy and in a couple of hours she awoke from her in-and-out slumber and went into the bathroom for a drink of water. When she returned to the bedroom, she crossed to the window and looked out at the street below, desperately wishing it would rain. Then, abruptly, she wrinkled up her nose. What was that? It must be her imagination. After last night, especially. She leaned toward the window again and breathed in.

Then she whirled around. "Stoney, wake up. I smell smoke."

An hour later Marian turned off the highway and headed into town. Yawning, she rubbed her eyes with her fingertips. Why had she waited so late to leave? She stretched her thighs languorously, pushed her toes against the floor of the car. Because they'd gone back to bed again after dinner. Which was wonderful—lasted so long, was as ripe with talk as with sex. Wonderfully idle talk. No mention of Maum Chrish, of the murder, of the past, of power, just chat chat chat until Marian dozed off, then woke up and saw it was after nine. She could have just stayed another night but she hadn't really wanted to; she wanted to see Maum Chrish again and she had told Harriet she would be back tonight.

Main Street was like a tomb as she drove through it, bisecting the triangle that outlined Essex. Nothing moving, no one on the sidewalks, not even another car. Then she thought about Charleston, about Susan, that wonderful old house in Ansonborough, Susan's two children. Jordan Taylor had introduced them, entirely by accident; he had handled Susan's divorce. I should have just stayed over, Marian thought, yawning again. But somehow she'd felt she ought to get home. Often she longed for Susan during the week but she was always glad to leave Charleston after a few days too. This was not the same driven love she'd felt for Eileen and it never would be. She would never live with Susan, and it wasn't just because of the kids. It was because both women preferred living alone. Theirs was a weekend marriage.

Often Marian felt she would spend the rest of her life alone, but the possibility no longer seemed tragic; after all, she had grown up watching a woman live alone, a woman who cast a shadow so long hardly anyone who followed her could fill it. In her way, and entirely unknown to her, Harriet Setzler had prepared Marian for the life she would choose—a life which, if Harriet knew everything, would scandalize her. Strange, Marian thought suddenly, how of all the people she had known for years in Essex, it was Anna McFarland she told. Anna who—it seemed clear now—had a few problems of her own.

Nosing her sportscar toward Aiken Avenue, Marian noticed that all the lights were on in the fire hall and she wondered if the men had a late poker game going. The wives were always complaining about the games; who was going to put a fire out if we ever did have one when those boys were drunk and had been up playing cards all night? Marian turned onto Aiken Avenue and drove slowly, thinking about whether this was the summer to leave Essex. What she had come home for was accomplished. Maum Chrish was or she wasn't, it didn't much matter anymore. She existed, that was enough. Probably she wasn't but she seemed like she was. Maybe that's what really counted—the people who seemed to be what they ought to be. Marian gazed at the houses on either side of her. If she left this time, she knew she wouldn't be back.

Then she saw it. Beyond her, down the street, a single flash of yellow and red. Above Harriet's house.

"What on earth?"

Marian stomped on the accelerator and the car shot out from under her and she took the next few blocks in a matter of seconds. She sailed past her house and braked sharply at the corner, slammed the car back into neutral, tore open the door, and jumped out.

Flames.

A small crowd stood in front of Harriet's house. Stopped beside it, on the cross street, was the largest firetruck of the Essex Volunteer Fire Department. Hoses ran from it across the back fence and disappeared out of view. Two men in yellow fire-retardant coats also stood atop extension ladders at the front of the house, their hoses aimed at the roof.

Marian started running. Flames licked at all the downstairs windows, ran up the clapboard sides of the structure, and reared out of the top of the chimney. Half of the sleeping porch had already fallen in on itself. The two ladders were now being pulled away from the roof, as other firemen dragged in another hose and began spraying the front porch.

Suddenly Marian stopped, her eyes glued to the fence in front of the house. Against it leaned Elizabeth Setzler's paintings. They lay in haphazard disarray and one was completely over-turned, but someone had gotten them out, mostly Harriet's favorites, the forest fire, the girl in the boat, some others. Marian swallowed. It was okay. Harriet must have gotten out too.

Marian saw Stoney and Jim in the crowd and ran toward them. They would know where Harriet was. Why oh why didn't I leave Charleston earlier? The question echoed like a mantra, as she lurched forward and grabbed Stoney's arm.

"Where is she?"

The look he gave her was a year long. He put his arm around her.

"Stoney . . ."

Marian saw Anna heading toward her through the crowd. She saw Jim Leland staring at her. Even Elsie Fenton turned toward her.

"She got the paintings out. *Where is she?*"

Finally Jim Leland said, "We think she went back inside again. Maybe to get another picture, I don't know. Now it's so bad nobody can get in."

Marian turned and pushed through the gate and raced toward the house. In a second she was across the grass heading for the steps. A piece of guttering fell off the roof and crashed onto the steps inches from her and she jumped. Then she ran on.

Jim shouted first. "Marian!"

Calling her name, Stoney and Jim both scrambled after her. She was on the porch now, heading for the front door. Ahead of Stoney, Jim reached the stairs just as the remaining guttering fell and it hit him and he wobbled, dazed. Then he threw it aside.

"Stop her!" a fireman yelled. "Don't let her open that *door*."

Jim grabbed Marian from behind just as she reached for the doorknob. She could see the wall of flame through the door's glass pane as Jim pulled her away. Then Stoney reached for her and threw his arms around her.

The two men led Marian to the bottom of the stairs. Anna rushed over and she and Marian clung to each other as they walked across Harriet's yard.

Stoney turned to Jim, his voice thick. "You saved her life."

The police chief looked surprised. He rubbed his bleeding right shoulder. "This can't be an accident, can it?"

Suddenly both men turned sharply. The firemen shouted warnings and ran for cover as a massive live oak, blackened and smoldering, teetered and then toppled over onto the ground.

Harriet Youmans Setzler had the last great funeral ever held in Essex.

We use it, we use her now, to date time. Such and such happened before Harriet was killed, that boy was born after Harriet passed away, hadn't seen the likes of that since Harriet's big funeral. People came from everywhere, from neighboring towns (who knows how many people had eaten those lime pies at one time or another?), from the farms, from the shacks out in the country, and even from inside the swamps. The airport in Charleston did an unusually brisk business, what with all the family arriving. Harriet had had six siblings and her three youngest sisters were still alive and they flew in from Florida. Her daughter and the daughter's husband and their two children arrived from New Hampshire in time for the inquest; her son Billy and his family drove in from Denver and they got to town the day before the funeral, and Jackson Setzler, with his new wife and three teenage girls in tow, finally got to town the day of the funeral. Cousins descended from Brunson and Belton and Ashboro; some hadn't seen Harriet in years but all remembered her. Emma Thomas had her boy Harry drive her up from Tallahassee. The Fenwicks came in from the farm—even Martha, who was almost never seen in public anymore, walked into the cemetery on Tex's arm. We were a mighty bunch. Some of us figured that's why it was such a downright pretty day for a funeral— warm but not unbreatheable, brilliant pink morning sunshine but low humidity for a change, we even had a little rain before sunrise. We figured Harriet somehow knew all these people were in town to pay their respects. She hadn't had that many of her family and friends together since the Setzler family reunion about ten years back—and even that gathering was a poor turn-out compared to this. We figured Harriet was pleased about all the to-do in her honor and so she'd ordered up a nice day for it.

There was only one thing we didn't talk about as we gathered together to see Harriet off. We didn't talk about the inquest. It was held three days after the fire, which totally destroyed the house before it was over. Harriet's body had been removed from the dining room just before the roof caved in, through the heroic efforts of fireman Jesse Morney. At the inquest it was determined that the fire resulted from arson; the rubble yielded an open gasoline can somewhere in the vicinity of the sleeping porch. Harriet, it was surmised, had been awakened by the smoke and had initially tried to save some of her belongings. Fifteen of the forty or more oil paintings survived, including eight which had been damaged. Apparently Harriet had gone back into the burning house and had been overcome by smoke. She couldn't call anyone; her phone line had been cut outside the house. No one could tell, from the rubble, whether anything had been taken. When the body was recovered, Harriet was wearing her customary jewelry—except for the diamond she wore on her right pinky finger. The conclusion of the inquest was that the arsonist was guilty of premeditated homicide.

Harriet's daughter Betty was taken aback by the funeral her stepmother's will requested. Harriet didn't want a service at the Lutheran church as everyone had expected. No, a graveside service was all she required—on a pretty day, of course. But she did want her casket pulled through town on a horse-drawn wagon first—it would deliver her to the cemetery like in the old days. Betty honored her mother's request for a closed coffin, but she would probably have forgone the wagon ride had it not been for Stoney and Marian, who insisted upon it and arranged the whole thing. And so, on the morning of Harriet's high-noon funeral, we stood on our sidewalks and watched her go by. Almost everyone in town. Marian in front of her house, Stoney and Anna in front of theirs, Elsie Fenton, the Loadholts, the Wilsons, Seth and his parents, up and down the street we were thick as flies on a picnic basket; many people from Willowbrook drove over to the old part of town so they could see the funeral wagon, and they brought their children. Some children threw flowers at the wagon but they were somber too, as though they knew they wouldn't see the likes of this again.

Some of us remembered FDR and JFK, when tragedy made

a nation a family for an instant. As with national leaders, we had never truly believed Harriet would die. People with the soft, sweet soul of an Emmas Thomas or a Sadie Thompkins died. But not legends. Legends were eternal, immune to mortality. The only possible reason Harriet Setzler was dead was because someone had killed her. Otherwise, she would never have succumbed; she would not have allowed it.

We watched the chestnut horse in its polished brass bridle pull the newly painted Fenwick wagon past us. Amos Tumley, who had once worked for both the Fenwicks and Harriet, held the reins, sitting straight and tall in a black suit. Behind Amos loomed that solitary bronze coffin, covered with an embroidered purple-and-white altar cloth made by the Lutheran Church Women's Circle. (Harriet's will said she wanted no flowers, that no florist ever grew any as pretty as those in her own front yard.) That morning Marian had given Amos a white rose for his lapel from the bushes Harriet had planted in Marian's back yard. It was the only adornment on the wagon, save for the coffin itself, which gleamed in the morning sunlight. As we stood and watched Harriet go out of our lives forever.

When the wagon had passed, however, our mouths tightened with anger, with a monstrous hatred for Harriet's killer. Harriet had been our yardstick. We always measured ourselves against her strengths and weaknesses, and so her presence gave us balance, equilibrium, at times a sense of grace. Without her we listed at a tilt.

Seth Von Hocke said it best. His parents released his bicycle on the day of the funeral, and he left his mother and father after a while and rode over to watch the wagon go down Laurens Avenue. Finally he ended up on the sidewalk with Stoney and Anna. Just as Harriet's coffin passed the McCloskey house, Seth looked up at Stoney and said, "It's a big wagon."

At the cemetery we lined up just outside the wrought-iron gates, the family and some of the older townspeople at the front, led by Heyward Rutherford. Behind them, the second line began with Marian in a cream silk suit, Stoney and Anna behind her along with other young couples whose step was lighter. The older group marched in evenly, but the second was a more disjointed, fragmented column. The Setzler plot was covered with a green canopy and we gathered beneath it for the short, traditional ceremony Harriet had mandated. Within a half hour the white-robed minister was making the sign of the cross above the casket. He reached down and scooped up a handful of Low

Country dirt and drizzled it across a corner of the casket. "Earth to earth, ashes to ashes, dust to dust; in sure and certain hope of the resurrection to eternal life through our Lord Jesus Christ; who shall change the body of our low estate, that it may be fashioned like unto his glorious body, according to the working whereby he is able even to subdue all things unto himself."

After the benediction people spilled out from under the canopy and gathered in small tight knots, some intersecting from time to time, to talk. Many people went over to say hello to Harriet's children and cousins; several stopped and spoke to Marian and Stoney about what had happened. Almost everyone seemed reluctant to leave. After a while Marian, who was surrounded by several people, noticed that the funeral home attendants were preparing to lower the casket into the gaping hole between William and Elizabeth. Marian glowered at the men. How dare they be in such a hurry. She gazed around and saw that no one else was paying attention to what the men were doing. It was over; in a way everyone was relieved. But it isn't over, she thought, looking back at the triple headstone. It isn't over at all. Abruptly she strode over to the gravesite. Someone should be there. Someone should be Harriet's witness.

Two men were kneeling beside the casket, adjusting the winches on the pulley which would lower the coffin into its vault. They looked up at Marian as she approached. She stopped at the foot of Harriet's casket, turned her head and eyed the flat tombstone with its military insignia perched at Elizabeth's feet. The men finished with the winches, and one of them got up and nodded at the other. Marian's hand shot out. Both men stopped instantly. Silent tears streamed down Marian's cheeks and she reached out and laid her hand on the coffin, just held it there against the cold metal for a moment. Then, because there was no other choice, she let go. She stepped back, still at the foot of the casket, and looked at the men again. Released by her eyes, they knelt down and turned the winch. And slowly Harriet's coffin disappeared into the earth.

Finally Marian turned and walked toward Jim Leland. She touched him on the arm and said, "Could I talk to you in your office tomorrow morning? Ask Bill Jenkins and Stoney to come if you would, and Anna McFarland too."

Stoney and Anna went to dinner that night at Fairfield Plantation. They hadn't planned to go out but at the last minute it just felt like the right thing to do, to get away from Essex for a few hours, especially away from their neighborhood, where it seemed the smell of smoke might linger forever. Stoney had gone to work that afternoon but it had been a wasted day; even Sumter Brownlow had been quiet and subdued. Anna had spent the afternoon with Marian but had finally left, sensing that Marian really wanted to be alone. Now Stoney and Anna sat in semidarkness overlooking the Salkhatchie River, the half-eaten prime rib still in front of them, the cabernet almost gone, as he reminisced about Harriet Setzler.

"You know, she scared me to death as a kid. I even think Dad was afraid of her." Stoney paused, smiled slightly, then added, "I never knew anybody who could be so kind and so intimidating at the same time. I can't imagine an Essex without Harriet Setzler. . . ." he trailed off. Then he added bitterly, "We're going to find who did this—he is not going to get away with it. Not this time."

The dark look in Stoney's eyes matched the one Anna had seen in Marian's eyes earlier that afternoon.

"Let's go home, Stoney."

They drove back in silence; there wasn't anything they could say to each other that helped. Upstairs later, in the bathroom, Anna thought about going back downstairs and getting a drink and sitting in the living room to listen to Mozart or the Pachelbel "Canon," as she sometimes did when depressed or unable to sleep. When she emerged from the bathroom, Stoney was already in bed, staring up at the ceiling. Anna sat beside him on the bed, in the silk gown he'd given her for their anniversary. She leaned down and kissed him. "Think I'll get a drink and go down and work for a while."

He put his arms around her and held her. "Don't stay up forever."

About to rise, Anna turned instead and leaned down and kissed him again slowly, gently, tenderly. She reached up and ran her lips over his forehead and down the bridge of his nose. "I am so sorry, Stoney." Over and over again she traced the contours of his face with her fingers, touching him again and again with softness, as though she might be capable of massaging the pain away.

They didn't speak. Anna just touched his face and he held her. After a while, unhurriedly, he leaned up and kissed the edges of the V-neck above her breasts the same slow way, almost ritualistic in his touch, as though partaking of a sacrament.

Slipping the smooth silk from her shoulders, he turned her onto her stomach and ran his fingers and lips up and down her back, across her rounded hips, down the backs of her legs to her feet, his hands holding her soles, running his finger back and forth against the soft underskin there. He turned her over and looked at her with visible longing. He ran his tongue over her breasts and down her stomach with mounting passion. His fingers circled her abdomen and she floated on the languid sensuality of his hands. All movements were dreamlike; even when he was inside there was no urgency, only a sense of natural ease. No one searched for the meaning of life; instead, they savored the experience of life. They moved gently, and she grew warm and he grew warm and suddenly all she could feel was the need to share this warmth, to give it back to him until he felt nothing else.

Afterward, he lay on his side like a saved man, with one arm around her, and stroked her arm for a long time without speaking.

Bill, Stoney, and Anna gathered in Jim's office the next morning at ten. Marian was late, because of a trip to Harriet's grave. Jim and Stoney both stood when Marian entered. She sat in one of the two seats across from Jim's desk. Anna, sitting in the other, reached over and squeezed her hand.

"Thanks for coming," Marian whispered to Anna. "I need you here."

Stoney crossed his arms over his chest and stood against the wall behind Jim's desk. Bill Jenkins perched on the low bookshelf behind the two seated women. Jim Leland looked at Marian for a second and then said, "I've been thinking about this all night, Marian. I called the SLED chief in Columbia and they're sending two guys down at the end of the week. If Turner is anywhere around here, we will find him. That's a promise."

"It isn't Turner, Jim." Marian took a deep breath. "I believe Leonard Hansen killed Harriet. And Sarah."

Stoney bolted forward.

"You've been listening to him, haven't you?" Jim said, indicating Stoney.

Marian looked at Stoney. "I wish I had."

"Well, I already know what Stoney thinks about Leonard, but we don't have one shred of evidence. An old scar Leonard gave him a hundred years ago doesn't prove a thing."

"For Christsake, Leland, let Marian talk." Bill Jenkins sighed and picked up his notepad.

Abruptly Marian unbuttoned her blouse until the top curve of her bare breasts was visible. Embarrassed, the men looked down. Marian stared at Jim. "You mean like this?"

Stoney looked up first. Between Marian's breasts was a tiny thin scar, about two inches long.

"Leonard," Anna exclaimed suddenly. "Oh God. It was him?" She looked at the scar on Marian's chest.

"He used a razor blade," Marian explained when Jim finally looked at her. She buttoned her blouse. "This was to frighten me into keeping my mouth shut."

"About what?" Jim asked.

"About rape."

Stoney walked over to Marian. "Why didn't you say something before?"

Marian stared at the floor. "I honestly didn't think it had anything to do with Sarah. I had suspicions but nothing concrete. I didn't figure out a connection until yesterday, when Anna told me what Harriet had said about telling Sarah something she shouldn't have. As far as I knew, Leonard was reformed; like all of you, I knew he had been a brutal teenager, I also knew he had blackmailed and raped me. But when he came back to town, he treated me with distant politeness, he stayed away from me mostly, and he never made even the vaguest reference to what had happened years ago."

"But you should have told us anyway," Jim said. "This puts an entirely different light on things. Beating up people as a kid is one thing. Rape is another."

"Don't you think I know that?" Marian cried. She gazed over at Anna. "You think a woman who's been victimized likes to talk about it, likes to bring it up? I don't even like to think about it. And as long as it didn't have anything to do with Sarah's murder, I saw no reason to put myself through this."

No one said anything for a second. Finally Stoney said, "Marian, we're sorry. We don't mean—"

"Oh Stoney, stop it. Stop trying to make up for the world's sins. It's presumptuous. And it's giving you gray hair."

"Here, here. Next thing he'll be fat," chimed Bill Jenkins. "That's what happened to me."

For a second everyone laughed nervously. Then Jim said, "I still don't see what this has to do with Sarah. Why do you think this is proof Leonard killed Sarah?"

Marian hesitated and looked at Anna again. She was suddenly glad Anna knew the parts of the story she was going to omit. "After Leonard raped me," Marian began, "I turned for help to the only person I had. I went home to Harriet's one night in torn clothes, bleeding. She bandaged me up and I told her what had happened. She was outraged."

Stoney interrupted, "Did Leonard know you told Harriet?"

"No, I don't think so. Not then. See, I swore Harriet to secrecy. I knew many people wouldn't believe me—a black girl accusing a white boy, no one did believe such things then. What I didn't know until after Harriet was killed was that she didn't keep her promise. She told Sarah Roth what Leonard had done to me. Sarah told Leonard's father, I believe. . . ."

"Who marched 'him' downtown," Anna finished, her eyes wide.

"And made him join the Marines," Stoney added almost at once. He looked at Anna for a second, then back at Marian. "But how did Leonard find out it was Sarah who told his father?"

"I don't know." Marian gazed toward the window, thinking of Harriet. Her eyes misted and she blinked.

"Sarah could have told Leonard when he lived with her," Bill suggested.

Marian's eyes were clear again. "She had him stay there out of guilt, I think. She always wanted to reform people. My guess is she felt guilty for having been responsible for Leonard being sent away in the first place."

"But why would Leonard decide to get even now?" Jim stared around the room. No one said anything for a moment and then Jim jumped up and opened his mouth.

Bill Jenkins was also on his feet. "The money," he said before Jim could get it out. "The money his father didn't leave him." Bill looked from face to face around the room. "Don't you bet finding out your son is a rapist might sour you on him forever? We all know Joe Hansen and Leonard never made up while they lived here. What if they never reconciled and that's why Joe didn't leave Leonard a dime—Joe made all that money and Leonard's mother is dead but Joe left all his money to a guy who worked for him. Why? Because he never forgave Leonard!"

Stoney walked toward Bill, matching the other man's thoughts the same way they matched strides when jogging. "Leonard came back to town to get the only thing his father did leave him.

An old house he couldn't even sell. Worth maybe $20,000 tops. Whereas the old man's estate''—Stoney looked back at Jim for confirmation, recalling a conversation they'd had about this several months ago—''was about $300,000, wasn't it? Leonard had to fix the house up just to get anything out of it and so he's been out there stewing about who's responsible for him losing out. Remembering why his father never forgave him. *And* who told his father.''

Jim said, ''If you're right, why did he kill Brockhurst, why cut up parts of a goat, why set fire to his own house?''

''To protect himself,'' Stoney said with vindication. ''I knew it. I knew he did it. He never changed, he just made us think he had.''

Then Bill added, ''He must have known Turner was spotted in Beaufort. So he made us think Turner was here by setting fire to his own house. Which gave him the perfect cover to kill Mrs. Setzler—the other person he would hold responsible. We were to believe Turner killed Mrs. Setzler.'' Bill's voice rose to a pitch. ''Leonard has had us all fooled. Except Stoney.'' He turned to Marian. ''You're in a hell of a lot of danger.''

Marian patted her purse with the derringer inside. She had carried it for years in honor of the man who had raped her. ''I'll be okay. I'll be fine once he's arrested.'' She looked away again, thinking of Harriet. ''If only I . . .''

Anna reached over and touched Marian's shoulder. ''If only we'd all really understood what was happening.'' Then she looked at Stoney and he held her gaze for a long time.

Jim cleared his throat. ''You know, this makes sense, we could be right. Or we may be just guessing—and Turner may still be around somewhere and he was only trying to rip Mrs. Setzler off and *he* set the fire to cover his tracks. It is hard to figure out why Leonard wouldn't have first gone after you, Marian. What I think is—''

Stoney exploded. ''*For God's sake, Jim.* Is he gonna have to kill Marian too?''

The police chief held up his hand. ''You might let me finish. I do think it's time I had a talk with Leonard.''

Mollified, Stoney said, ''You can't go out there alone.''

Jim nodded. ''Thanks.'' Then he smiled. ''Maybe you are the prodigal after all.''

It was a moment before Stoney answered. ''No, I don't think so.''

Shotguns stored in the patrol car, Stoney and Bill and Jim sped out of town to pick up Leonard Hansen, while Anna and Marian walked home together to wait for it to be over.

Seventeen

"DAMN," STONEY CRIED out as he and Jim and Bill pulled up in front of Leonard Hansen's house. "His truck's gone, he's not here."

The three men slid out of the patrol car and stared at the house. It looked much as it had the night it had been on fire: the hole in the roof still gaped inconsolably at the gray skies above it like an open can of sardines. Tools and debris and even a flashlight used that night lay strewn across the smoke-damaged porch. "One thing's for sure," Bill said, eyeing the police chief, "he hasn't been spending his time cleaning up."

"Which doesn't necessarily mean he's been busy killing Harriet Setzler," Jim answered. All during the drive out to the country, however, he had had the sinking feeling that Stoney and Marian were right about Leonard. Which unnerved him, given how much time he'd spent with Leonard since Leonard's return to Essex. He should have noticed something.

Stoney strode up onto the porch and knocked on the door, turning back to Jim and Bill. "No way he's here."

In a moment the other two men joined Stoney on the porch and Jim knocked this time. He turned and stared out at the yard. "He isn't at work, I called before we left the office. We didn't see him in town. So where can he be?" Jim opened the screen door and pushed on the wood door. It gave, creaked open. He turned back to Stoney and Bill. "I don't have a warrant but I think we've got cause to look around."

The other two nodded and followed Jim inside. To Stoney, the house looked much as it had the afternoon he'd searched it, except for the hole in the ceiling and two empty Jack Daniels bottles on the floor in front of the ragged sofa in the living room. Jim picked up one of the bottles. He hadn't seen Leonard take

a drink since he got back to town, even though everyone knew
Leonard had made quite a career of it as a teenager. Jim put the
bottle down and crisscrossed the room several times; it contained little other than the lumpy sofa, old newspapers, and a
brand-new 25-inch Sony television. Perhaps if they waited,
Leonard would show up and would have an explanation for what
Marian had told them. There was still Ricky Gibson's alibi for
Leonard—which had satisfied Brockhurst. Would it have satisfied him if he'd heard Marian's story? For a second Jim desperately wished the SLED agent were there. He was sure Brockhurst
would not have been nearly this nervous about confronting
Leonard Hansen. Brockhurst hadn't grown up with him either.

Stoney plundered around the kitchen while Bill examined the
bedroom. Then Jim and Stoney heard a piece of furniture being
moved in the bedroom, and Bill emerged carrying a long vinyl
case. He unzipped it while the other two men watched. "It was
under the bed," Bill said, splitting the case open. "Empty."
He looked over at the others. "Looks like it's for an assault rifle.
My guess is he has it with him."

Jim tried to stay calm. "Leonard was in Nam. Makes perfect
sense he'd have a gun. Half the country owns at least one."

"An assault rifle?" Stoney exclaimed, staring at Jim. "Which
he's carrying around with him?"

"You don't know that for sure."

"Jesus, didn't what Marian say mean anything to you? Don't
you care that Harriet Setzler is dead?"

Jim glowered at Stoney. "Of course I do. But we have got to
be sensible. We have to be cautious and careful, we have to
think straight. Or we're gonna fuck up." He stopped, nodded
at Stoney. "This is my responsibility. People like you care too
much. Idealists. You go too damn far. You turn things into a
holy cause. Nothing is more dangerous."

"Hey, guys." Bill held up his hands in a time-out.

Stoney turned and walked back into the disheveled kitchen,
where the new wood cabinets were only half-installed. Was Leland going to do anything? Or was he too scared of Leonard?
Funny about Jim. At Harriet's house he had saved Marian's
life—with no thought to his own safety. But now he was backing
off on Leonard. Stoney sighed; he no longer believed that the
town would be the same again when the murderer was caught.
He had realized this as he watched, from a distance, Harriet
Setzler's body descend into the hot summer earth. He couldn't
fix things now. All he could do was stop Leonard.

The three men wandered around the house for a few more minutes. In the bedroom Bill opened Leonard's closet and stared at the clothes, at the shoes, at the two boxes on the closet shelf which he pulled down and checked. Porn magazines mostly. And several photos of a naked woman, one of which had been cut in half right across the woman's breasts. In the living room Jim found several half-empty cigarette packs and various matchbooks and several phone numbers on torn scraps of paper. The phone numbers weren't local. Also an old *TV Guide*, a paperback spy novel, a newspaper clipping about the Vietnam War Memorial in Washington. Nothing that would aid an indictment. Regular stuff belonging to a regular bachelor. In the kitchen Stoney even opened the ancient white refrigerator and the kitchen cabinets, both of which were nearly empty; the man had not cooked much in here. There were no suspicious-looking knives.

Abruptly all three men froze in their respective rooms at the sound on the road outside. A moving vehicle. Stoney sped in the living room just as Bill came out of the bedroom. All three men rushed to a window. Outside a pickup truck had stopped a hundred yards short of the house and was now backing up to turn around. In a moment it tore back down the highway in the direction it had come from.

"He saw your car, Jim." Stoney rushed out onto the porch. The truck was already out of view.

Jim and Bill were on the porch in a second. "You sure it was Leonard?" Jim asked.

"I'm not absolutely positive," Stoney admitted. "But who else would suddenly stop and turn around and go back where he came from?"

Jim scrambled down the stairs. "Come on, you two."

Within seconds the three men were in Jim's car, heading down the dirt road after the truck.

Four hours later Stoney pulled up, alone in Jim's patrol car, in front of the McCloskey house. Before he could get out, Anna and Marian came running down the steps.

When Anna saw Stoney behind the wheel, she jerked open the driver's door. "God, are you all right? We've been half out of our minds worrying."

Before Stoney could answer, Marian asked, "Did Jim bring him in? Is he locked up?"

Stoney shook his head no. He put one arm around each woman and the three of them walked back up the steps and into the house. Anna made Stoney a huge roast beef sandwich while he and Marian sat at the kitchen table, talking quietly. But Stoney kept his eyes on Anna the whole time she moved back and forth from the refrigerator to the kitchen counter to the bread box. He kept remembering the night before, in bed, and for a moment he wished Marian weren't there, so that he could go to Anna and hold her. Then he shook himself and reached for the glass of water she handed him. He looked up at her and their eyes locked. She didn't look away.

"We went to his house," Stoney said between bites of sandwich, "and he wasn't there. We did find a gun case though—minus the gun. Anyway, we were checking all over the house—he hadn't done a thing to the place since that night it was on fire, he hadn't even cleaned up or put a temporary cover over the hole in the roof. Then we heard a car. Only it was a truck. By the time we got to the window the truck was backing up, it turned around and headed back out the same way it had come in."

Marian spoke first. "Was it Leonard?"

Stoney drank more water. His chambray shirt was dirty and stained with sweat under the arms. "It had to be. He must have seen Jim's patrol car."

Anna filled Marian's glass with more iced tea. "So what happened?"

"We followed the truck. But it was fast as hell—we never did get close enough to tell if it was Leonard's but it had to be— who else would have been driving that fast? Anyway, the truck finally turned on Mill Creek Road." Stoney turned to Marian. "You know that rutted old two-lane that goes back into the swamps?"

Marian nodded. "That's the only place it goes. It ends in there."

"Right. We thought he was crazy. Well, we went in after him. Went all the way to the end of the road and didn't find him. It was like he vanished. He must have taken that truck into the swamps. But he couldn't go far with it—too many trees. So Jim and Bill and I walked into the woods and started looking for it. We couldn't find one damn thing. No truck, no Leonard, no nothing."

Anna shivered. "Is he still in there?"

"Far as we know. Only . . ." Stoney hesitated.

"You can't be positive," Marian said, "that it really is Leonard until you find the truck, can you?" When Stoney nodded, she added, ''And we can't truly be positive it was Leonard who killed Harriet until you find him.''

Again Stoney nodded. ''But there's no way out of there except on foot.'' He swallowed the last of his sandwich. ''Jim sent me back to get help. I've got to call Buck Henry—see if he'll put out an APB and send some men to help. We're gonna need flashlights and stuff. I've already been by Heyward's and he's getting a few people together to go on out now. Once it gets dark, Leonard will be a lot harder to find.''

''Y'all need to be careful in those swamps at night,'' Marian said, putting words to Anna's thoughts too. ''You can't see a damn thing, you're likely to step on a cottonmouth moccasin.''

Stoney wiped his mouth with his napkin. ''It hasn't exactly been safe around here. Until we find him, I want you two to stay here together. Keep all the doors and windows locked and Silas inside. Don't go out and don't open the door for anyone. There's no guarantee Leonard won't slip away and circle back to town.''

He got up and walked over to the other side of the kitchen. The Marlin .22 rifle still leaned against the wall, where Jim Leland had left it the night before Harriet was killed. Stoney picked it up and pulled the chamber back. Then he walked out of the room. When he came back, he had a small plastic box of shells. He looked at the two women, who were still at the table. ''I'm gonna leave this here but it won't be any good to you unless you know how to use it.''

''I know how,'' Marian said, but she did not mention the small pistol in her purse.

Stoney looked at her. ''Anything—I mean *anything*—tries to get in this house before I get back, I want you to shoot it. Can you do that?''

''Without a moment's hesitation.''

Then Anna stood up and stared at Stoney. ''Stop treating me like a child. If that man tries to get in this house, I can shoot him too.'' She stopped abruptly and they all stared at each other. Then Anna said softly, ''This is what's happened to us, isn't it?''

Nobody said anything. In a few moments Stoney went back into the living room to call the Ashton sheriff and several other people. He stayed on the phone for almost forty-five minutes. Then he went upstairs to the bedroom and got out three light-weight jackets (would this oversized one fit Bill?)—if they were out there into the night they would need protection from insects.

He made a mental note to check for some insect repellent in the garage when he went to gather up the flashlights. Anna and Marian were making sandwiches and filling plastic bottles with water. Maybe he should take a bottle of brandy too. Stoney stared into his and Anna's closet blankly, trying to think what else he should take with him. Then he noticed Anna's silk night-gown hanging on a peg on her side of the closet and the memory of the previous night flooded him again like a sudden fever. He reached for the silk and held it to his face for a second and breathed in.

Downstairs Stoney gathered the flashlights and insect repel-lent and stuffed them, along with the three jackets, into a nylon flight bag. Marian and Anna had packed a hamper full of food and Stoney walked into the kitchen to retrieve it, stopping to kneel down to pet Silas. "You take care of things here," he instructed the dog under his breath. "I mean it this time."

When Stoney stood up, Marian was behind him. "I'm going with you," she said. "I know those swamps as well as anyone."

"No," Stoney said. "You're staying here with Anna. Please, Marian. I need you to do that."

Marian stared at him a second and was about to argue but then changed her mind. In a few moments Stoney and Anna walked out to the patrol car alone. He put the flight bag and the hamper of food in the back seat. Beside the hamper Anna saw another rifle, with a larger bore than the Marlin inside the house. She raised her eyebrows and he said, "Belongs to Jim."

"Stoney, I'm scared for you."

He put his hands on her hips and pulled her to him, burying his face in her hair. "I'm scared too. But I'll be all right, I'll be with Jim and Bill and everyone else. You and Marian stay put; if you have any trouble, call Buck Henry's office number—he's leaving a deputy on duty there."

"You promise me you'll be okay? You won't do anything scary?"

"I won't do anything stupid, Anna. Everything's scary."

She nestled deeper against him until his abdomen was tight against hers and the feel of his sex made her breathe harder and she realized, abruptly, that in the midst of all this terror all she wanted to do was lie down with him inside her. He moved her hips with his hands until her heat made him feel better and he wondered if he would have pulled up her skirt on the street right then and there if he hadn't had to go. Then he stepped back and got in the car and started it up, his eyes still on her as he drove away.

Nearly twenty men met in the swamps that evening, at the end of Mill Creek Road. But by the time they had gathered and organized, it was almost dark. As they moved around deciding who would search where, the trees parted and the brilliant half-moon broke through, a stark white hammock outlined by the blackened sky. As clouds passed, the moon turned blue, then lavender, then gray. Soon the clouds transformed the entire sky into waves of light and dark, like the violent heavens of medieval religious paintings.

Lanterns set on the ground glowed against the backdrop of black trees, and everyone who moved about in their shadows reflected a surreal halo on his face, like the ghostly illuminated specters of some undiscovered underworld. Jim Leland and Buck Henry stood in the light of one lantern, surrounded by two Ashton deputies and Ed Hammond, Heyward Rutherford, and Bill Jenkins. All of the men were armed and carried a flashlight, which poked out of their jackets or dangled at the end of their hands. Other men were gathered behind them in smaller groups, several men from Ashboro and several farmhands from the Fenwick's place, even Ricky Gibson and two of his cronies who didn't believe it was Leonard out there but who couldn't resist a chase through the swamps.

Jim was saying to Buck Henry, "Leonard probably knows these swamps like the back of his hand. He hunted here as a kid. We won't have any idea which direction he's taken until we find his truck."

The Ashton sheriff nodded. "As long as he stays in here, we should be able to find him. There are only two ways out; he could go back to town, but I put a man at the end of Mill Creek Road. Or he could follow the Coosa River downstream. Nobody—I don't care how well he knows the swamps—could keep from getting lost without staying close to the river."

"What's to keep him from stopping where the Coosa crosses I-95?" Bill Jenkins asked. "He could hitch a ride on the interstate and be long gone."

Buck Henry shook his head. "He probably knows we're watching the interstate. I don't think he'll go near it. I think he'll follow the river to Beaufort and slip into Georgia by a back road somewhere. Or he'll wait for us to give up and he'll go back to where he hid his truck and just drive outta here pretty as you please.''

''Then we can't go home,'' Stoney said with determination, joining the others. ''You know, he could just go back to his house. Act innocent, like none of this ever happened.'' Stoney paused. ''I don't like to think of him going back to town. But he'd have to go through town to get home again.''

''Where's Marian?'' Jim asked.

''With Anna. At my house. They have a rifle and the dog.''

Bill Jenkins rolled his eyes. ''Silas? That dog's a wimp.''

''That's probably why he can run circles around you,'' Stoney shot back and for a moment all the men chuckled, relieved by the change in tension.

They decided to pair up and fan out in a half circle, moving through the woods toward the river. Two shots fired in rapid succession would mean something had been found. Any other gunfire would be regarded as dangerous. If no shots were fired in the next three hours, they would meet back here to discuss what to do next. Watches were synchronized, insect repellent shared, sandwiches and water bottles doled out, flashlights and rifles checked one last time. Then everyone began moving forward.

They were searching the swamps some distance north of where Maum Chrish lived, and as Stoney and Bill walked into the darkness, the night sounds of the woods dimmed, the scurrying of rabbits and squirrels and raccoons faded and then stopped. The noise of the searchers seemed to have expatriated every living creature within miles. It was too quiet, unnaturally quiet.

''Jesus Christ,'' Bill breathed, ''it's creepy as shit in here. I keep thinking I see snakes in the trees—it's those damn vines wrapped around everything. They *are* just vines, aren't they?''

Stoney gazed up into the trees and shivered. He saw what Bill meant. He swallowed and stared at the black water. Reeds sprouted from it like Medusa's hair. His blood pumped harder and he nearly stumbled over the roots of a live oak in front of him. Mosquitoes buzzed at his face and he swatted at them. Now and then he aimed his flashlight at the ground, checking for snakes.

Abruptly Bill grabbed Stoney's arm and held him still, putting a finger to his own lips.

A skunk waddled past the two men and disappeared into the brush.

Bill let out a long sigh. "Hope he gets Leonard."

They walked farther into the woods, holding back the giant overgrown bushes in order to pass. After a while Stoney reached into his pocket and drew out a pack of chewing gum and handed Bill a stick. They chewed nervously, moving faster into the dark swamp. Below them the ground was spongy and they gingerly stepped around the muddier spots. After an hour they paused briefly and wiped sweat from their foreheads.

"You know there's one thing Leland didn't tell us," Stoney said a few minutes later when they'd resumed their trek.

Bill looked over at him in the darkness, but Stoney stared straight ahead and added, "He didn't tell us what to do if we found him."

Anna and Marian were lying on the carpet in the living room of the McCloskey house with lights on all over the house. Outside, spotlights glowed front and back. The doors were locked and dead-bolted and the curtains were drawn in almost every room except the living room, which had no drapes. But, sprawled on the floor, the two women couldn't see out the front windows and no one passing by could see them—which was the way they preferred it tonight.

Anna was leaning against the sofa, her legs outstretched, Silas nestled beside her. Every now and then her eyes wandered from the television across the room to the front door and then back down to the watch on her wrist. It was after ten. How long would they stay out there? She stared for a moment at the carpet beneath her. This was the one place in the house she felt safe. For days after she and Stoney had made love here the room had smelled like sex and even now she thought she could detect the vague scent in the air. She wondered if Marian noticed.

The black woman was stretched out on the floor, in a long rayon tunic, her head atop a throw pillow, an empty bowl of popcorn beside her. When the theme music faded on the television screen, she looked up at Anna and moaned, "I cannot watch another movie. My eyes are beginning to cross."

Anna got up and punched the VCR and the TV off. "I know. Me too. How 'bout some wine? As long as we're in prison, we might as well get sloshed. Why on earth aren't they back yet?"

Marian didn't answer. None of her possible responses sounded good, even to her. She rose and followed Anna into the kitchen. When they both had a glass of white wine, Anna said, "We could go to bed, only I know I'll never get to sleep."

"Me neither. Show me your studio, show me some pictures."

Anna looked surprised. "Really?"

"Yeah. When you're famous, I can say I saw your early work, and that I know how it all came together for you."

"Right." Anna walked toward the studio door. "You probably don't need to start saving my autograph yet."

They entered the studio and Marian crossed immediately to the windows, parted the curtains, and looked out at the pond. Steam rose from the warm water, wispy apparitions that moved in and out among the live oaks, and the moon hung in the sky like a secretive half-closed eye. Nothing moved. The yard was deathly still, as though everything out there held its breath, waited.

"I'm worried about her," Marian said in a whisper. "Maum Chrish. She's out there. And so is he."

Anna stood behind Marian at the window. "Why wouldn't she be okay?"

"What if Leonard isn't finished? He still has to pay me back. Everyone knows she's my mother now. What if he tries to get me through her? Take Harriet from me and then her too?"

Anna put her arm around Marian. "Stoney and all those men are out there. She'll be all right."

The black woman turned around. "Show me some pictures. Anything to make time pass."

They sat down in front of the pine worktable where Anna's most recent work was spread out haphazardly. First she showed Marian the Daufuskie pictures. "The ad agency didn't like them. In fact, they'll probably never give me another assignment."

"Well, I like them." Marian thumbed through the photos. "You should have used these at Career Day."

"I hadn't taken them then."

"Anna, why didn't you use your own pictures?"

The other woman looked up and thought for a second. "Protection, maybe. I guess I do a lot of that."

Abruptly Anna got up. "I've got something else to show you. Maybe this isn't the best time or maybe it is." Anna disappeared into her darkroom. Inside, in the dim red light, she stared up at the pictures hanging from the drying line. Harriet Setzler in a hat in front of a live oak, Harriet in her porch swing, Harriet leaning against her fence talking about the old days and that peculiarly distant look she would get when she did so—as if talking about the old days reincarnated them. The double exposures, Harriet in the hat superimposed on a crowded view of rush hour at the Atlanta airport, Harriet in the garden joined to a protest march Anna had shot in D.C. in the late sixties. Slowly Anna took down all of the pictures, one by one. Carefully she stacked them and then she took them back outside. Wordlessly she laid them in a row on the table in front of Marian.

Marian looked at each picture, one by one, exactly as Anna had removed them from the drying line. The black woman didn't say anything. Then she started over again, staring at each picture again, beginning with the first and studying each one in turn until she got to the last one again. When she looked up at Anna, her eyes were moist.

"Can I have one of these?"

Anna swallowed and nodded. In a few minutes she showed Marian some of her old work and they were going over her Washington pictures when Silas abruptly growled in the kitchen. Both women stopped and looked at each other.

"Silas?" Anna called.

The dog started to bark. The floor shook from his jumping.

Anna and Marian scrambled into the kitchen. Silas was sniffing the back door. "Aarruggh. . . ."

"What is it, boy?" Heart hammering, Anna moved toward the rifle against the wall.

Then Silas stopped. He walked back and forth in front of the door twice and then moved away from it, went back to his favorite corner, and lay down.

Marian and Anna again moved in unison to the back door and stared out the window. Everything was perfectly still.

"I guess he's just nervous," Anna said, her voice unnaturally high. "It was probably a stray dog."

"Yeah," Marian said. "That's probably what it was."

They poured themselves more wine and went back into the studio. Marian's hand shook as she set her wineglass back down on the worktable. She noticed a manila envelope on the far end of the desk and pointed toward it. "More pictures?"

Anna stared at the envelope. Her eyes widened. Christ. She forgot she left them out. The nude pictures of her. She had taken them out of her files the day she was developing the pictures of Harriet—she had been trying to decide whether to show them to Stoney or whether to destroy them. "Uh, those are sorta different pictures," she managed at last.

"Bad shots? X-rated? What?"

Anna giggled nervously. "Sorta. They're nude studies. I did them a long time ago."

"Can I see them?"

"Marian, they're—" Anna stopped. Was she ashamed of them? No, they were terrific work. Was she afraid to let her lesbian friend see her naked?

She pushed the envelope toward Marian, who took the pictures out and looked at each one carefully. Anna began to sweat. Finally Marian laid the last photograph down on the table. Then she looked over at Anna. "You knew what it felt like and you wanted to know what it looked like."

"How the hell do you know that?"

Marian smiled. "We're not different in our inquiry. Just in the way we found out." She tapped the pictures. "These are wonderful. Very sensual. They should not be locked up."

Jesus. How did she know that too? Anna wondered. She looked at Marian and Marian smiled back at her.

When it got to be eleven o'clock, they decided to try to get some sleep. Leaving Silas to guard the kitchen, they walked upstairs and parted in the hall after Anna showed Marian the guest room. "I'll be right down here," Anna said, indicating her own bedroom, unsure whether she was reassuring Marian or herself.

"Try to get some sleep." Marian stretched; all her muscles were tense. "I bet they'll be back before long. You can't find anything in those swamps at night."

Anna flashed an ironic half smile. "I don't know whether I hope Stoney comes back soon so I know he's okay or whether I want him to stay out there as late as it takes to find Leonard."

She told Marian good night and walked into her bedroom, crossed to the bathroom, and washed her face and brushed her teeth. Retracing her steps, she stopped and stared out at the street below. The later it got, the more she worried. She turned down the spread and plumped the pillows absently. Then she went to the closet to hang up her blouse, noticed the royal silk gown when she opened the door. It reminded her of Stoney. She turned around, slid her skirt and underwear off, and climbed into bed nude. Sleep, just let me sleep. She turned on her side and slipped one arm under her pillow. She closed her eyes. Somewhere out there in this dark night was the man she loved. And another man who killed people.

Anna turned onto her stomach and pressed her body into the sheets. She could feel the hardness of her nipples beneath her and she wondered if it was nerves. Or having Marian look at the naked pictures of her. A while back she would never have avowed that that excited her—she would have been too worried about what it meant. Now she didn't care. Now she just wanted to press herself against the sheets and feel them slide up across her bare thighs and back. She didn't want to think at all.

Finally she fell asleep. She dreamed about a college professor and his wife she and Stoney had known in Maryland. An art professor who had encouraged Anna's photography. In the dream they were back in College Park having dinner with the couple but they were all nude and she came to understand—slowly— that she was to make love to her old professor while Stoney and the wife looked on. It seemed perfectly logical that she should do so. Soon he and she were standing and he was taking her from behind, near the dining room table while Stoney and his wife had dessert. Cherry cheesecake. Anna had the feeling that she would have sex with everyone in the room before it was over and despite the erotic possibilities there was something uncomfortable about that knowledge too. Then she started bleeding. Profusely. There was blood all over her. Her professor had gone too deep. Blood was running down her legs, forming a huge pool on the floor and—

Anna sat up in bed. Blood. It was all she remembered of the dream. She looked around the room frantically. She threw the covers back and jumped out of bed and ran to the window. Stoney. Blood. She peered out the window and looked in the direction of the swamps.

Eighteen

WHEN JIM LELAND and Ed Hammond reached the Coosawhatchie River, Jim fired two shots into the air. It was time to regroup. He stared at the river for a moment; in front of him a dead tree spanned it like a bridge. At his feet, beneath the shallow water but visible in the diffuse moonlight, lay a tangled network of underwater plants. Here and there bleached white tree stumps also protruded from the dark water like decaying skeletons, with vines snaking around them in necrophiliac embrace. Farther out the river was completely opaque, its surface sealed by a slimy green silt.

And that infernal buzz—mosquitoes. Jim itched all over.

Being in the swamps made him feel like a child again—unprotected, uninformed, unsure. The supernatural seemed frighteningly logical here. For a moment he remembered a black man who died when he was a boy; Jim and his parents attended the funeral because the man had worked for them. They arrived at the man's small shack later, on the edge of the swamps, to pay their respects. Jim grasped the front doorknob to go inside, only to find that it had been reversed. The inside part was outside. "So old Sam's spirit can't get back in," a huge woman who was standing at the door told him. "We done buried old Sam's hat and his knife and extra clothes wid him too—so he don't come back after them neither." Later Jim would learn that after everyone left that day all the dishes and cooking utensils were emptied and scoured so Sam's spirit wouldn't have access to food and water and would go on where it was supposed to go. Which was also why an oil lamp had been left burning on Sam's grave that night, so he could see his way to heaven.

In here—thirty years later—every bit of that made sense to

309

Jim. In fact, if he lived in here, he'd do the exact same thing after a funeral.

Soon the other men began to straggle in, looking tired and anxious and itchy. The police chief and Buck Henry spoke to each group and then walked over to talk by themselves quietly. Several of the men, Stoney and Bill among them, sat down on fallen logs and tipped their water bottles back until water ran down their sweaty faces. Flashlights were doused, two of the Ashboro fellows and Ricky Gibson smoked in silence, and every so often one man or another would walk away a few feet and take a leak. No one said much, no one talked. The later it got, the more somber everyone seemed, as if such a long stay in this dark world had altered the mind, the senses, the perceptions. Even Heyward Rutherford, in his spiffy L. L. Bean outdoor clothes, didn't have a single "great" thing to say.

Finally Jim walked over to where everyone was sitting. "Buck and I think we should split up again and follow the river. We're bound to find the truck sooner or later."

So the searchers teamed up again, this time moving in different directions along the riverbank. Silently Stoney and Bill headed south. The Coosa was narrow where they walked, filled with debris and dead trees. Looking into it, Stoney got the same crawly feeling along his shoulderblades he used to get in certain rough neighborhoods in D.C. He knew Leonard could be hidden anywhere: in the woods to Stoney's left, farther up the river, anywhere. With an assault rifle aimed at them. Stoney stumbled abruptly and his right ankle turned in a muddy hole he hadn't noticed. Slowly he withdrew his foot. Testing his ankle again, he breathed in with relief. The swamps had a distinctive smell— loamy, damp, elemental, almost sensual. The longer he stayed in here, the more he felt he carried that smell on him. It mixed with the sweat on his arms and seeped into his pores. Became part of him.

"Christ Almighty, my feet hurt," Bill said after a while. Suddenly he shone his flashlight into the woods on his right, arced it from tree to tree.

"What's the matter?"

"I dunno. Thought I heard something." Bill moved forward, aimed the flashlight deeper into the woods. "I guess it was an animal—or something." In a moment he turned around and rejoined Stoney. "That 'or something' is making me nuts."

"I know. Me too."

"Sorta seemed like a lark at first, you know? Go in the

swamps like kids and get the bad guys. Doesn't feel like a lark anymore."

Stoney stopped for a minute and listened. "I keep thinking I'm hearing things."

"We start seeing things, I'm going home."

As they walked on, Stoney gazed at the live oaks submerged in the river like penitents wading toward baptism. He thought about Anna too, worried about her and Marian being alone in town. Then he stopped dead. He heard—something.

Drums. In the distance somewhere. Someone was beating a drum. Maybe two drums.

Stoney didn't say anything to Bill, who was ahead of him studying the soaked ground with his flashlight, looking for footprints. The drums grew louder and suddenly Bill froze in his tracks. "Shit. What the hell is that?"

"Drums."

Bill turned. "*Whose* drums?"

Stoney didn't answer. His heart raced and sweat rolled down his forehead. It was dark and close and hot and the trees crouched over them like enemies, and it was so humid, so damp and wet. Snakes came instantly to mind. So did ritualized killings. Exorcisms. They had stepped back in time and their innate senses, so veneered with civilization and education, were dulled and useless. This was an alien world of water and earth and giant trees and anguish. He and Bill and all the others were intruders. They had entered a realm they did not understand, in which they were not welcome. Leonard had brought them here on purpose.

Stoney and Bill stopped by the river to rest and Stoney fidgeted with the nylon bag over his shoulder, and then he handed the bottle of brandy to Bill, who uncorked it and tipped it back. He coughed and gave the bottle back to Stoney. "If we keep going this way," Bill said, "eventually we'll end up in the Atlantic."

"If we don't get lost first." Stoney drank from the bottle and recorked it.

They began walking south again, almost tiptoeing now. "What if we never find him?" Bill asked. "What if we never know?"

"We're going to find him," Stoney said firmly. He moved ahead of Bill, striding resolutely into the darkness, his rifle tight to his side and his flashlight beam in front of him. They walked in silence for almost an hour, shining their flashlights on both sides of them and then down at the ground below, stopping to veer off into the brush once or twice. Stoney was so tired now his eyes glazed over and he swore for a moment that he saw someone in front of him. He jerked back—it looked like a woman. Blood. She had blood on her. Then the vision disappeared and Stoney picked up his pace, looking back at Bill from time to time to urge him on. They walked for another hour and twice more Stoney thought he saw the woman. He didn't recognize her but now he was certain he could smell blood.

"Come on, Jenkins. Let's find him," he cried vehemently when the woman faded away again.

Bill Jenkins stared at his friend and wondered if Stoney hadn't been out here too long.

They walked on.

Anna woke up because she knew someone was in the room with her. She could hear him moving around but in the darkness she could not see him. He was in the shadows, safely out of the way of the moonlight streaming through the window. Her first thought was to grab Stoney until she remembered Stoney wasn't there beside her, then she thought about calling Marian, but she didn't want the man to know she was awake. Right now he made no move toward the bed and as long as she was quiet and still, maybe it would be all right. Maybe he would leave her alone.

The man walked out of the room. Into the bathroom.

Oh God. Anna expelled a long sigh of relief. Stoney. Oh God, it was Stoney. He was home. It was okay. She sat up and called to him and he walked back in and sat down on the bed and held her for a minute. "Bill and I left at three—I was so tired I started seeing things. Some of the guys are still out there. Heyward Rutherford—of all people—found the truck. Jim thinks Leonard will just hole up in there until we quit looking. I'm going back after I sleep awhile."

As he kissed her, Anna noticed the wild smell of the swamp on his skin. He rose to take his shower. When Anna heard the water running, she got up and walked naked into the bathroom and pulled back the shower curtain. He didn't say anything as she climbed in with him, just embraced her and leaned against her as though too exhausted to speak or bathe. The water ran down across them and Anna breathed in the swamp smell as it seeped inside her. For a long while they stood holding each other, letting the water run across their skin.

* * *

Down the hall Marian tossed fitfully. She had heard voices in Anna's room and knew Stoney must be home. They had not found Leonard; one of them would have told her if they had. Would they find him at all?

Marian closed her eyes again, trying to sleep. Her eyes opened. *No.* She would not think about it, she would not remember it, she would not open that window. She had nailed it shut years ago and it had stayed shut, even when she talked to Anna. Why now, why tonight, why here? She turned over and closed her eyes once more—and then the window stood wide open and she spiraled downward. Falling down faster and faster. A blinding white light burned behind her eyes and she blinked, but still it burned and refused to fade. She lay beneath it naked, her legs pinned wide. The smell of river and damp loam. And whiskey. A white boy holding a bottle up. He was grinning. "Come git it, Maarriooonnn."

He always said her name like it was a joke. As if she had no right to it.

She lay there waiting for it to be over. Then his voice thickened. He unzipped his pants and drew out his engorged penis. "Lookit. You can't wait, can you? You love white meat. That's how you convince yourself you're white, ain't it?" Then he tackled her, yanked her legs farther apart, rammed himself inside. She vowed she would not scream. No matter how much it hurt. He would not see any emotion.

"You black bitch," he whispered over and over again in her ear, his voice slurring, his eyes closed. He wanted her but he hated himself for wanting her; to want her was to want the worst thing in his world, black pussy. In a moment he withdrew again abruptly and emptied himself across her stomach.

Marian opened her eyes. Suddenly she knew what she had to do.

Slowly Anna began to bathe Stoney. She soaped up her hands and washed his face with a soft sponge; she took the shampoo from the windowsill and lathered his hair and ran her fingernails back and forth through it, then trailed them across his shoulders and back down his chest. His arousal was immediate, which amazed him given how tired he was. But he said nothing, just stood there and let her hands work on him. She kneaded his shoulders and his back and his chest, working the soap deep into the hair on his chest, and she wasn't sure when she stopped bathing him and he started touching her. But suddenly they stopped and knew they had to have each other now, fast and quick, and deep.

He half picked her up and eased inside her and she cried out and then remembered Marian and didn't care and cried out again every time he went deeper. He held her away and then pulled her back again and again, until she could not speak and he could no longer hold her.

In bed later they lay cradled together like spoons as he moved inside her, rubbing her back with his fingernails, up and down, up and down, until she shivered under his touch. Sometimes he just lay still, not even wanting to move. Inside her he felt safe, at peace. Filled, she felt completed, no longer alone.

They passed much of the night finding themselves in each other again. They lay in suspended intersection, searching for a fusion so complete nothing could endanger it. Sometimes he dozed but then he would awaken and feel her move, stimulating him in his sleep; she would shift to deepen their connection and he would move with sudden fervor. But they would deliberately slow again. She would reach behind her and stroke his thigh, he would rub the back of her neck or caress her breasts, her abdomen. Both thought of the eventual joy but neither moved toward it, because neither wanted to let go and part. Tonight their desire for each other was so intense that fulfillment lay in never satisfying it.

Marian felt exhausted the next morning and she didn't feel much better when she got back to her own house.

Where was he? The man who raped her and took Harriet away.

She stared out her front window, still tired. She could not just go through this day like other days. There was no routine now. The normal world had ended with Harriet's murder. Marian knew she ought to go out back and check on the new garden, but she didn't want to. She wanted to find Leonard. She wanted someone to pay for the emptiness she felt.

Soon Marian walked into her bedroom and changed her clothes. Within minutes she was in her car speeding out to the swamps. When the trees closed in around her, however, she wanted to turn back. Coming out here wasn't the same as when she had visited Maum Chrish before Harriet was killed—now everything was different. Now she almost regretted the days she'd spent here; she should have been with Harriet, she should not have divided her loyalties like that. But her life would always be split, wouldn't it? Between what she was and was not, who she could be and who she couldn't be. She slowed down and stared at a live oak tree along the roadside. The gods had sent her Maum and had taken Harriet away, leaving her incomplete again. Marian smiled with irony. At Maum Chrish's hearing she had preached that completeness was multifaceted; yet she had somehow missed the point herself.

In a moment she zoomed across the bridge she and Anna had once walked over and braked to a stop. She got out, slid her purse strap over her shoulder, and took the path into the woods. It was daylight, she had the gun, Leonard would be sleeping now, waiting for dark. She hoped.

God it was hot. That rain on the day Harriet was buried had hardly made a dent in the drought. Marian stared up at the sunshine. It stopped at the tops of the trees; the only thing that got inside here was the heat, the humidity. She began to sweat. She hated Leonard being in here. Again. Like all those years ago. Now the place was ruined for her again; Leonard had charged the atmosphere with something far more sinister than any water moccasin or voudou curse.

When Marian reached the clearing, the fire was burning and she heard the drumbeats. She recognized the discordant Petro rhythm; the sound was some distance away, maybe down at the Oyotunji village which practiced Yoruba voudou. They were using the exultant beat of throwing off slavery to pass a message down the river. That evil was in the woods. The white men didn't know it but the black men were helping them.

Maum Chrish's house looked empty as Marian strode up to it and called out. No one responded, so she climbed up the steps and peered inside the doorway. Then she walked inside. A ceremony had recently taken place. Cornmeal edged the *vèvè* on the floor and there was the distinct smell of blood. Marian's heart tightened and then she said to herself, it was only a chicken, it was only an offering.

She walked back outside and suddenly Maum Chrish was here—just standing in the middle of the yard in front of the garden whose produce was overflowing despite the drought. She appeared so abruptly that for a moment Marian imagined she had simply materialized before her eyes. Marian shook herself and moved down the steps. Maum Chrish was all in white—white caftan, white *agousséan* scarf over her shoulder, white turban. Preparing for purification. Marian walked toward her.

"You are the one who's come," Maum Chrish said, exactly as before.

"Yes," Marian said. "I've come for help. There's someone in the woods. He hurts people."

"The night of the Dark Satellite." The other woman nodded, staring up at the sky as though the moon were above them at midday. Marian looked up too and suddenly she did see the moon—or was it really the sun? She couldn't be sure but it looked more like the moon; the sunshine above the trees seemed to emanate from a white half-globe.

"They look in places where God is. He is where God has gone."

Marian gaped at Maum Chrish. "Leonard? They're looking for him in the wrong place? Where is he?"

"Where God is gone," Maum Chrish intoned again.

Where God is gone, Marian thought. Almost everywhere. She walked closer to the other woman. "I don't understand."

Maum Chrish turned toward the river behind her. She pointed downstream. "The cemetery, the crossroads, Grans Bwa."

Marian repeated. "The cemetery, the crossroads, and the spirit of the forest."

And suddenly she *knew*. It was what he would do. They thought he would hide in the swamps. So of course he would leave them.

Marian turned to go, but Maum Chrish stopped her. Wordlessly the taller woman angled around and walked back to her house. Marian knew she should wait. In a moment Maum Chrish reappeared. She was carrying a black camera bag, which she handed to Marian with a long lingering look.

The men met again that morning at ten at the end of Mill Creek Road. Most arrived together, in twos and threes and even larger groups. By now everyone in the county knew that the Essex killer (as the Ashboro *Times* was calling him) was cornered somewhere in the swamps. People who had never even heard of Leonard Hansen showed up to help look for him. Before going into the woods there was an easy camaraderie among men whose paths didn't often cross except in church or at the voting booths on Election Day. They showed up in jeans and khakis and overalls and greasy workpants, all anxious to help, men who weren't about to be left out of the biggest thing to happen in Ashton County in two decades. They laughed and slapped each other on the back, the way men sometimes do

en out in the woods without women, carrying guns and eating
d pissing wherever they want.

But the minute they actually separated into pairs and began
mbing the woods, the jocular mood vanished. The swamps
ren't quite as forbidding in daylight but even so there was a
eternatural suspense about the interior that suddenly quieted
en the most boisterous. The swamps did that—unearthed some
ne-shared memory that both attracted and frightened men and,
the very least, unevened their footing. They stepped more
utiously, moved more stealthily.

They were covering the lower end of the Coosawhatchie to-
y, which was where Leonard's truck had been found. The
er virtually ran in circles here. Today they had dogs and the
gs ran in circles as well, plunging after various scents that so
· had led nowhere. Miles were covered more quickly in day-
ht and several footprints were spotted, sending the dogs into
frenzy which ended on the other side of the river. The dogs
st the trail there, sniffed in a dozen different directions but
ways circled back.

Bill and Stoney joined Heyward Rutherford and Jim Leland
metime in the afternoon and the four of them fanned out,
ecking the riverbank like miners pawing a pan of gold. Hey-
ard was grumbling about how Essex would never recover if
s didn't end soon, how it would hurt business, how no one
uld move into town (and presumably buy his houses and use
at new car wash he was still determined to build).

Stoney got tired of listening to Heyward and angled around
face Jim. "What if he didn't follow the river?"

Sweat rolled down Jim Leland's face. He felt like punching
oney. "He *had* too. Nobody but an animal could find their
y around here without it."

"Jim, we have to think like Leonard. He knows this country,
's almost a bird dog himself. He can get in and out of here by
ell."

"Then which goddamn way did he go?"

"I agree with Jim," Bill said to Stoney. "If Leonard's that
uch at home here, he's even more likely to stick with the
er." Bill leaned down and rubbed his sore right calf, thinking
out how hungry he was. "I mean, the river affords protection,
wer. Walk away from it in any direction and you become more
posed. Before long you'll end up in a town. Most likely one
these poor-as-dirt black towns. I don't think Leonard would
liberately go in one of those. Do you?"

Stoney, against his will, had to agree. He and Bill walked on ahead of Jim and Heyward.

When Stoney and Bill were beyond hearing, Jim mumbled under his breath, "I'm damn tired of Stoney's shit. He thinks I won't do anything. Well he's wrong. I'll do what has to be done and I'll do it my own way."

Suddenly all four men looked up. They stared at each other as the shot rang in their ears. They waited, each man barely breathing. They waited for the second shot.

Marian pounded on the door of the McCloskey house. Where could Anna be today of all days? Not that the other woman had looked very rested at breakfast. Marian smiled. The walls of even old houses were but so thick. And the way Stoney and Anna kept looking at each other over breakfast, well, there was no mistaking that look.

Marian beat on the door again. Where *was* she?

Then the door opened with a jerk. Anna stared at Marian. "Sorry. I was in the darkroom."

Marian strode through the door, whirled around, handed Anna a black camera bag. "Your Nikon. I went to see Maum Chrish and she gave it to me. How can you work today?"

Anna stared at her camera bag, then looked up. "You were out there? Alone? Are you crazy?"

"Anna, when is Stoney coming back?"

"I'm not sure."

Marian paced up and down the hall. "Surely he'll come back later—they'll need more food and water if they don't find him before dark." Marian stopped, sighed. "How long can this go on?"

"Come on back to the kitchen. Have you eaten anything to-day?"

Marian shook her head and followed Anna. They made a tuna sandwich and split it, ate it standing at the kitchen counter. Sitting down would have seemed too normal, too everyday. "Anna, I think they're looking in the wrong place. I don't think Leonard's in the swamps."

Anna paused in midbite, her eyes wide. "Why not?"

"Maum Chrish told me he wasn't there. What she said was sorta—abstract. But I believe I know what she meant. I think I know the place she was talking about." Marian gazed at the kitchen doorway, toward the hall. "I should tell the men who she said. I should tell Stoney and Jim. Do you know where they've gone to look?"

Anna shook her head. "They went back to the same place, I think."

Marian nodded. "Mill Creek Road. I'll go out there then."

"You'll never find them. Stoney said they were spreading out all over the place. You better just stay here. We'll hear something. He said he'd come home before dark if they hadn't found Leonard by then."

Marian looked at her watch. "That's hours from now. Leonard might get away by then."

"Where do you think he is?"

"There's this place he mentioned to me once when we were"—she didn't want to say when we were kids, it made them seem too innocent and chummy—"he mentioned it a long time ago. When I first knew him. The old Sheldon Church ruins. His parents punished him once and he ran away from home and hid out there for a few days—because there was a place to sleep and a water pump." Marian turned to Anna. "But the Sheldon Church is outside the swamps, damn near to Beaufort."

"Could he get there on foot?"

"Hell yes. Go down the Coosawhatchie until the swamp turns into marshes and you're there. It's shorter following the river than going by the highway. But you have to turn at an unmarked intersection to get to the church." Marian remembered Maum Chrish's voice. "The crossroads."

"But wouldn't somebody notice him there?"

"It's not a real church, Anna. It's the abandoned ruins of a church built in the 1700s. It was burned by the British during the Revolution and rebuilt only to be burned again by Sherman in 1865. It's an historical site but it's so out of the way nobody ever goes there. And there is an old cemetery. Which is surrounded by woods," Marian said to herself. "The Grans Bwa."

Anna trembled. At both Marian's tone and the look in her eyes.

"Everything around here," Marian said suddenly, thinking of the rebuilt and reburned church, so like the town, "happens twice. Whatever happens comes around again."

Then she grabbed Anna. "Don't you see? Where God has gone?"

"What?"

"That's what Maum Chrish said. Leonard was—where God has gone. Like a church no longer used. Or abandoned."

In a few minutes Anna called Buck Henry's number but there was no answer. Marian called several other people around town, talking to wives and mothers mostly, asking for information about where the men were, if any of them had returned home, if any of the women had heard anything. The rest of the afternoon, to get their minds off the waiting, Anna baked a walnut cake with an obscene amount of butter and sugar in it. Afternoon shadows fell across the back yard and still Stoney hadn't come back. Anna stared out the back kitchen windows and said softly, "It's going to be dark soon."

When Stoney walked in the front door an hour later, she ran into the living room and threw herself at him. "Thank God, you're home. Did you find him?"

Stoney shook his head and leaned into Anna, smelling her hair. He held her tight against him; every time he breathed in, he breathed in her; she filled his senses so deeply his head ached. Then he looked up and saw Marian and smiled, without releasing Anna. The three of them walked into the kitchen and Stoney ate two pieces of the cake. Then he said, "Thought we had him at one point. Someone was shooting. Only when we got there it was just Ricky Gibson killing a copperhead." Stoney hunched over the kitchen table. "The longer it takes, the more I'm scared he's gone. And we'll never know for sure."

"Yes we will," Marian exclaimed. She told Stoney about her visit to Maum Chrish's house and what the other woman had said. Stoney listened carefully and Marian noticed how tired his eyes looked. The men were worn out. They needed help. "I'm going back with you," she said. "You can take me with you, or you can make me stay behind. In which case I'm going out there on my own."

Stoney didn't argue. Instead he went upstairs to wash his face and lie down for half an hour. He'd just close his eyes for a few minutes and he'd be ready to go again.

An hour later Stoney called Bill Jenkins' house. Anna and Marian had refilled the water jugs and made more sandwiches. Quietly Stoney spoke to Anna while Marian finished packing up the food. "I want you to go over to Bill's house until I get back. I've called Diane and she said she'd appreciate the company."

"I'd rather go with you."

"I know that. But that's not a good idea. And I don't want you in this house alone."

At the Jenkins' split-level a few minutes later Stoney walked

Anna to the door and kissed her so fiercely she was left breathless afterward. And frightened. She had to be sure things would be all right and so she held him a moment longer; she asked no questions, now she just sought reassurance in his touch.

He backed away with his solemn eyes still on her. Anna wanted to beg him not to go. But instead, she stood and watched as he and Marian disappeared into the fading evening sun.

Nineteen

STONEY AND MARIAN shot down the Savannah highway toward the swamps. Crouched over the Rover's steering wheel, Stoney was already tired from walking the swamps most of the last forty-eight hours, and now and then he stared into the windshield and thought he saw drops of blood splattered on the glass. He shook his head and focused on the road.

"I called Ed Hammond," he said to Marian after a while. "He came home with me and I dropped him off at his house. I told him—on the phone—what you said about the Sheldon Church. He's going back out to meet Jim and he'll tell the rest of them. I imagine they'll all head down there. Hell, we've looked everywhere else."

Marian didn't answer. She was thinking about the last look Maum Chrish had given her that afternoon. There had been something unspoken in her eyes as Marian was leaving and Marian had struggled all afternoon to understand what it might mean, what it might have to do with locating Leonard. But she couldn't figure it out. She had tried to project into Maum Chrish but she just couldn't get in. She stared up at the moon. As darkness fell, the light of the Dark Satellite patterned the road with patches and dribbles, which they resolutely followed south.

The deeper they penetrated the woods, the larger and thicker the trees seemed until it was hard to tell where the road ended and the swamps began. They crossed low concrete bridges like fugitives, unseen by anyone. Only two cars, going in the opposite direction, passed them, and the sudden headlights invaded the Rover like split-second passing images on a television. Then the light was gone again and the darkness resumed. The trees were older the farther south they drove, as though all life had begun at the sea. These trees leaned like shrunken old people and many were dead. The swamps were thicker too, the smell deeper and loamier and darker. Old cemeteries lay so close to the low-lying road here that sometimes floods unearthed a casket and left it floating in a small inlet for days—like a Norse death-ship launched into the ocean to journey to heaven. Gnats and mosquitoes papered the windshield and at one point Stoney had to turn on the wipers to get rid of them. For a moment he imagined it was raining, but only insects slicked the glass between him and the darkness. Abruptly he remembered going to Harriet's in the middle of the night months earlier, finding footprints under her sleeping porch. He had told her everything would be all right. Now he saw her face again as it had looked that night. The boldest of the bold alone and afraid.

Stoney glanced at Marian. She was staring out the windshield too, immobile, as though she were somewhere far away. He wanted to ask her why, mother or no, she had ever come back to this godforsaken place, to this town with its secrets and swamps, but it felt like prying and so he didn't ask. He wondered if she felt what he felt. That cool breeze. It was so humid sweat trickled down his leg into his socks but from somewhere he also felt an uncannily cold air pocket. It circled around the back of his neck and whirled down his arms to blow across his hands on the steering wheel. No matter how he turned, he felt that cold breeze encircle him and it filled him with dread. Above them the trees crowded in closer and Stoney wondered if the cooler wind came from them, if some old juxtaposition of hot and cold currents was causing the prickly sensation on the back of his neck. The tree branches reached down to the car like the hands of the starving—begging for food, aggressive in their need, ripping at the Rover in desperation. Cold hands scratching and clawing, breathing out a cold wordlessness.

He had to talk. "You sure this is the way?"

Marian nodded. "Before long we'll be out of the trees."

And she was right. She, too, was glad when the sky opened up; now the trees were fewer, which meant they were nearing the end of the Coosawhatchie Swamp. Marian saw some cattails along the side of the road and she almost laughed aloud. The swamps were giving way to partial marshes, they had made it through. She could see over the trees now. The moon could get in again and at least there was light. And beside them stretched a small inlet, flat and slick with green slime.

"There's one thing I don't understand," Stoney said. "The marshes are so visible. He can be seen so easily here."

"But only if someone's looking for him."

They passed more low savannas with reeds sprouting out of them and herons swooping low for nocturnal feeds. Although many people came to the marshes to fish, almost no one lived along this particular section; this land was even more untenable than the swamps. The ground was always giving way, returning to the ocean.

Abruptly Stoney braked at a stop sign. The highway ended here and they had two choices—go right or go left. He turned to Marian. "Which way is it?"

"The crossroads," she whispered.

"But which way?"

"I don't know. I've never been here, I've just heard about it."

"For God's sake, Marian. You should have told me that." Stoney reached for the glove box and rummaged through it, looking for a South Carolina map. "I know I used to have a map in here, it probably has the Sheldon Church on it."

"I'm sorry. I just thought—I thought I'd just know where it was."

"Well, I hope to hell Jim and Bill and the rest have a map."

"Jim must know where it is. Boys used to hunt near it when we were growing up."

Stoney slammed the glove box shut. "Well, we're going to have to use the trial-and-error method."

They got out of the Rover and walked beyond the stop sign into the intersection and stared in both directions. Nothing but darkness. Here the marshes receded again and all the land fronting the intersection was thickly forested. There were no lights on the crossing two-lane road and no cars, no signs, nothing.

"Suppose we split up and you go one way and I'll try the other?" Marian suggested. "I'll walk down this way," she pointed to the right, "and you ride down the other way and if you find anything you circle back and pick me up."

"No way. I'm not about to leave you out here alone."

"Stoney, we can't waste *time*. If we don't cover both directions, he may get away." A pause. "Besides, I know this area much better than you do."

"No. Absolutely not."

They went back to the Rover. Inside, Marian snapped open

her purse and took out the loaded derringer. "I'll be okay by myself. I've got this. And extra bullets."

Stoney stared at the gun and thought for a few moments. Then he looked down the dark road. Finally he said, "Okay, just for a little while. But you take the Rover. And stay in it. I mean that, Marian. Don't get out. You find the church, you come back and get me."

Stoney climbed out of the vehicle, a flashlight and Jim Leland's rifle in his hands. Marian slid into the driver's seat and Stoney waited until she started the engine. Then he slammed the driver's door shut. "You be damn careful. He's not afraid of anything."

Marian slipped the Rover into first gear. "I'll be okay. You're the one I'm worried about. You're on foot." Marian hesitated, then added, "Stoney, if you have to, shoot first."

"I just don't buy it," Jim Leland said to Bill Jenkins and Heyward Rutherford. "Makes no sense at all for Leonard to go down to the Sheldon Church."

Bill swatted at the gnats flying around his face. He felt like he'd sweated off ten pounds and the frigging bugs must have eaten away at least another five. "I'm just telling you what Ed said. Marian believes he's there."

Jim wondered if he'd done the right thing. Putting so much stock, despite his misgivings, in Marian's opinion. Telling everyone to follow the river as they had earlier, but to advance southward now as rapidly as possible. When the river ended, at the marshes, they would be almost exactly at the Sheldon Church. So that part did make sense. If Leonard followed the river, then he would also end up there. And would need a new place to hide—someplace out of the way, with lots of cover. Of course, Buck Henry had looked down his nose at the whole thing. They were to follow the advice of a schoolteacher who'd obtained her information from a half-looney voodoo queen? Was this the kind of police work that went on in Essex all the time?

Jim shivered when he heard the drumbeats again. Lordy, he wished they'd quit that, whoever was doing it. Over and over again just this one drum beating. Just when he thought it had stopped, it started up again. It sounded like a death knell, the way the bell in the tower of the Lutheran church had once been rung for dead people. People over sixty never stopped talking about the way it had rung over and over again for Elizabeth Setzler in the twenties. Jim listened again. Thummm—

thummm—thummm. Did that sound give Buck Henry the willies too? The Ashton sheriff had finally agreed to send his men toward the church, so they would all end up there eventually. Probably at about the same time, give or take. Coming through the swamps, they might even beat Stoney and Marian. If Leonard was there, it would be good to have everyone together. On the other hand, Jim knew that if he got to the church first and found Leonard, then this would be *his* arrest. Leonard Hansen, who had tricked him, who had even offered to *help* him, would be arrested and behind bars. Leonard would kill no more. Not in the town where he was police chief.

Abruptly Jim froze. What was that?

Bill and Heyward, ahead of him, stopped too.

"What is that?" Bill's voice was almost inaudible.

"I don't know," Heyward cried. "Sounded like something moving."

"Quiet!" Jim bent low and held his rifle up to his chest and carefully unhooked the safety, signaling with his eyes for the other men to do the same.

Then they heard it again. The sound of hard and heavy footsteps. Tree limbs snapping back. Something running.

Jim listened. Whoever it was, he was close. Buck Henry had those damn dogs way upstream and they had Leonard right here! Jim stared at Heyward and Bill, wondered if they were the backup men he'd have chosen.

The moon suddenly shot out from behind a cloud and illuminated the three men. Bill Jenkins jerked back from the light. "Which way?"

"I can't tell." Jim's head pounded, and he bit his lip so hard it bled. He pointed. "He could be over there. Or on the other side of the river." The police chief straightened his shoulders abruptly. "You two cross the river and check there. I'll go this way."

Bill Jenkins looked doubtful, thinking about Jim alone. He also thought about confronting Leonard himself with only Heyward to help. Then he saw the story it would make if he were personally involved in Leonard's capture and he forgot Jim and turned to scramble across the river, dragging Heyward with him. Jim watched them go, then turned in the other direction and started running.

Leonard Hansen knelt down beside the rusted water pump, which sat on a raised brick platform, and worked the iron handle

p and down for several seconds. Water coughed in the lines
nd finally shot out of the spout. Leonard cupped his hands and
rank deeply, still kneeling, his rifle butt resting against his
igh, the barrel cradled in the crook of his right arm. He pumped
e handle again and leaned his head under the spout, allow-
g the water to run down his cheeks and across the back of his
eck. Slowly he wiped his face on his shirt sleeve and sat back
n his haunches, his right hand nervously gripping his weapon.

He never heard the approach, just the voice. "Don't move,
eonard. Not an inch."

Leonard froze, his hand tightening on his rifle. The voice was
ehind him. Leonard turned his head slightly; in his peripheral
ision he saw a figure in the shadows. A gun, perhaps a rifle,
as pointed at his back.

"I said, *don't move!*"

Leonard sat perfectly still but eased his hand toward the safety
n his rifle.

"Pick up your rifle and toss it to your right."

Leonard waited but didn't move.

"Throw your rifle to the side. *Now.*"

Leonard stood, his back still turned. "I'm lifting it up," he
aid, holding the gun out from his body. "I'm going to toss it
ver toward that tombstone." Slowly he angled in the direction
f a nearby grave. "Here goes." He flung his right arm wide
ut didn't let go of his weapon; instead, he slowly pivoted to
ice the gun still aimed at his chest.

"Throw it down, Leonard. Or I'll fire. I swear I will."

Leonard stared but didn't raise his rifle. "No you won't." He
miled but the hand holding his downturned firearm trembled
lightly. "If you had the guts, you'd 'a already done it."

They stood for a moment in complete silence. Then, "You
astard. You killed all of them, Sarah and Brockhurst and Har-
iet. They knew what kind of man you really are—and it cost
iem their lives."

"Got it all figured out, have you?"

"Not just me, everybody knows. About the money your fa-
ier wouldn't leave his own son, how Sarah told him about the
ape years ago. Everybody'll be here in a minute. They're going
o lock you up for the rest of your life."

Leonard glanced toward the ruins of the Sheldon Church.
ehind the building was another way out of the grounds. He
ared at his accuser. "I shoulda took care of you a long time
go," he growled.

"Drop your rifle, Leonard. I mean it."

Leonard smiled. "No you don't. You don't have it in you Takes guts you ain't got."

"But you do, of course. You're brave enough to rape teenag girls and kill frail old ladies."

"Go fuck yourself."

"Drop your rifle."

Leonard stepped forward and breathed, "Except for the dam noise, I'd shoot you through the head right now." He brushe past and started walking up the path toward the church.

"Stop right *there*!"

Leonard kept walking. He heard footsteps behind him b he didn't stop. When he got to the church, he paused for second and turned around. "I *will* take care of you now if have to. Beats the shit outta crawling around old houses tha stink of catpiss, or carving up goats for stupid fools who' believe any—"

The sharp sound lasted only a second, then he felt it.

All the searchers were now near the church. They all hear it clearly. The shot so loud it was handed off by the trees one b one until everyone covered their ears. Not one shot, not two but three. Then a silence as thick as dirt.

Buck Henry careened out of the swamps with his two deputie and grabbed the map sticking out of his back pocket. The thre men ran east through the woods and then found a paved road They followed the road for half a mile; then the sheriff notice a six-foot-high rusted wire fence on their right. "That's it."

The men sprinted alongside the fence until they reached th open gate and the stone steps leading into the enclosure Abruptly they all halted. In the distance moonlight outlined th ruins of an old brick church, a ghoulish shell minus its roof an windows, crumbling red brick walls missing a corner here an there, twenty-foot arched holes missing their stained glass and four mammoth columns out front that were now detache from the rest of the structure. The building was surrounded b live oaks, and a thick mist that was indistinguishable from th ghostlike strands of Spanish moss lay upon the churchyard lik a mantle.

They started toward the church. On their left was an old fashioned water pump, its greenish-iron handle still up, wate dripping from the spout. Someone had recently taken a drink

Buck Henry stared at the pump; then he saw a single tombstone, leaning and illegible, to one side of it. Then he saw another. The church had no formal graveyard; its grounds were so expansive that the dead had been buried randomly, in isolated pockets of the yard that suddenly appeared out of nowhere.

"Buck, somebody's down there. At the church."

The sheriff stared down the worn dirt path. The mist was so clouded it was hard to see the structure, just those decapitated columns sticking out of the treetops. But then he saw the people too. He relaxed, slowed down. Many of the men were already here. They were all very still, so Leonard Hansen either wasn't here or had got away. But the shots. Who fired them? And why was everyone just standing around?

As Buck Henry and the two deputies walked forward, the mist rose from the ground, the cold nightbreeze meeting the hot earth, and it curled around the live oaks that lined the pathway to the church, wove in and out among the long tendrils of gray moss, some of which hung almost to the ground. The inside of the church was a grassy mall with one cement catafalque grave commemorating the founder of the church. Beyond the building, to its right, three other rectangular tombs stood in a circle like friends meeting on a streetcorner. One of the catafalques was damaged; several pieces of the top slab had fallen inside, leaving a gaping hole the size of a shoebox in the top of the tomb.

It was around this tomb that everyone had gathered. Buck Henry saw the Essex police chief and the town council president and that fellow who ran the newspaper. He saw Ricky Gibson, who had once worked on his car, and he saw the doctor and Stoney McFarland and that schoolteacher (a woman had no business out here at night). He saw some of his own men but the guys with the dogs hadn't arrived yet; he saw one or two farmers whose names he could never place. All of these men were standing very still and they were all staring at the broken catafalque.

Then Buck Henry saw why.

Everyone looked up when they heard the sheriff approach. Now they stared at him. Quickly Buck Henry dropped to his knees beside the catafalque. And leaned over a body.

The sheriff stared at Leonard Hansen. The man's eyes were open and there were two bullet holes in the right side of his skull. There was no need to put a finger to the pulse in his neck. Buck Henry stood up heavily. Then he squatted back down again and picked up the assault rifle that lay beside the dead man. It was cold.

The sheriff motioned to Jim Leland. The police chief stepped forward and the sheriff asked, "Who shot him?"

Jim Leland stared down at Leonard. "I'm not sure."

"Well, the man's rifle hasn't been fired. We have to know what happened."

Jim stared down at Leonard's body again. Something glinted up at him in the moonlight. "What's that?" He reached down and held up Leonard's limp left hand. On it was a small diamond ring which was obviously too small; it was stuck on the knuckle of Leonard's left pinky finger. Jim leaned back up; he had never seen Leonard wear a ring before. He walked over to Marian and said something and the two of them approached Leonard's body again.

Marian stared down at the dead man. Jim held up Leonard's hand and she stared at it. Then she gasped, her hands covering her mouth. "Harriet's ring." She dropped down beside Leonard's body and hit the dead man's chest over and over again. "Why did you have to kill her? Goddamn you, *why*?"

Jim dragged Marian away and walked her back over to where Stoney was standing. He and Stoney stared at each other for a moment. "I guess you were right all along."

Stoney didn't say a word, he just stared at Leonard's body.

Jim crossed back to Buck Henry. The sheriff said, "We have to find out who shot him so we can file a report. Likely as not, it was a case of self-defense. But we have to answer for his death."

Jim nodded but he didn't say anything.

Buck Henry turned and faced everyone. "I have to know who shot Hansen."

No one said a word.

"You know we can't just leave it this way. His gun wasn't fired so we have to explain what happened. I want whoever shot this man to raise his hand now."

No one did.

"I know you probably didn't mean to kill him—just to stop him. There's nothing to worry about. But you've got to speak up."

Almost imperceptibly men moved away from each other, just inches, fractions of inches, just enough space to cast sidelong looks at each other without anyone noticing, and they wondered what would happen to them if no one owned up to the shooting.

The khaki-clad sheriff sighed and shook his head. He walked back and forth in front of Leonard's body, stopped once in while to say something to one of his deputies. Then he addressed the other men again. "You know there are ways of finding out, ways of identifying that bullet. Ways of finding out who was carrying the rifle with the right bore. But it seems a damn shame to waste all that effort—look what this man has already cost us— when it could all be cleared up right now if one of you would just speak up and tell me what happened."

Silence. More imperceptible movement. Now the distance between those who stood in the churchyard was large enough that shadows could get inside it. The people stood scattered like the tombstones, isolated from each other. And they did not answer.

Buck Henry finally sent one of his men back to radio for the coroner. The deputy moved past the others and was soon swallowed by the mist. Then the Ashton sheriff spoke directly to Jim, "You got any ideas?"

Jim shook his head.

The bigger man gazed down at Leonard Hansen's body, then finally looked up at the assemblage. "I'm going to ask y'all one more time. Who shot this man?"

Silence.

"Goddamnit. Now who did this?"

After waiting for a response and getting none, Buck Henry turned around again and sighed. When he angled back toward the group, he said, more quietly, "It's not that I blame you. You saw his gun and panicked, maybe that's how it happened. It was self-defense, you were apprehending a known and armed killer. It's simple," he finished, almost pleading now. "Please. Just tell me that."

"It's never simple," someone said.

"Who said that?"

The sheriff searched each face and saw that he was not going to get an answer.

Before dawn broke, Buck Henry personally felt each firearm to see if any were warm, but it was too late to tell which had been fired now. Leonard Hansen's body was removed, the group still standing around watching. Then, finally, everyone left. But they did not go out of the church as they'd come inside its gates, or as they'd first entered the swamps two days before. They walked singly now, not in groups, not slapping each other, not even talking. Even those who would ride back to Essex together walked alone now. They would get in the same car and ride back through the murky morning but they would not ride together.

They would look at each other furtively and they would wonder. But only one of them would know. And so they would ride side by side but singly. And they would speak again but they would not talk.

Stoney dropped Marian off at her house and then drove on to Bill's to pick up Anna. Diane Jenkins had already taken Anna home, she said, staring at Stoney at her front door. "Stoney, what happened out there?"

"Bill didn't tell you?"

"He said somebody shot Leonard dead. That's not what I mean. Bill is—I don't know, distant, different. He's asleep now."

Stoney gave Diane Jenkins no answer. He just drove on home in the early morning light. He was so tired he left the Rover in front of the house and climbed the steep stone steps to the front porch. Then he saw it. At his own front door. Her. He was beside her bed, he was looking down . . . oh God there was so much blood, Jesus blood everywhere, on the headboard, on the sheets, on the cotton blankets, on her neck, her face, the floor, drops of red trailing across the rug like footprints, it was all over the room, and she was bleeding, cuts on her face, her neck, her eyes were open but Christ she didn't see and there were torn seams in the skin along her neck and God in heaven she was dead and cut and there was this smell this smell and she was so full of blood and there was this—

Stoney grabbed his front storm door and shook it violently, holding on, trying to make the image go away. He closed his eyes. They flew back open. That was all he could see, whether his eyes were open or closed. The room. Sarah's face. The woman of blood. God oh God he even stabbed her in the eye! I will not look at this, I won't. He closed his eyes tight but there it was, Sarah's face. He opened his eyes again and saw Sarah's face on the surface of the front door. He snapped his eyes shut. Then he saw Monkey. He saw Harriet—and he beat on the door harder, almost tore it down.

When Anna found him, he looked at her in terror. Then he saw she had no blood on her. He allowed her to lead him inside where she made him lie down on the sofa. She held his hand. He tried to talk but found he had no words, and so he just held on to her hand as she stroked the contours of his cheekbone until he fell asleep.

"Maybe we can't trust the world anymore, Stoney," she whispered to him once. "But I do trust you."

He slept all day. When he woke up, he was uncertain what day it was, uncertain whether the darkness meant it really was night or not. Day and night didn't seem to mean much anymore. He rose and went to take a shower and toweled his hair dry and shaved and then looked at himself in the mirror for a long time.

Anna was standing in the doorway when he walked back in the bedroom. He was naked except for the white towel tied round his waist and it reminded her, suddenly, of Maum Chrish's white scarves. It made her want to cry, that white cloth. As did the strong stomach muscles running up the sides of his chest like ladders. Her eyes mirrored the ache he had seen in his own in the bathroom and for a few minutes they just gazed at each other, taking their time, knowing exactly what that ache meant.

Slowly she unbuttoned her blouse, but they didn't speak. He watched as she peeled her clothes away and stood in front of him. He reached over and took her hand and kissed it and they talked with the pressure of their fingertips. Their touch was sometimes sad but never tentative. Then they were together almost at once, without speaking. Their passion was hot, desperate, and demanding. Over and over again they brought each other up and they could hear the cicadas outside and smell the moist earth through the window. He felt immersed in an incredibly warm sea, a tide that caught and held him, lapped at the edges of his consciousness until he began falling rapidly, spiraling into a deep tunnel where there was no sense of danger, no explanations or circumlocutions, no blood, no fear of landing against a hard and implacable surface. As he plummeted, she soared. She ascended higher and higher into spacelessness, weightlessness, where there is no consciousness, only the sure and steady hand of sensation. That sensation was given air and light, allowed to breathe, and so it divided into a thousand different levels, a hundred dimensions. She could feel the difference between them even as she winged beyond and began to splinter into space, reveling in the loss of herself. As they moved in opposite directions, they drew together even as they drew apart.

And they had waited so long. She cried out over and over again, until sudden and intense tears erupted, so thankful was she for the simple complexity of pleasure. But the next tremor came and soon she was laughing and crying at the same time and he shouted then and took so long, went so deep, even he was laughing before it was over. The floorboards beneath the bed creaked and moaned, in the kitchen Silas howled, and Stoney and Anna laughed together until they cried again.

Epilogue

A FEW YEARS have passed on by now and we look pretty much like we always did. The middle of town is still a triangle that almost nobody can cross without getting damn near run down from at least six different directions. Heyward and Sumter Brownlow meet in the diner every Thursday at noon to talk about redesigning Main Street so it'll work better. The ladies go to Venny's Beauty Shop and get their hair snipped and blown around while they read the old copies of *People* and *Soap Opera Digest*. Boys still whizz by on BMX bicycles with stray dogs yelping behind them. The Lutheran church is presently arguing with the Baptists about who really owns that parking lot they've been sharing for years which now needs repaving. Bill Jenkins has enlarged the Essex *Telegraph*, even has two full-time reporters working for him now, one of whom does the books too. Sadie Thompkins died last year and that no-count gal she raised showed up for the funeral, to everyone's surprise. Elsie Fenton is running the library these days and almost nobody likes that, her being so scatterbrained and usually late opening up; thank goodness the town council hired a high school girl to help her, one of Diamond's nieces that everybody says is smart as a whip. Heyward Rutherford did finally demolish Sarah's store but the garden club talked him out of a car wash at the last minute; retired now as town council president, Heyward apparently can't decide what to do with the land and so people have been quietly planting different parts of it, hoping it will become a park before Heyward notices.

It still hurts to remember, though. That land is a pointed arrow shot into the heart of long-term memory. So is Harriet's house. A new couple from Charleston (he's to set up a drafting department at the community college in Ashboro) fell in love with the neighborhood and bought the lot. They've rebuilt the house much as it was before. They were even able to salvage a little of the lumber and both chimneys, only they added more bathrooms and turned the sleeping porch into something they call a "solarium." The new owners painted the house burgundy with gray shutters—Harriet would have hated such modernity but all in all they seem to hold the place right dear. The garden isn't much anymore, except for the hardier of Harriet's flowers, which began to shoot back up little by little a year or so after the fire. The azaleas are short and stumpy now, regrouping, and the fifteen paintings Harriet saved that night hang on the walls of the library.

Some of us who survived that summer are also long gone. Marian, Stoney and Anna, and Jim Leland all left within a year of Leonard Hansen's death. Marian is Dr. Davis now, heads up some kind of an experimental program in the Chicago city schools; she was invited back to speak at the graduation ceremonies of the high school last year but she didn't stay long. Jim Leland finally did get married, of all things, and he and his new wife, who used to teach math at the high school, moved to Spartanburg and opened up a restaurant; they come back to see relatives right often. Stoney and Anna returned to Washington. Seems Anna's pictures are doing real well; a book of them, including some photos of Harriet and of Maum Chrish's house, was published just three months ago. Rumor is Stoney went back to school and became a history professor, but they've never been back to visit.

Maum Chrish just disappeared. No one has ever seen her again. After that last night, a reporter from Ashboro went out to the swamps to try to talk to her; the fellow had heard Marian say Maum Chrish told her where Leonard would be. But the old swamp woman was just gone. Marian went out there a few days later. She said everything in the shack was exactly the same. The ship model was still hanging from the rafters, the pieces of white cloth were still in the trunk. But the woman was gone. Most people assumed she'd just taken off temporarily—what with so many folks roaming around in the swamps after Leonard, and probably she'd be back when everything quieted down again. Only Marian felt differently. And she was right, nobody's seen Maum Chrish since.

Yeah, we look right much the same. We were a quiet town and then something loud and noisy happened and now time has rowed in and rowed out again. We miss Harriet and Sarah; we don't seem to have as many old ladies around anymore; they go to nursing homes more often now. But we've adjusted to our loss, and the earth has settled flat over the graves. Sometimes, at twilight, walking down Aiken Avenue under the live oaks, you can almost imagine it never happened.

Almost.

There never was an investigation into the shooting of Leonard Hansen. There was no inquest. The two bullets which had gone through Leonard's body (one apparently missed) were never recovered, and Buck Henry wrote up the death as accidental. Someone in pursuit of Leonard Hansen had fired upon the suspect under the jurisdiction of the Ashton County Sheriff's Office, to protect himself and to stop a known killer. Harriet Setzler's diamond ring, as well as the Rothenbarger silverware found later in the cellar of Leonard's house, were conclusive proof that he had killed her and Sarah. Brockhurst's murder, on the other hand, remains an unsolved case in Ashton County; Buck Henry still believes J. T. Turner might have been responsible and once a year or so he studies the file on it again and carefully questions any burglary victims in the area.

I would like to say we've stopped trying to figure out who really killed Leonard. I truly would. But I can't. Nor can I speak for anyone anymore except myself. I'm no longer the mouthpiece of this town. (At one time I practically *was* Essex.) But people can't come to me anymore to find out what we're all thinking. Our collective consciousness is gone. Which is the primary scar that summer left on us. We don't talk much these days, not like we used to. We live only in our own pocket now. We're not too sure of things anymore. Next time we probably won't be as shocked, which is a way of saying we probably won't be as shocked, which is a way of saying we probably won't care as much. But that summer changed us forever. Before it, as naturally as the rites of birth, circumstance sliced our fingers and joined our blood in an act of faith and loyalty. We were one, a town of shared blood. Then circumstance betrayed us and soured the blood like ruined wine. Our blood does not flow one from the other anymore: it is now a solitary river which joins no sea, an act of love forever contained and selfish.

What I'm trying to say is, we don't know exactly who killed Leonard. I don't even know who everyone else *thinks* did it. I only know who I think did it. I believe it was whoever lost the most—like idealism, the security of sanctuary, the unsullied memory of childhood.

So the Pizza Hut is moving in and the bank has added another teller and pretty soon Seth Von Hocke will be in high school. And Harriet lies where she always wanted to be—beside William. (Trying to annoy Elizabeth on the other side, no doubt.) People go by the Setzler plot often, to remember, to tell stories about Harriet to their children. Which may be how the odd thing happened. I refer to the small live oak sapling that has grown up behind the Setzler headstone. The tree is almost four feet tall now, first live oak that's been planted around here in decades. Seth says sometimes it looks to him like old Mrs. Setzler herself is rising up out of the ground to check on what everybody's up to.

But of course, that's ridiculous.